Copyright © 2020 by Gavin Aung Than
Original interior design by Gavin Aung Than and
Benjamin Fairclough © Penguin Random House Australia Pty Ltd.

All rights reserved. Published in the United States by Random House Children's Books,
a division of Penguin Random House LLC, New York. Originally published by Puffin Books,
an imprint of Penguin Random House Australia Pty Ltd., Sydney, in 2020.

Random House and the colophon are registered trademarks of Penguin Random House LLC.
RH Graphic with the book design is a trademark of Penguin Random House LLC.

Visit us on the Web! rhcbooks.com

Educators and librarians, for a variety of teaching tools,
visit us at RHTeachersLibrarians.com

Library of Congress Cataloging-in-Publication Data is available upon request.
ISBN 978-0-593-17516-3 (trade pbk.)
ISBN 978-0-593-17513-2 (hardcover)
ISBN 978-0-593-17515-6 (ebook)

The artist used Adobe Photoshop to create the illustrations for this book.
The text of this book is set in 11-point Sugary Pancake.
This edition's cover and interior design by Sylvia Bi and colorization by Sarah Stern

MANUFACTURED IN CHINA
10 9 8 7 6 5 4 3 2 1
First American Edition

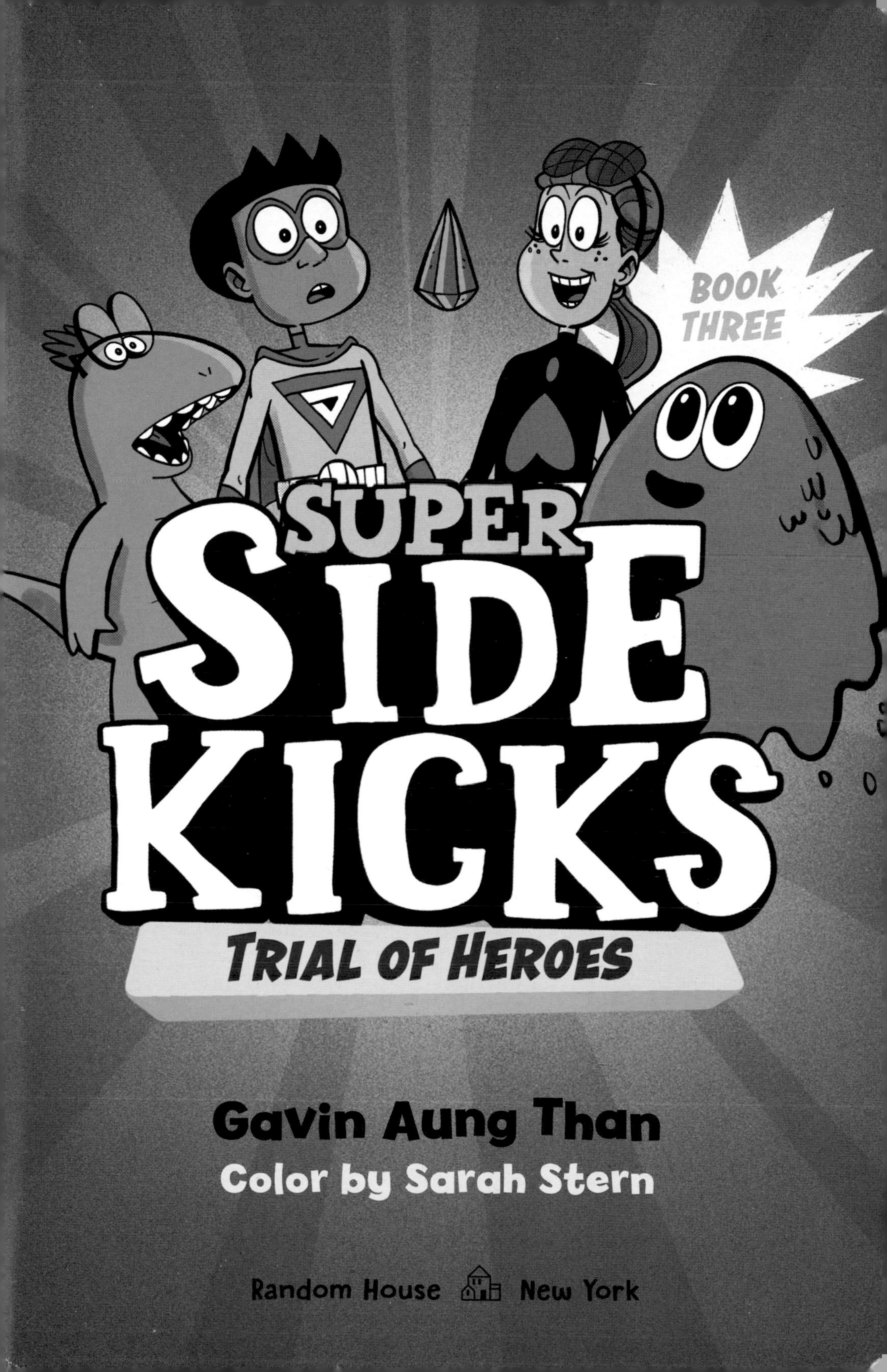
BOOK THREE

SUPER SIDEKICKS

TRIAL OF HEROES

Gavin Aung Than

Color by Sarah Stern

Random House New York

PREVIOUSLY . . .

Four superhero sidekicks were sick of being bullied
by their selfish grown-up partners, so they decided
to form their own team. They are the . . .

SUPER SIDEKICKS!

JUNIOR JUSTICE

Born leader. Expert martial artist. Brilliant detective.
Assisted by Ada, the world's most advanced belt buckle.

FLYGIRL

Acrobatic flyer. Bug whisperer. Cricket lover (the sport and
the insect). Uses dangerous bug balls to subdue enemies.

DINOMITE

Dinosaur shape-shifter. Physics professor. Poetry
connoisseur. Would rather be reading a book.

GOO

Limitless stretch factor. Untapped power potential.
Still has nightmares about his past as a bad guy.

THE GROWN-UPS

Captain Perfect, the world's most beloved
(and obnoxious) superhero; Rampagin' Rita,
simple yet scary strong; and Blast Radius,
who hasn't met a problem he couldn't
solve by blowing it up.

Chapter

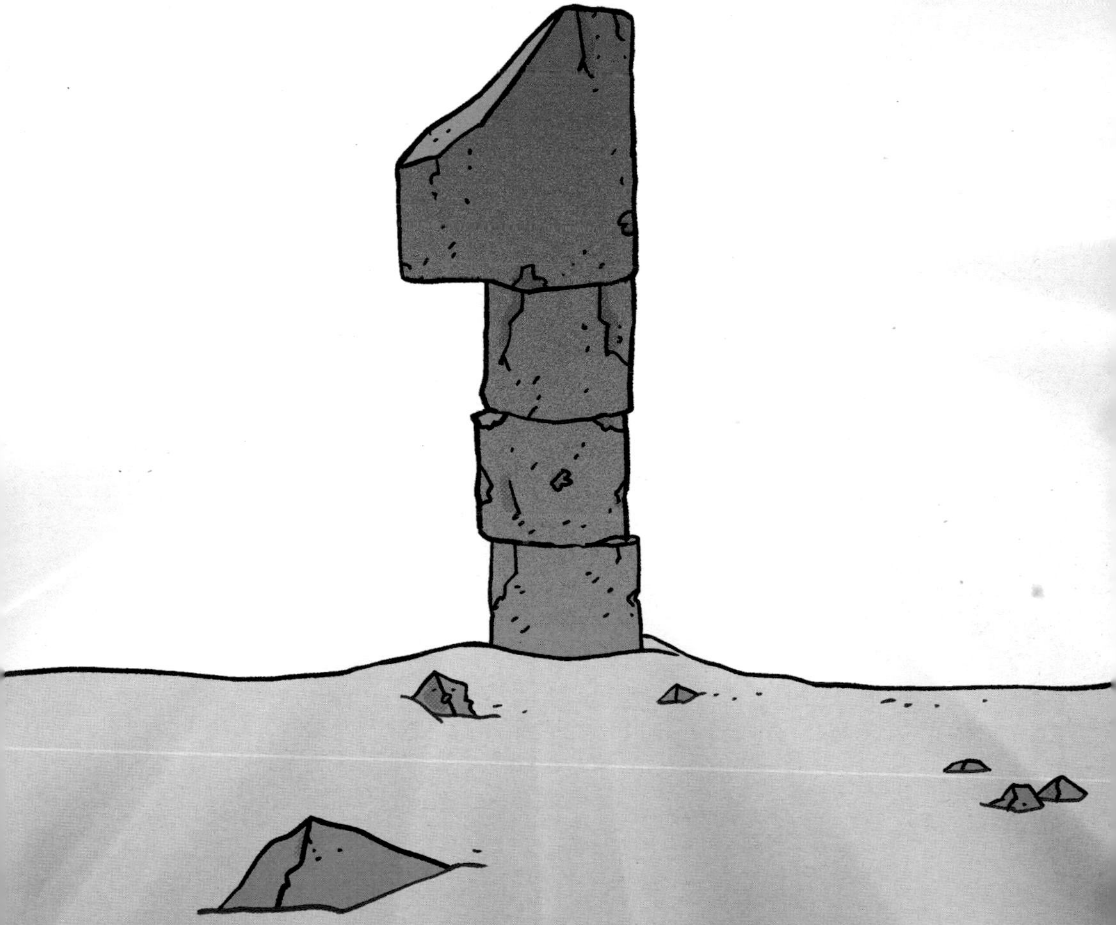
1

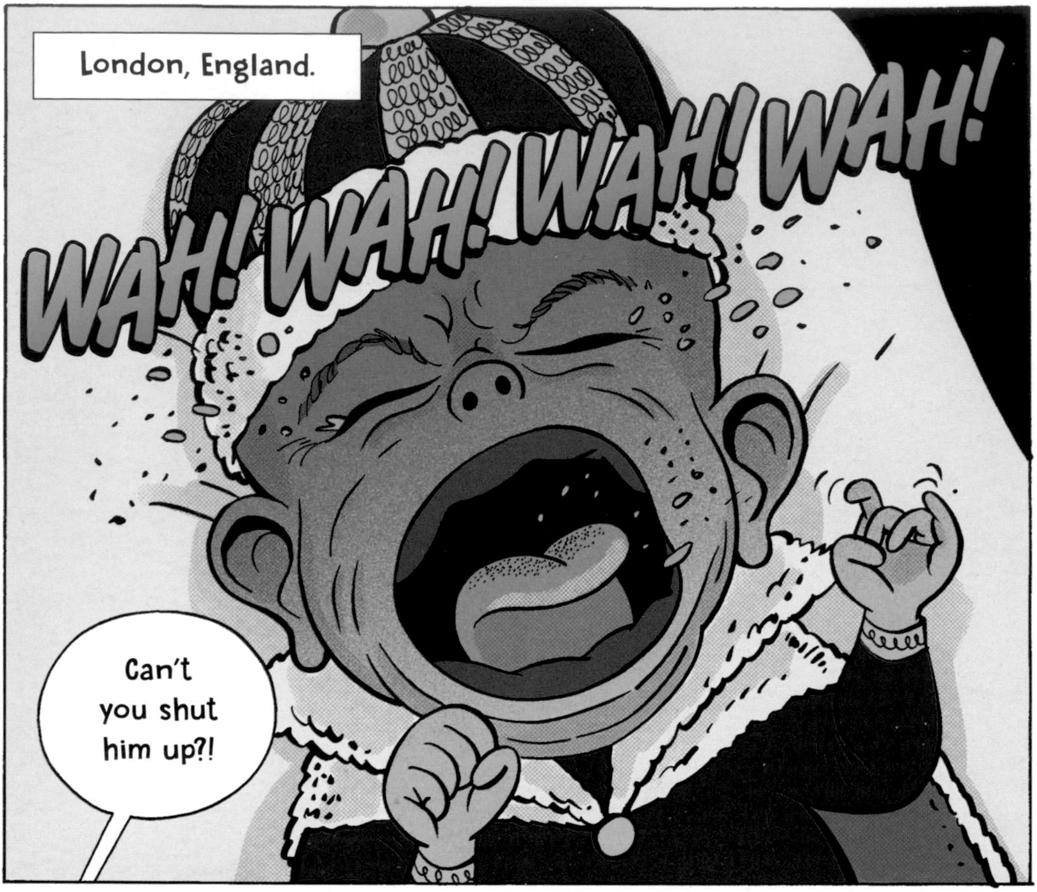
London, England.
WAH! WAH! WAH! WAH!
Can't you shut him up?!

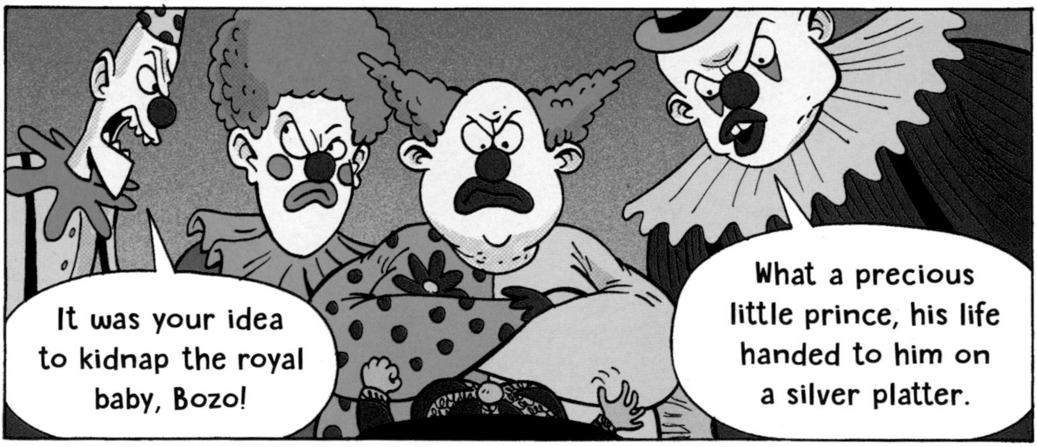
It was your idea to kidnap the royal baby, Bozo!
What a precious little prince, his life handed to him on a silver platter.

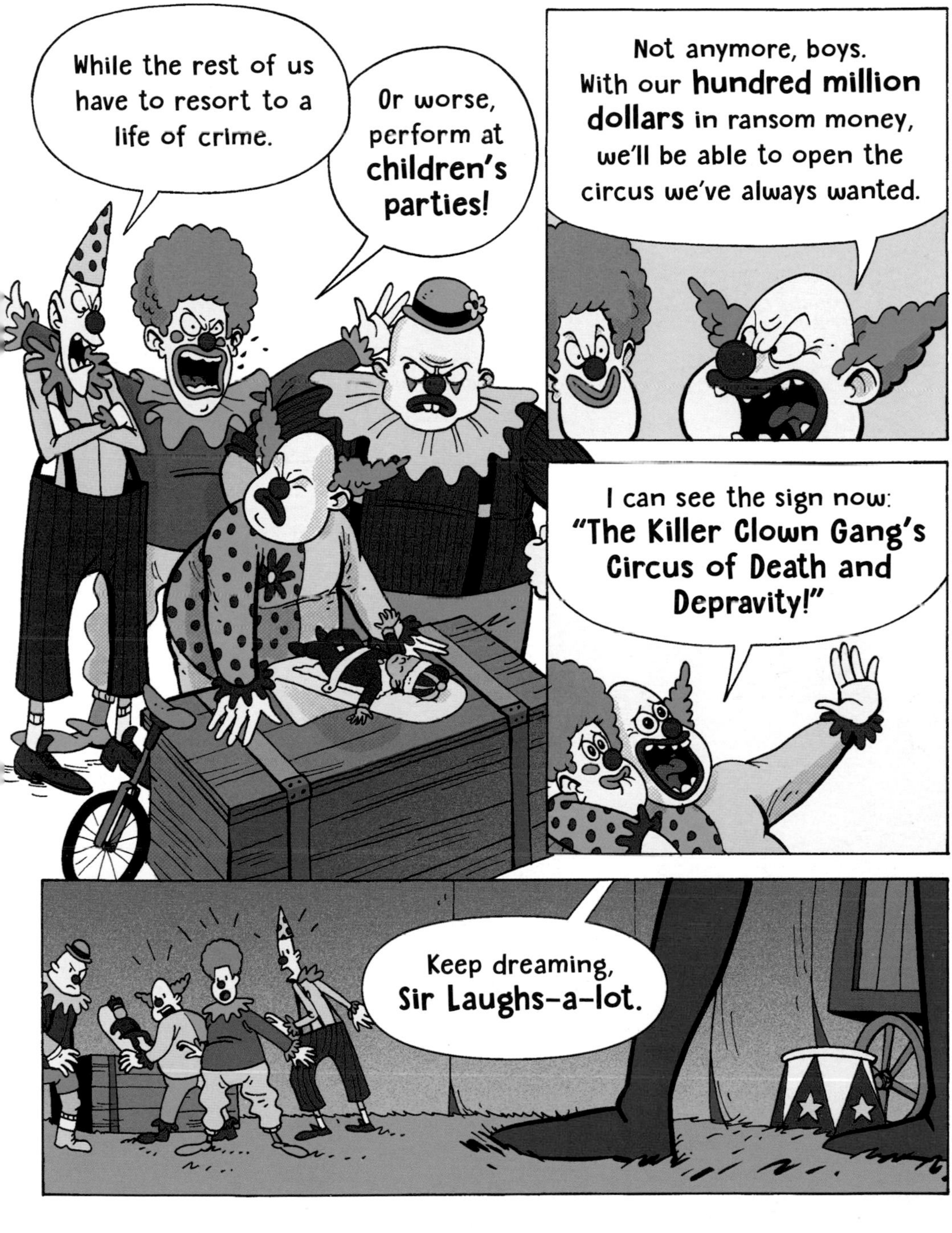
While the rest of us have to resort to a life of crime.
Or worse, perform at **children's parties!**
Not anymore, boys. With our **hundred million dollars** in ransom money, we'll be able to open the circus we've always wanted.
I can see the sign now: **"The Killer Clown Gang's Circus of Death and Depravity!"**
Keep dreaming, **Sir Laughs-a-lot.**

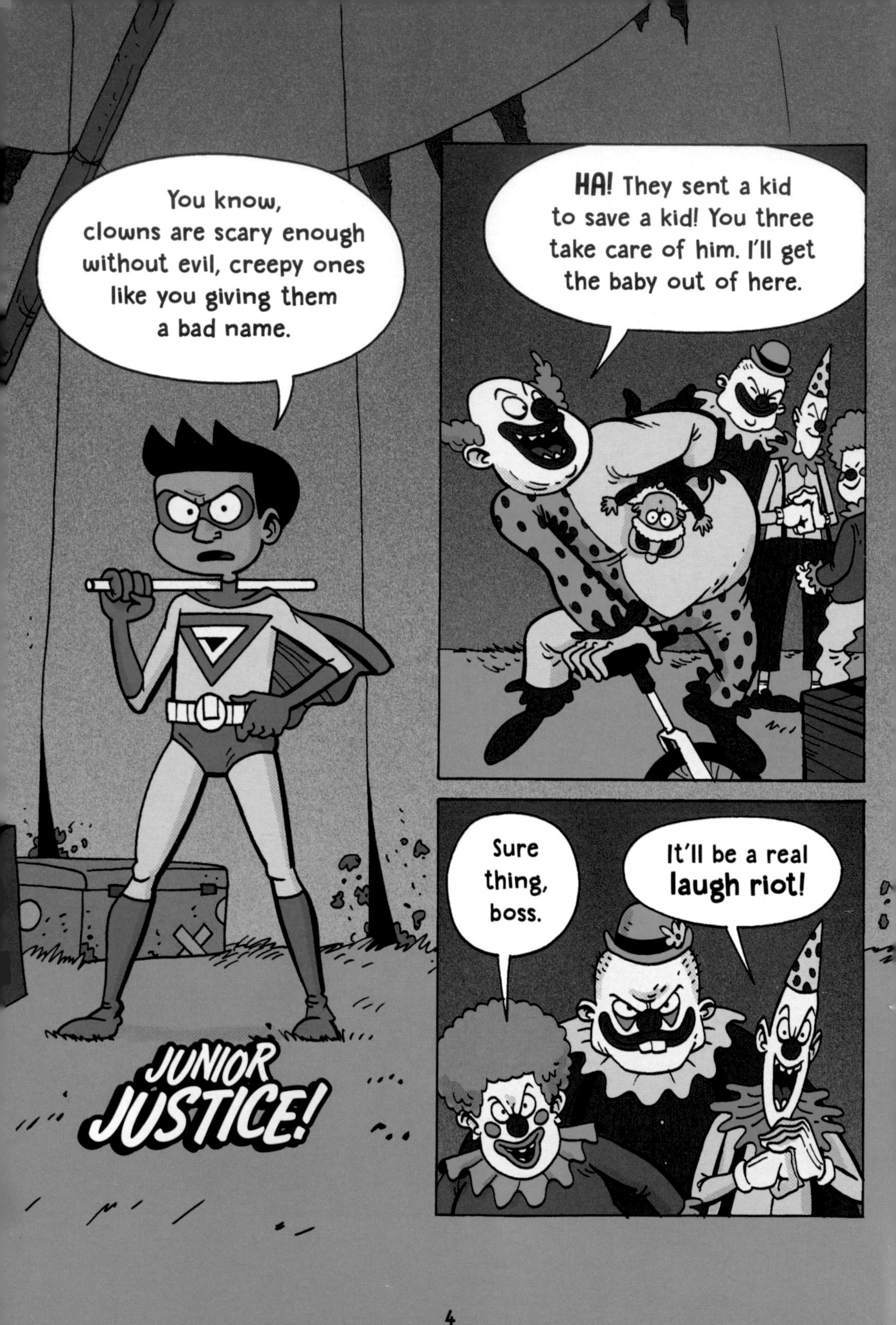
You know, clowns are scary enough without evil, creepy ones like you giving them a bad name.
JUNIOR JUSTICE!
HA! They sent a kid to save a kid! You three take care of him. I'll get the baby out of here.
Sure thing, boss.
It'll be a real laugh riot!

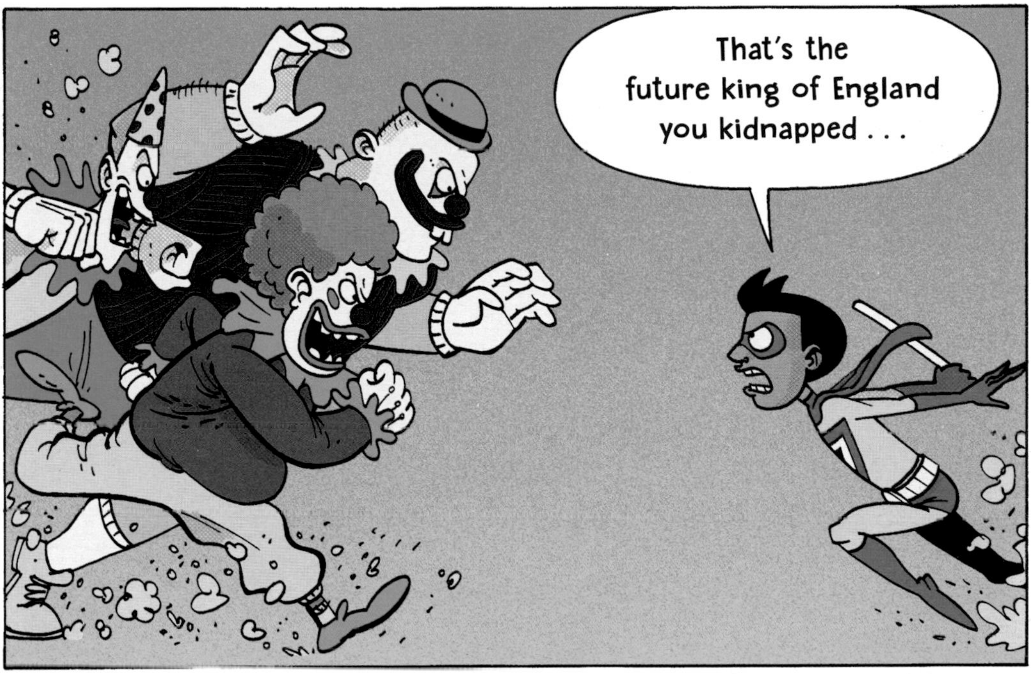
That's the future king of England you kidnapped . . .

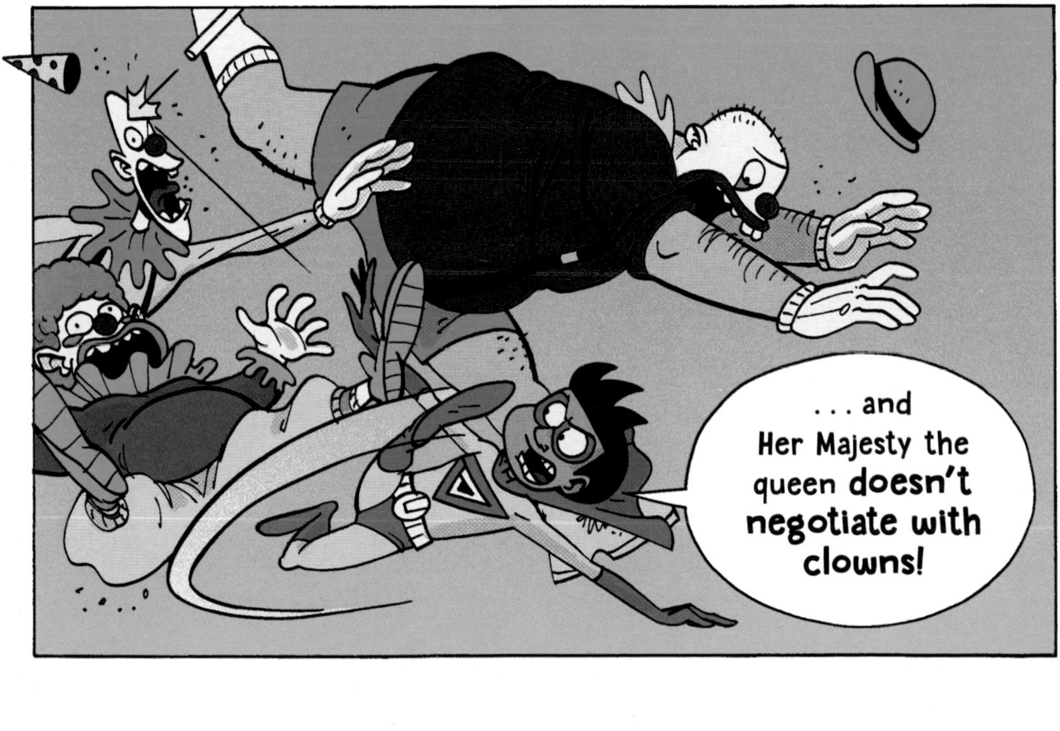
. . . and Her Majesty the queen doesn't negotiate with clowns!

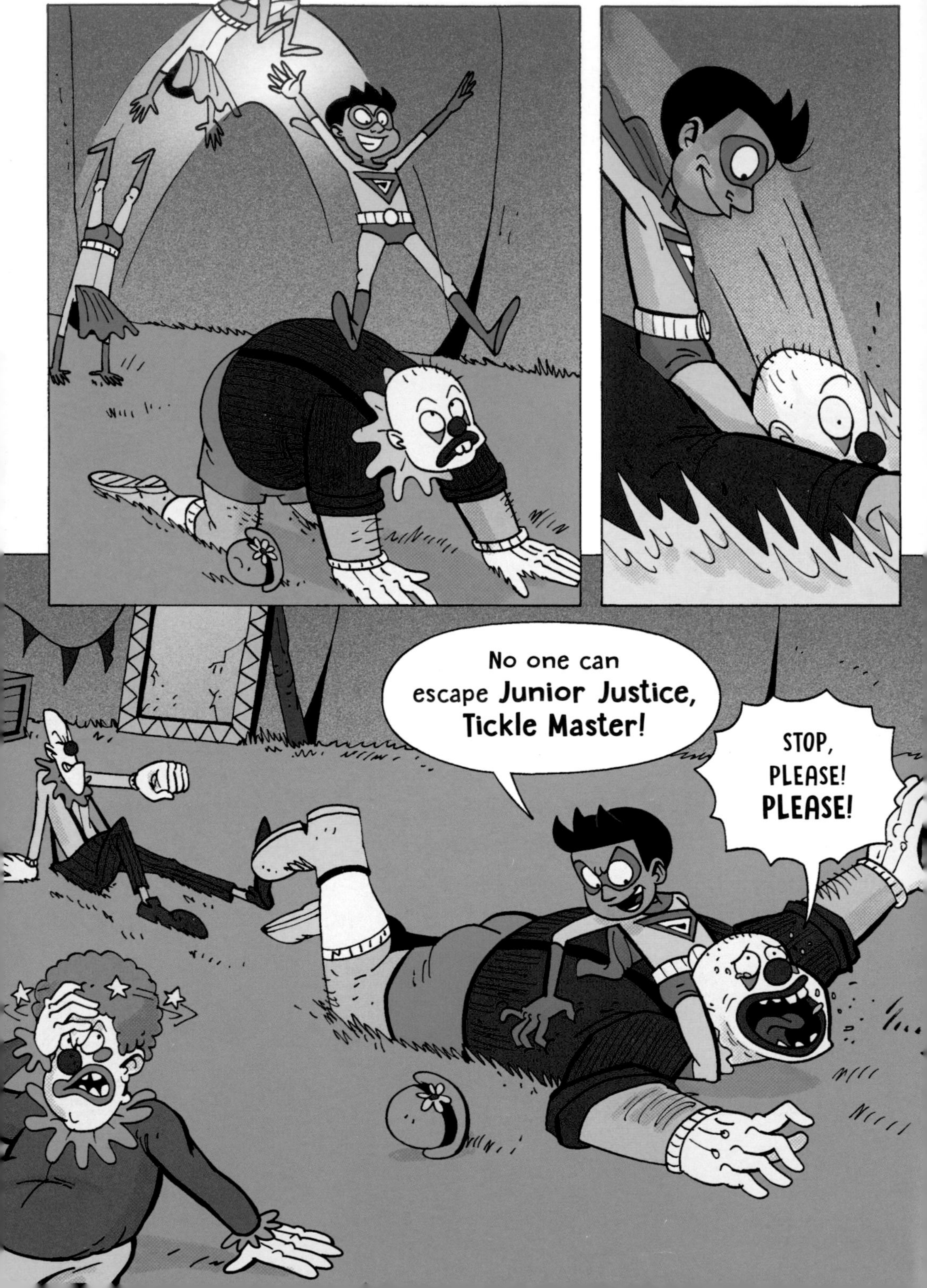
No one can escape Junior Justice, Tickle Master!
STOP, PLEASE! PLEASE!

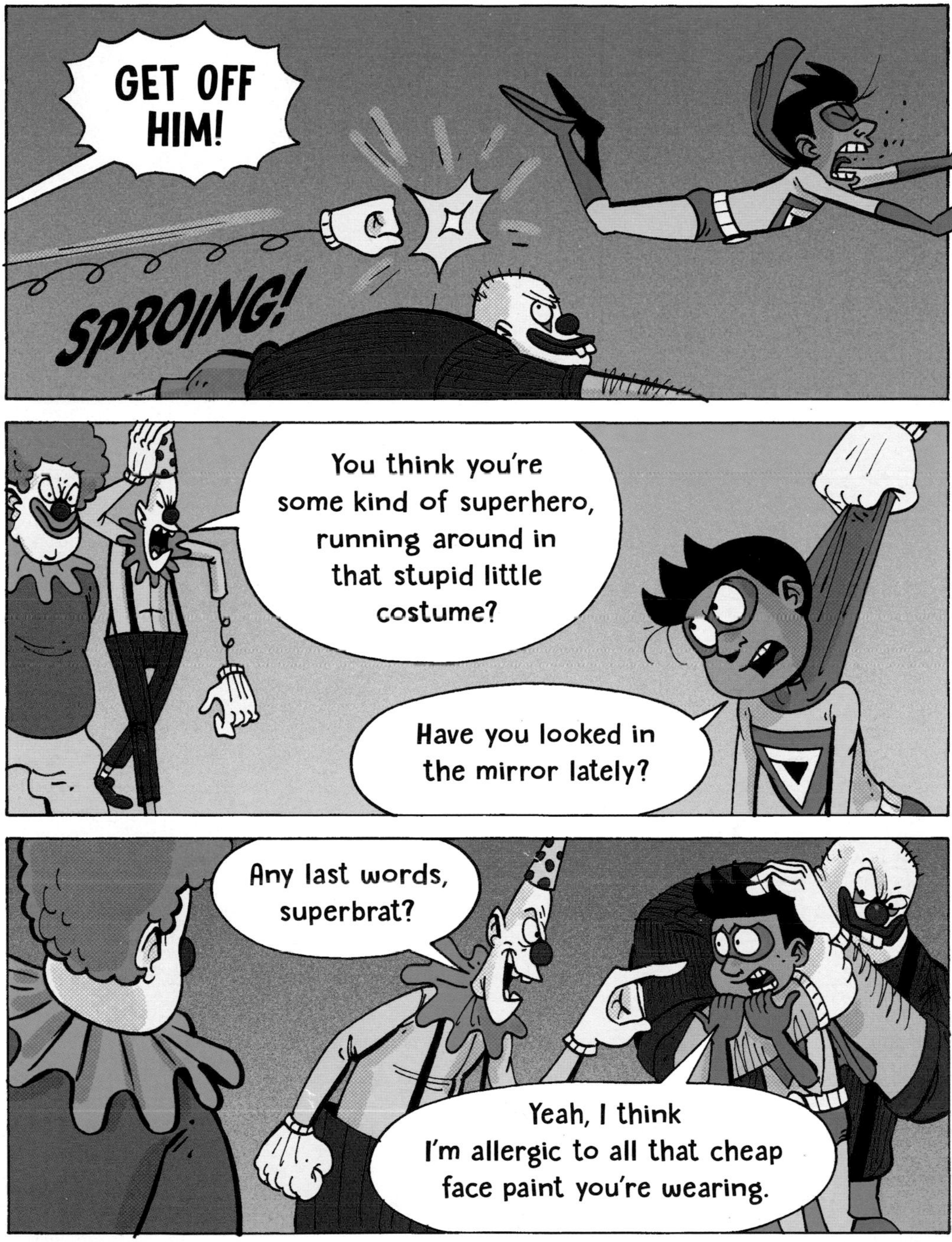
GET OFF HIM!
SPROING!
You think you're some kind of superhero, running around in that stupid little costume?
Have you looked in the mirror lately?
Any last words, superbrat?
Yeah, I think I'm allergic to all that cheap face paint you're wearing.

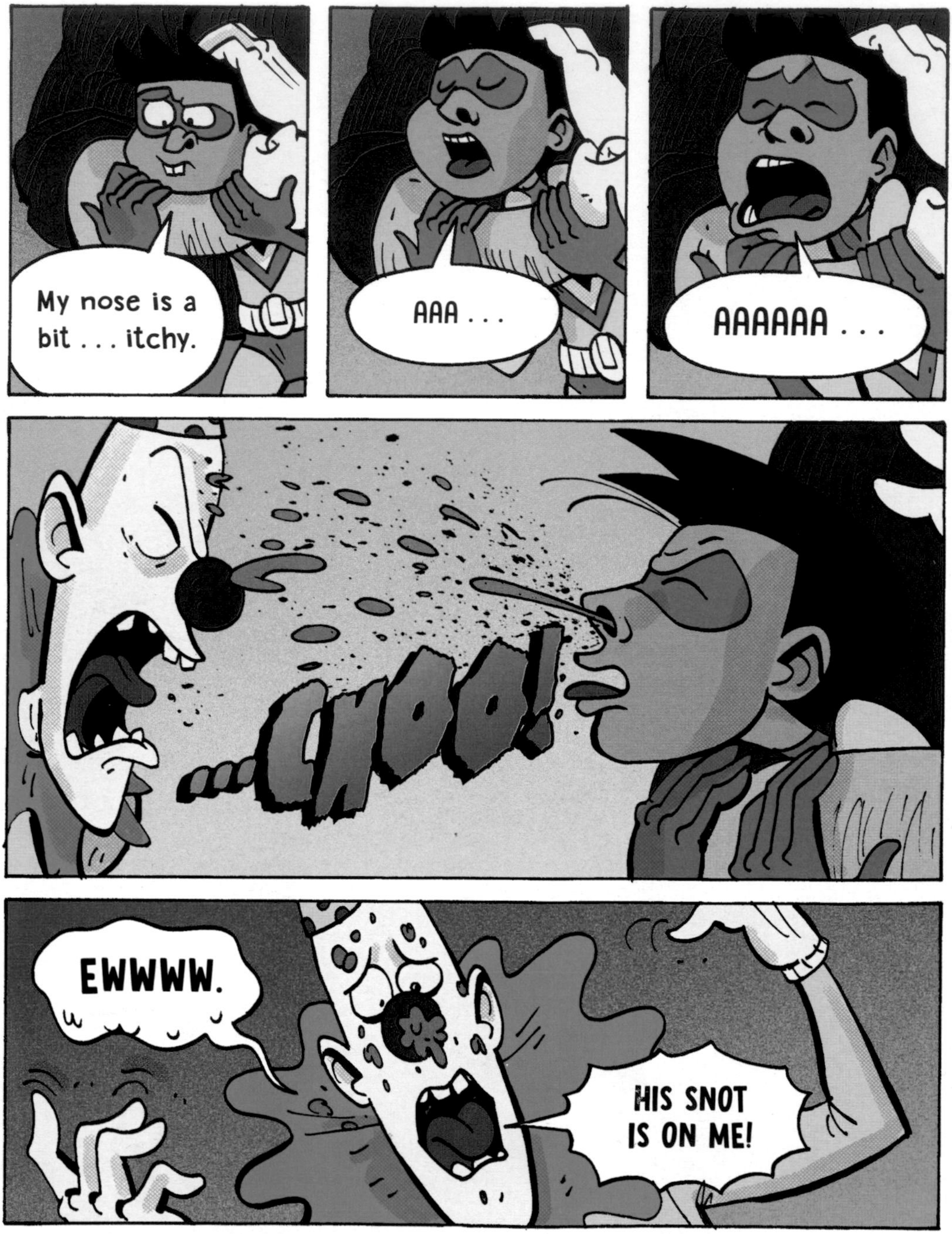
My nose is a bit . . . itchy.
AAA . . .
AAAAAA . . .
. . . CHOO!
EWWWW.
HIS SNOT IS ON ME!

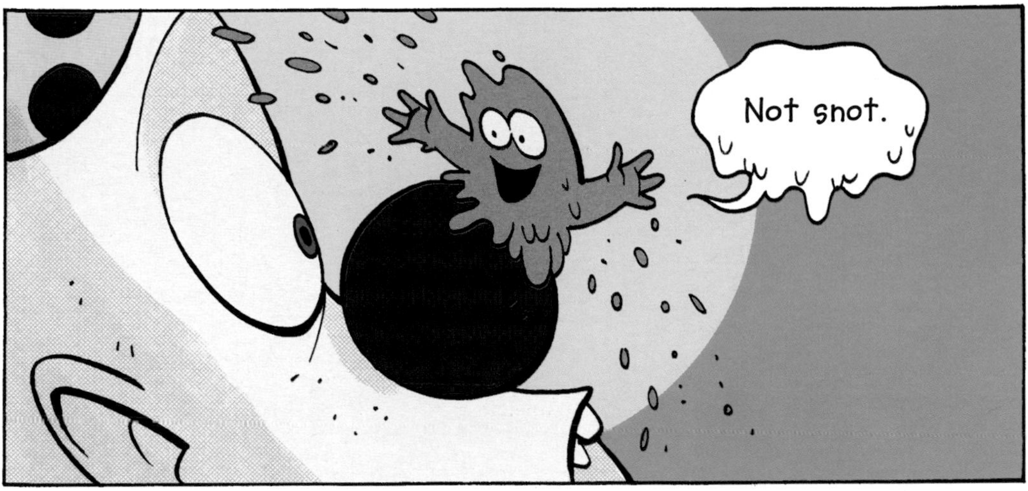
Not snot.

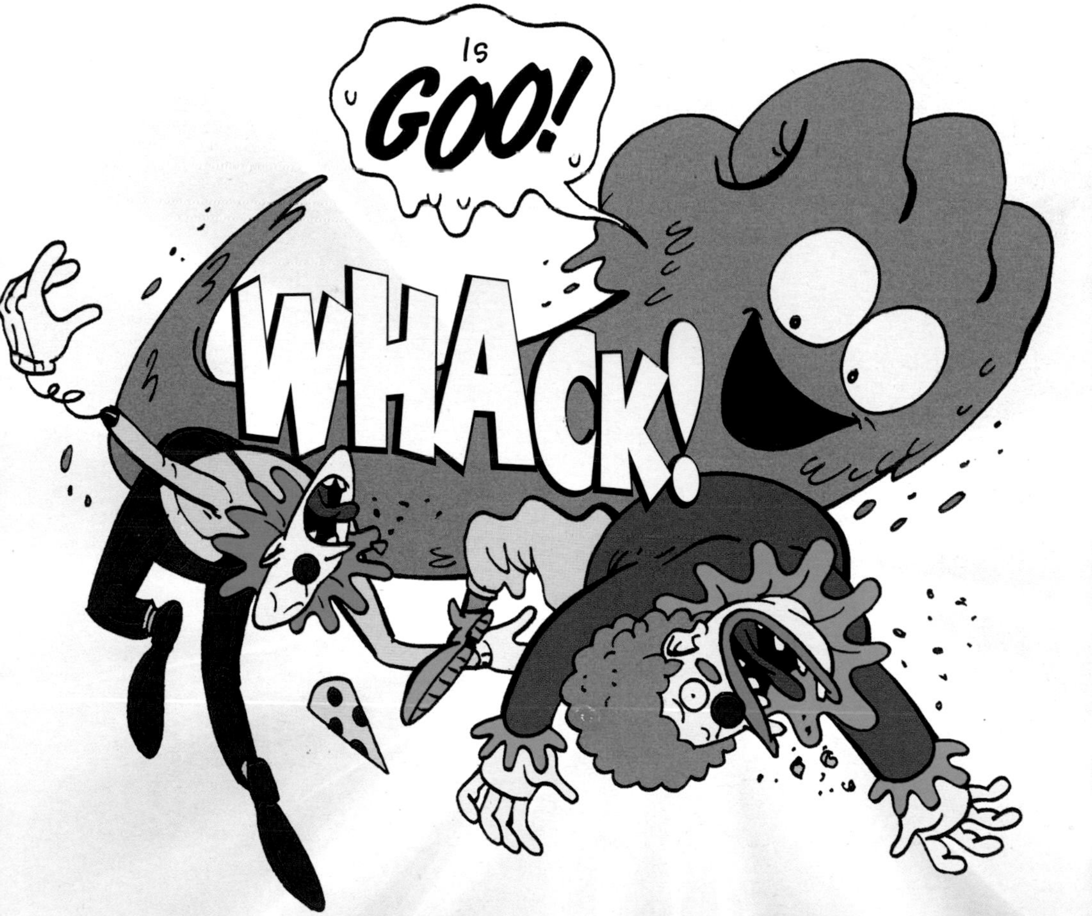
Is GOO!
WHACK!

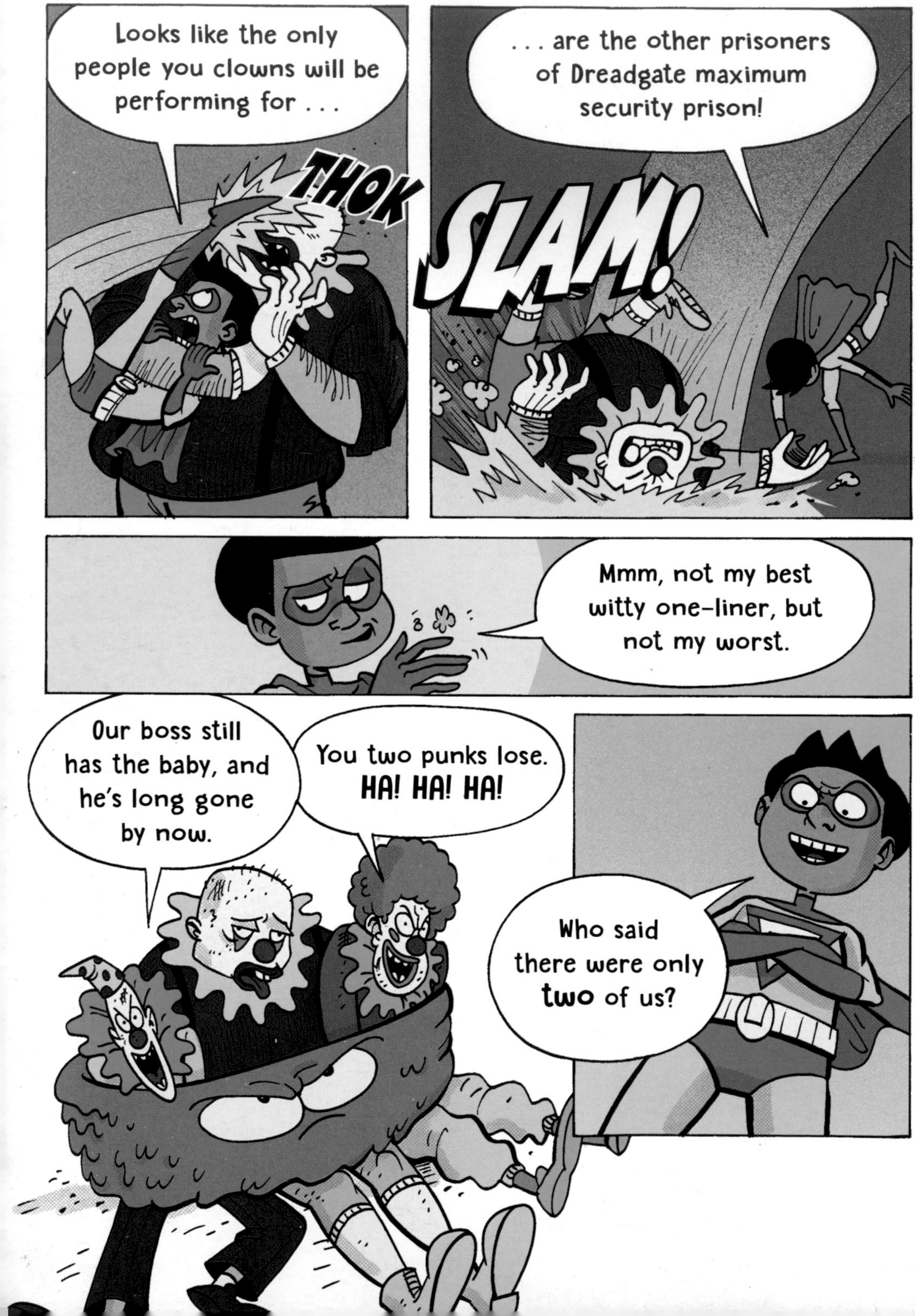
Looks like the only people you clowns will be performing for . . .
THOK
. . . are the other prisoners of Dreadgate maximum security prison!
SLAM!
Mmm, not my best witty one-liner, but not my worst.
Our boss still has the baby, and he's long gone by now.
You two punks lose. HA! HA! HA!
Who said there were only **two** of us?

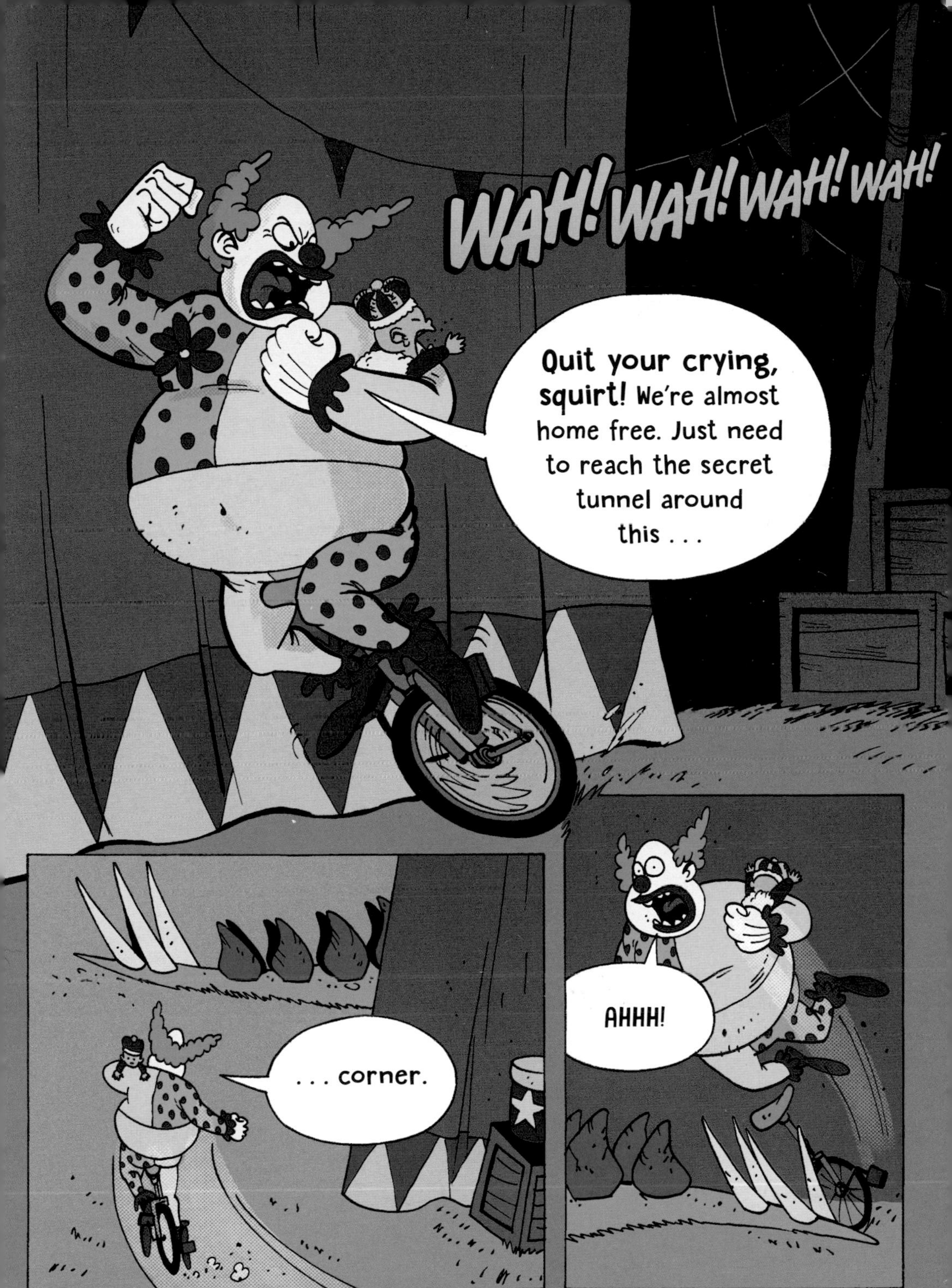
WAH! WAH! WAH! WAH!
Quit your crying, squirt! We're almost home free. Just need to reach the secret tunnel around this . . .
. . . corner.
AHHH!

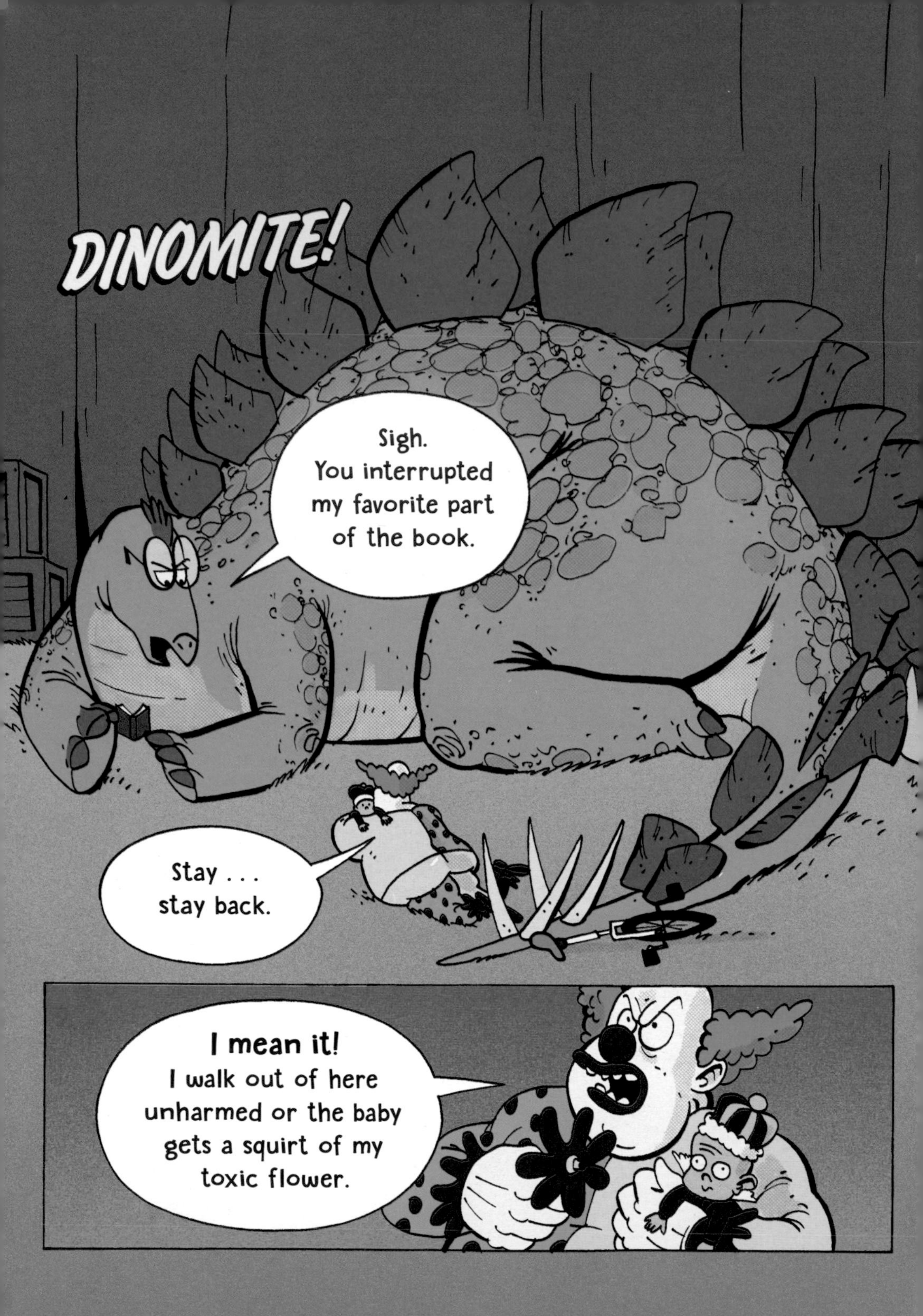
DINOMITE!
Sigh. You interrupted my favorite part of the book.
Stay . . . stay back.
I mean it! I walk out of here unharmed or the baby gets a squirt of my toxic flower.

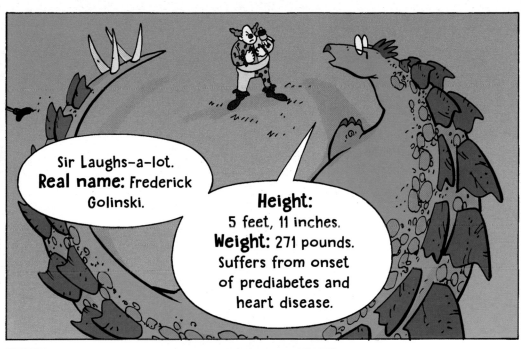

Sir Laughs-a-lot. **Real name:** Frederick Golinski.

Height: 5 feet, 11 inches. **Weight:** 271 pounds. Suffers from onset of prediabetes and heart disease.

Tsk tsk, too many of those carnival snacks, Frederick? Also allergic to **eggs, aspirin,** and **beestings.**

. . . anything?

THOK
THOK
THOK

Yeah, so? What does that have to do with . . .

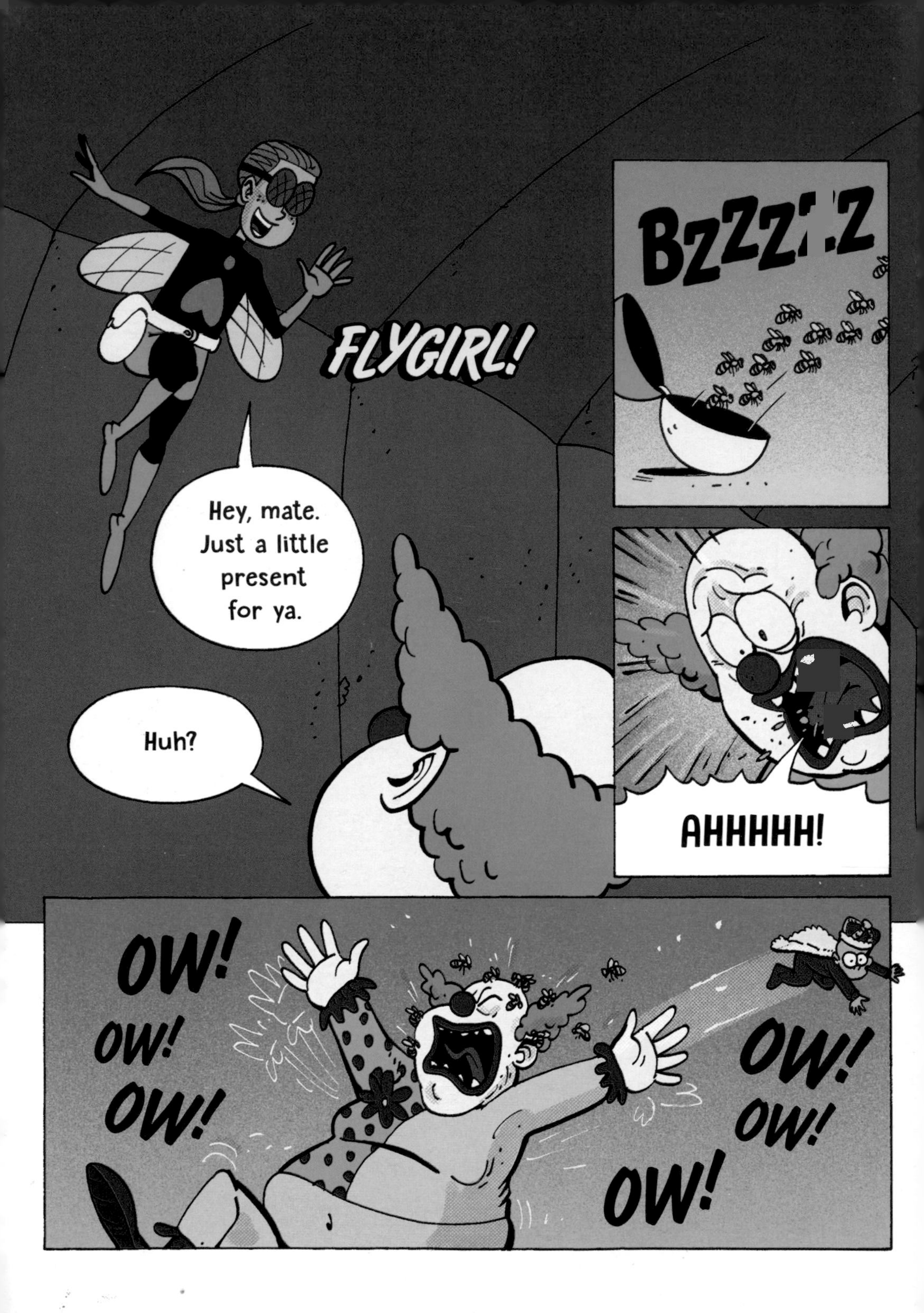
FLYGIRL!
Hey, mate. Just a little present for ya.
Huh?
AHHHHH!
OW!
OW!
OW!
OW!
OW!
OW!

Sheesh, you're a pretty ugly prince.
Relax, Frederick. This is a shot of epinephrine. You'll be fine in an hour, and an ambulance is on the way.
I'M GONNA DIE! GET ME TO A HOSPITAL!
Ngh ngh ngh eck.
Heavens above! That stench is repugnant.
PEE-YEW, the royal baby just dropped a royal load!

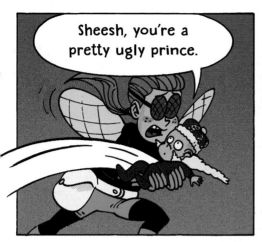

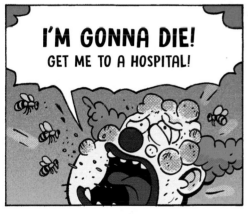

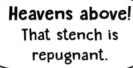

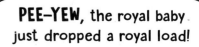

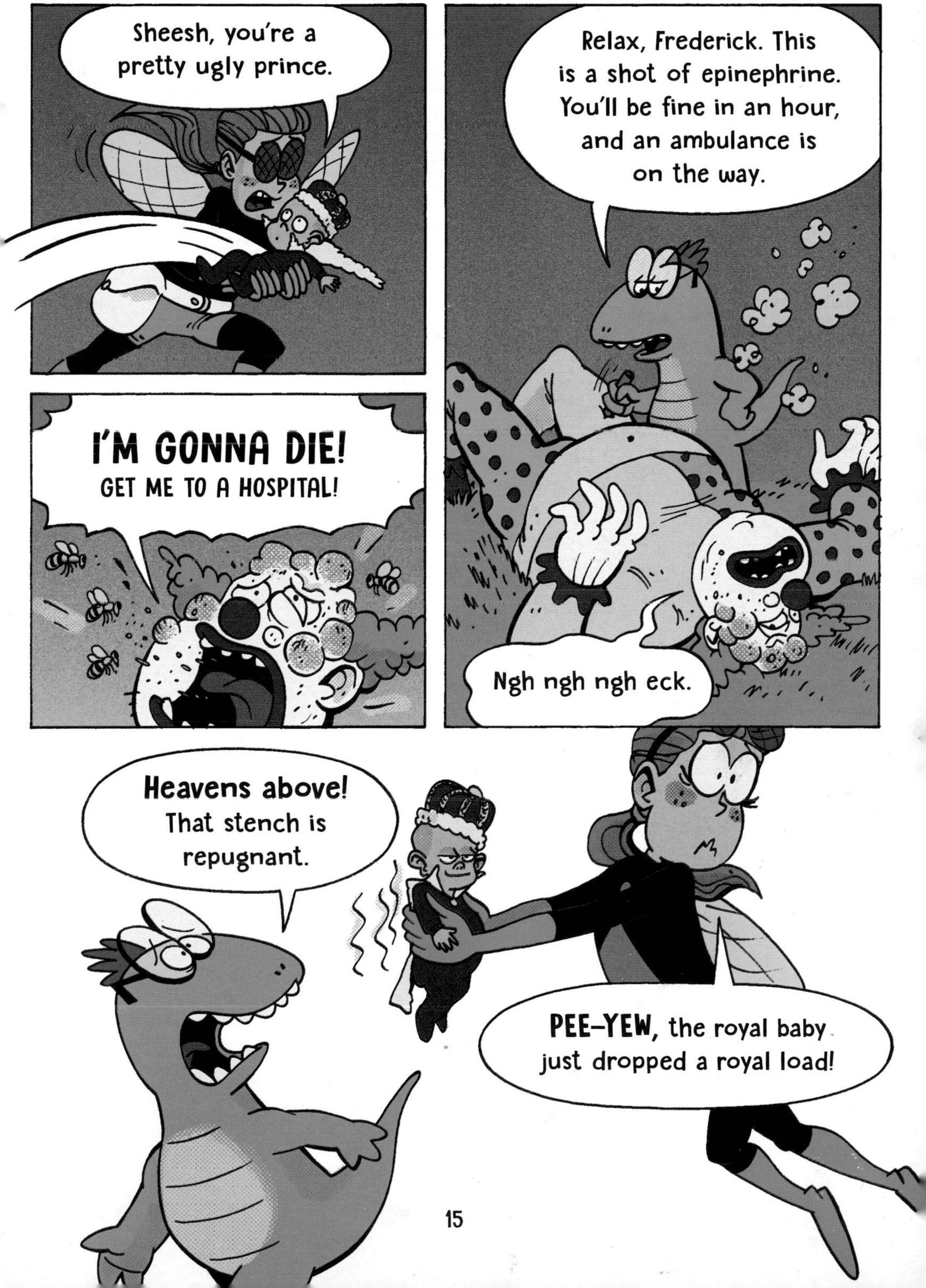

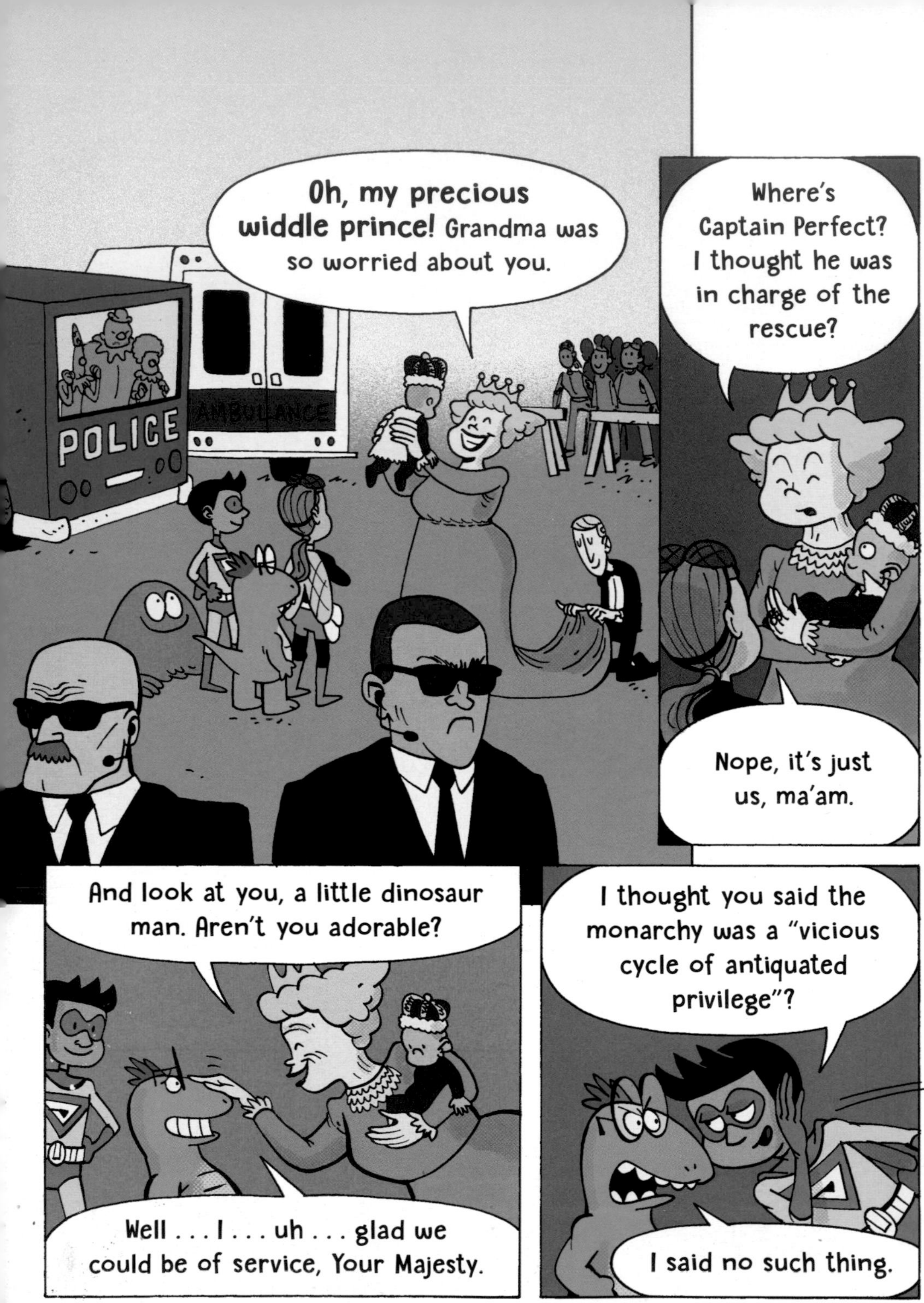
Oh, my precious widdle prince! Grandma was so worried about you.
POLICE
AMBULANCE
Where's Captain Perfect? I thought he was in charge of the rescue?
Nope, it's just us, ma'am.
And look at you, a little dinosaur man. Aren't you adorable?
Well . . . I . . . uh . . . glad we could be of service, Your Majesty.
I thought you said the monarchy was a "vicious cycle of antiquated privilege"?
I said no such thing.

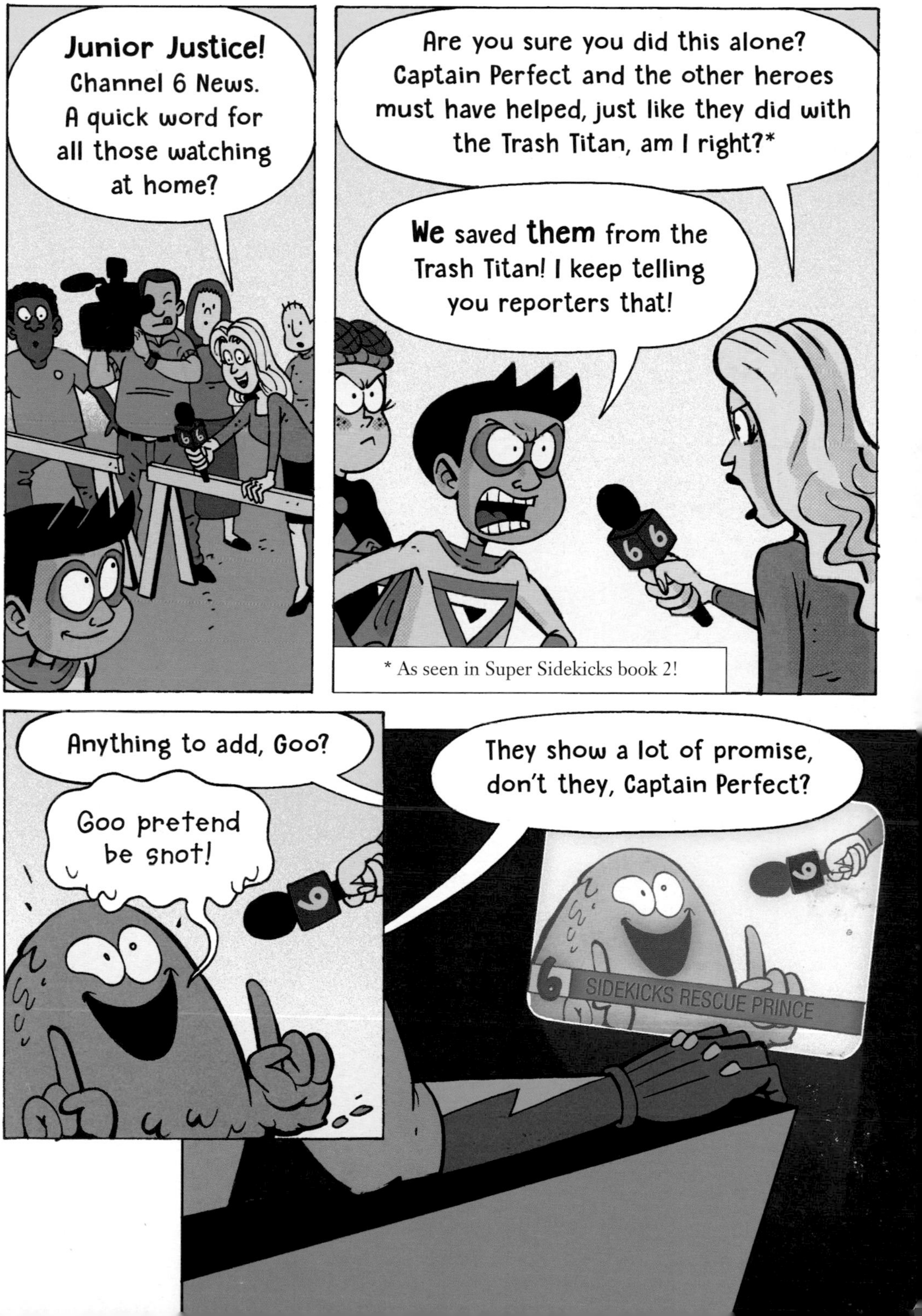
Junior Justice! Channel 6 News. A quick word for all those watching at home?
Are you sure you did this alone? Captain Perfect and the other heroes must have helped, just like they did with the Trash Titan, am I right?*
We saved them from the Trash Titan! I keep telling you reporters that!
* As seen in Super Sidekicks book 2!
Anything to add, Goo?
Goo pretend be snot!
They show a lot of promise, don't they, Captain Perfect?
SIDEKICKS RESCUE PRINCE

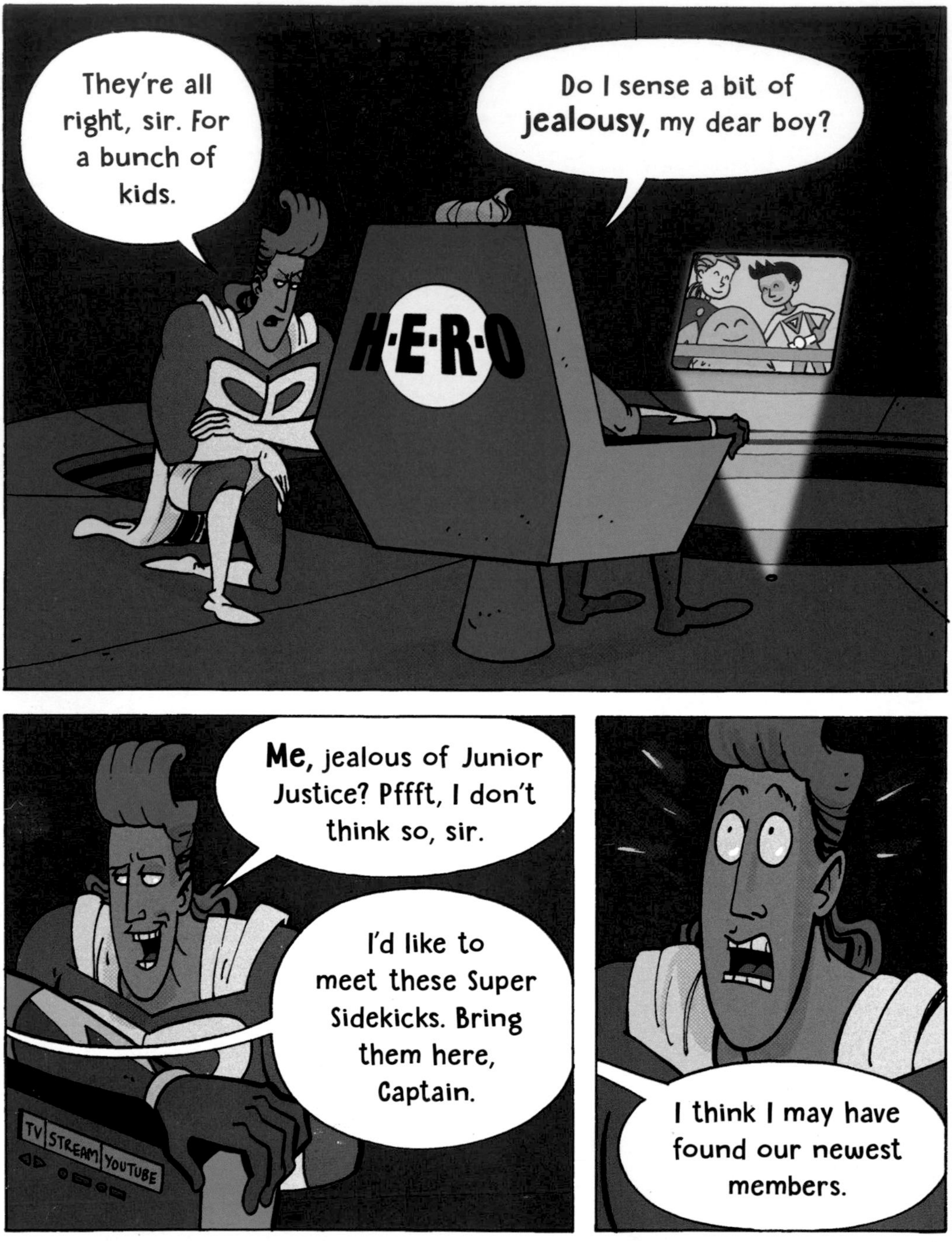
They're all right, sir. For a bunch of kids.
Do I sense a bit of jealousy, my dear boy?
H·E·R·O
Me, jealous of Junior Justice? Pffft, I don't think so, sir.
I'd like to meet these Super Sidekicks. Bring them here, Captain.
TV STREAM YOUTUBE
I think I may have found our newest members.

Chapter

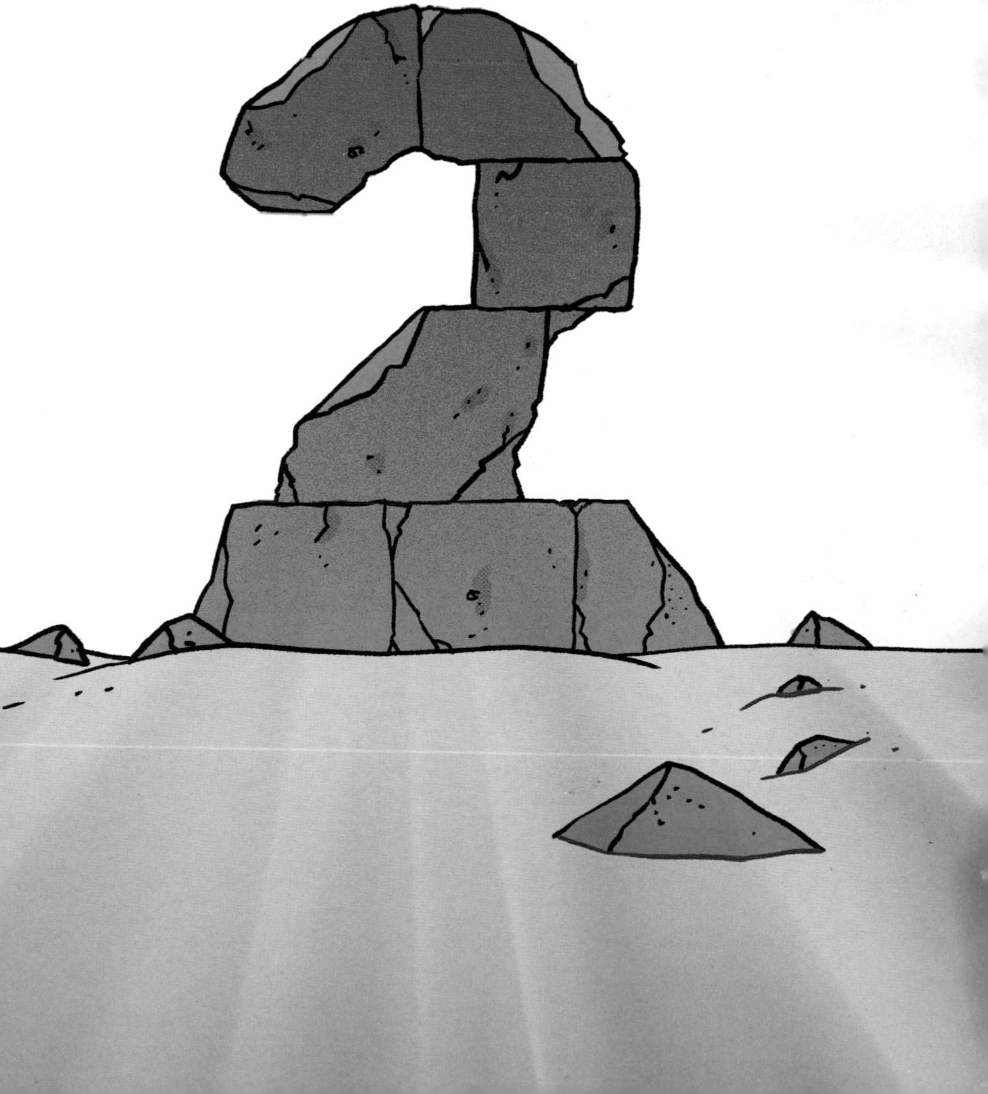
2

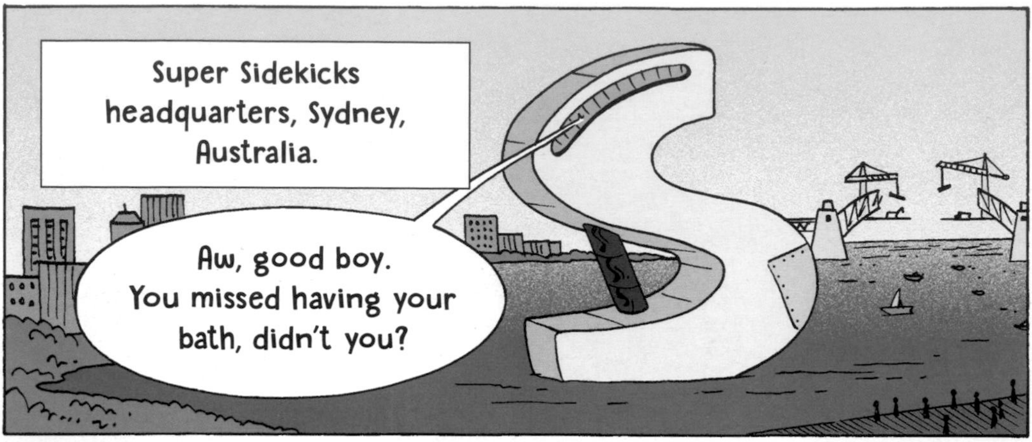
Super Sidekicks headquarters, Sydney, Australia.
Aw, good boy. You missed having your bath, didn't you?

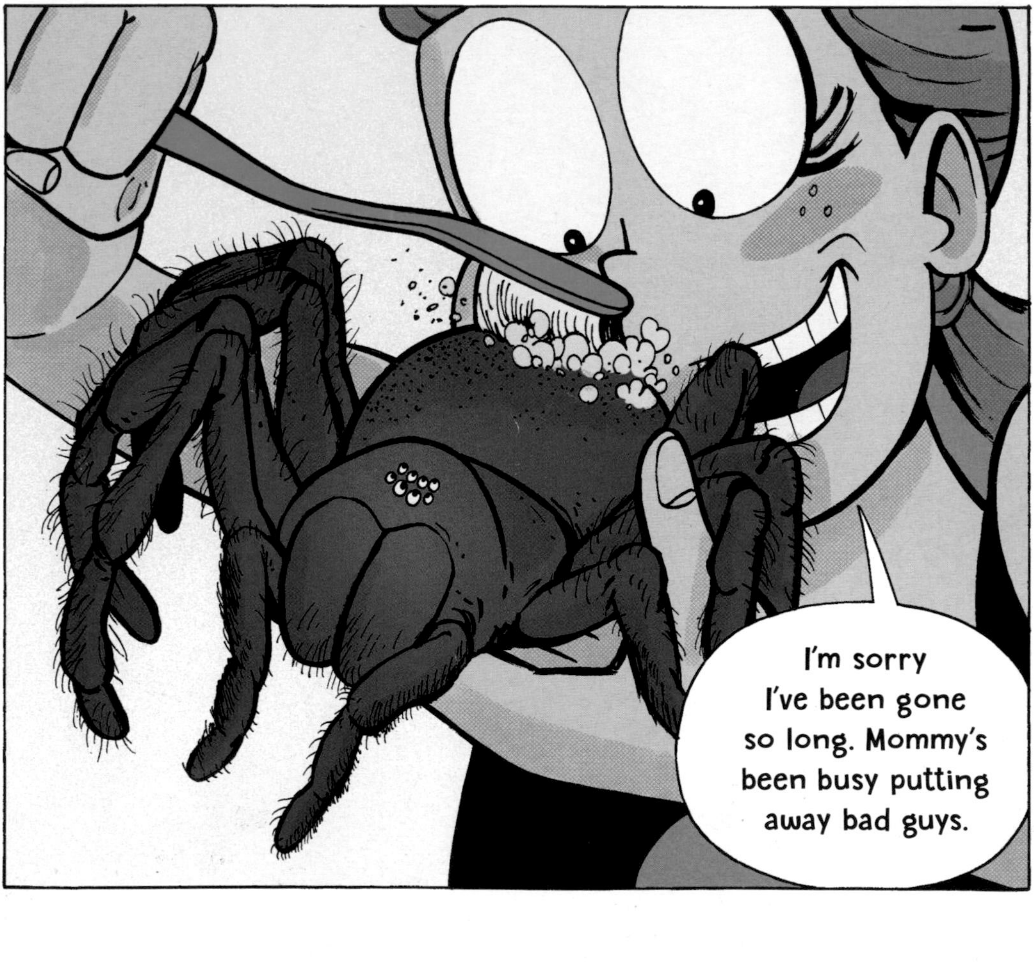
I'm sorry I've been gone so long. Mommy's been busy putting away bad guys.

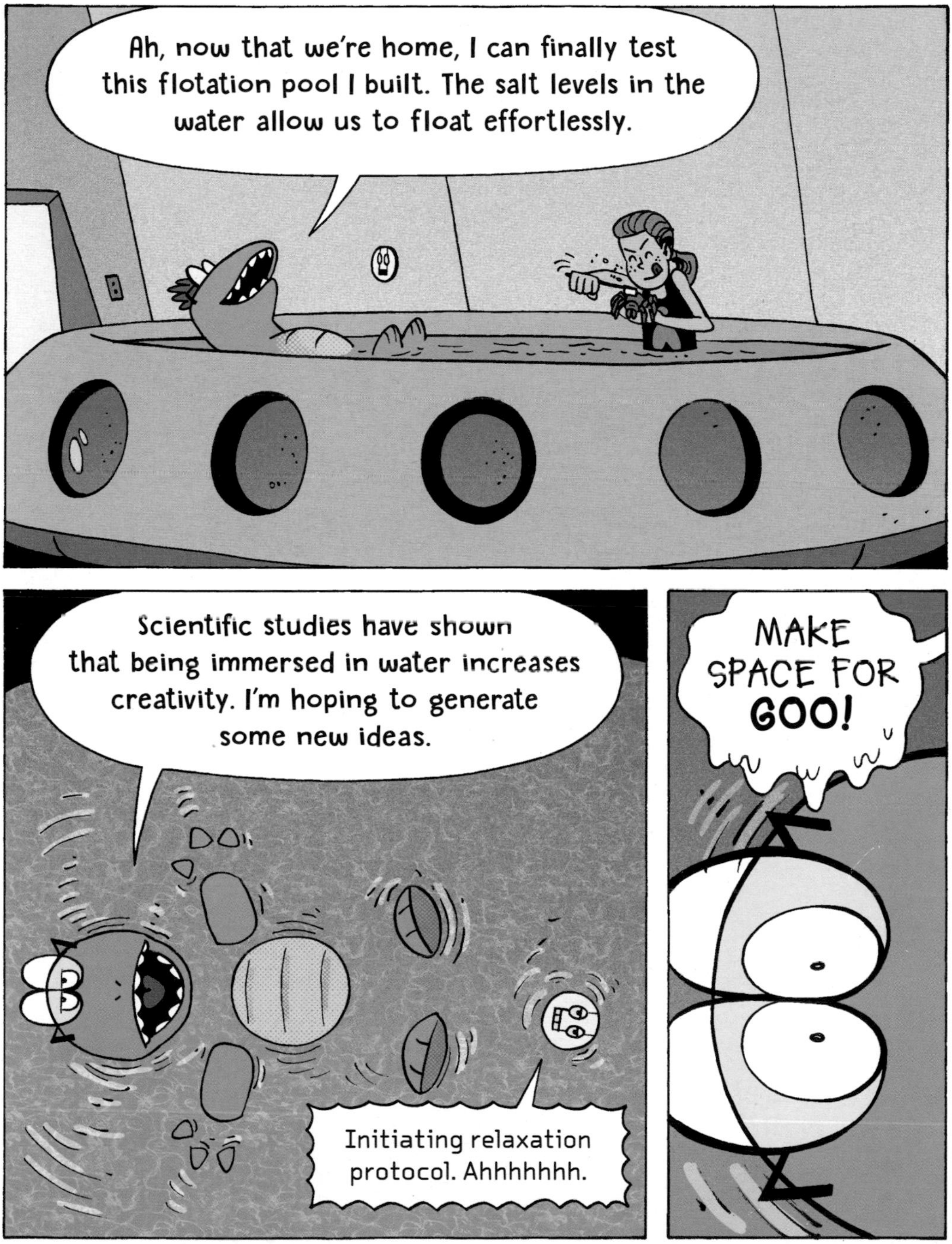
Ah, now that we're home, I can finally test this flotation pool I built. The salt levels in the water allow us to float effortlessly.
Scientific studies have shown that being immersed in water increases creativity. I'm hoping to generate some new ideas.
Initiating relaxation protocol. Ahhhhhhh.
MAKE SPACE FOR GOO!

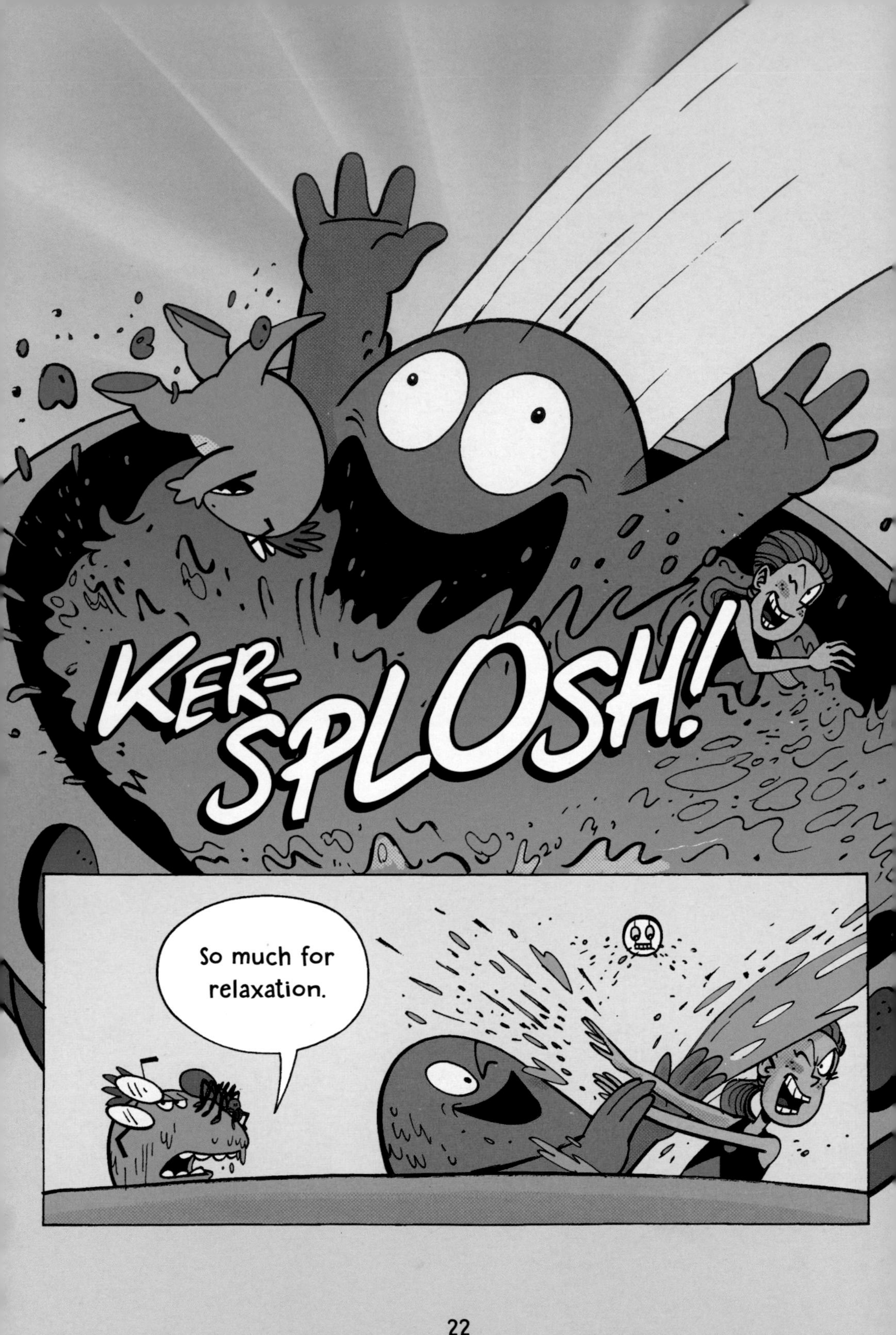
KER-SPLOSH!
So much for relaxation.

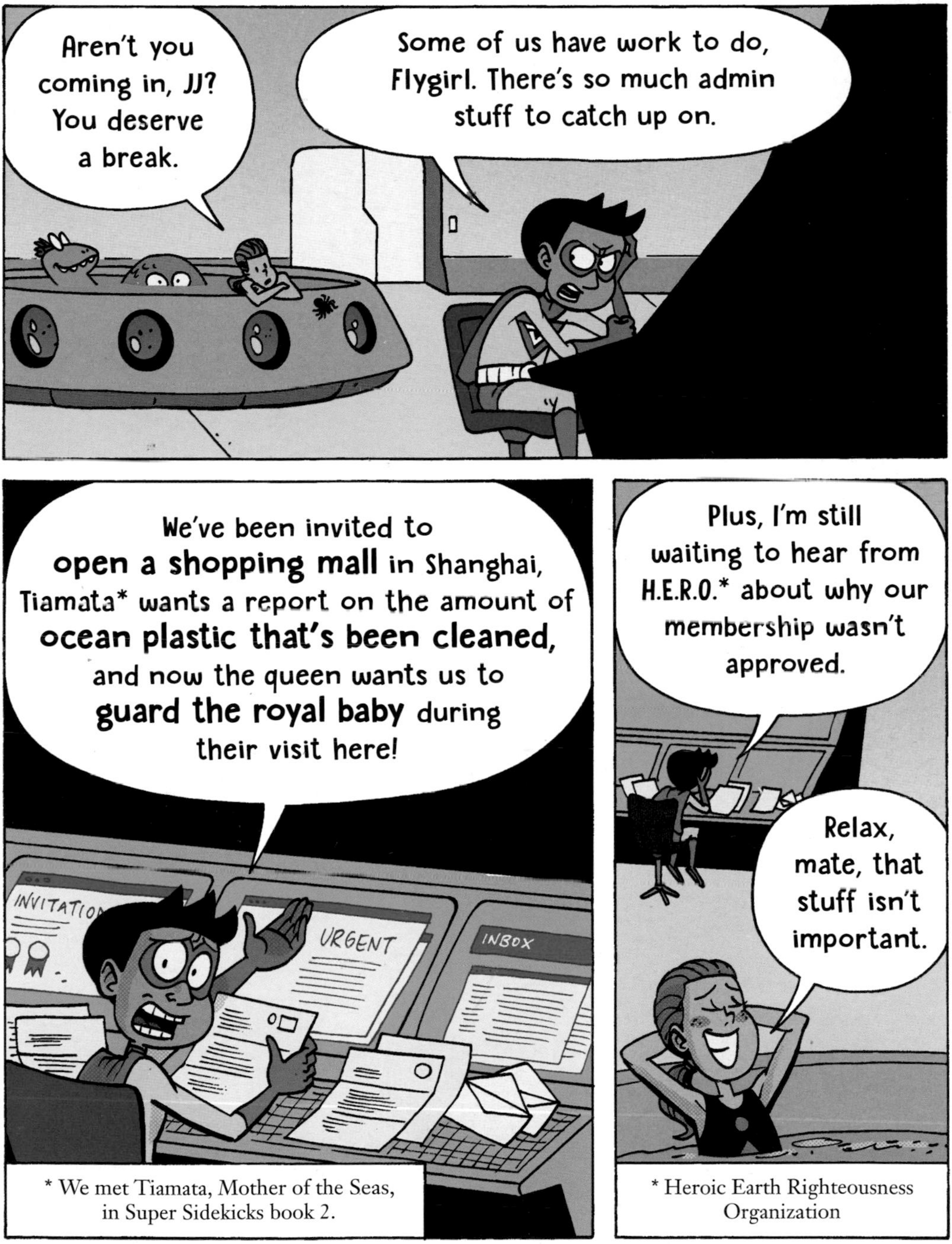
Aren't you coming in, JJ? You deserve a break.
Some of us have work to do, Flygirl. There's so much admin stuff to catch up on.
We've been invited to open a shopping mall in Shanghai, Tiamata* wants a report on the amount of ocean plastic that's been cleaned, and now the queen wants us to guard the royal baby during their visit here!
INVITATION
URGENT
INBOX
Plus, I'm still waiting to hear from H.E.R.O.* about why our membership wasn't approved.
Relax, mate, that stuff isn't important.
* We met Tiamata, Mother of the Seas, in Super Sidekicks book 2.

* Heroic Earth Righteousness Organization

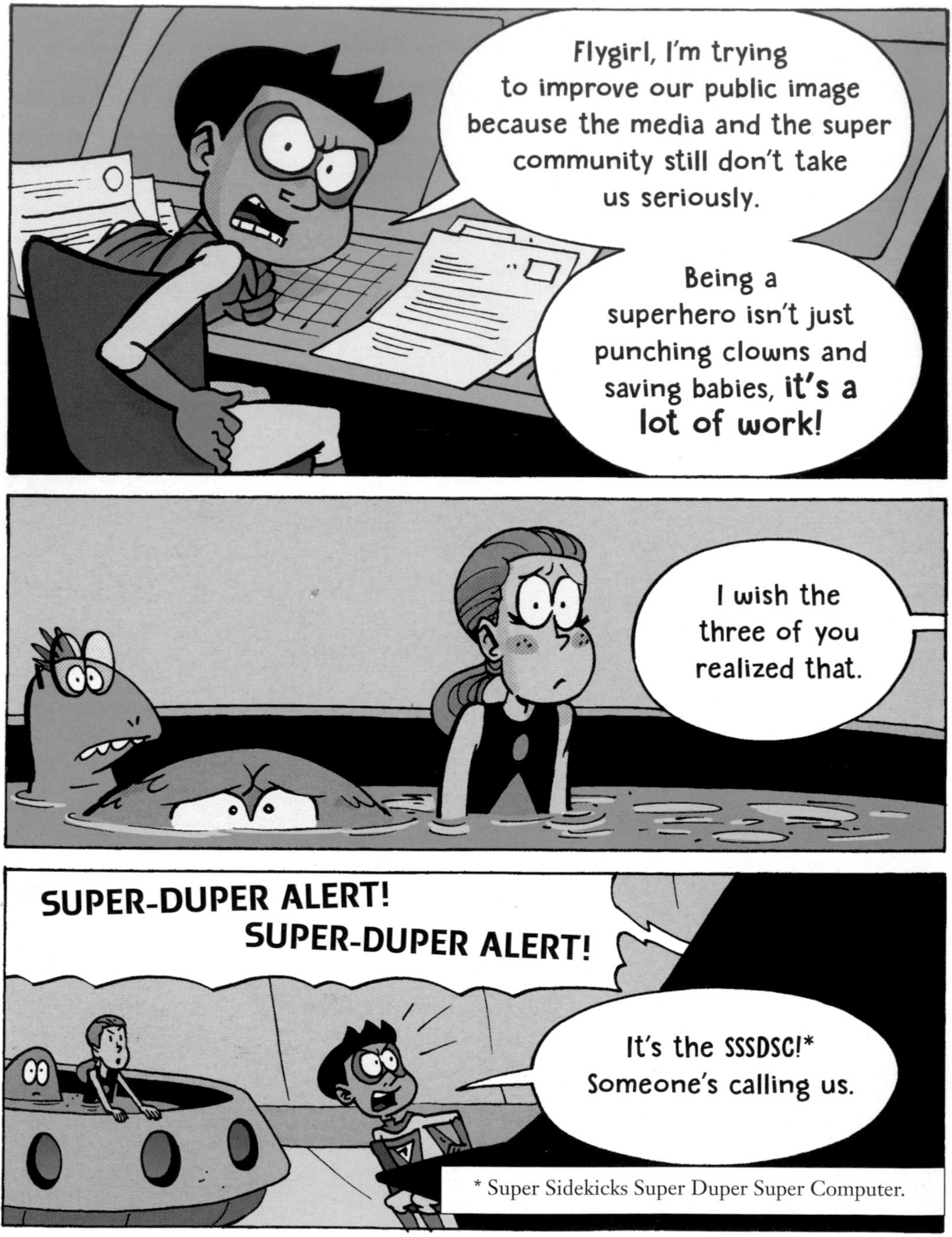
Flygirl, I'm trying to improve our public image because the media and the super community still don't take us seriously.
Being a superhero isn't just punching clowns and saving babies, **it's a lot of work!**
I wish the three of you realized that.
SUPER-DUPER ALERT!
SUPER-DUPER ALERT!
It's the SSSDSC!* Someone's calling us.
* Super Sidekicks Super Duper Super Computer.

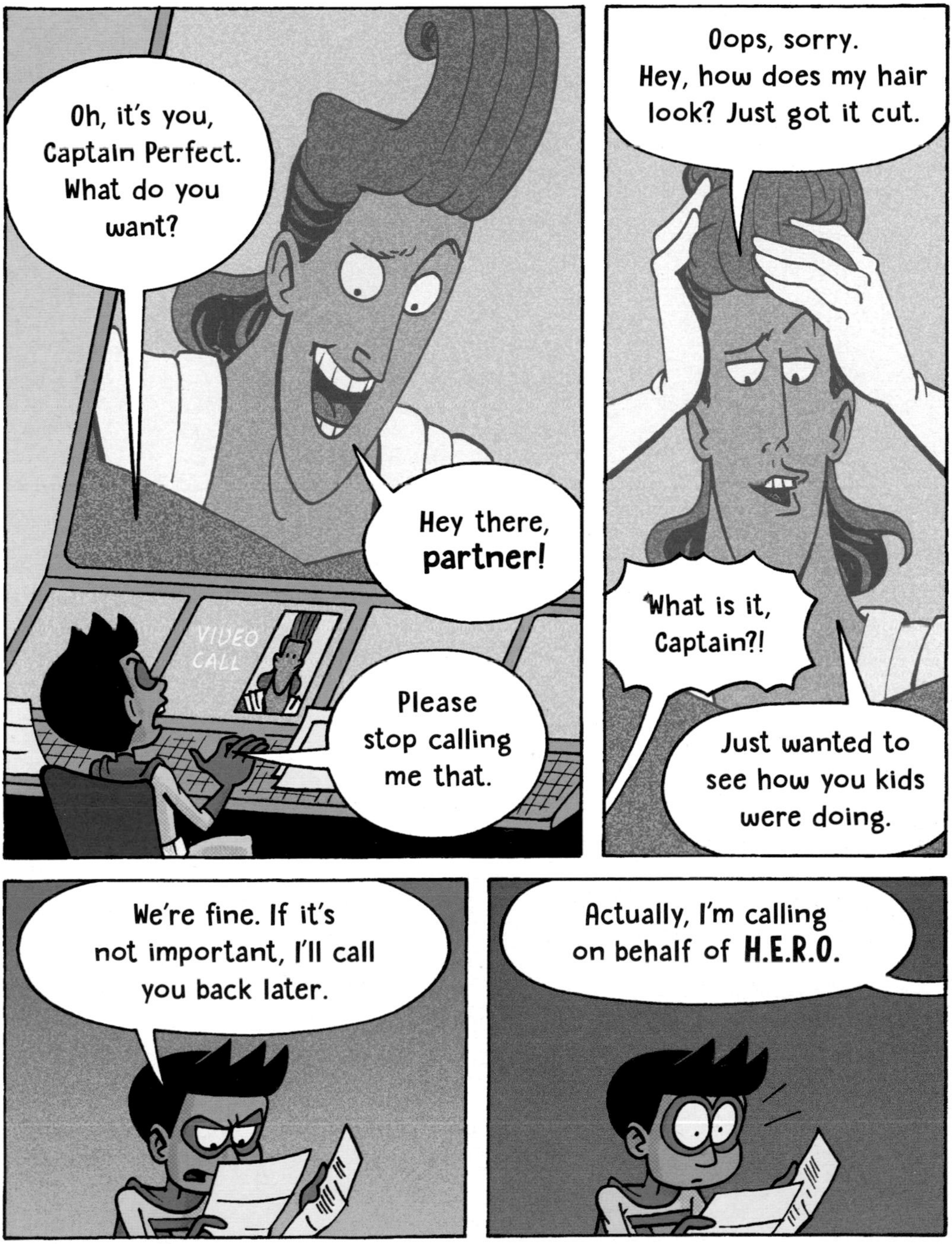
Oh, it's you, Captain Perfect. What do you want?
Hey there, partner!
VIDEO CALL
Please stop calling me that.
Oops, sorry. Hey, how does my hair look? Just got it cut.
What is it, Captain?!
Just wanted to see how you kids were doing.
We're fine. If it's not important, I'll call you back later.
Actually, I'm calling on behalf of H.E.R.O.

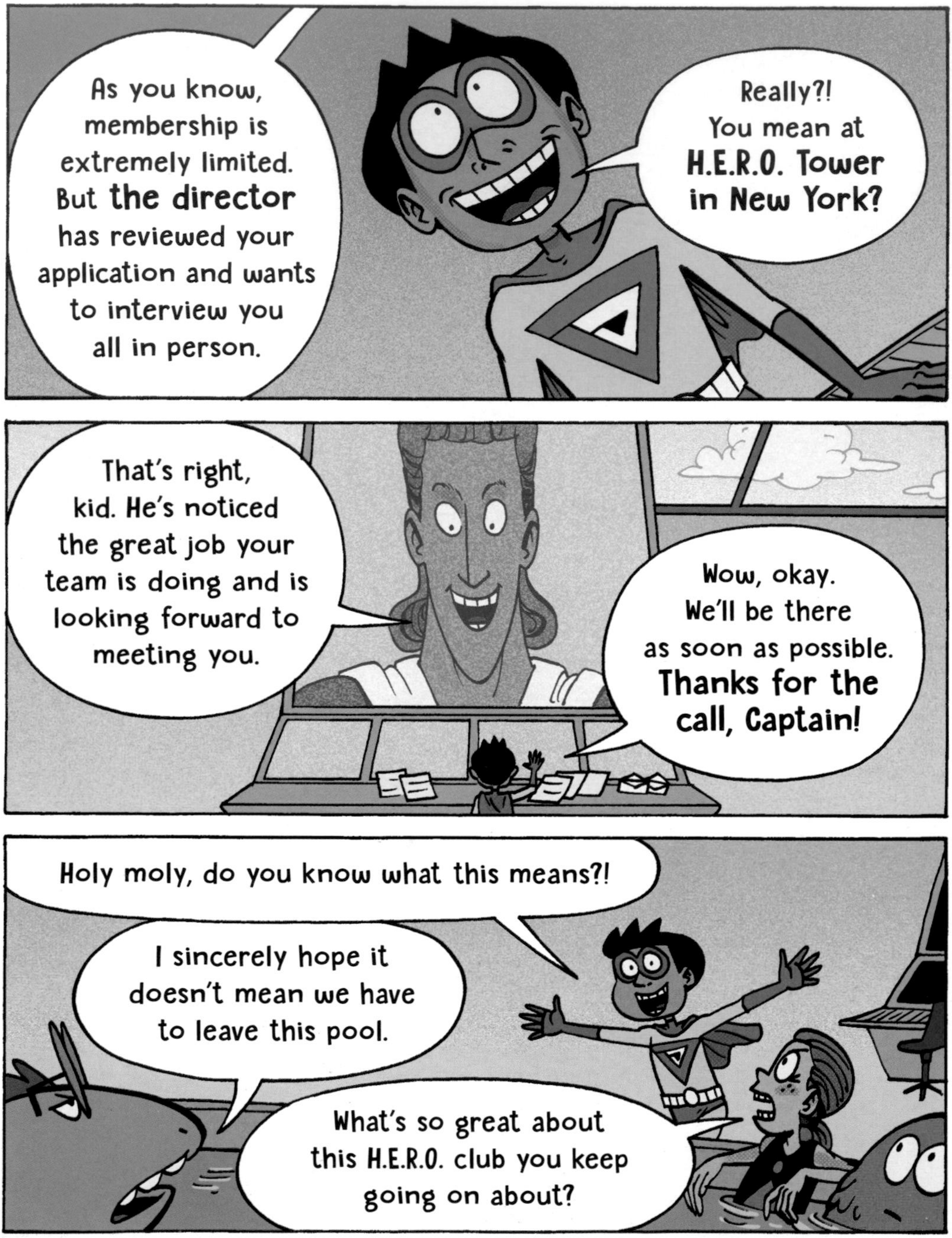
As you know, membership is extremely limited. But the director has reviewed your application and wants to interview you all in person.
Really?! You mean at H.E.R.O. Tower in New York?
That's right, kid. He's noticed the great job your team is doing and is looking forward to meeting you.
Wow, okay. We'll be there as soon as possible. Thanks for the call, Captain!
Holy moly, do you know what this means?!
I sincerely hope it doesn't mean we have to leave this pool.
What's so great about this H.E.R.O. club you keep going on about?

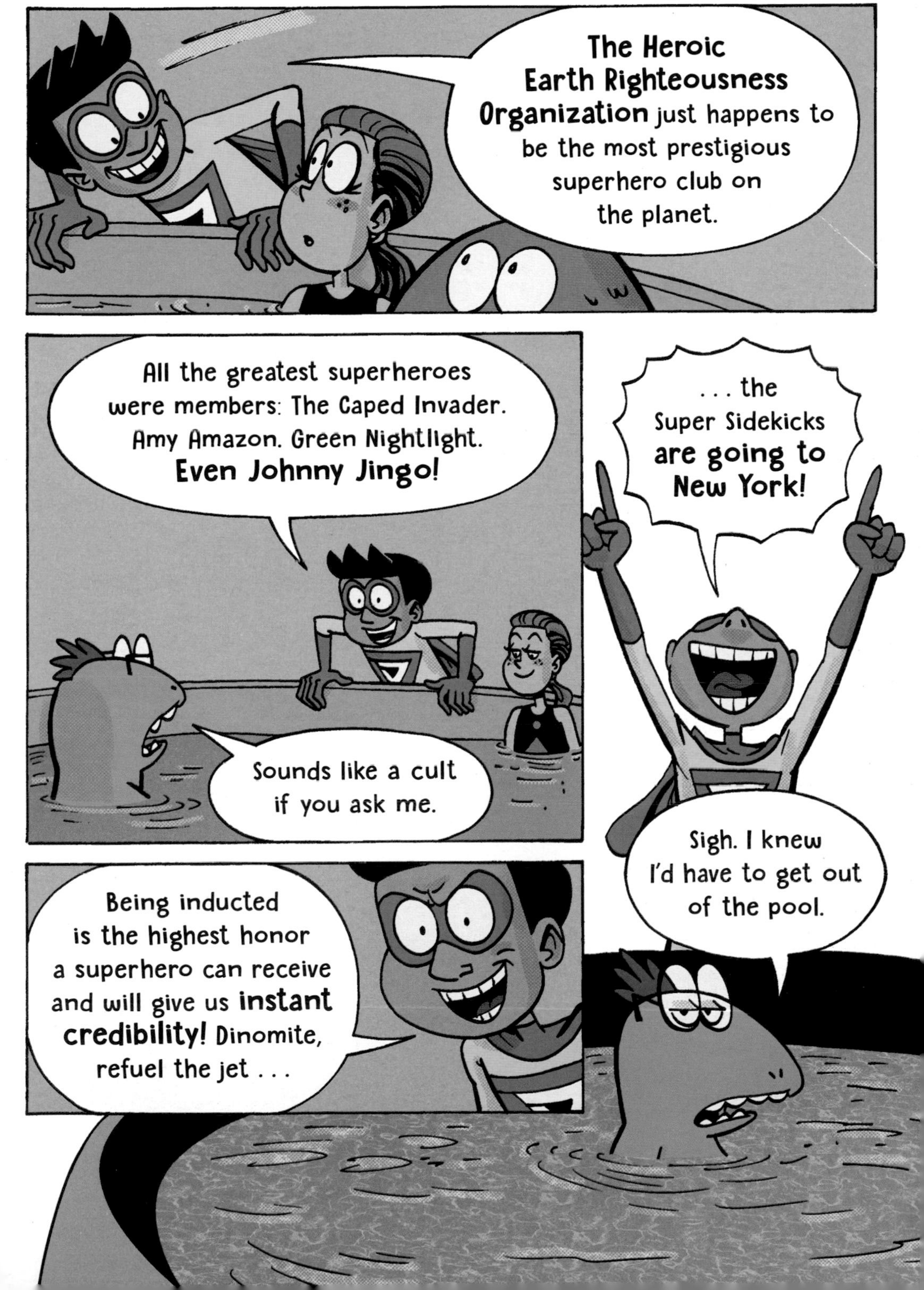
The Heroic Earth Righteousness Organization just happens to be the most prestigious superhero club on the planet.
All the greatest superheroes were members: The Caped Invader. Amy Amazon. Green Nightlight. Even Johnny Jingo!
Sounds like a cult if you ask me.
. . . the Super Sidekicks are going to New York!
Being inducted is the highest honor a superhero can receive and will give us instant credibility! Dinomite, refuel the jet . . .
Sigh. I knew I'd have to get out of the pool.

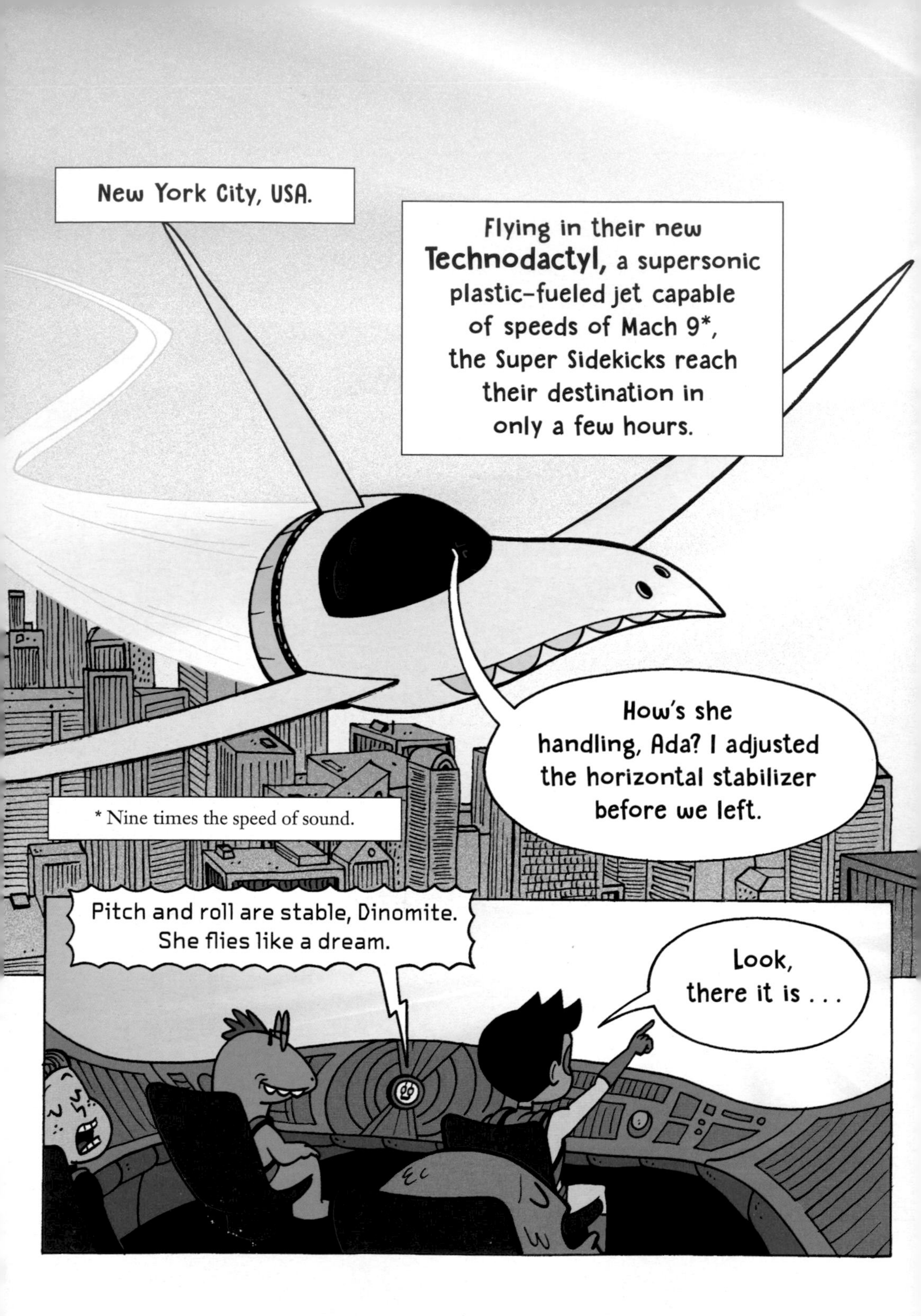
New York City, USA.
Flying in their new Technodactyl, a supersonic plastic-fueled jet capable of speeds of Mach 9*, the Super Sidekicks reach their destination in only a few hours.
How's she handling, Ada? I adjusted the horizontal stabilizer before we left.
* Nine times the speed of sound.
Pitch and roll are stable, Dinomite. She flies like a dream.
Look, there it is . . .

H.E.R.O. Tower!

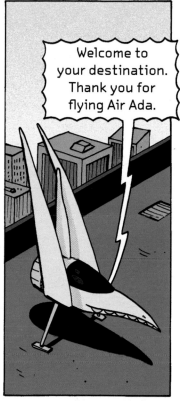

Welcome to your destination. Thank you for flying Air Ada.

How do I look? Is my mask straight? Does my cape have any creases?

Junior Justice so handsome!

Chill out, mate. I've never seen you this nervous before.

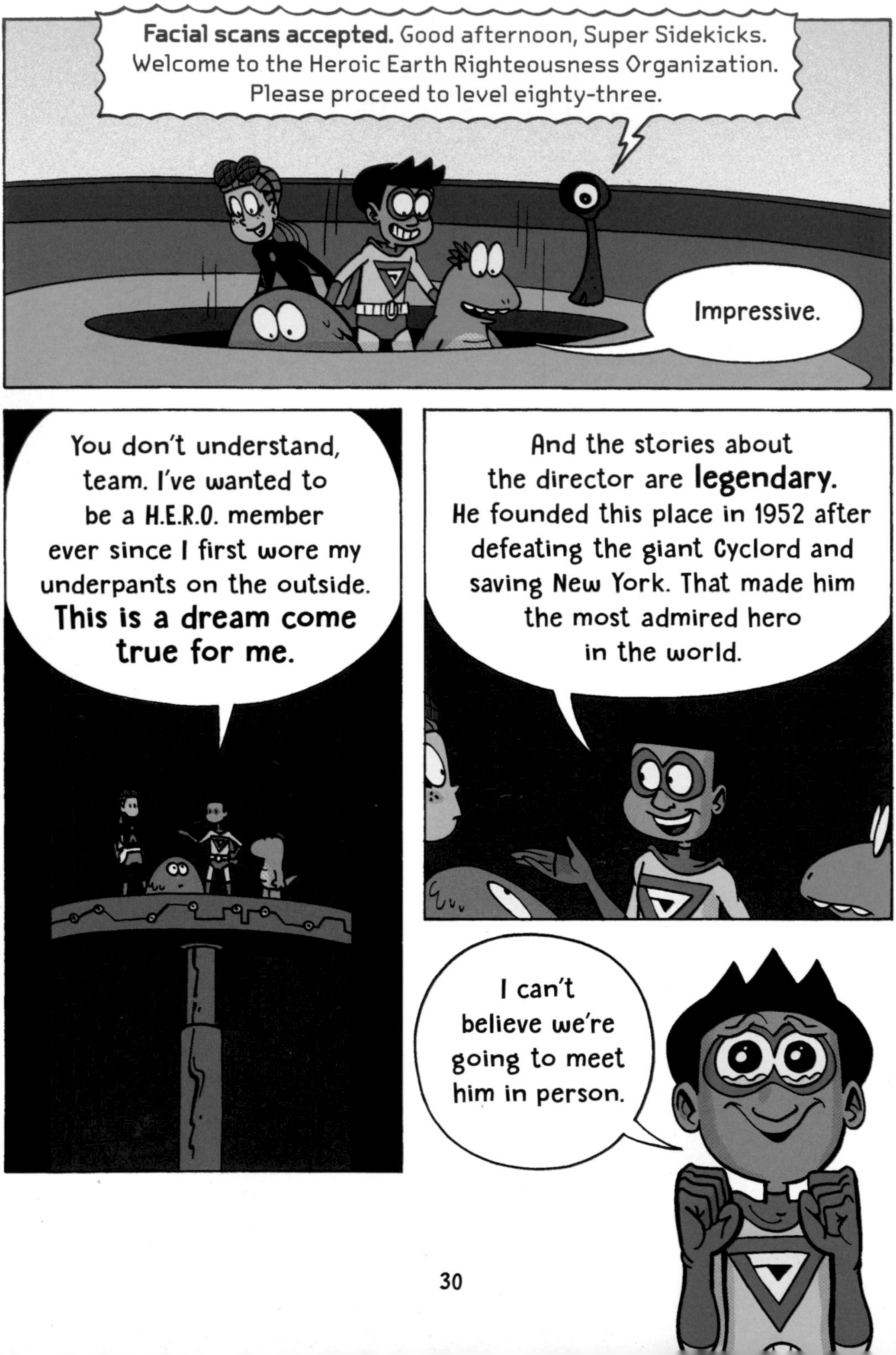
Facial scans accepted. Good afternoon, Super Sidekicks. Welcome to the Heroic Earth Righteousness Organization. Please proceed to level eighty-three.
Impressive.
You don't understand, team. I've wanted to be a H.E.R.O. member ever since I first wore my underpants on the outside. **This is a dream come true for me.**
And the stories about the director are **legendary.** He founded this place in 1952 after defeating the giant Cyclord and saving New York. That made him the most admired hero in the world.
I can't believe we're going to meet him in person.

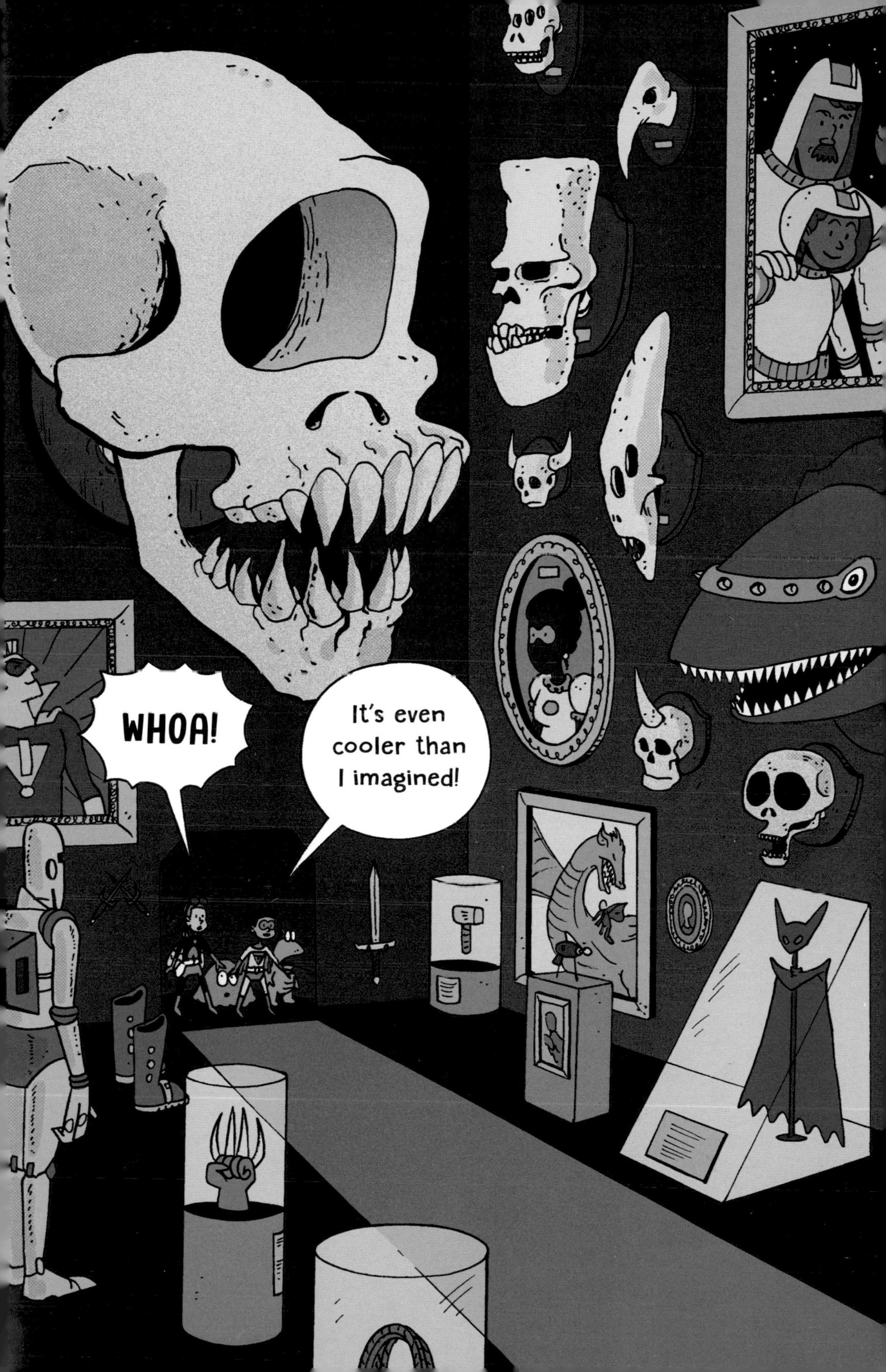
WHOA!
It's even cooler than I imagined!

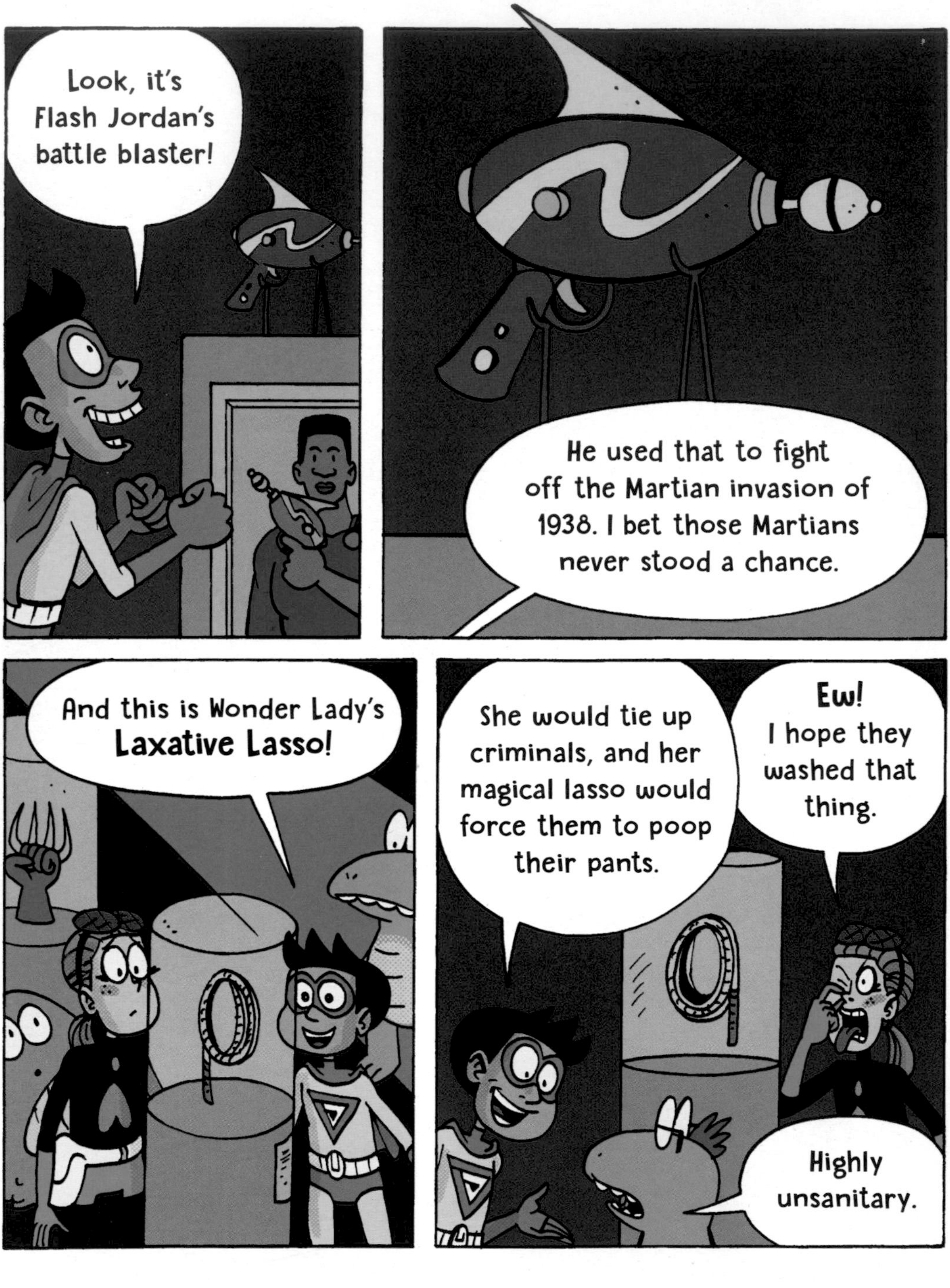
Look, it's Flash Jordan's battle blaster!
He used that to fight off the Martian invasion of 1938. I bet those Martians never stood a chance.
And this is Wonder Lady's **Laxative Lasso!**
She would tie up criminals, and her magical lasso would force them to poop their pants.
Ew! I hope they washed that thing.
Highly unsanitary.

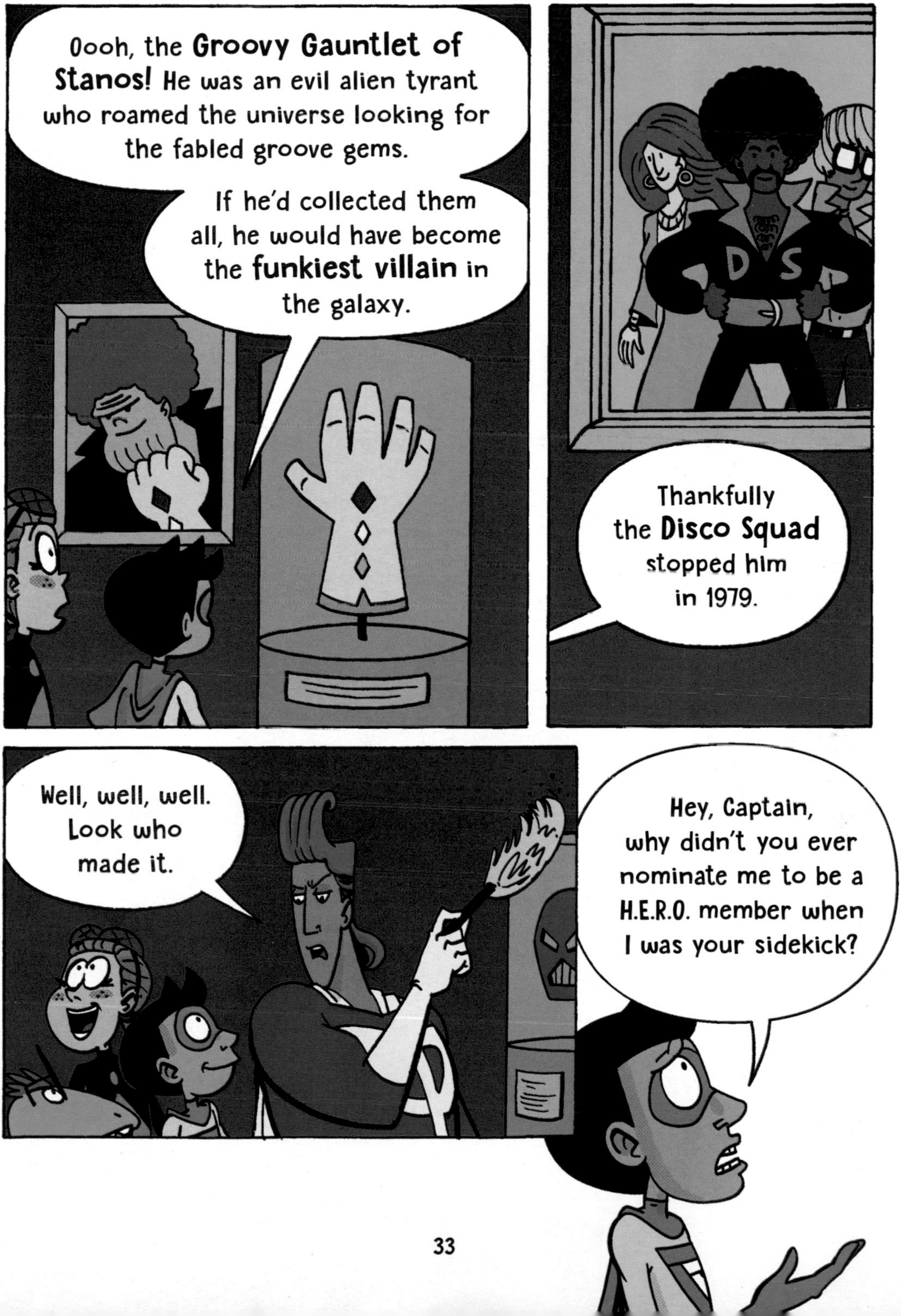
Oooh, the Groovy Gauntlet of Stanos! He was an evil alien tyrant who roamed the universe looking for the fabled groove gems.
If he'd collected them all, he would have become the funkiest villain in the galaxy.
D S
Thankfully the Disco Squad stopped him in 1979.
Well, well, well. Look who made it.
Hey, Captain, why didn't you ever nominate me to be a H.E.R.O. member when I was your sidekick?

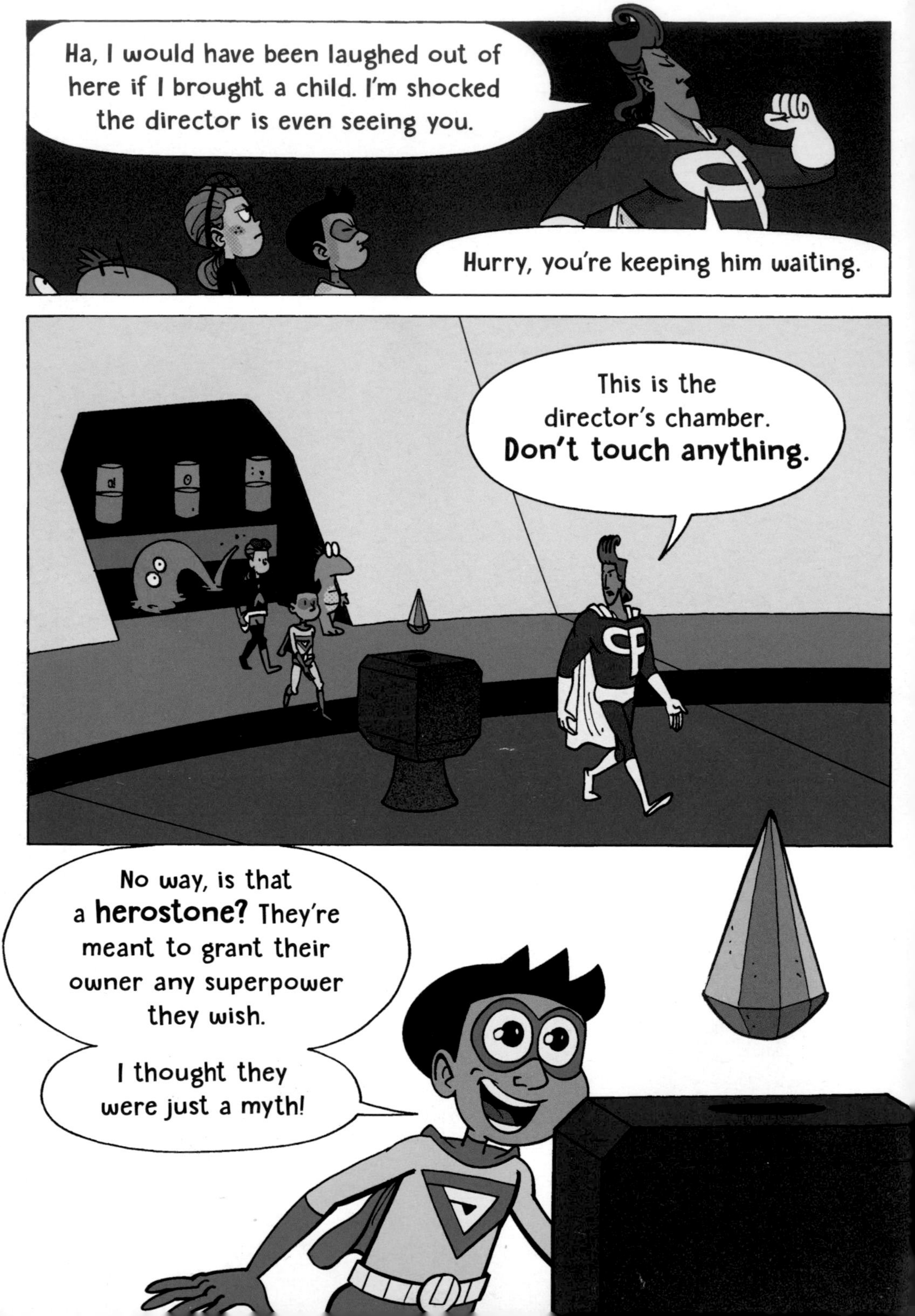
Ha, I would have been laughed out of here if I brought a child. I'm shocked the director is even seeing you.
Hurry, you're keeping him waiting.
This is the director's chamber. **Don't touch anything.**
No way, is that a **herostone?** They're meant to grant their owner any superpower they wish.
I thought they were just a myth!

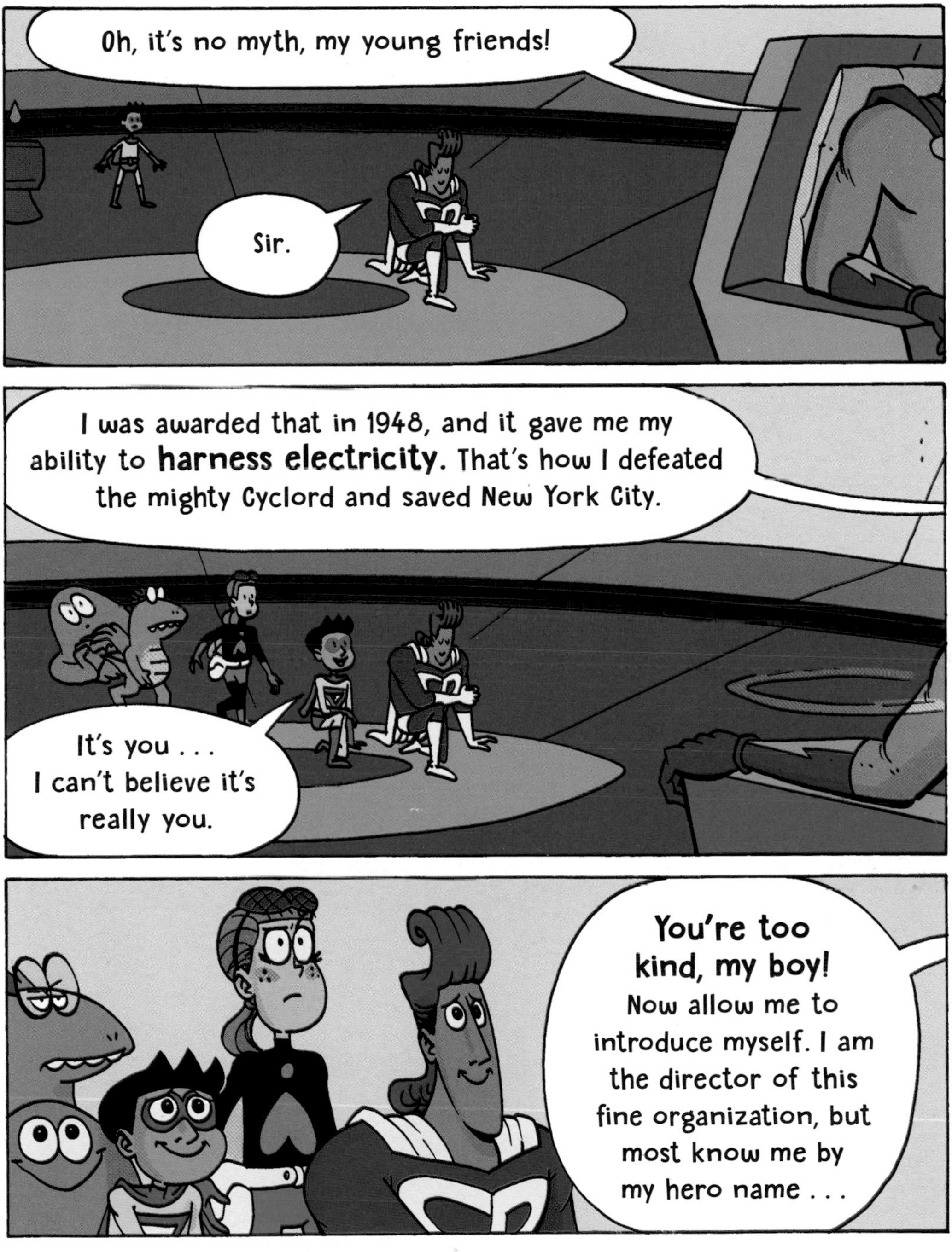
Oh, it's no myth, my young friends!
Sir.
I was awarded that in 1948, and it gave me my ability to **harness electricity.** That's how I defeated the mighty Cyclord and saved New York City.
It's you . . . I can't believe it's really you.
You're too kind, my boy! Now allow me to introduce myself. I am the director of this fine organization, but most know me by my hero name . . .

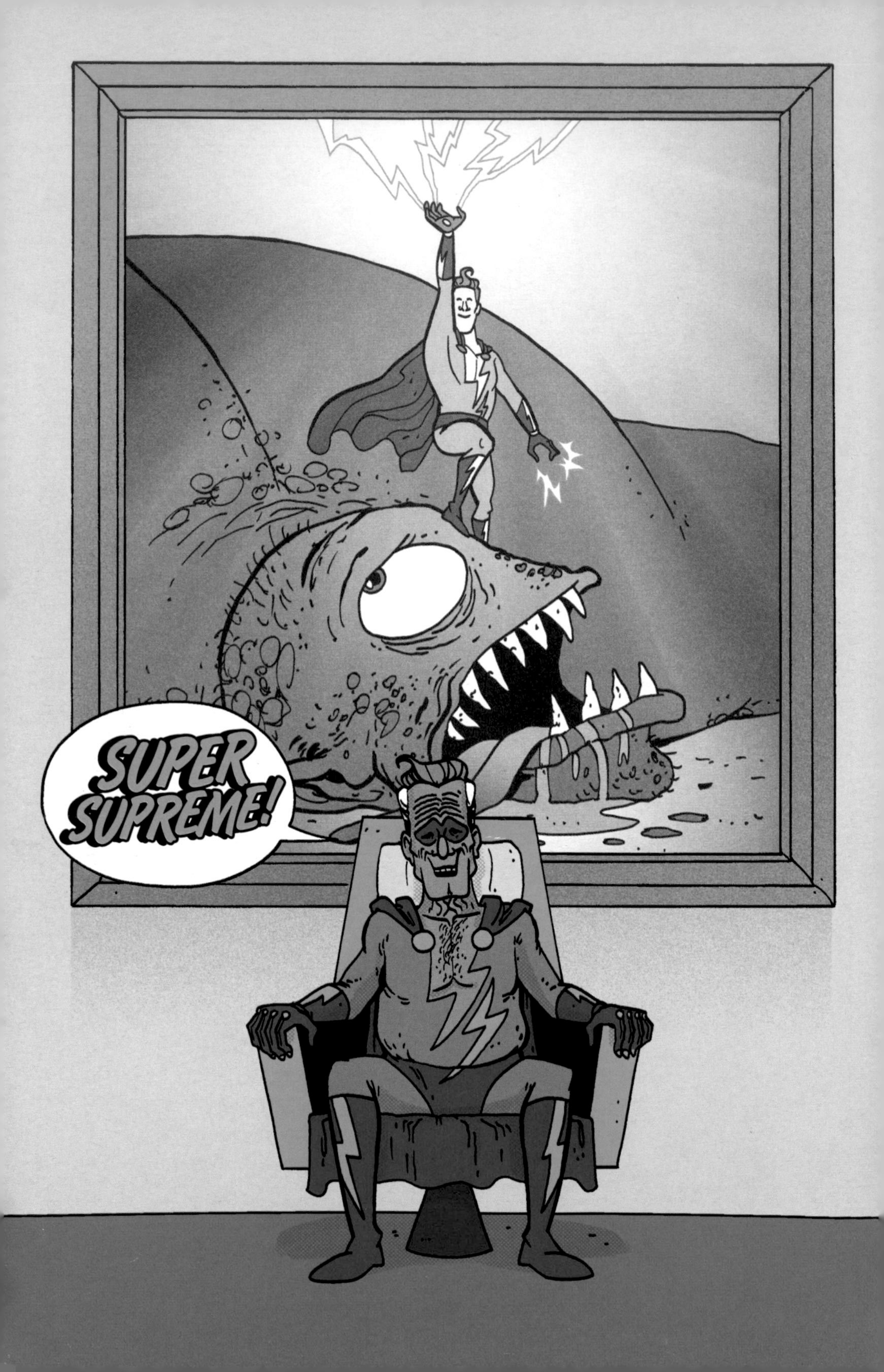
SUPER SUPREME!

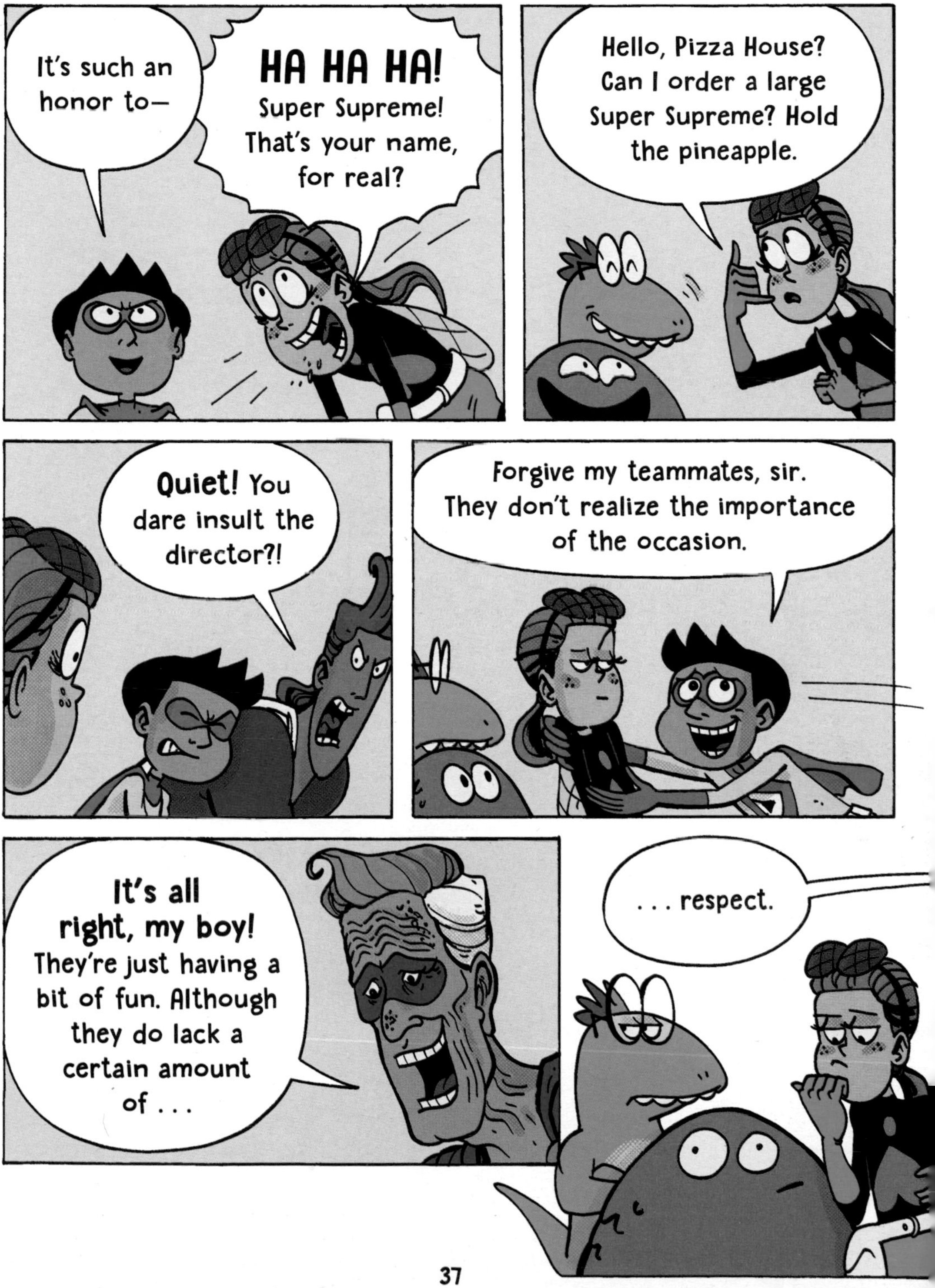

It's such an honor to—
HA HA HA! Super Supreme! That's your name, for real?
Hello, Pizza House? Can I order a large Super Supreme? Hold the pineapple.
Quiet! You dare insult the director?!
Forgive my teammates, sir. They don't realize the importance of the occasion.
It's all right, my boy! They're just having a bit of fun. Although they do lack a certain amount of . . .
. . . respect.

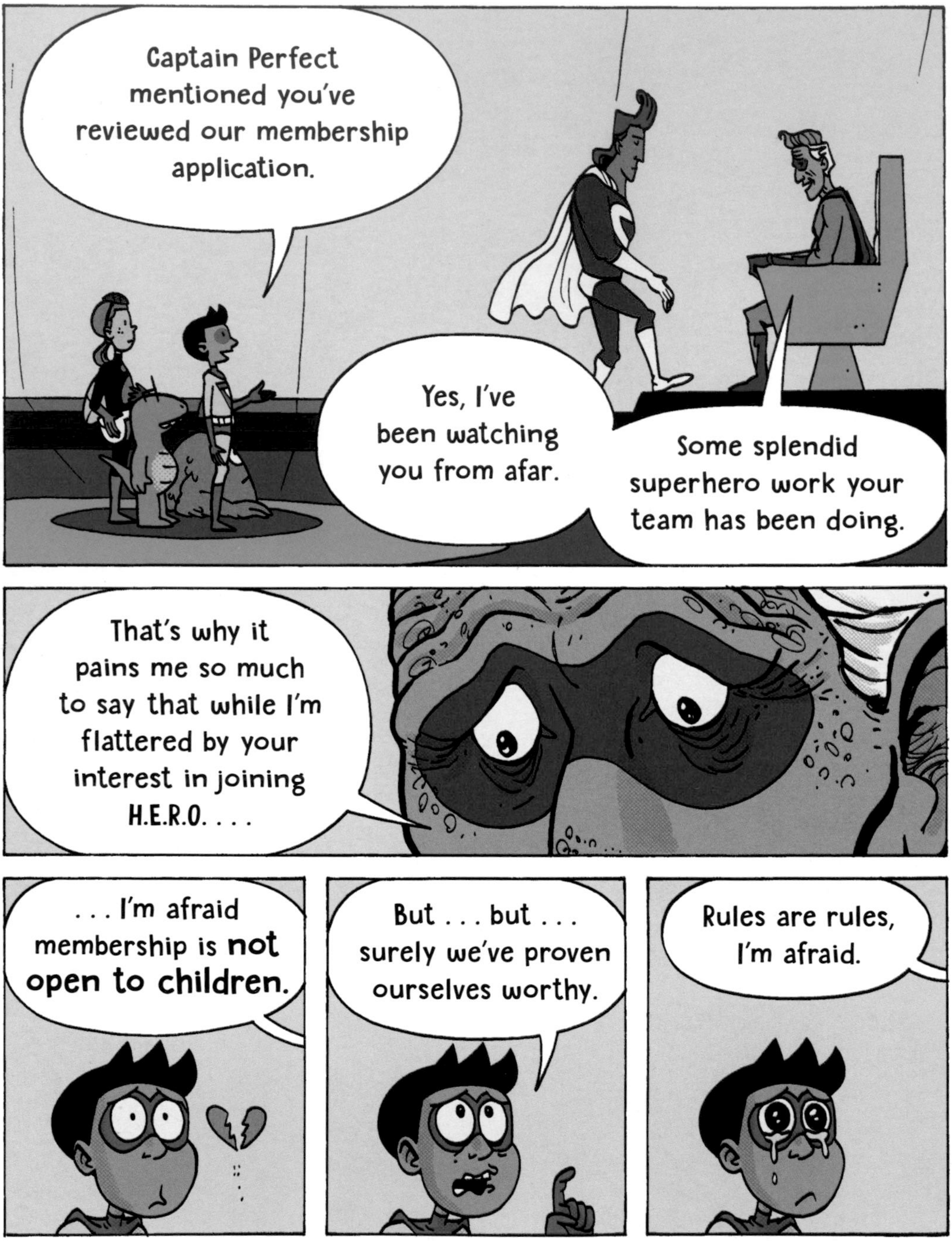
Captain Perfect mentioned you've reviewed our membership application.
Yes, I've been watching you from afar.
Some splendid superhero work your team has been doing.
That's why it pains me so much to say that while I'm flattered by your interest in joining H.E.R.O. . . .
. . . I'm afraid membership is **not open to children.**
But . . . but . . . surely we've proven ourselves worthy.
Rules are rules, I'm afraid.

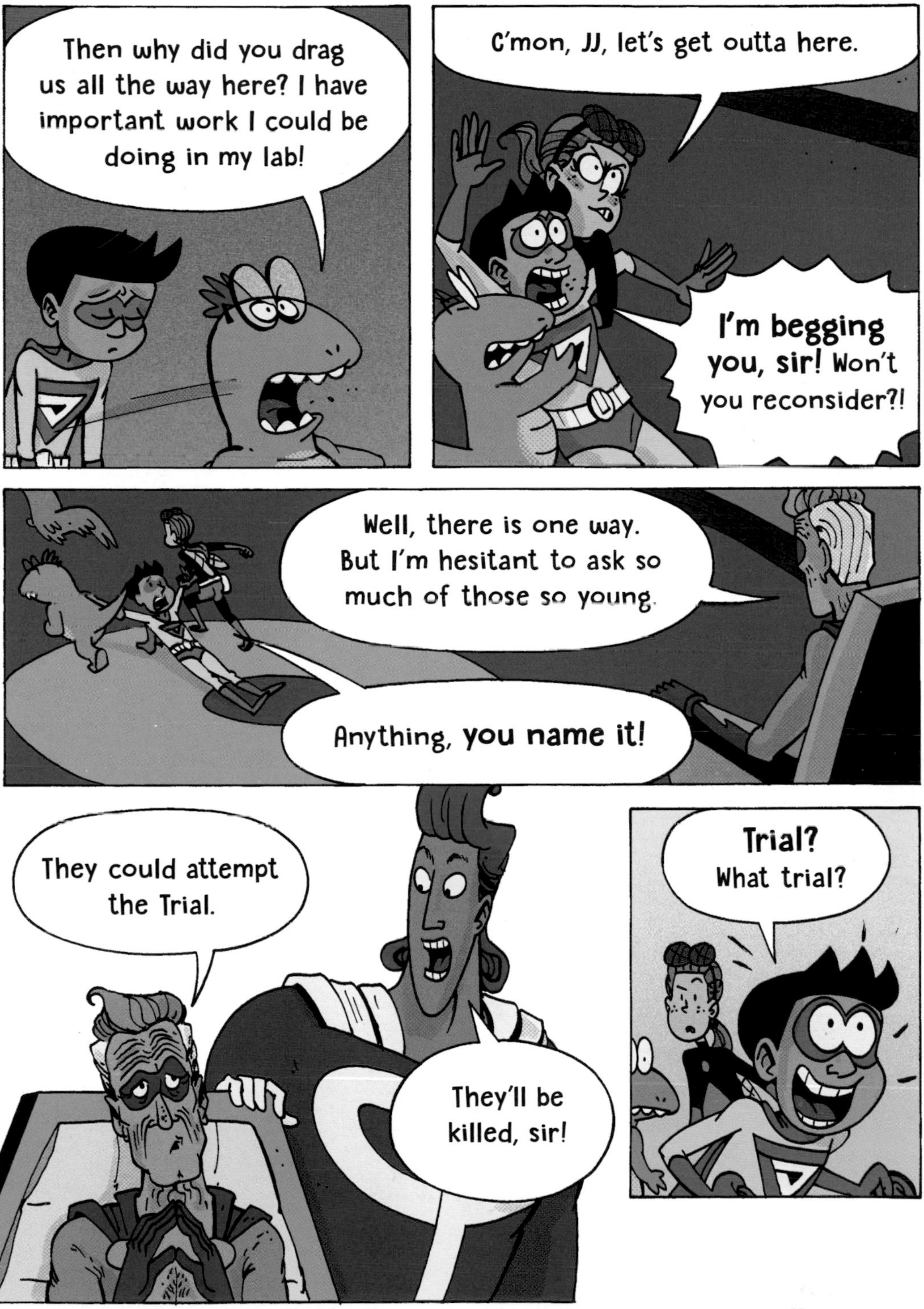
Then why did you drag us all the way here? I have important work I could be doing in my lab!
C'mon, JJ, let's get outta here.
I'm begging you, sir! Won't you reconsider?!
Well, there is one way. But I'm hesitant to ask so much of those so young.
Anything, you name it!
They could attempt the Trial.
They'll be killed, sir!
Trial? What trial?

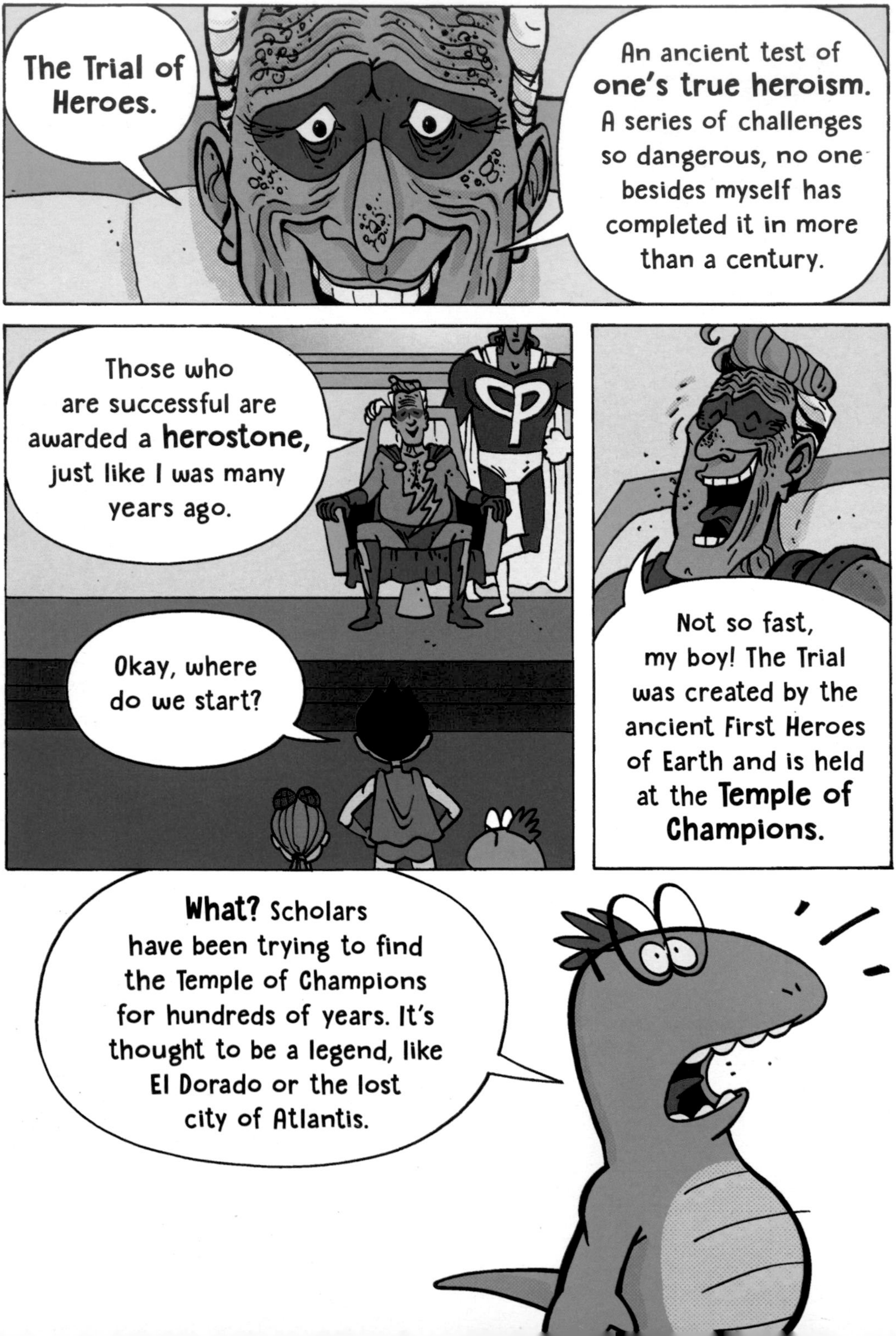
The Trial of Heroes.
An ancient test of one's true heroism. A series of challenges so dangerous, no one besides myself has completed it in more than a century.
Those who are successful are awarded a herostone, just like I was many years ago.
Okay, where do we start?
Not so fast, my boy! The Trial was created by the ancient First Heroes of Earth and is held at the Temple of Champions.
What? Scholars have been trying to find the Temple of Champions for hundreds of years. It's thought to be a legend, like El Dorado or the lost city of Atlantis.

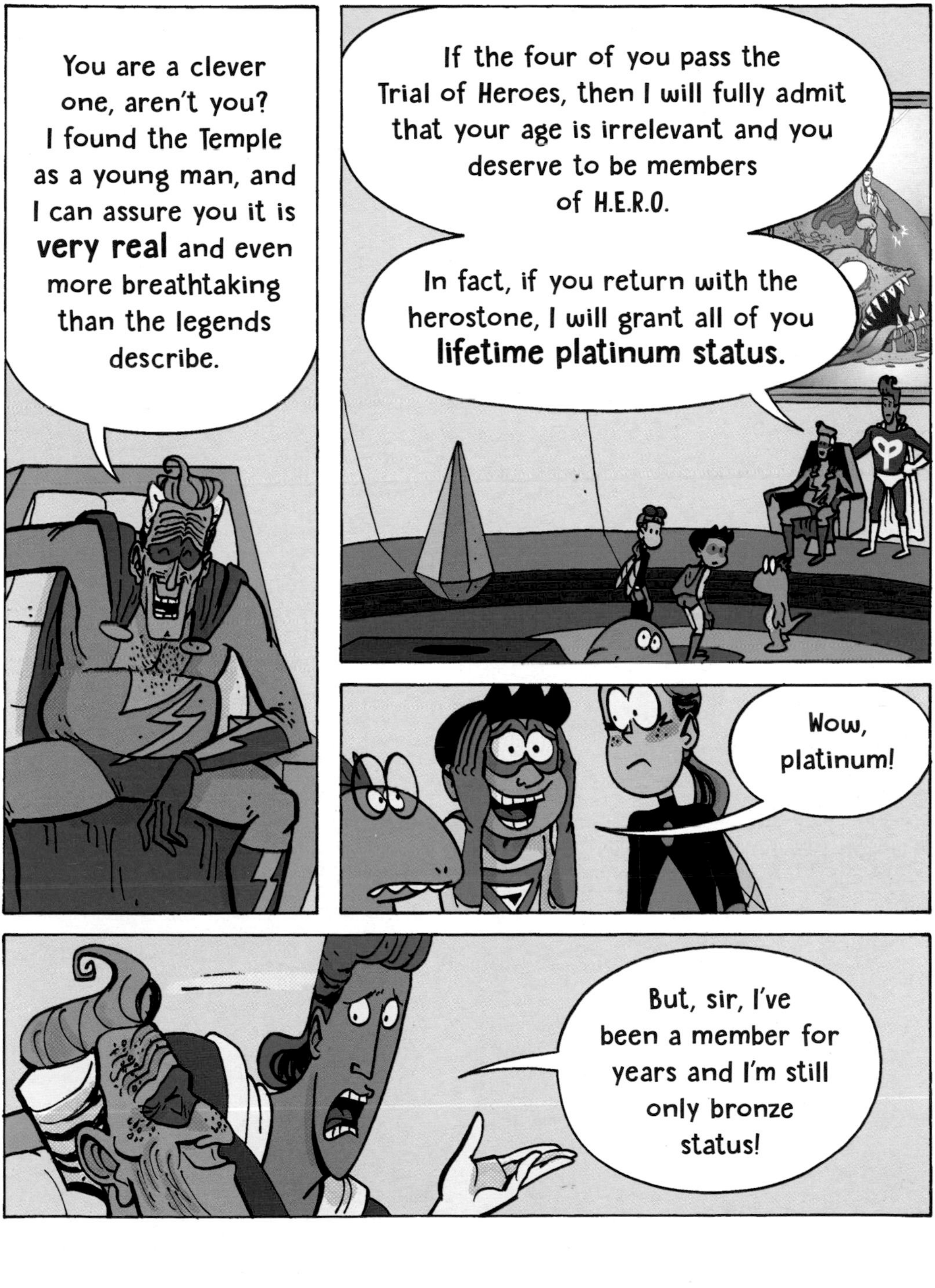
You are a clever one, aren't you? I found the Temple as a young man, and I can assure you it is very real and even more breathtaking than the legends describe.
If the four of you pass the Trial of Heroes, then I will fully admit that your age is irrelevant and you deserve to be members of H.E.R.O.
In fact, if you return with the herostone, I will grant all of you lifetime platinum status.
Wow, platinum!
But, sir, I've been a member for years and I'm still only bronze status!

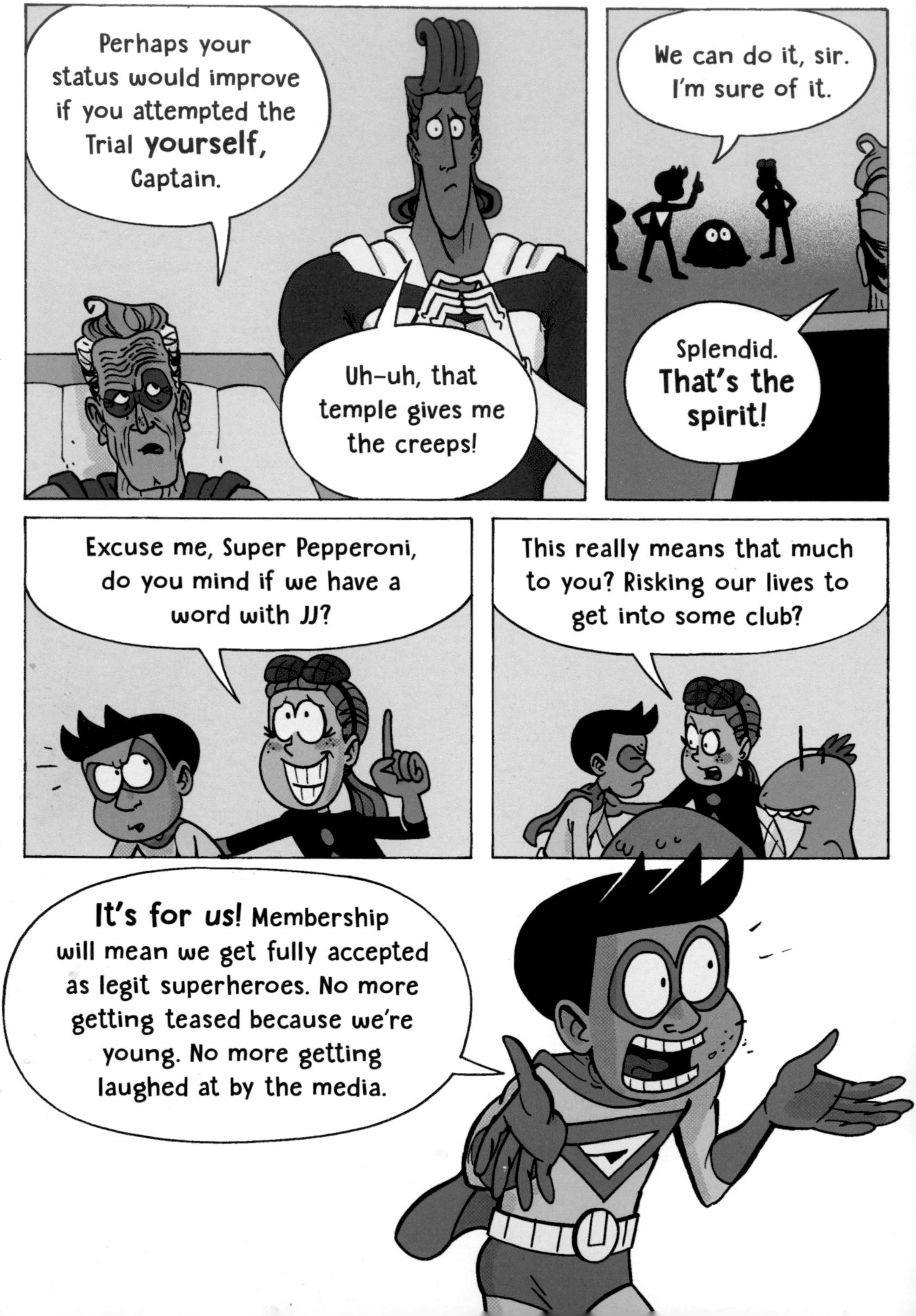
Perhaps your status would improve if you attempted the Trial **yourself,** Captain.
Uh-uh, that temple gives me the creeps!
We can do it, sir. I'm sure of it.
Splendid. **That's the spirit!**
Excuse me, Super Pepperoni, do you mind if we have a word with JJ?
This really means that much to you? Risking our lives to get into some club?
It's for *us!* Membership will mean we get fully accepted as legit superheroes. No more getting teased because we're young. No more getting laughed at by the media.

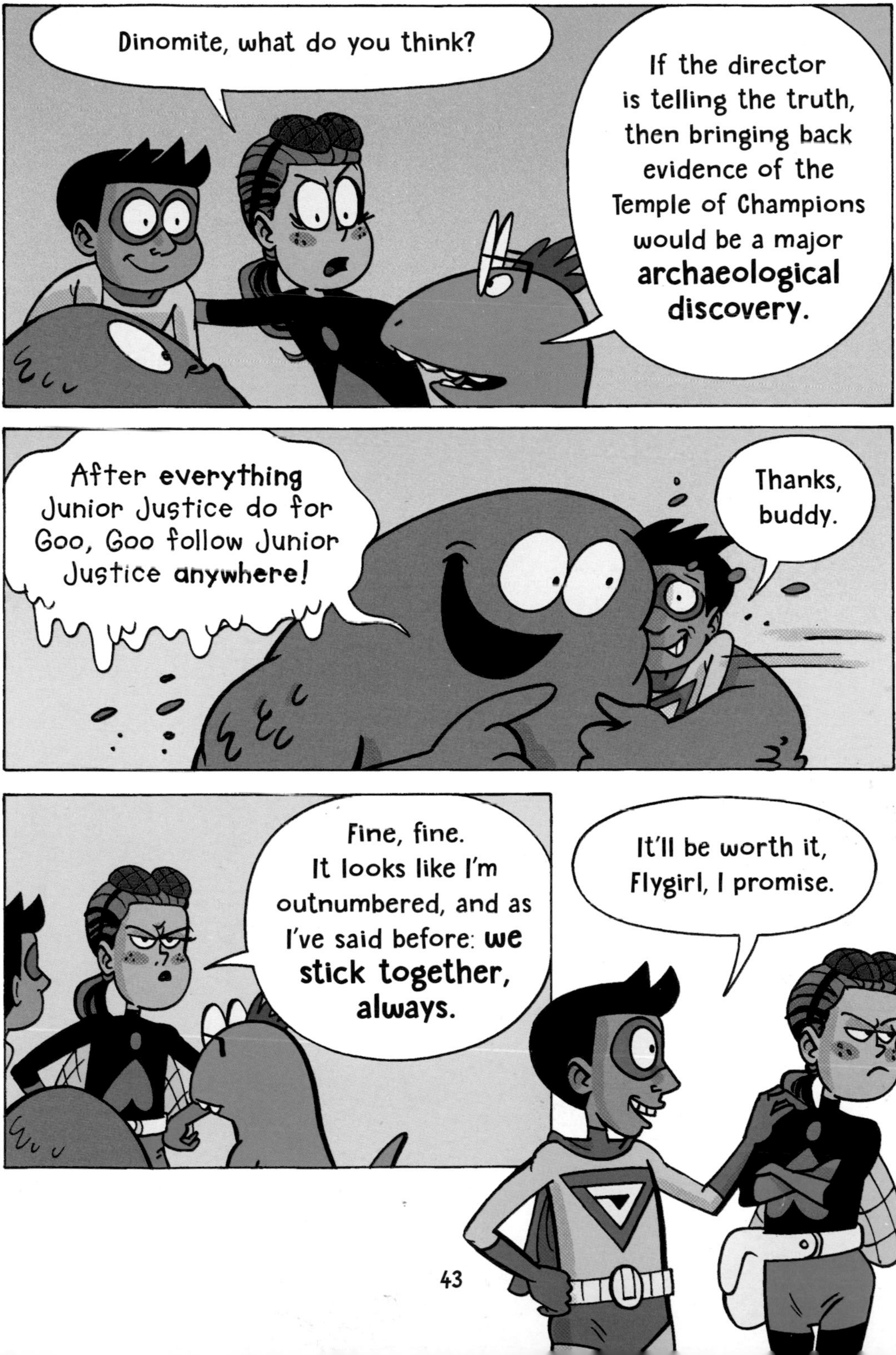
Dinomite, what do you think?
If the director is telling the truth, then bringing back evidence of the Temple of Champions would be a major archaeological discovery.
After everything Junior Justice do for Goo, Goo follow Junior Justice anywhere!
Thanks, buddy.
Fine, fine. It looks like I'm outnumbered, and as I've said before: we stick together, always.
It'll be worth it, Flygirl, I promise.

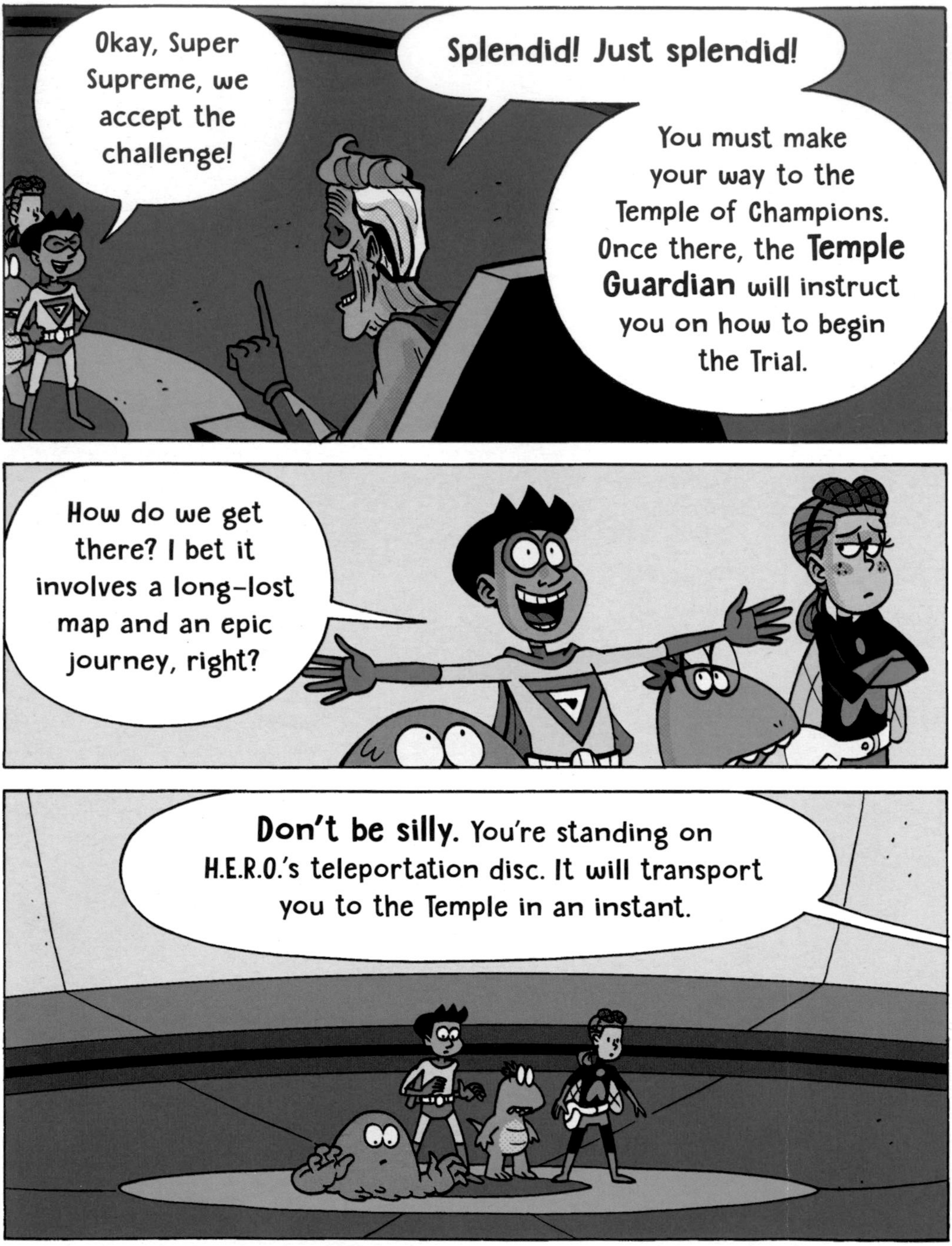
Okay, Super Supreme, we accept the challenge!
Splendid! Just splendid!
You must make your way to the Temple of Champions. Once there, the **Temple Guardian** will instruct you on how to begin the Trial.
How do we get there? I bet it involves a long-lost map and an epic journey, right?
Don't be silly. You're standing on H.E.R.O.'s teleportation disc. It will transport you to the Temple in an instant.

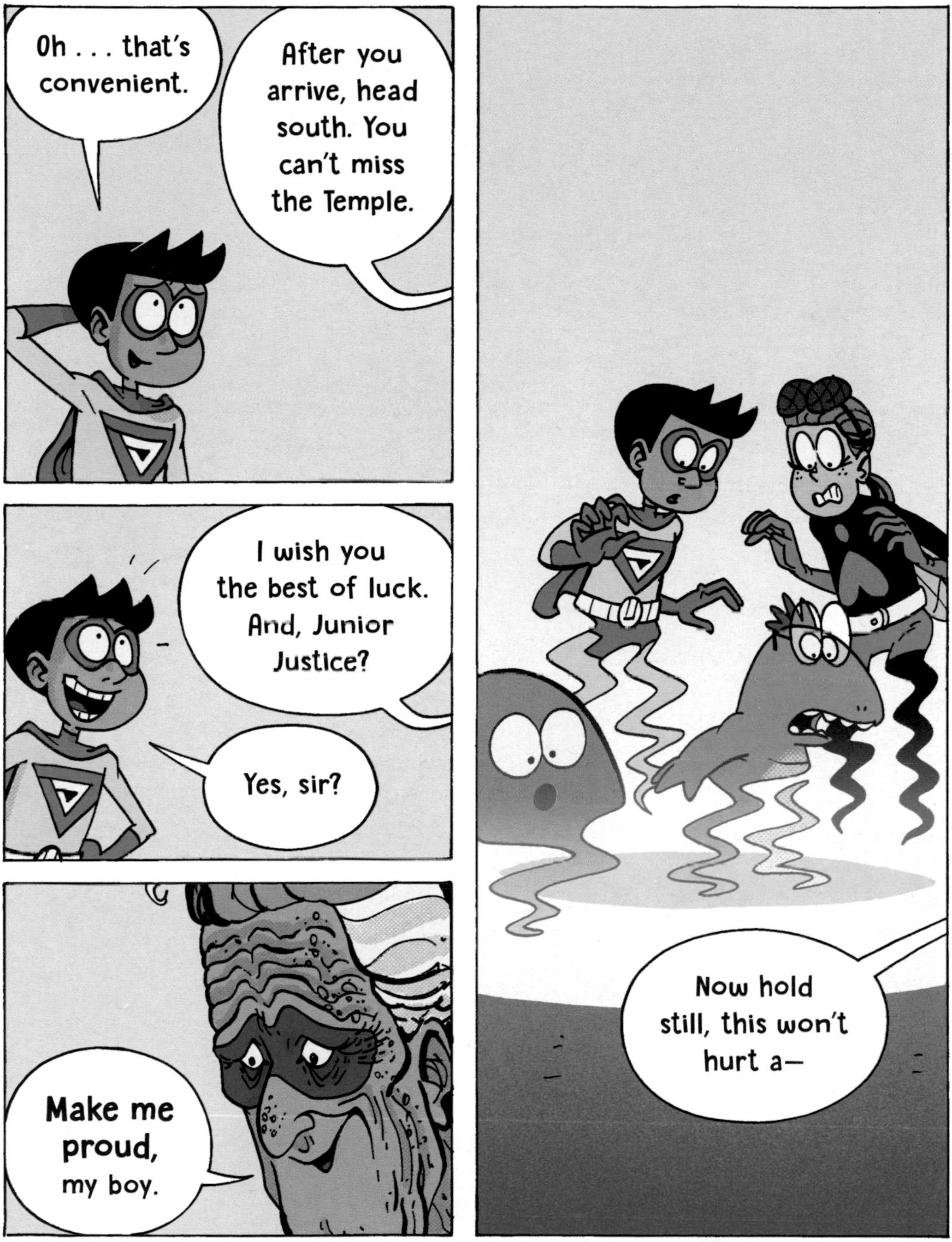
Oh . . . that's convenient.
After you arrive, head south. You can't miss the Temple.
I wish you the best of luck. And, Junior Justice?
Yes, sir?
Make me proud, my boy.
Now hold still, this won't hurt a—

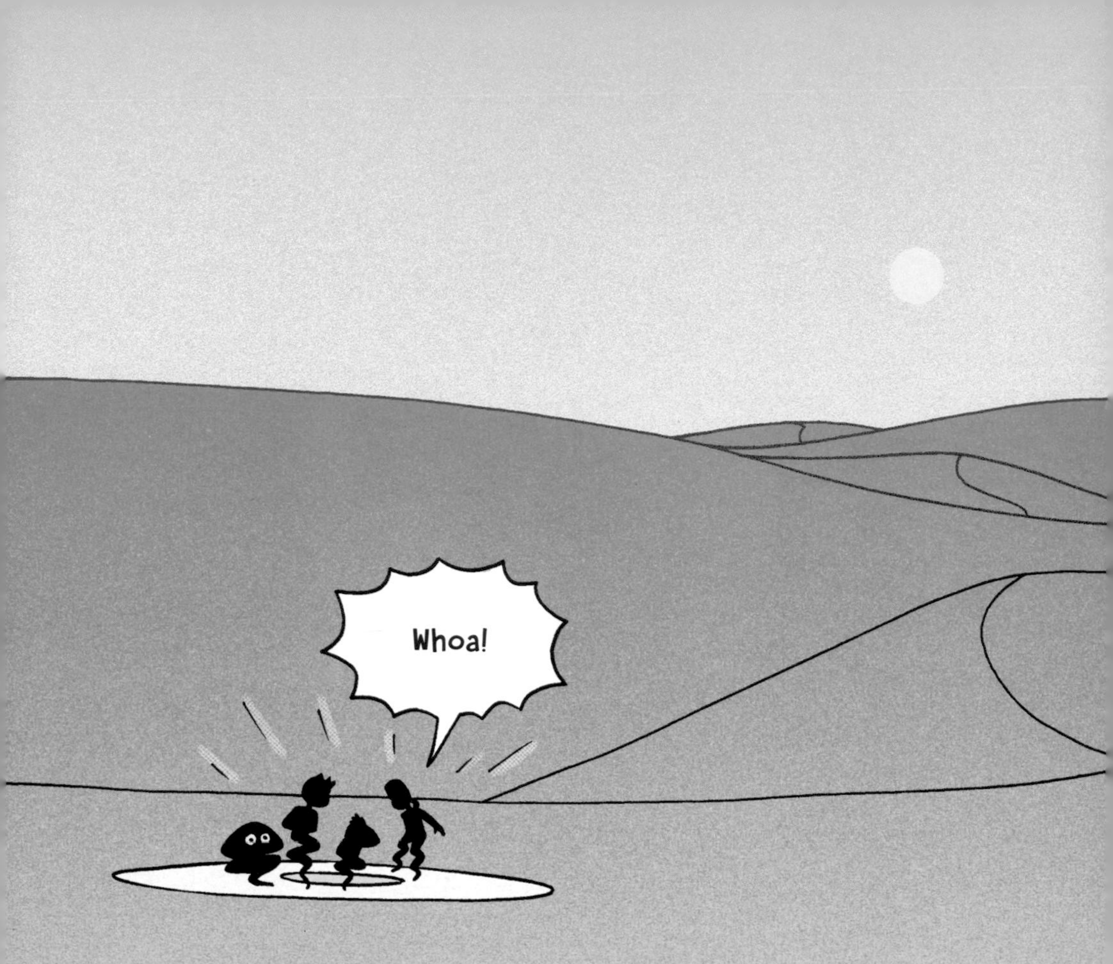
Whoa!

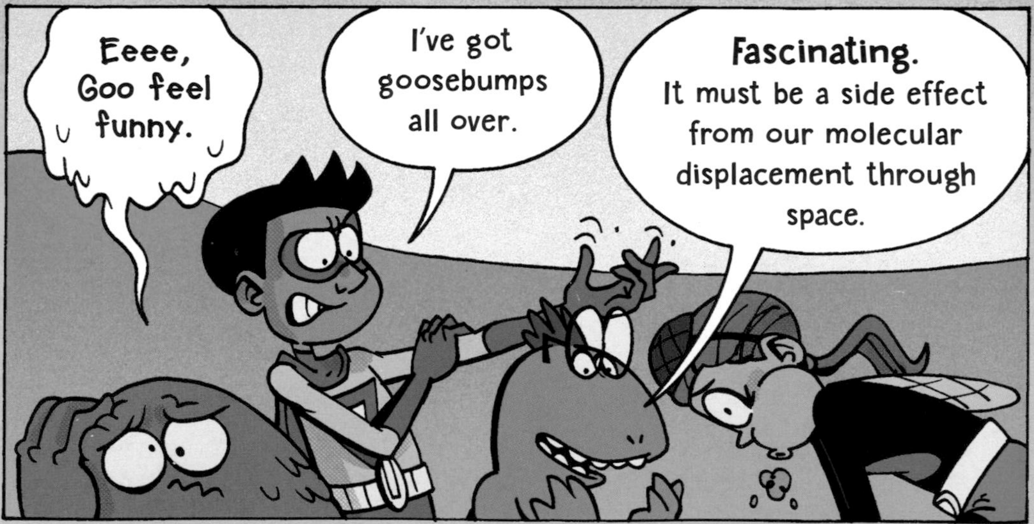
Eeee, Goo feel funny.
I've got goosebumps all over.
Fascinating.
It must be a side effect from our molecular displacement through space.

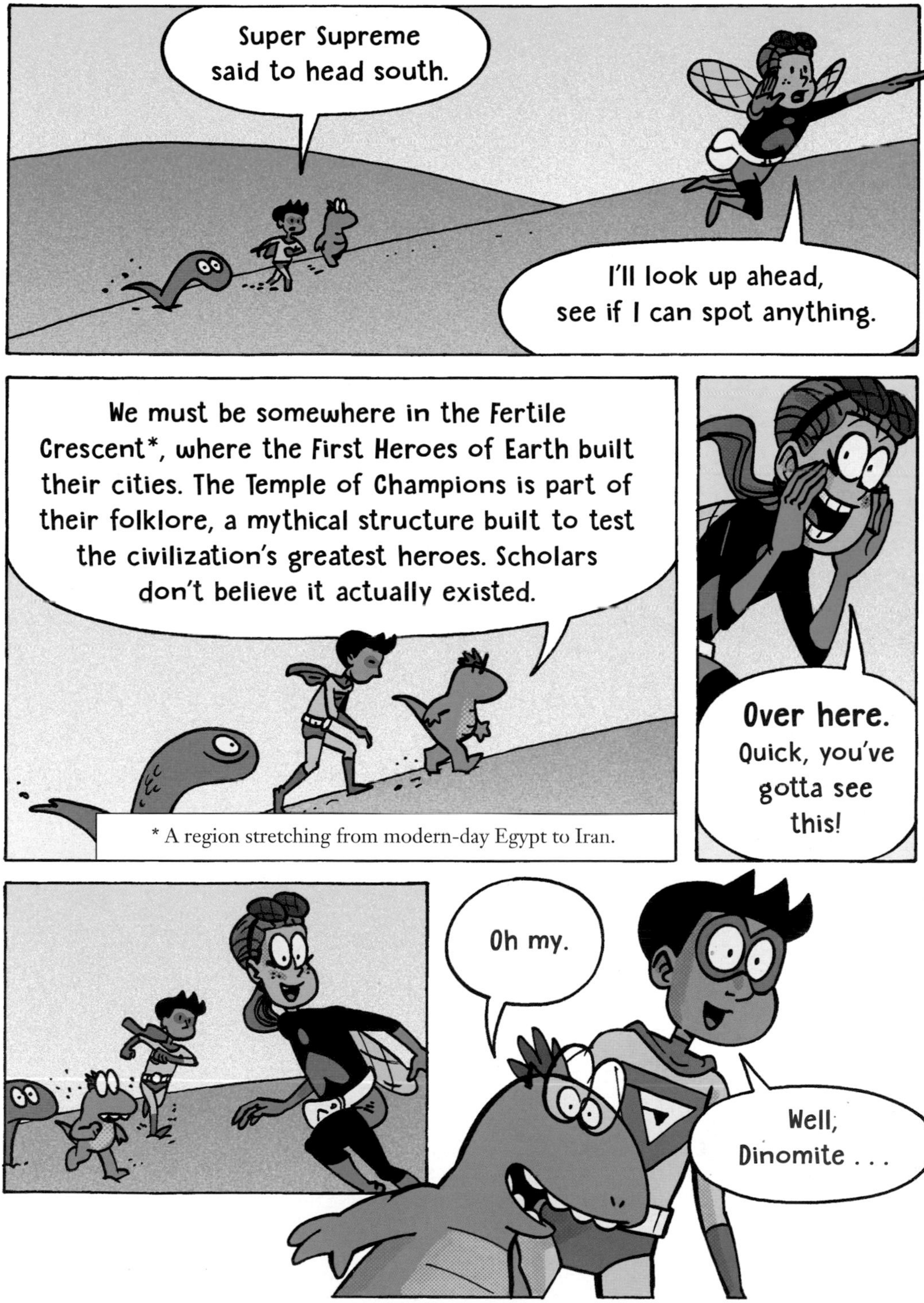
Super Supreme said to head south.
I'll look up ahead, see if I can spot anything.
We must be somewhere in the Fertile Crescent*, where the First Heroes of Earth built their cities. The Temple of Champions is part of their folklore, a mythical structure built to test the civilization's greatest heroes. Scholars don't believe it actually existed.
* A region stretching from modern-day Egypt to Iran.
Over here. Quick, you've gotta see this!
Oh my.
Well, Dinomite . . .

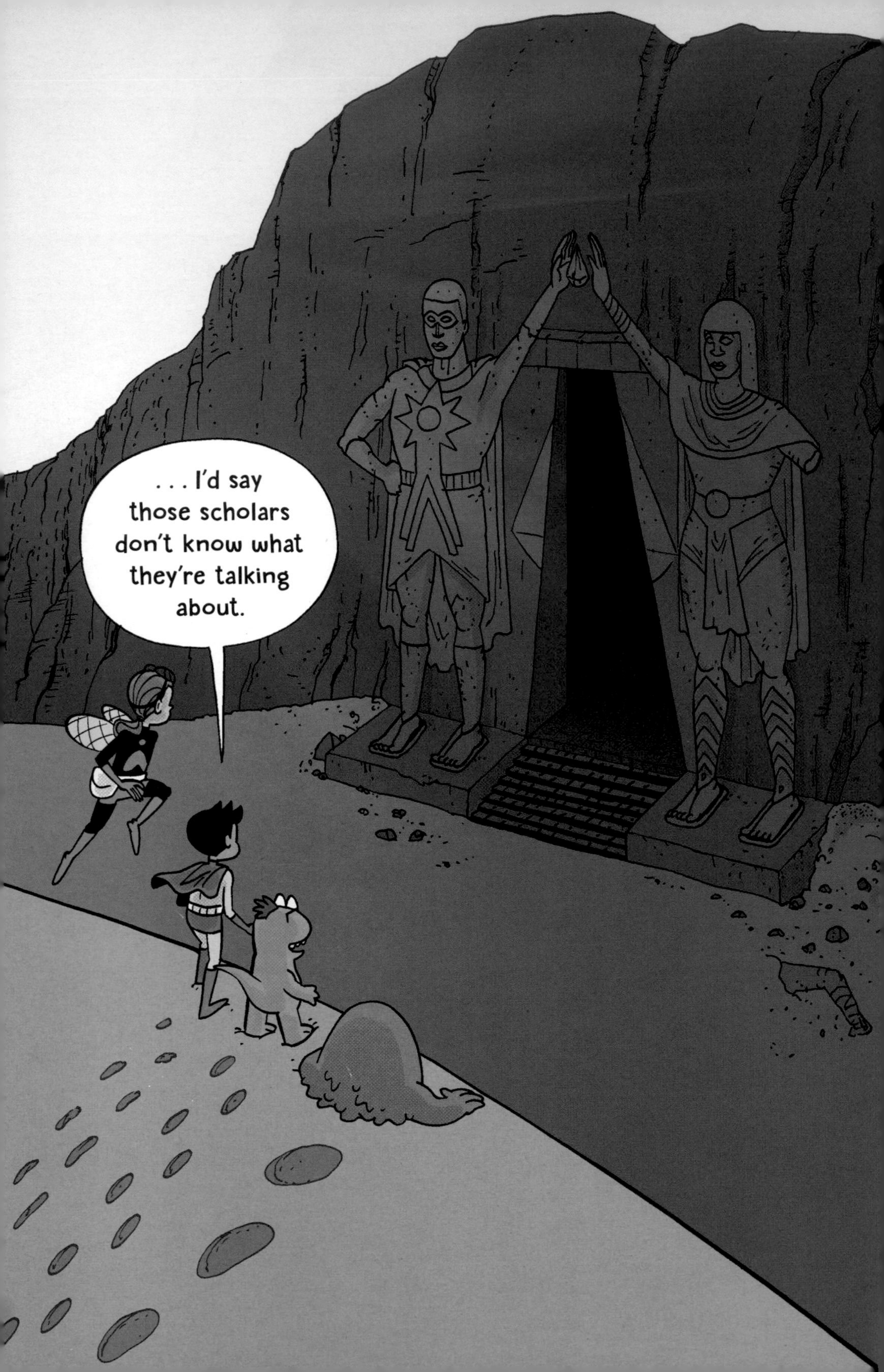
. . . I'd say those scholars don't know what they're talking about.

Chapter

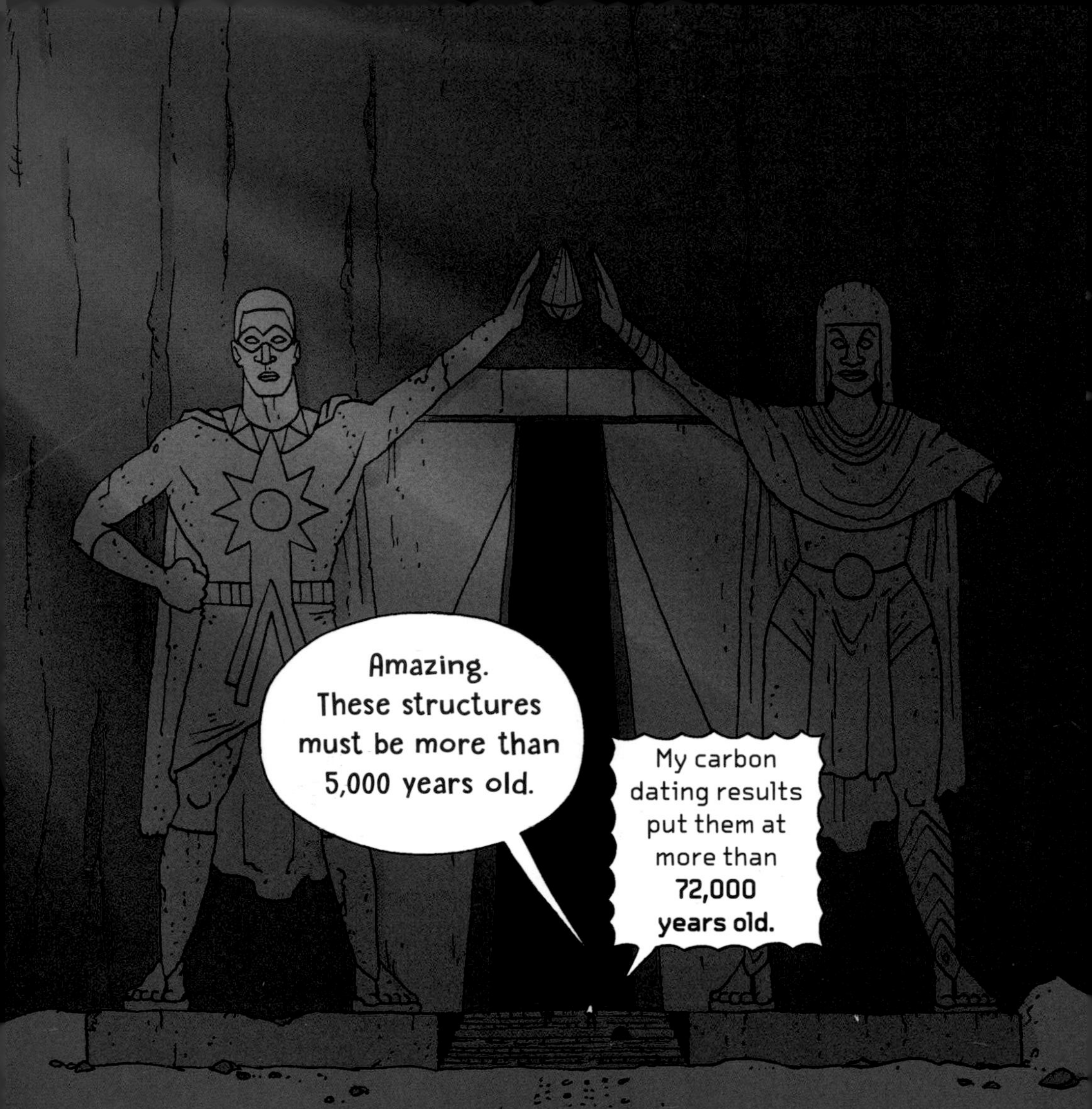
Amazing. These structures must be more than 5,000 years old.
My carbon dating results put them at more than **72,000 years old.**

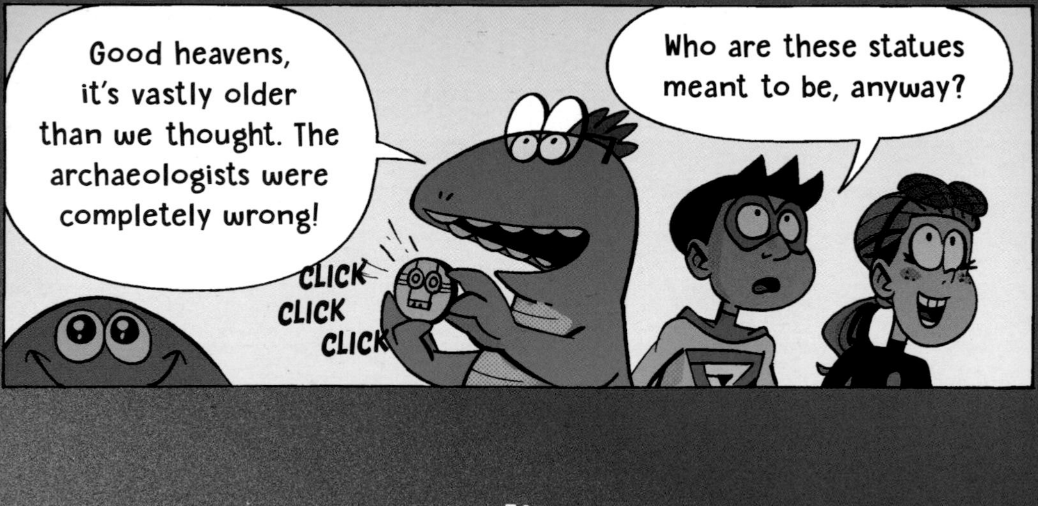
Good heavens, it's vastly older than we thought. The archaeologists were completely wrong!
CLICK CLICK CLICK
Who are these statues meant to be, anyway?

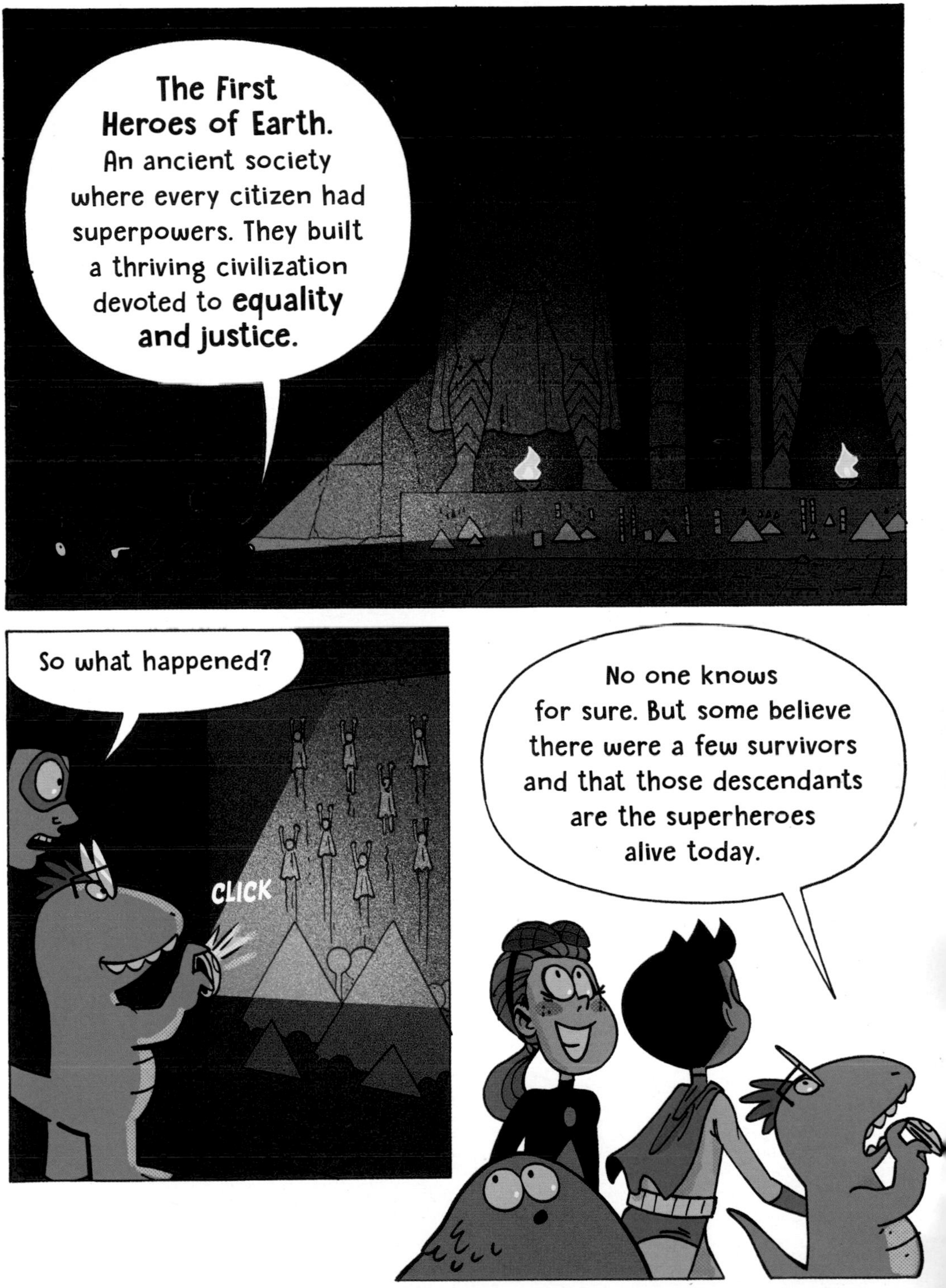
The First Heroes of Earth. An ancient society where every citizen had superpowers. They built a thriving civilization devoted to equality and justice.
So what happened?
CLICK
No one knows for sure. But some believe there were a few survivors and that those descendants are the superheroes alive today.

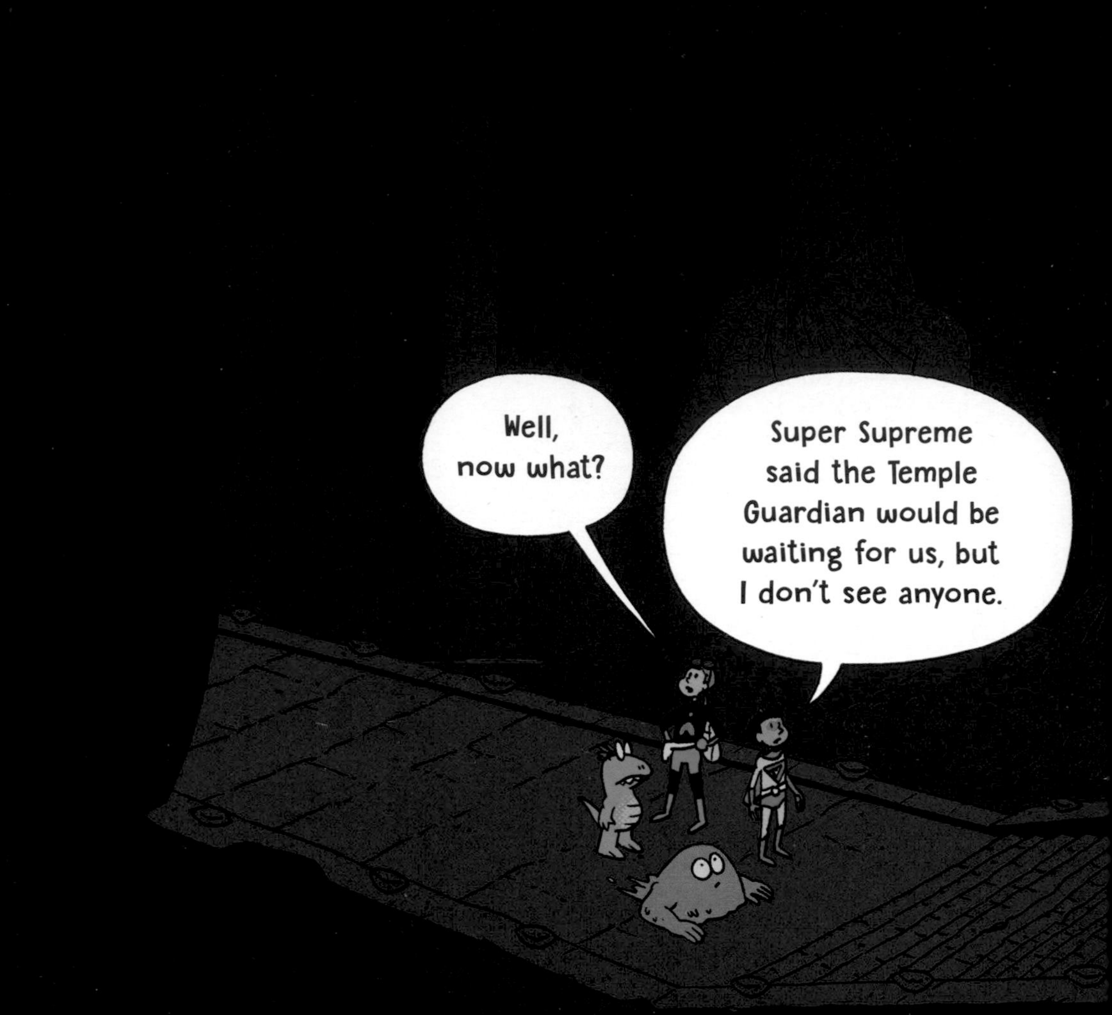
Well, now what?
Super Supreme said the Temple Guardian would be waiting for us, but I don't see anyone.

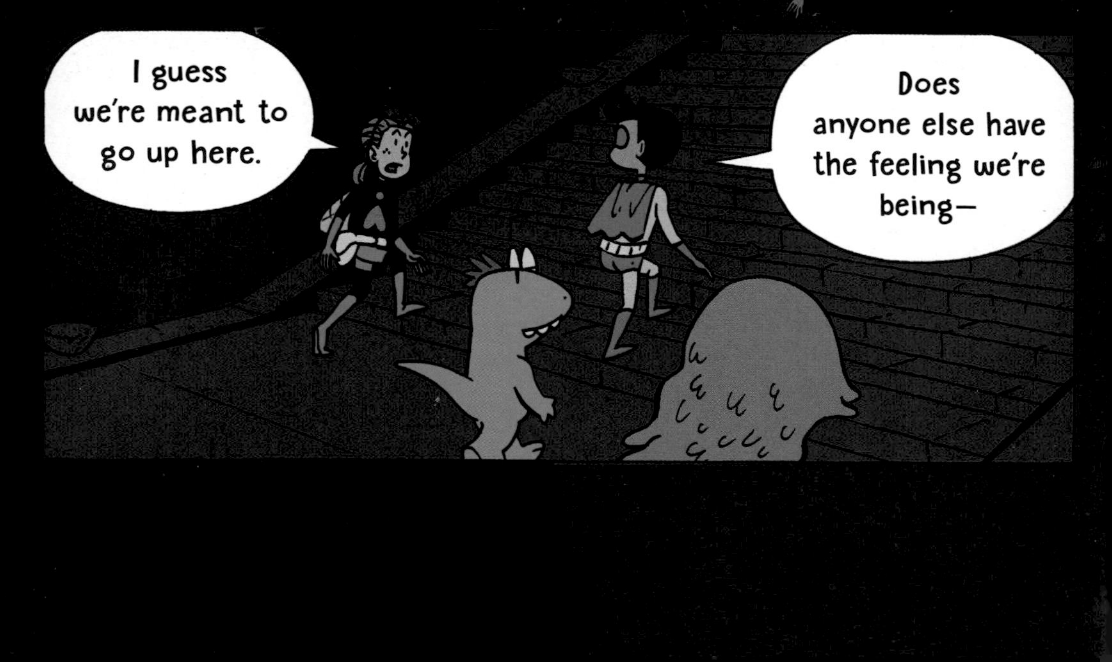
I guess we're meant to go up here.
Does anyone else have the feeling we're being—

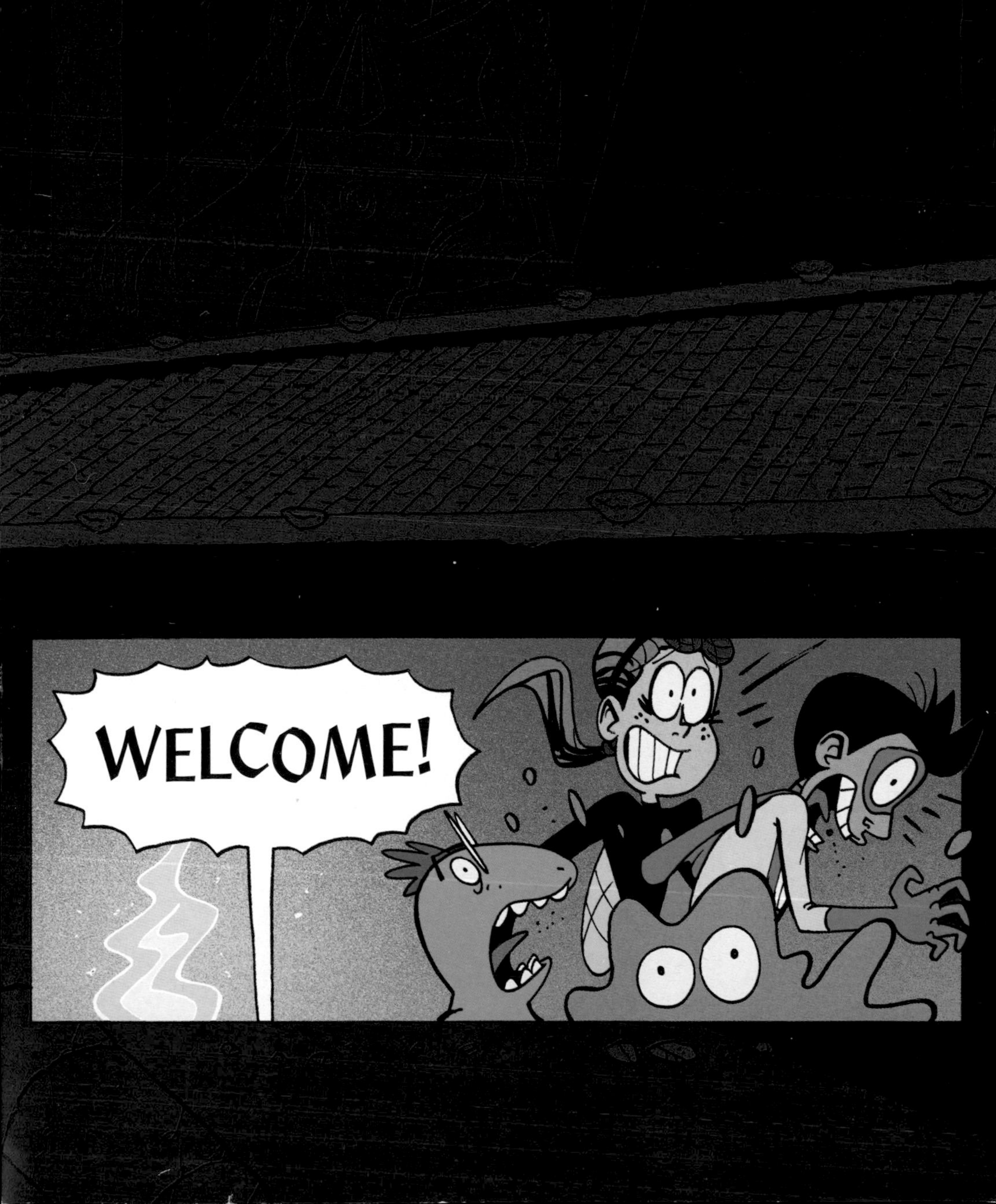
WELCOME!

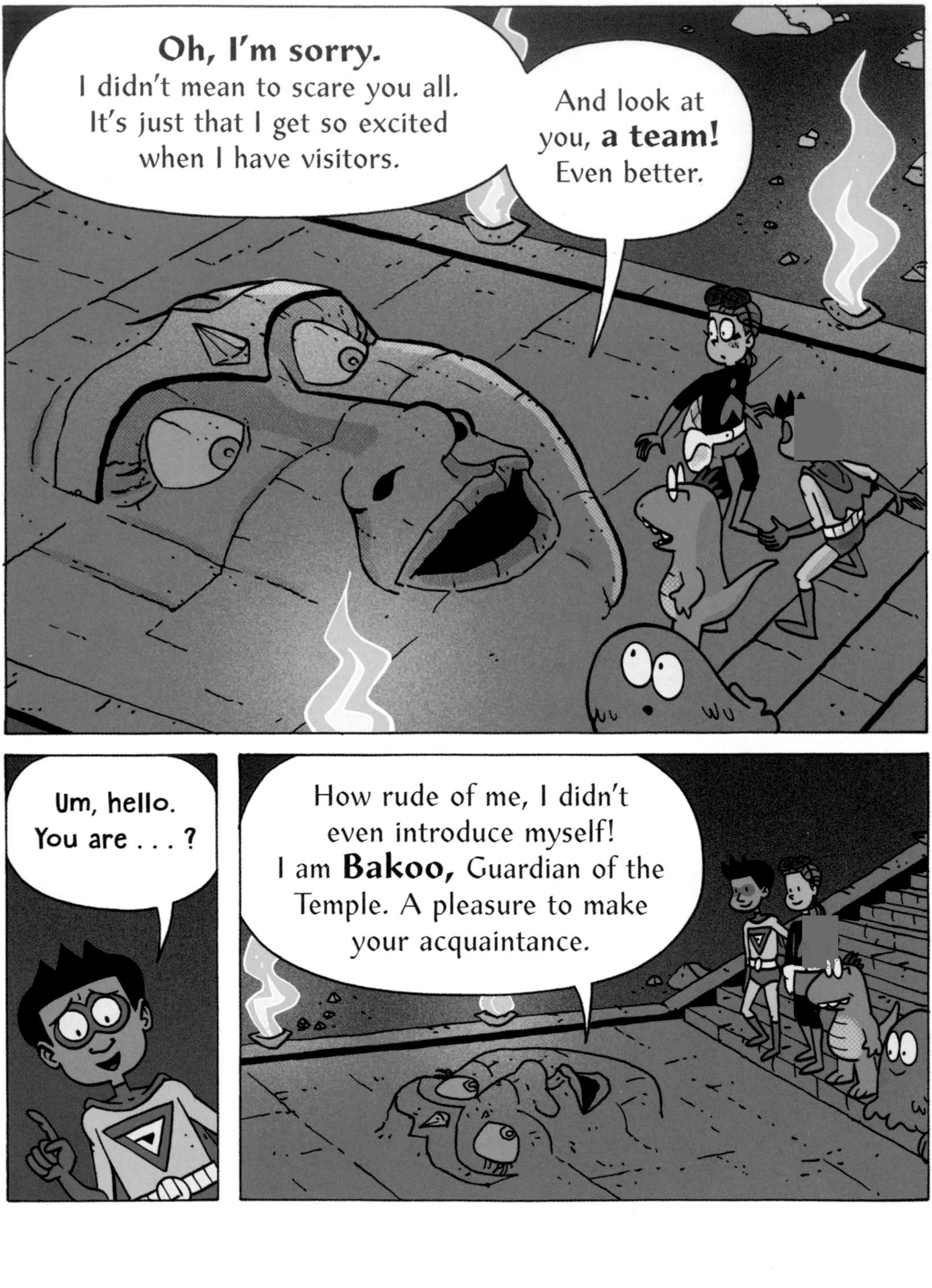
Oh, I'm sorry. I didn't mean to scare you all. It's just that I get so excited when I have visitors.
And look at you, **a team!** Even better.
Um, hello. You are . . . ?
How rude of me, I didn't even introduce myself! I am **Bakoo,** Guardian of the Temple. A pleasure to make your acquaintance.

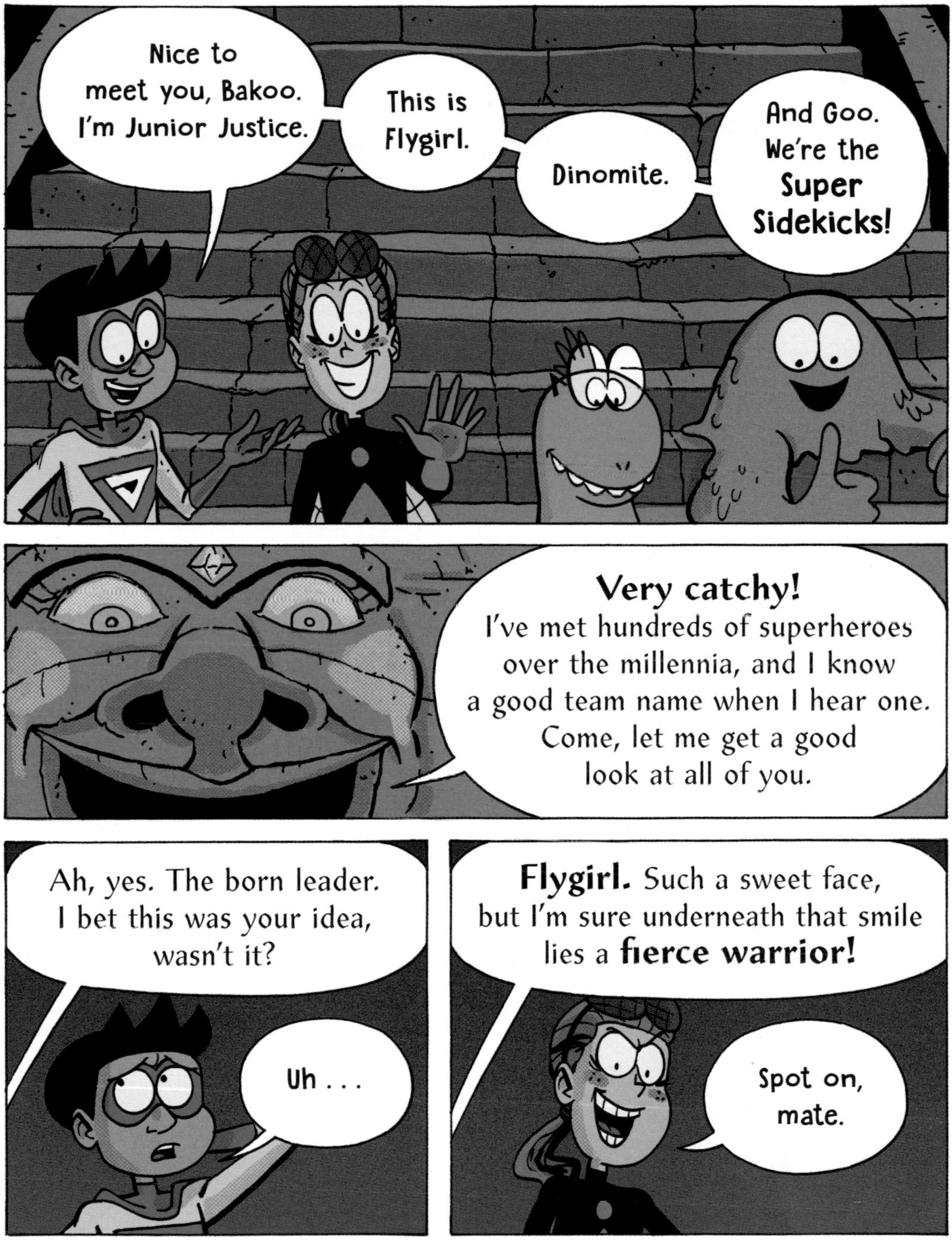
Nice to meet you, Bakoo. I'm Junior Justice.
This is Flygirl.
Dinomite.
And Goo. We're the Super Sidekicks!
Very catchy! I've met hundreds of superheroes over the millennia, and I know a good team name when I hear one. Come, let me get a good look at all of you.
Ah, yes. The born leader. I bet this was your idea, wasn't it?
Uh . . .
Flygirl. Such a sweet face, but I'm sure underneath that smile lies a fierce warrior!
Spot on, mate.

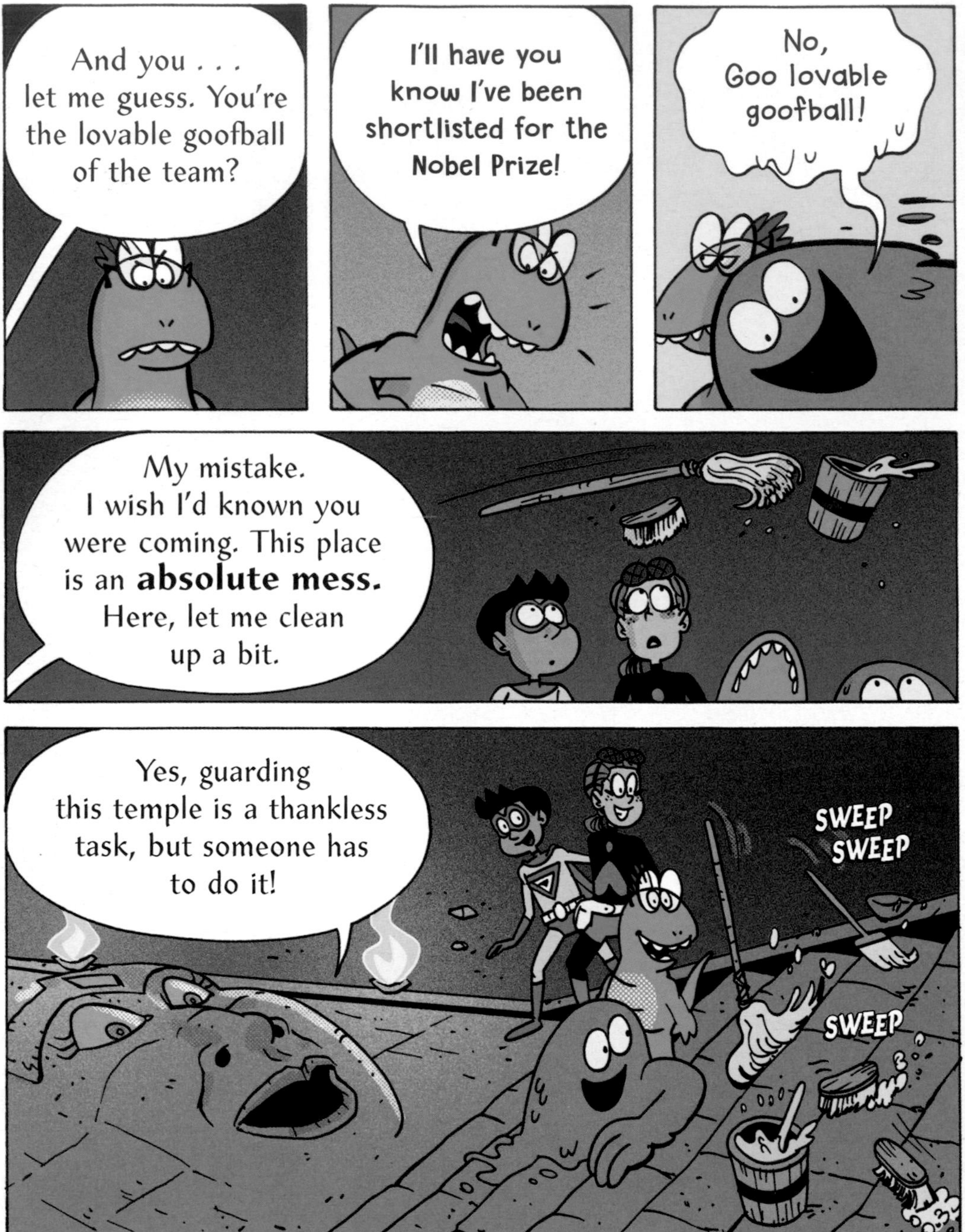
And you . . . let me guess. You're the lovable goofball of the team?
I'll have you know I've been shortlisted for the Nobel Prize!
No, Goo lovable goofball!
My mistake. I wish I'd known you were coming. This place is an **absolute mess.** Here, let me clean up a bit.
Yes, guarding this temple is a thankless task, but someone has to do it!
SWEEP SWEEP
SWEEP

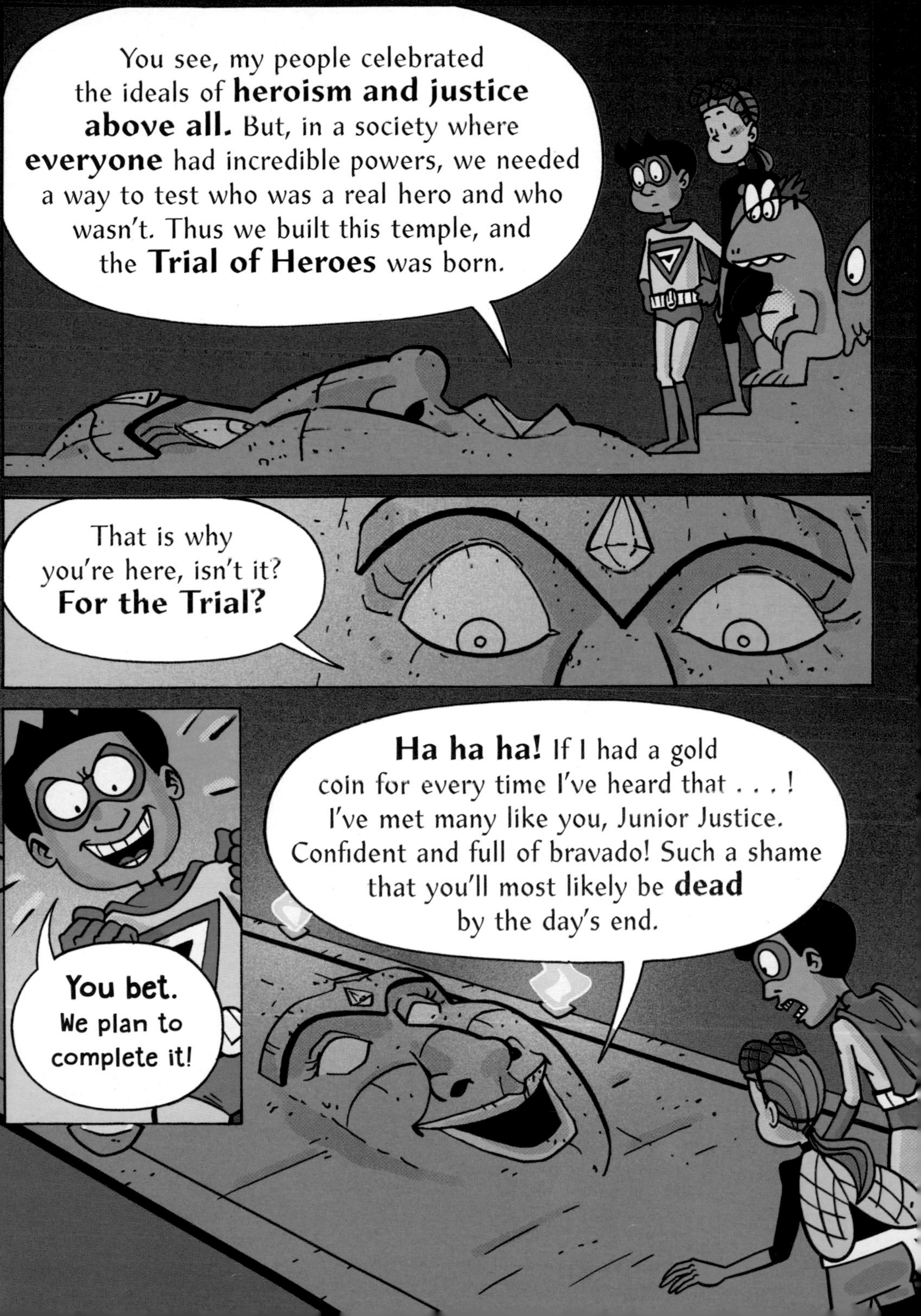
You see, my people celebrated the ideals of **heroism and justice above all.** But, in a society where **everyone** had incredible powers, we needed a way to test who was a real hero and who wasn't. Thus we built this temple, and the **Trial of Heroes** was born.
That is why you're here, isn't it? **For the Trial?**
You bet. We plan to complete it!
Ha ha ha! If I had a gold coin for every time I've heard that . . . ! I've met many like you, Junior Justice. Confident and full of bravado! Such a shame that you'll most likely be **dead** by the day's end.

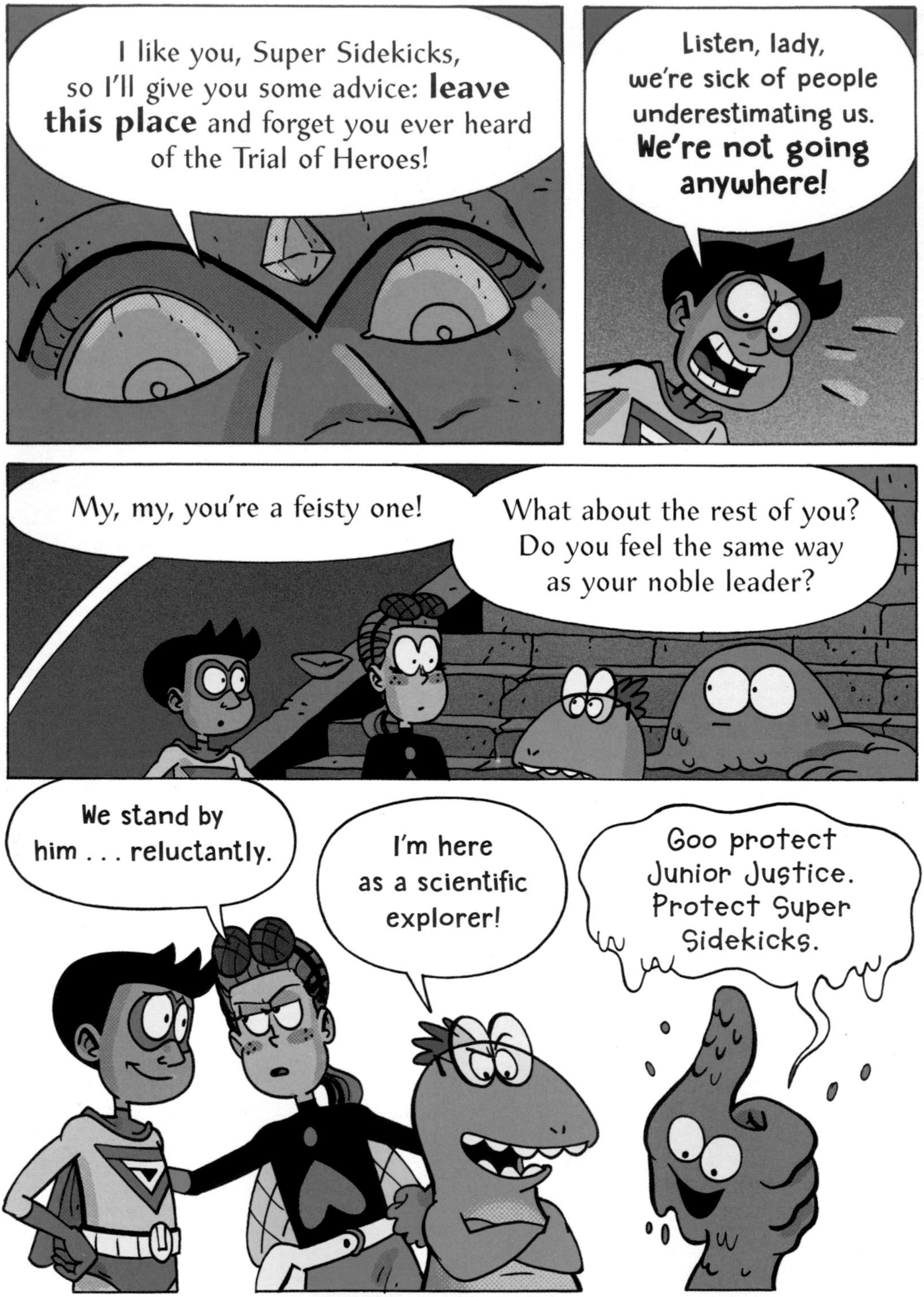
I like you, Super Sidekicks, so I'll give you some advice: **leave this place** and forget you ever heard of the Trial of Heroes!
Listen, lady, we're sick of people underestimating us. **We're not going anywhere!**
My, my, you're a feisty one!
What about the rest of you? Do you feel the same way as your noble leader?
We stand by him . . . reluctantly.
I'm here as a scientific explorer!
Goo protect Junior Justice. Protect Super Sidekicks.

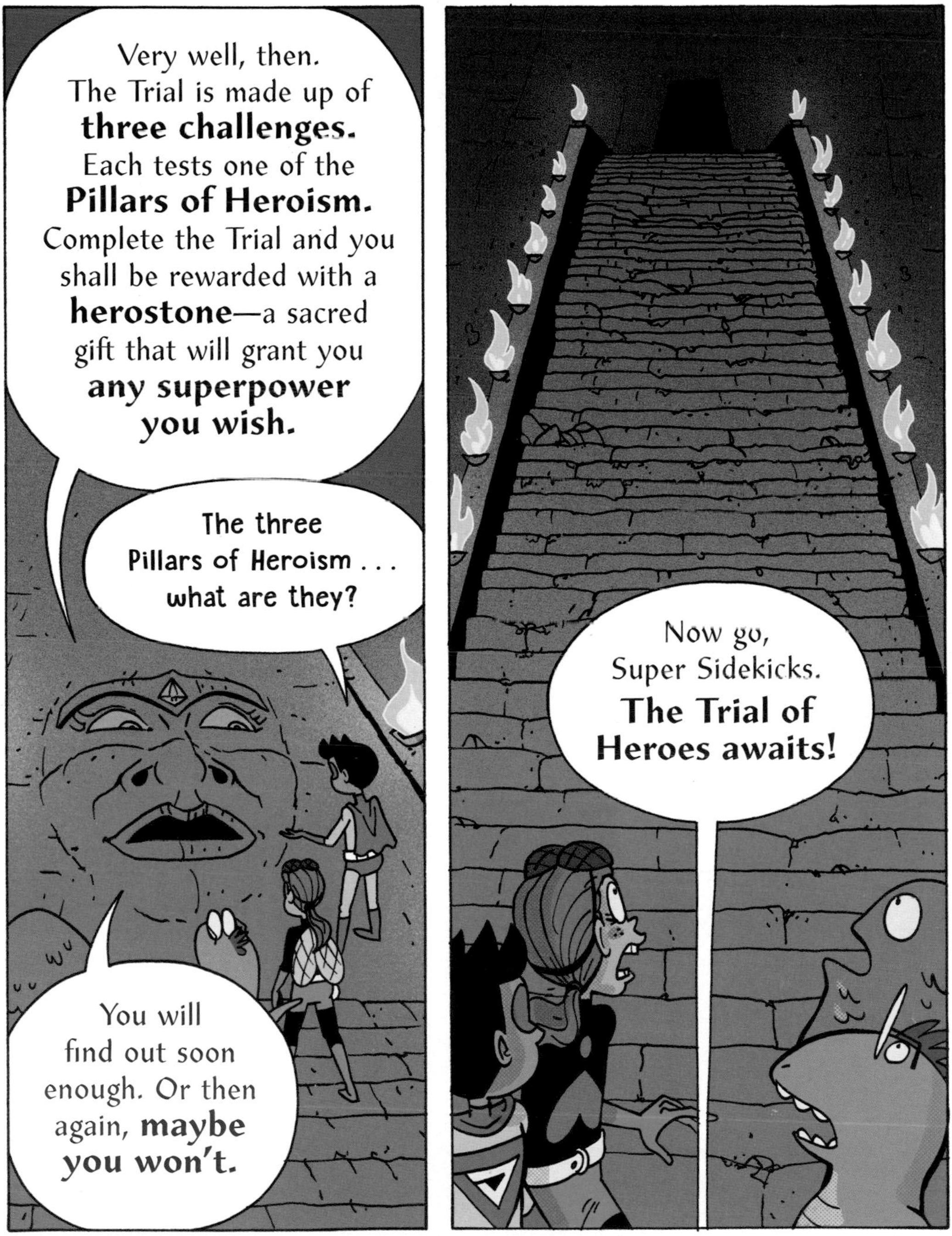
Very well, then. The Trial is made up of **three challenges.** Each tests one of the **Pillars of Heroism.** Complete the Trial and you shall be rewarded with a **herostone**—a sacred gift that will grant you **any superpower you wish.**
The three Pillars of Heroism . . . what are they?
You will find out soon enough. Or then again, **maybe you won't.**
Now go, Super Sidekicks. **The Trial of Heroes awaits!**

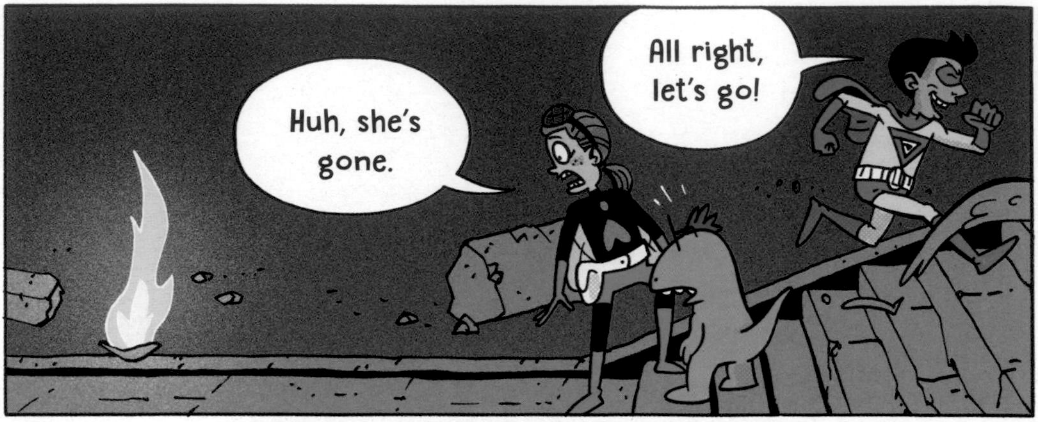
Huh, she's gone.
All right, let's go!

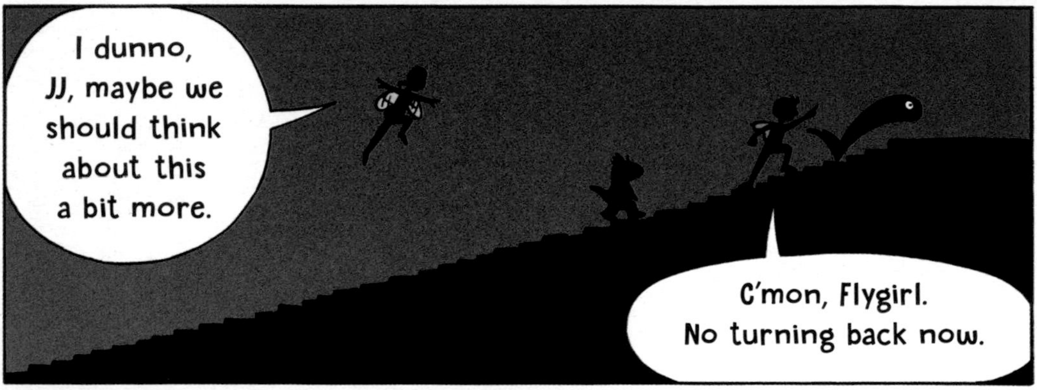
I dunno, JJ, maybe we should think about this a bit more.
C'mon, Flygirl. No turning back now.

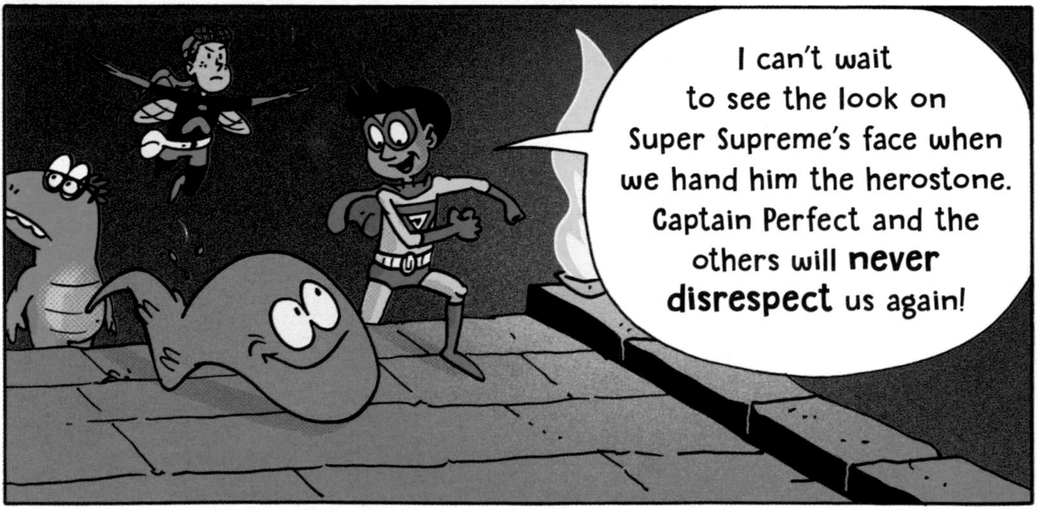
I can't wait to see the look on Super Supreme's face when we hand him the herostone. Captain Perfect and the others will **never disrespect** us again!

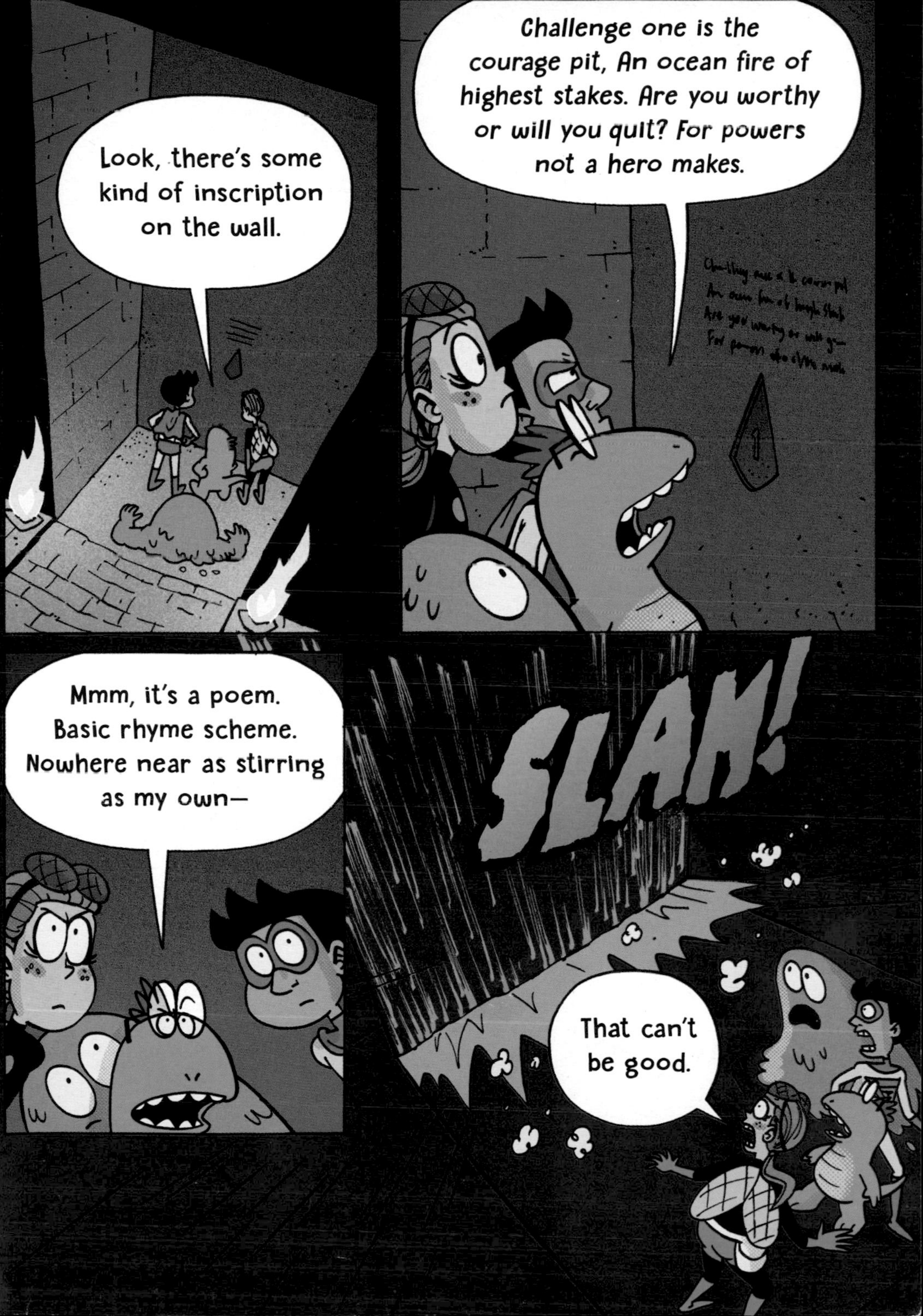
Look, there's some kind of inscription on the wall.
Challenge one is the courage pit, An ocean fire of highest stakes. Are you worthy or will you quit? For powers not a hero makes.
Mmm, it's a poem. Basic rhyme scheme. Nowhere near as stirring as my own—
SLAM!
That can't be good.

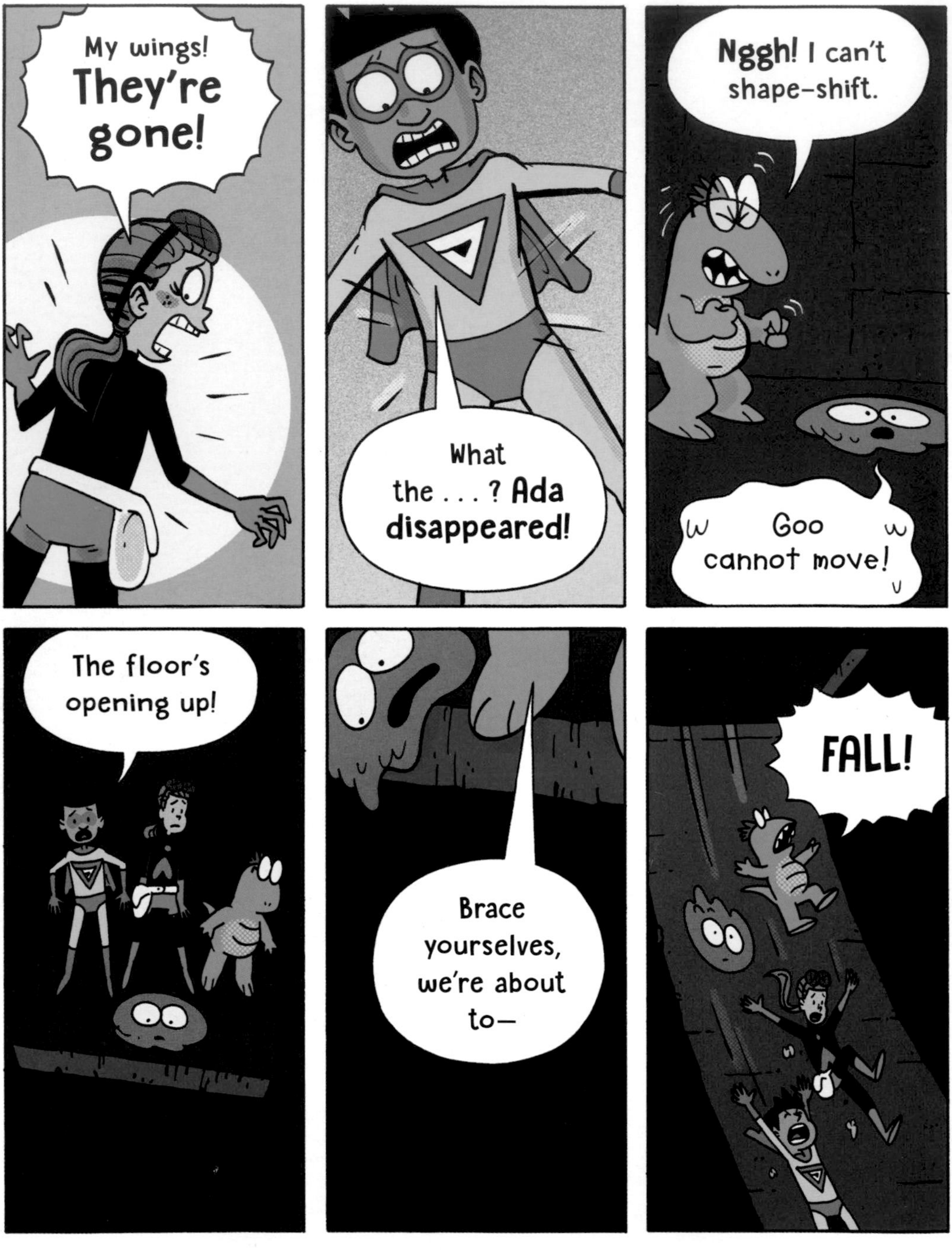
My wings! They're gone!
What the . . . ? Ada disappeared!
Nggh! I can't shape-shift.
Goo cannot move!
The floor's opening up!
Brace yourselves, we're about to—
FALL!

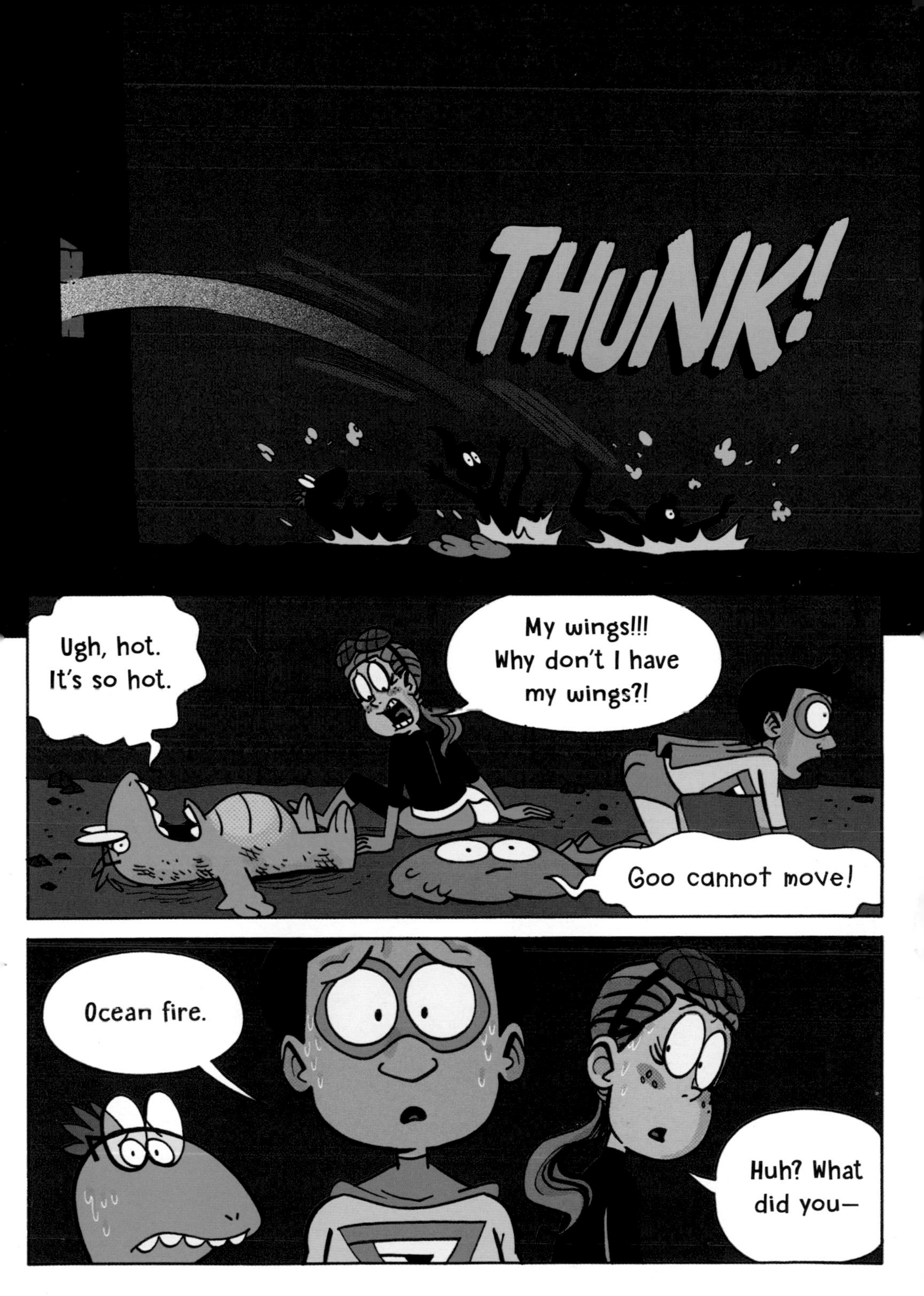
THUNK!
Ugh, hot.
It's so hot.
My wings!!!
Why don't I have
my wings?!
Goo cannot move!
Ocean fire.
Huh? What
did you—

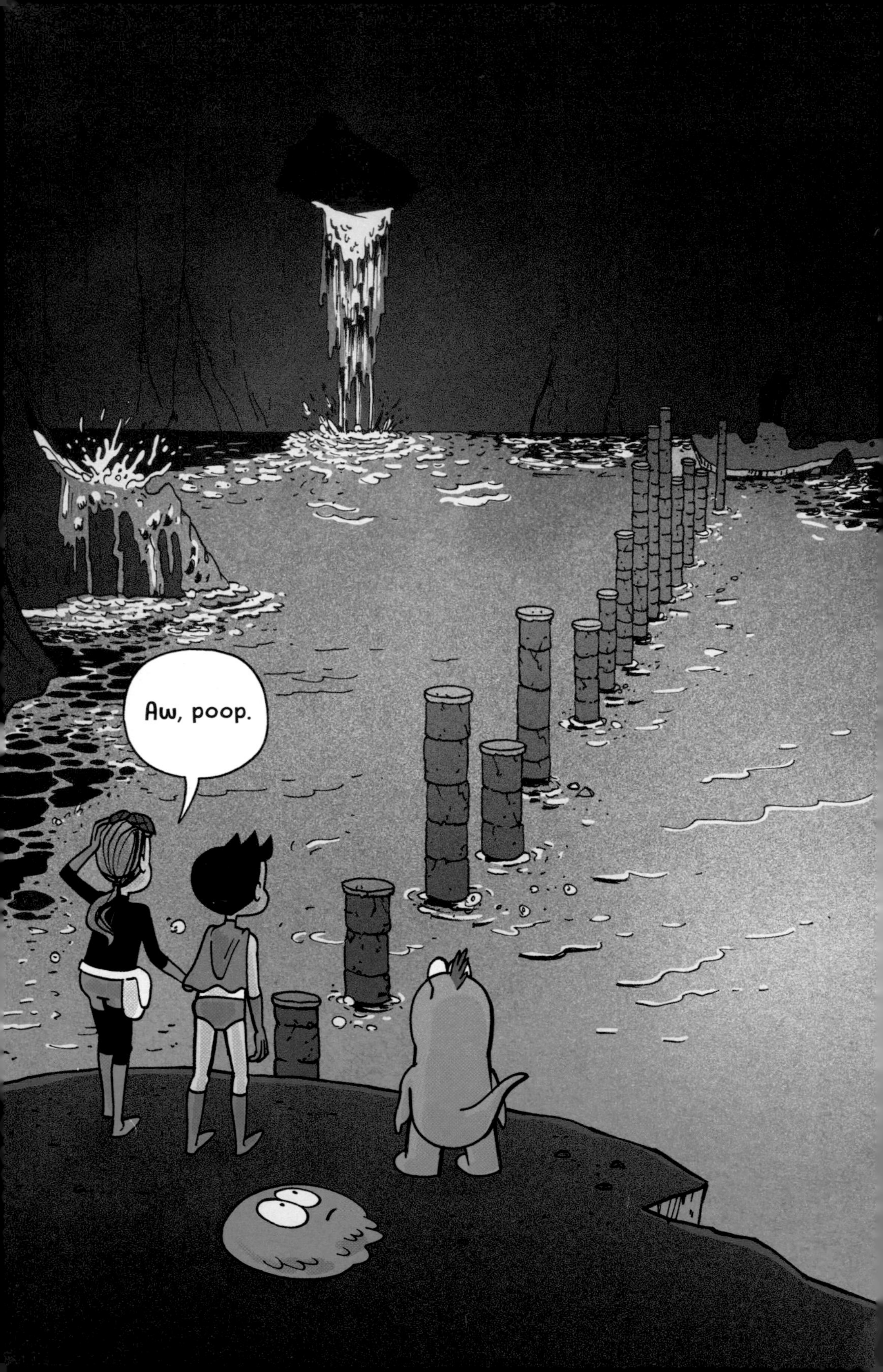
Aw, poop.

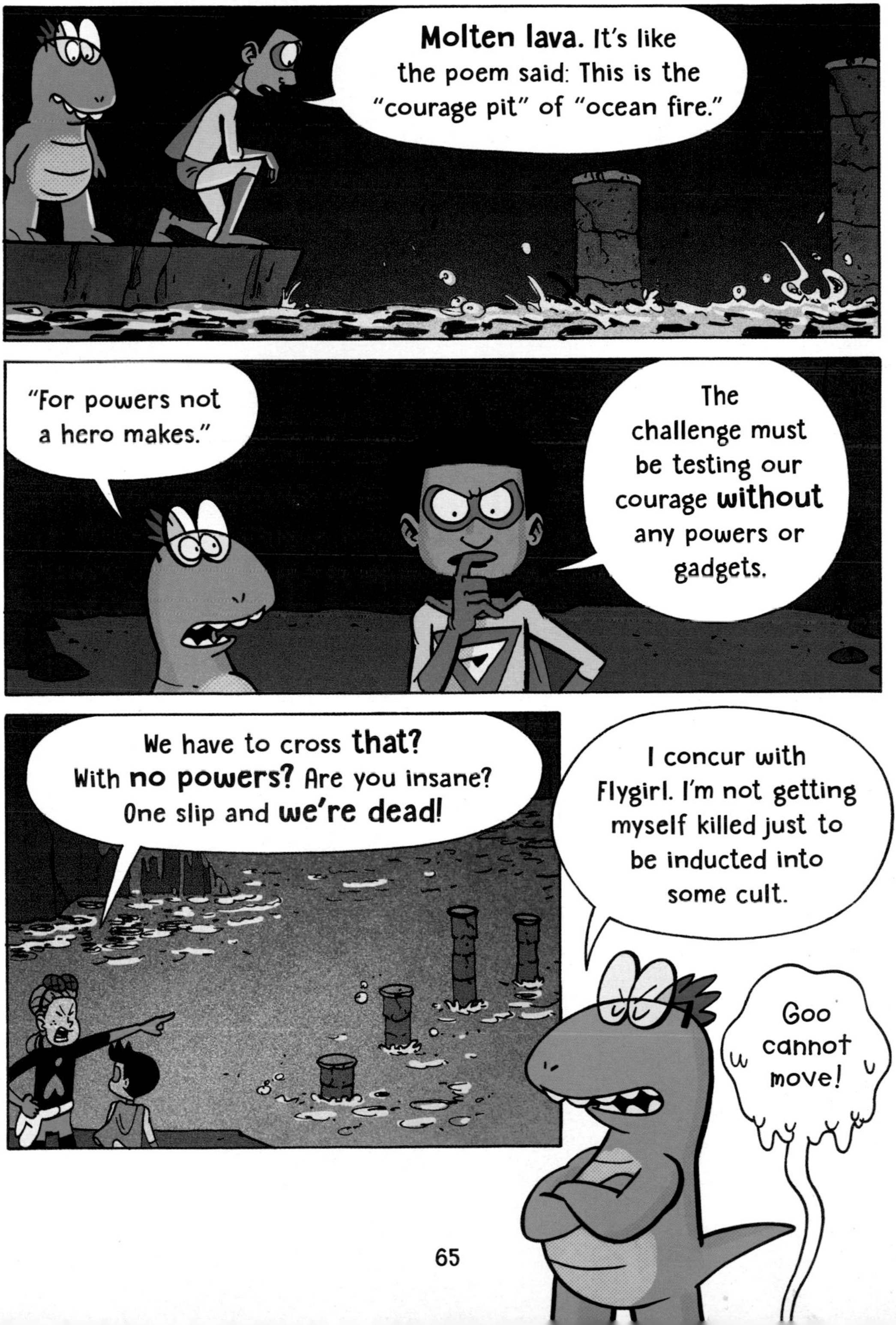
Molten lava. It's like the poem said: This is the "courage pit" of "ocean fire."
"For powers not a hero makes."
The challenge must be testing our courage **without** any powers or gadgets.
We have to cross **that?** With **no powers?** Are you insane? One slip and **we're dead!**
I concur with Flygirl. I'm not getting myself killed just to be inducted into some cult.
Goo cannot move!

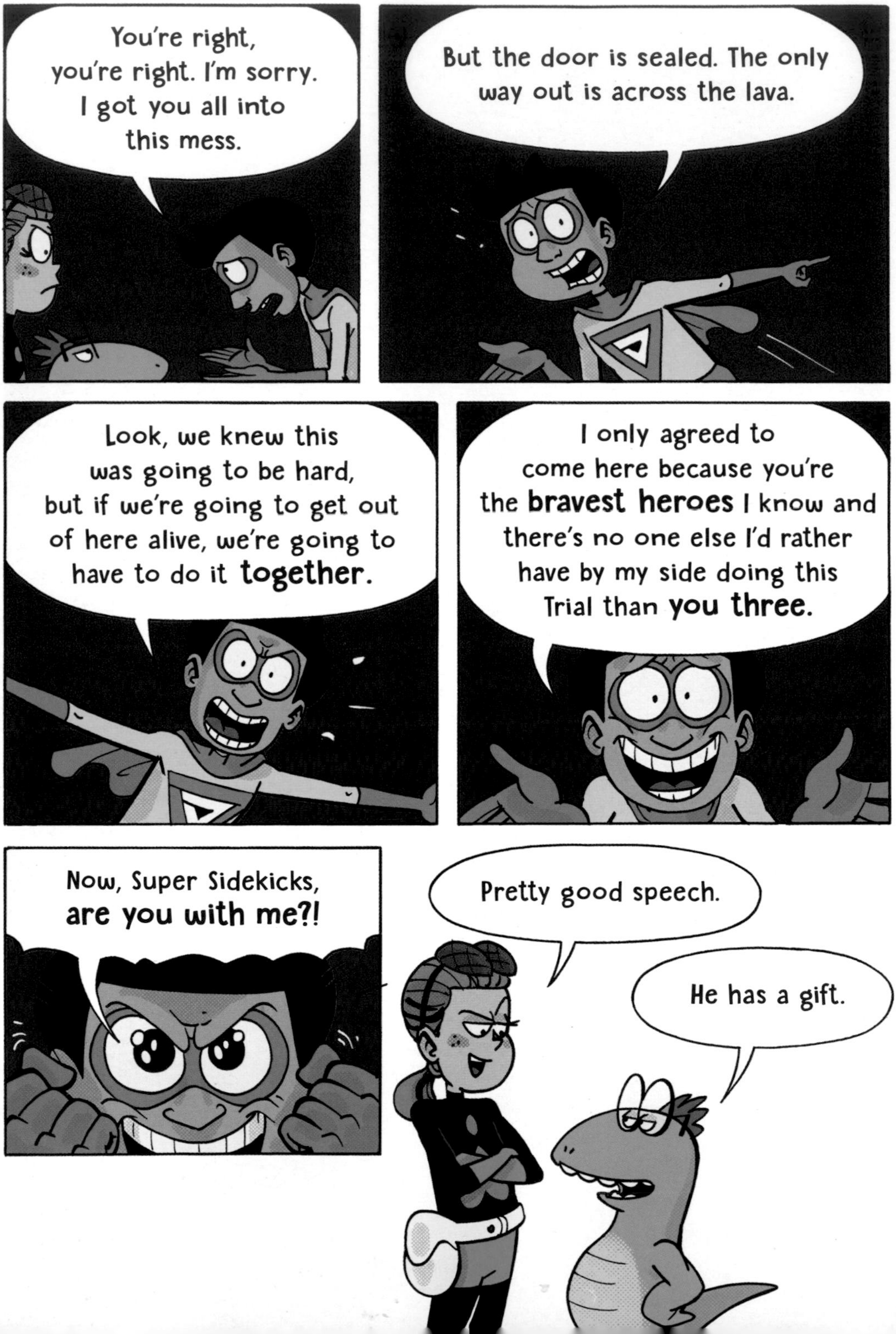
You're right, you're right. I'm sorry. I got you all into this mess.
But the door is sealed. The only way out is across the lava.
Look, we knew this was going to be hard, but if we're going to get out of here alive, we're going to have to do it **together**.
I only agreed to come here because you're the **bravest heroes** I know and there's no one else I'd rather have by my side doing this Trial than **you three**.
Now, Super Sidekicks, **are you with me?!**
Pretty good speech.
He has a gift.

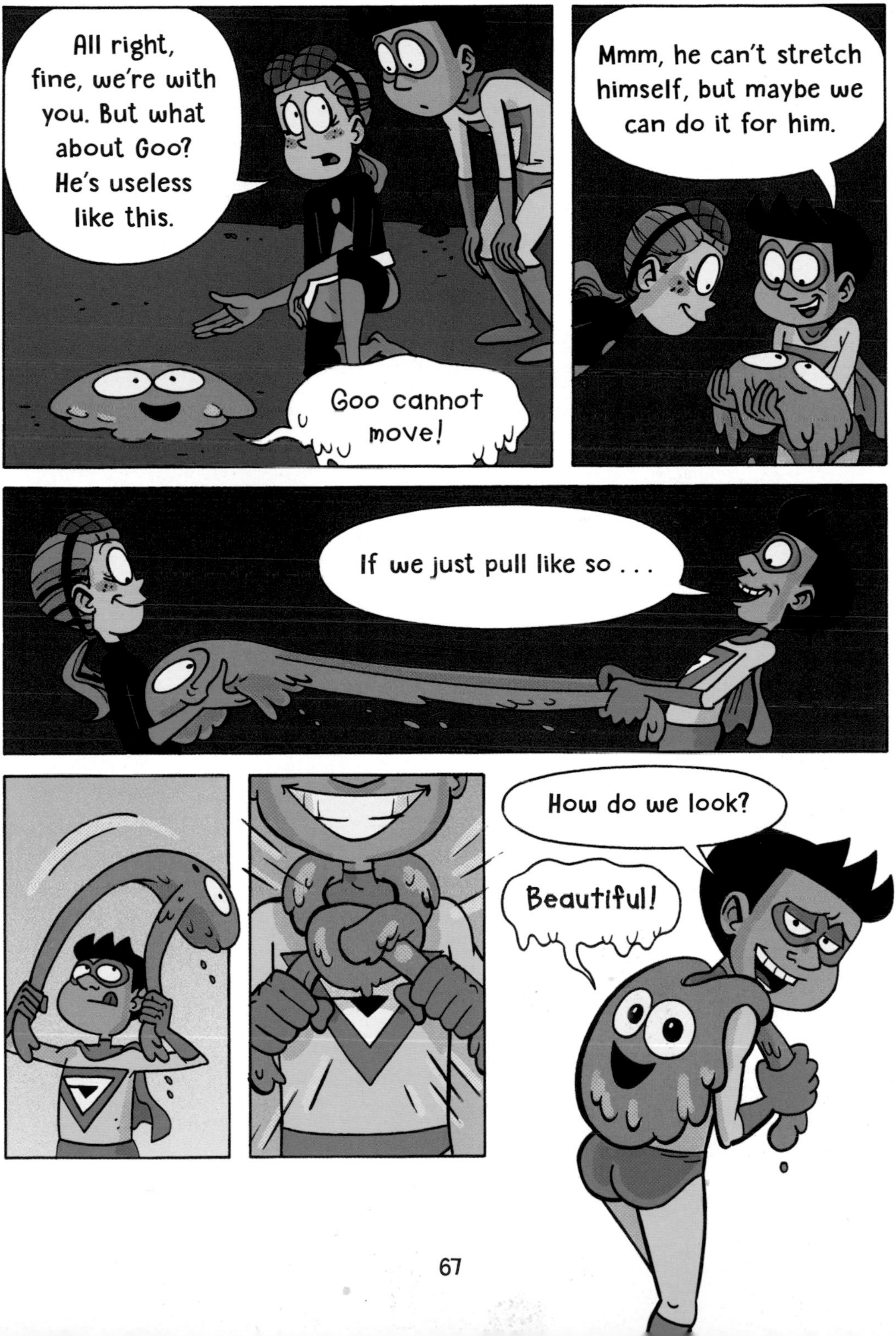
All right, fine, we're with you. But what about Goo? He's useless like this.
Goo cannot move!
Mmm, he can't stretch himself, but maybe we can do it for him.
If we just pull like so . . .
How do we look?
Beautiful!

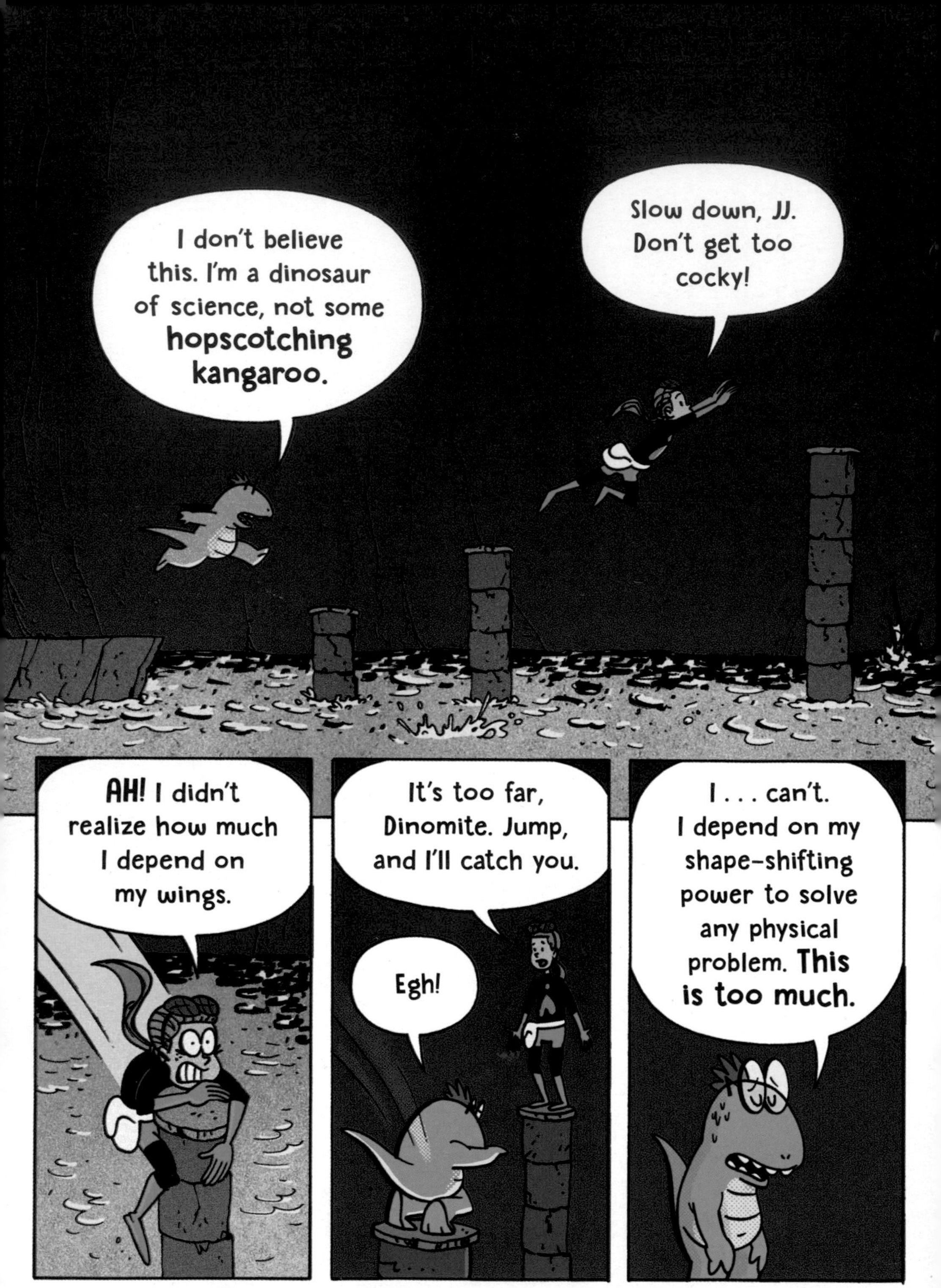
I don't believe this. I'm a dinosaur of science, not some **hopscotching kangaroo.**
Slow down, JJ. Don't get too cocky!
AH! I didn't realize how much I depend on my wings.
It's too far, Dinomite. Jump, and I'll catch you.
Egh!
I . . . can't. I depend on my shape-shifting power to solve any physical problem. **This is too much.**

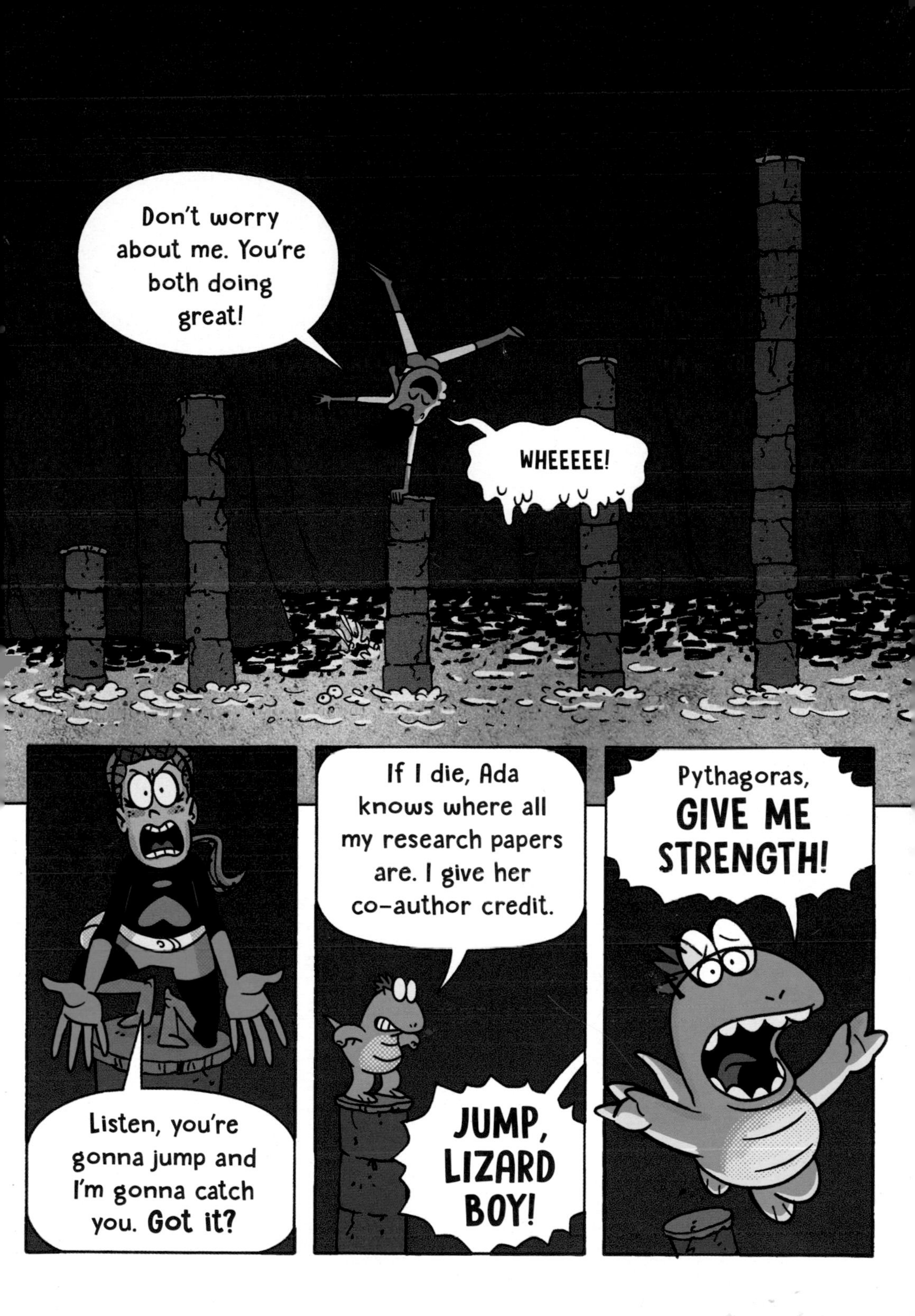
Don't worry about me. You're both doing great!
WHEEEEE!
Listen, you're gonna jump and I'm gonna catch you. Got it?
If I die, Ada knows where all my research papers are. I give her co-author credit.
JUMP, LIZARD BOY!
Pythagoras, GIVE ME STRENGTH!

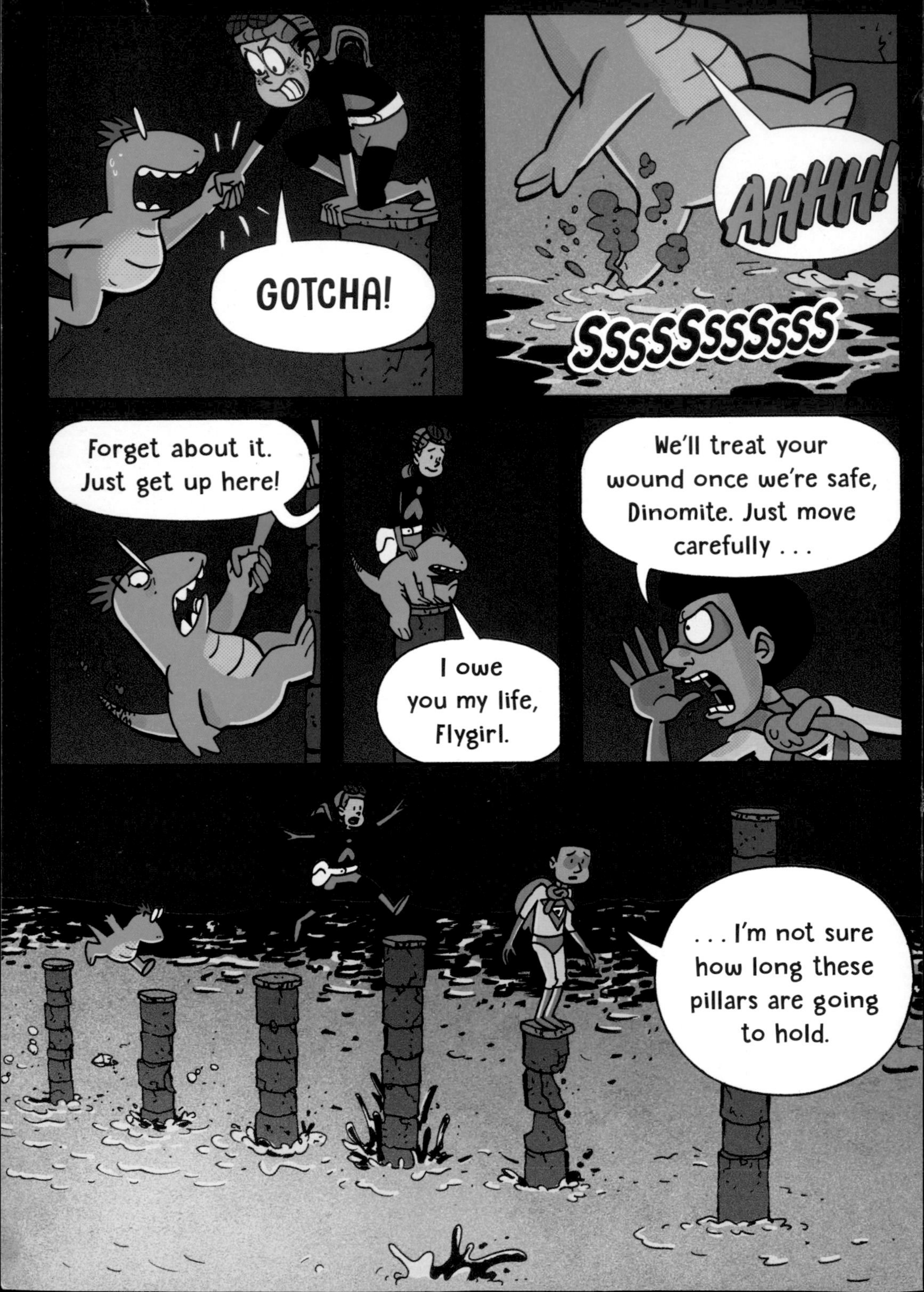
GOTCHA!
AHHH!
SSSSSSSSSSS
Forget about it. Just get up here!
I owe you my life, Flygirl.
We'll treat your wound once we're safe, Dinomite. Just move carefully . . .
. . . I'm not sure how long these pillars are going to hold.

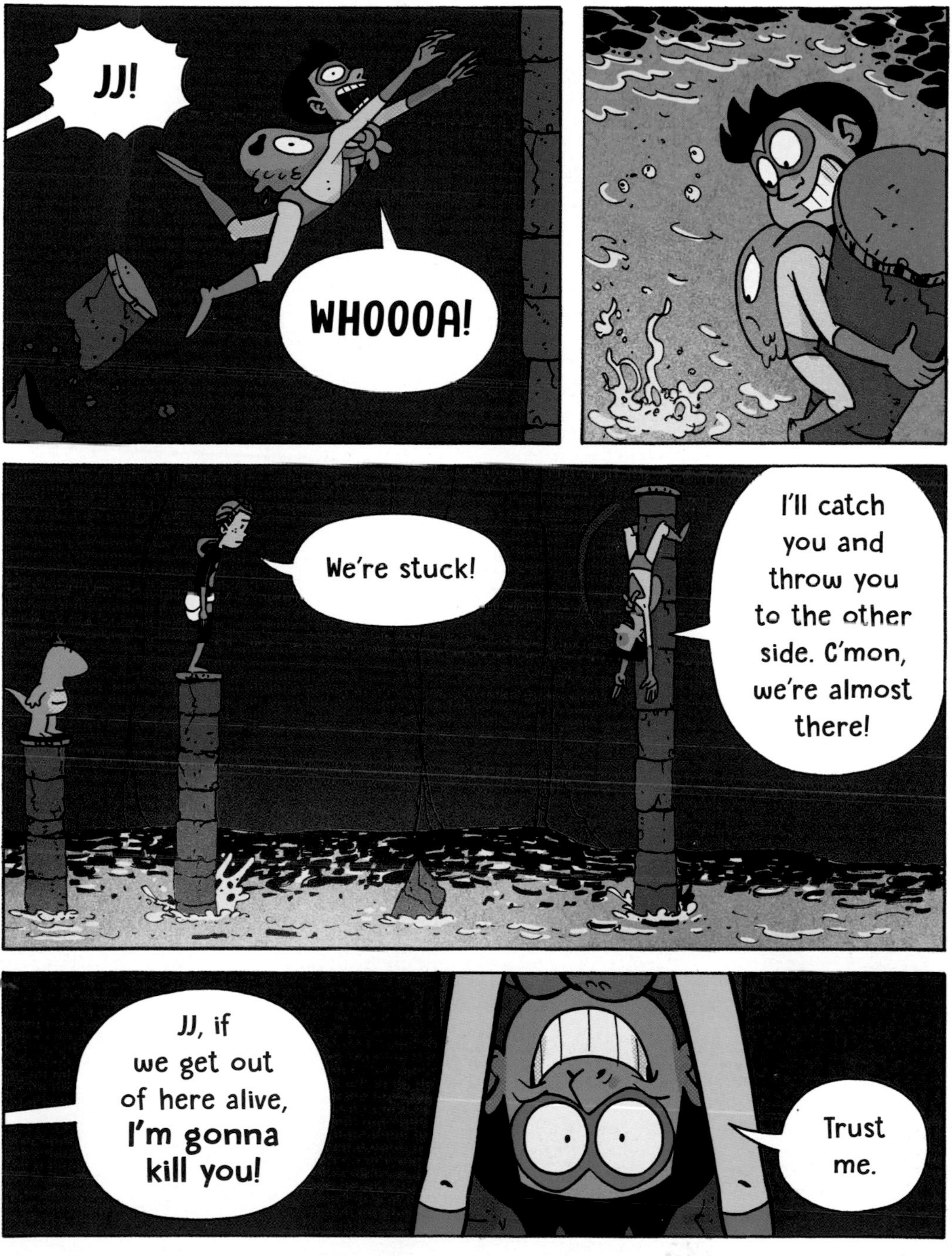
JJ!
WHOOOA!
We're stuck!
I'll catch you and throw you to the other side. C'mon, we're almost there!
JJ, if we get out of here alive, I'm gonna kill you!
Trust me.

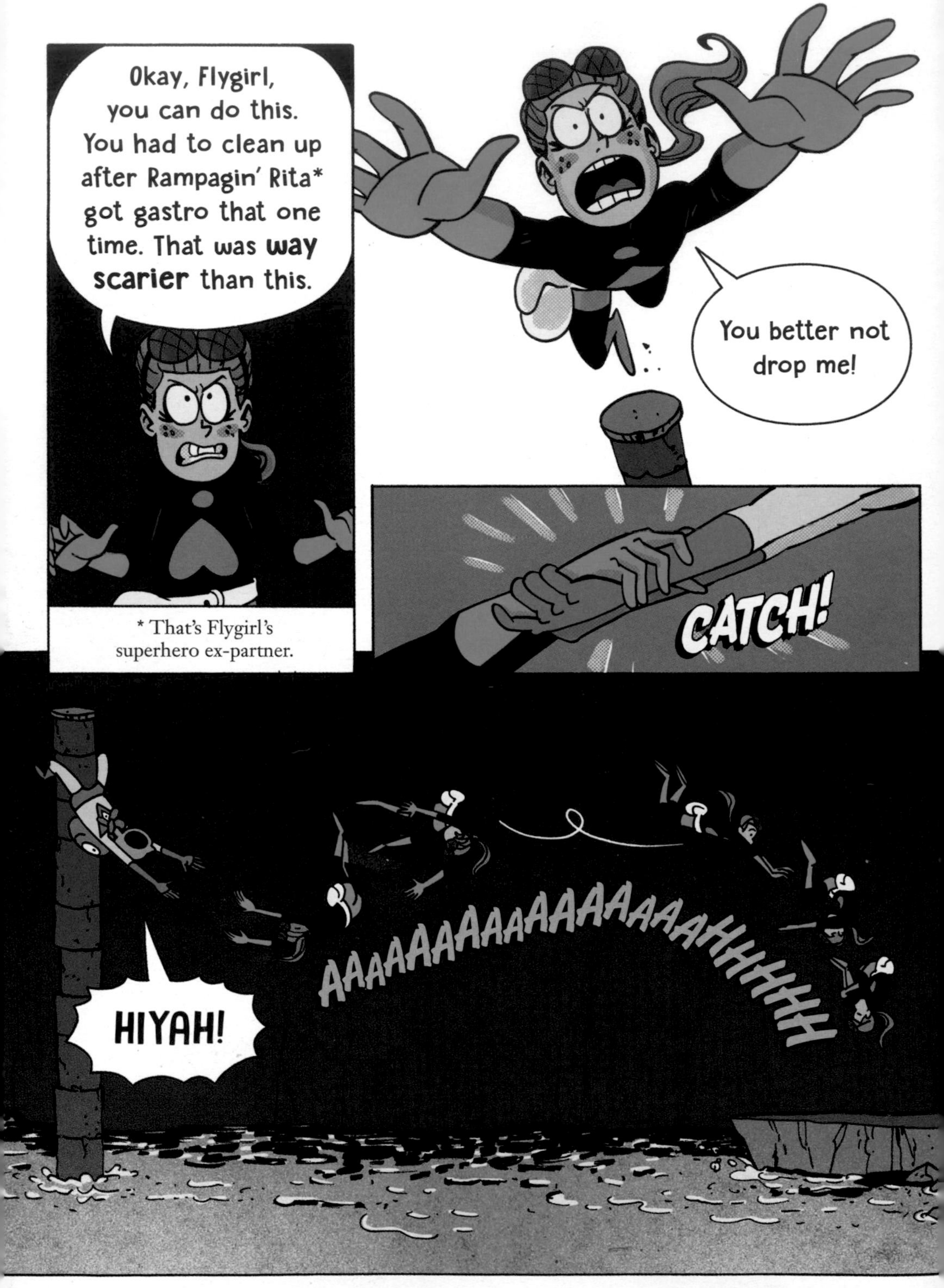
Okay, Flygirl, you can do this. You had to clean up after Rampagin' Rita* got gastro that one time. That was **way scarier** than this.
You better not drop me!
CATCH!
HIYAH!
AAAAAAAAAAAAAAAAAAAHHHHHH
* That's Flygirl's superhero ex-partner.

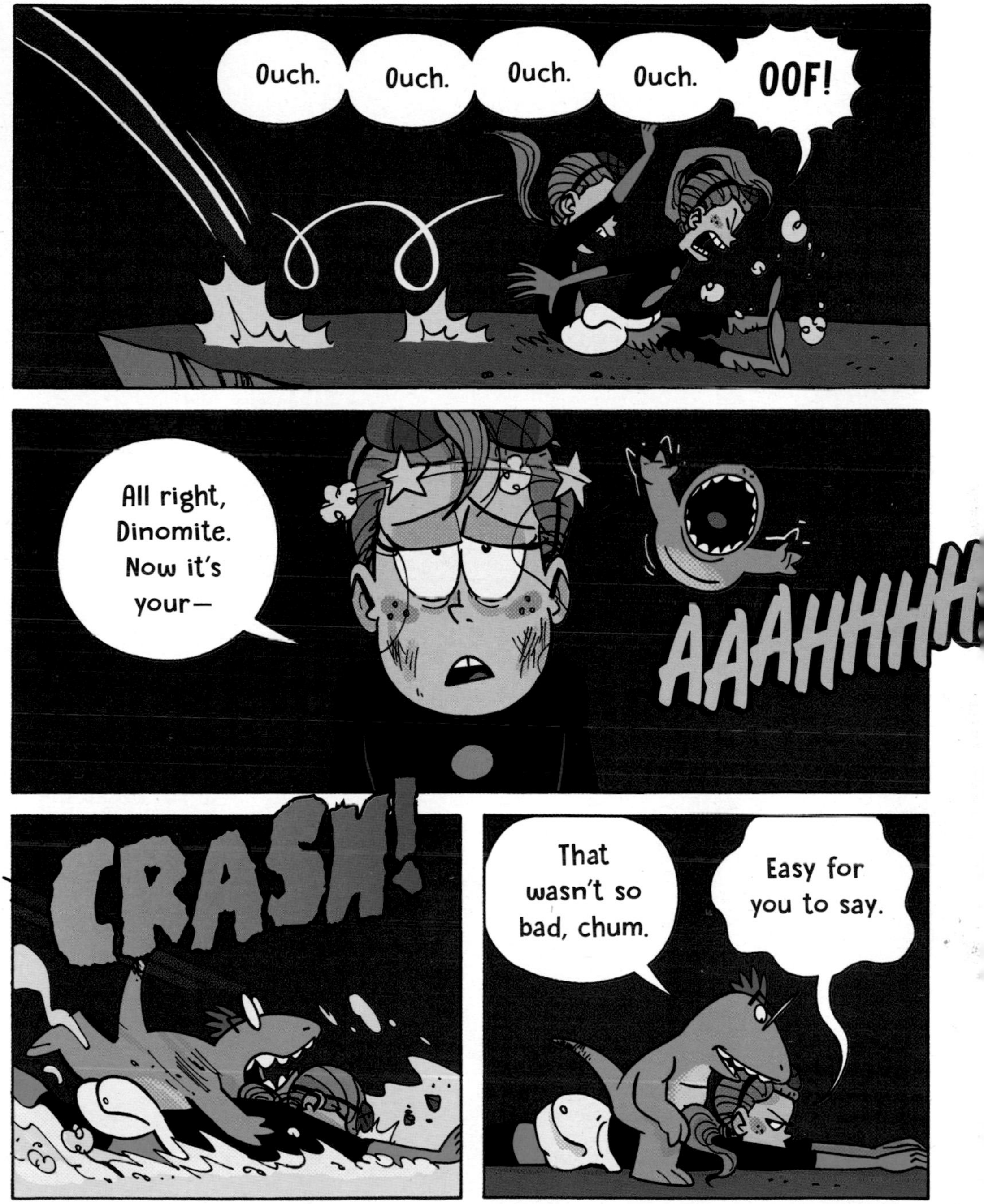
Ouch.
Ouch.
Ouch.
Ouch.
OOF!
All right, Dinomite. Now it's your—
AAAHHHH
CRASH!
That wasn't so bad, chum.
Easy for you to say.

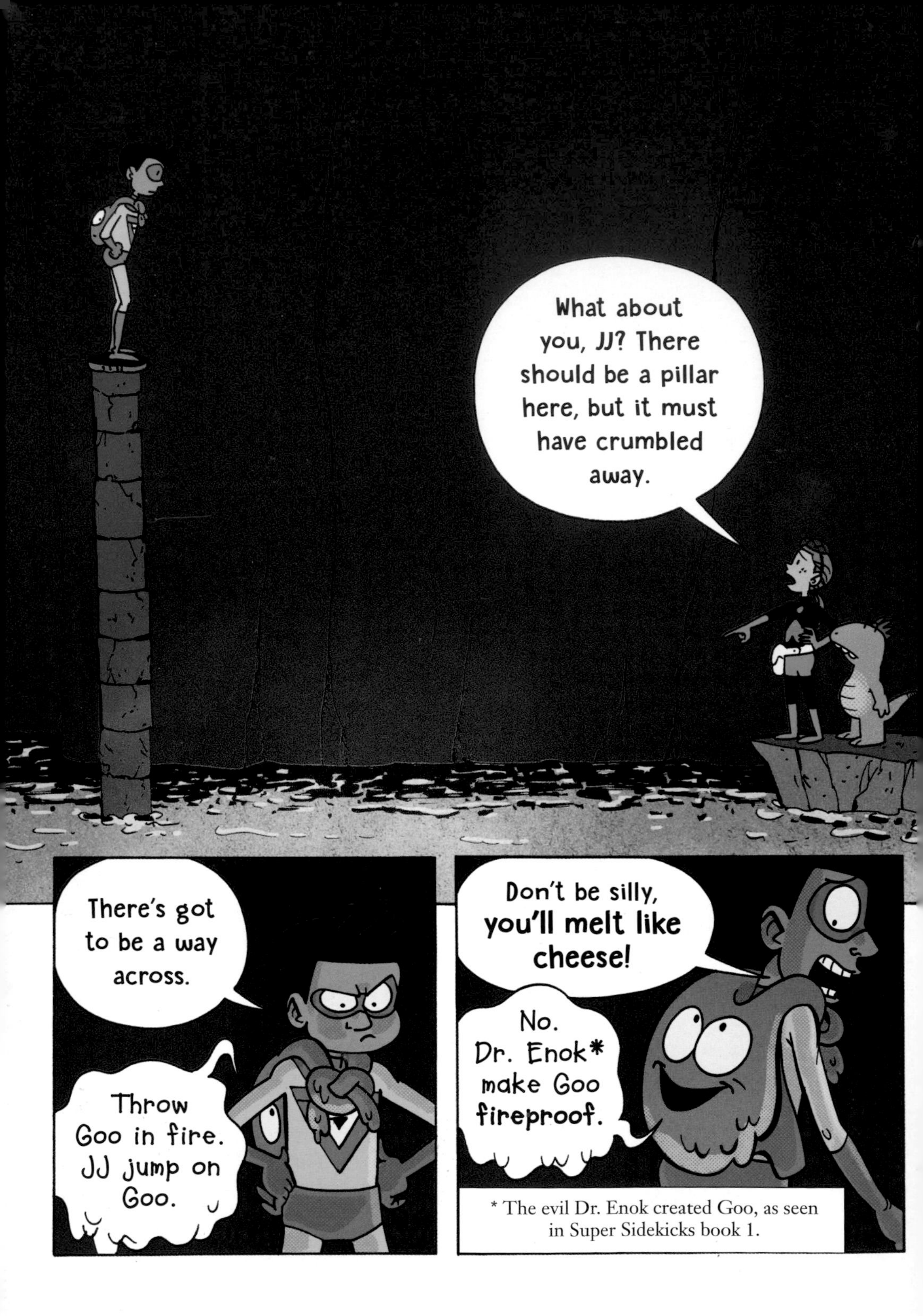
What about you, JJ? There should be a pillar here, but it must have crumbled away.
There's got to be a way across.
Throw Goo in fire. JJ jump on Goo.
Don't be silly, you'll melt like cheese!
No. Dr. Enok* make Goo fireproof.
* The evil Dr. Enok created Goo, as seen in Super Sidekicks book 1.

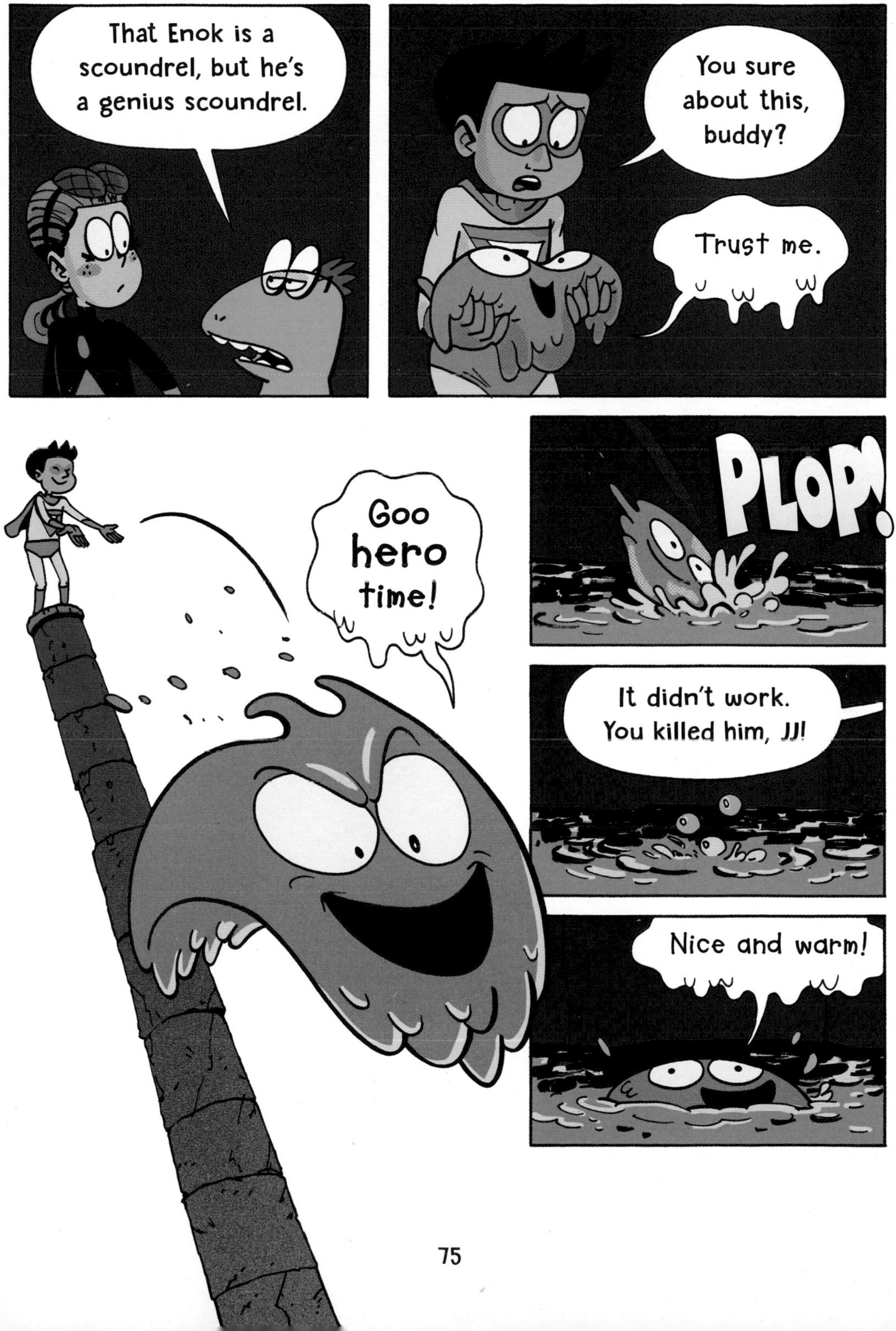
That Enok is a scoundrel, but he's a genius scoundrel.
You sure about this, buddy?
Trust me.
Goo hero time!
PLOP!
It didn't work. You killed him, JJ!
Nice and warm!

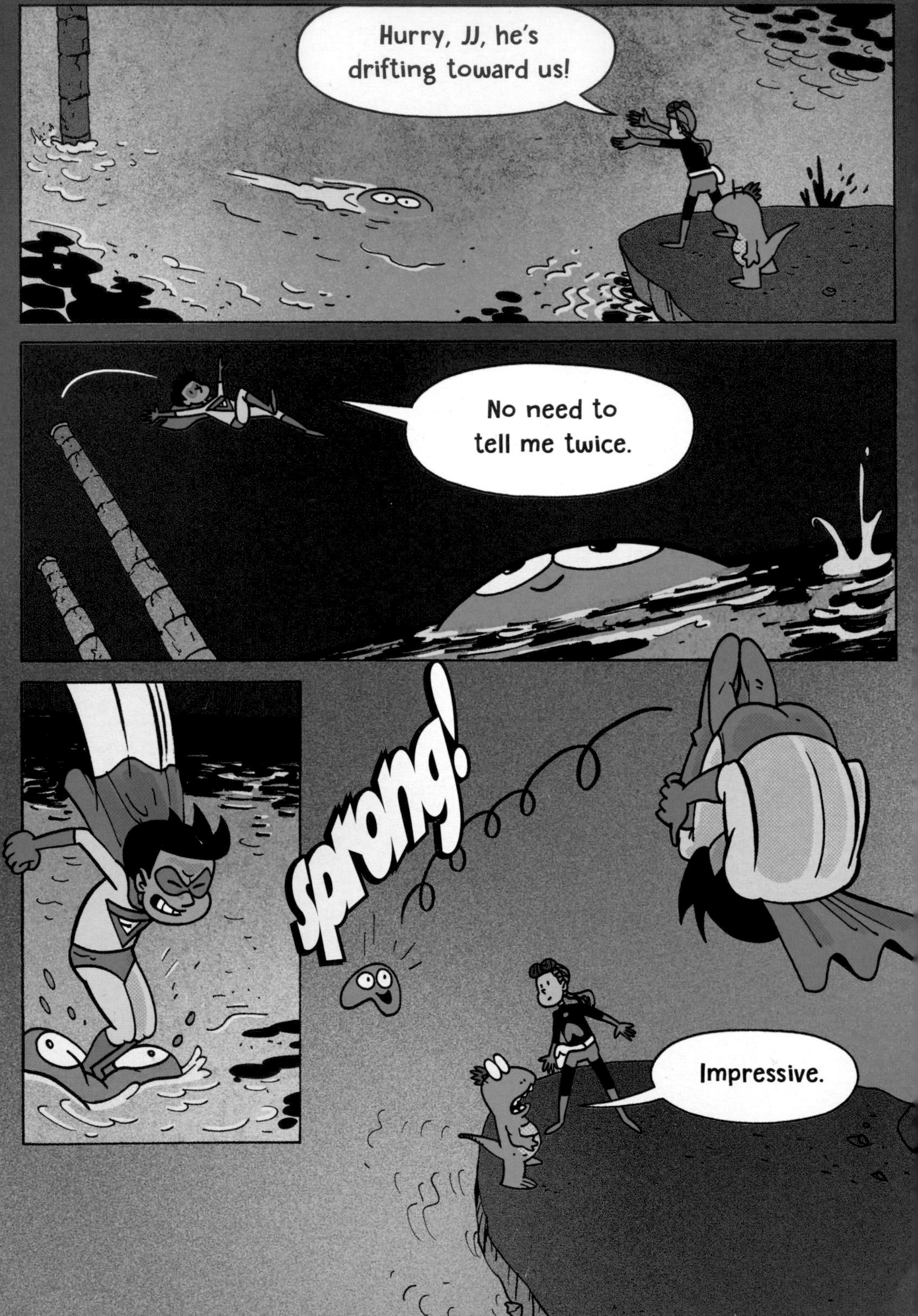
Hurry, JJ, he's drifting toward us!
No need to tell me twice.
sprong!
Impressive.

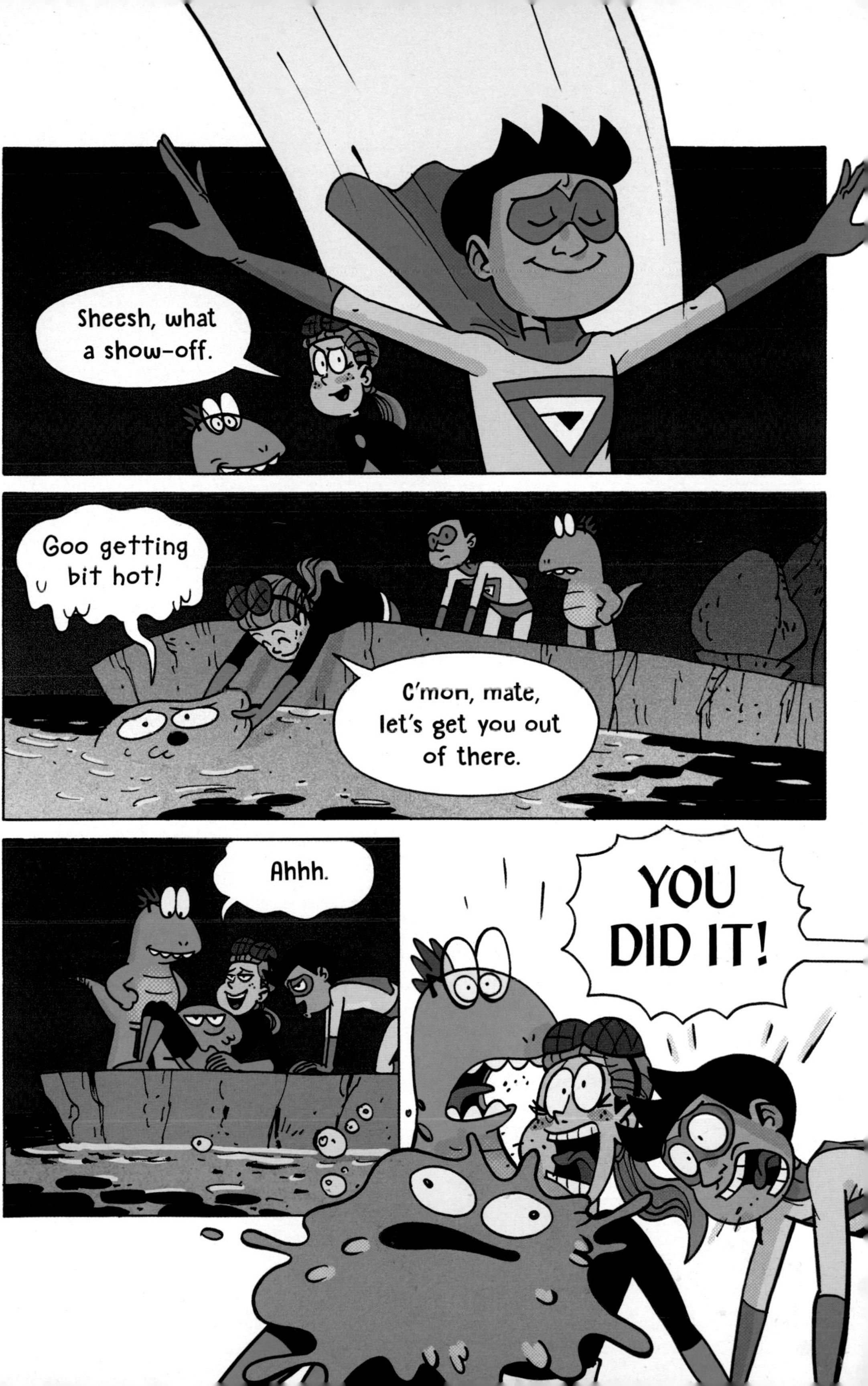
Sheesh, what a show-off.
Goo getting bit hot!
C'mon, mate, let's get you out of there.
Ahhh.
YOU DID IT!

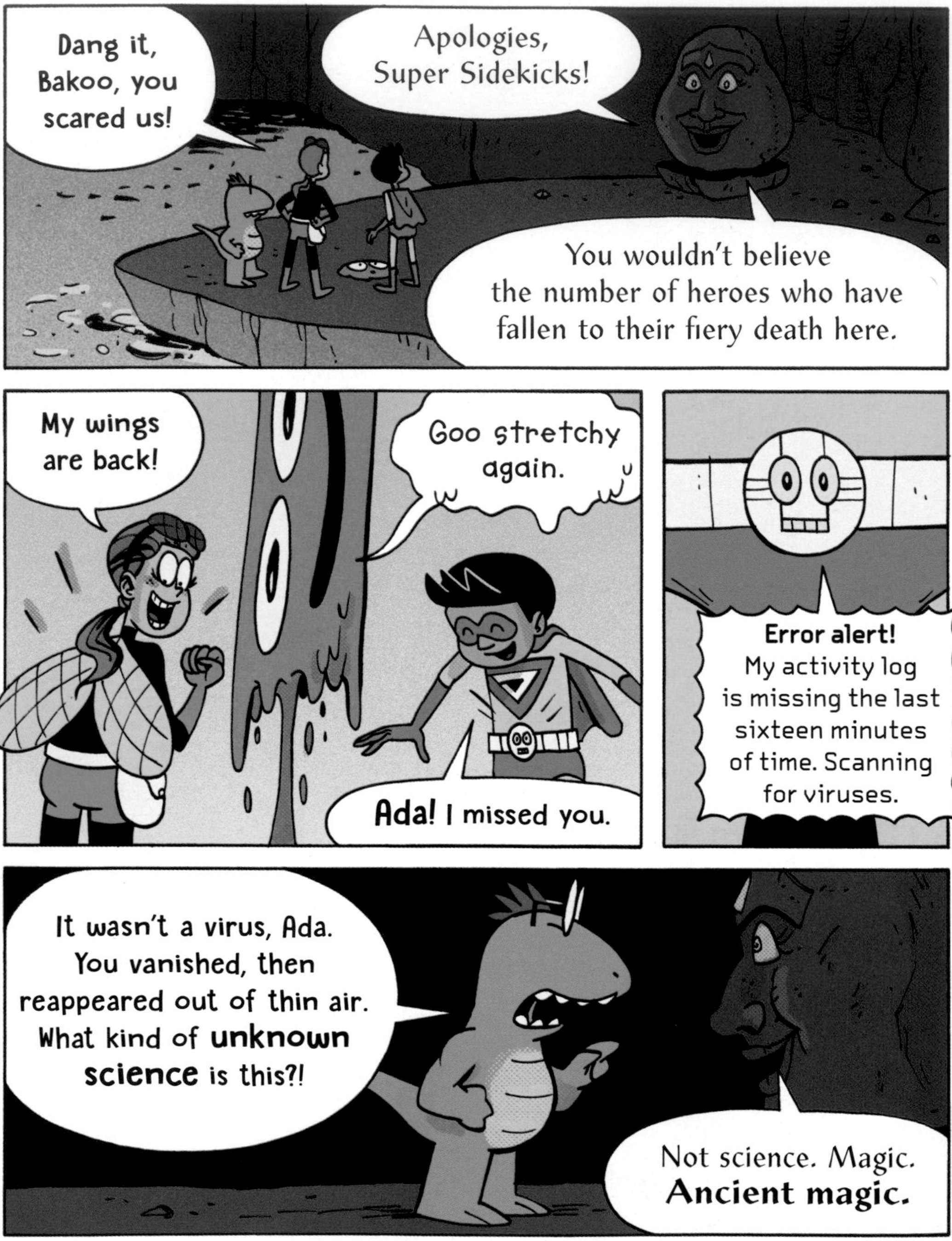
Dang it, Bakoo, you scared us!
Apologies, Super Sidekicks!
You wouldn't believe the number of heroes who have fallen to their fiery death here.
My wings are back!
Goo stretchy again.
Ada! I missed you.
Error alert! My activity log is missing the last sixteen minutes of time. Scanning for viruses.
It wasn't a virus, Ada. You vanished, then reappeared out of thin air. What kind of unknown science is this?!
Not science. Magic. Ancient magic.

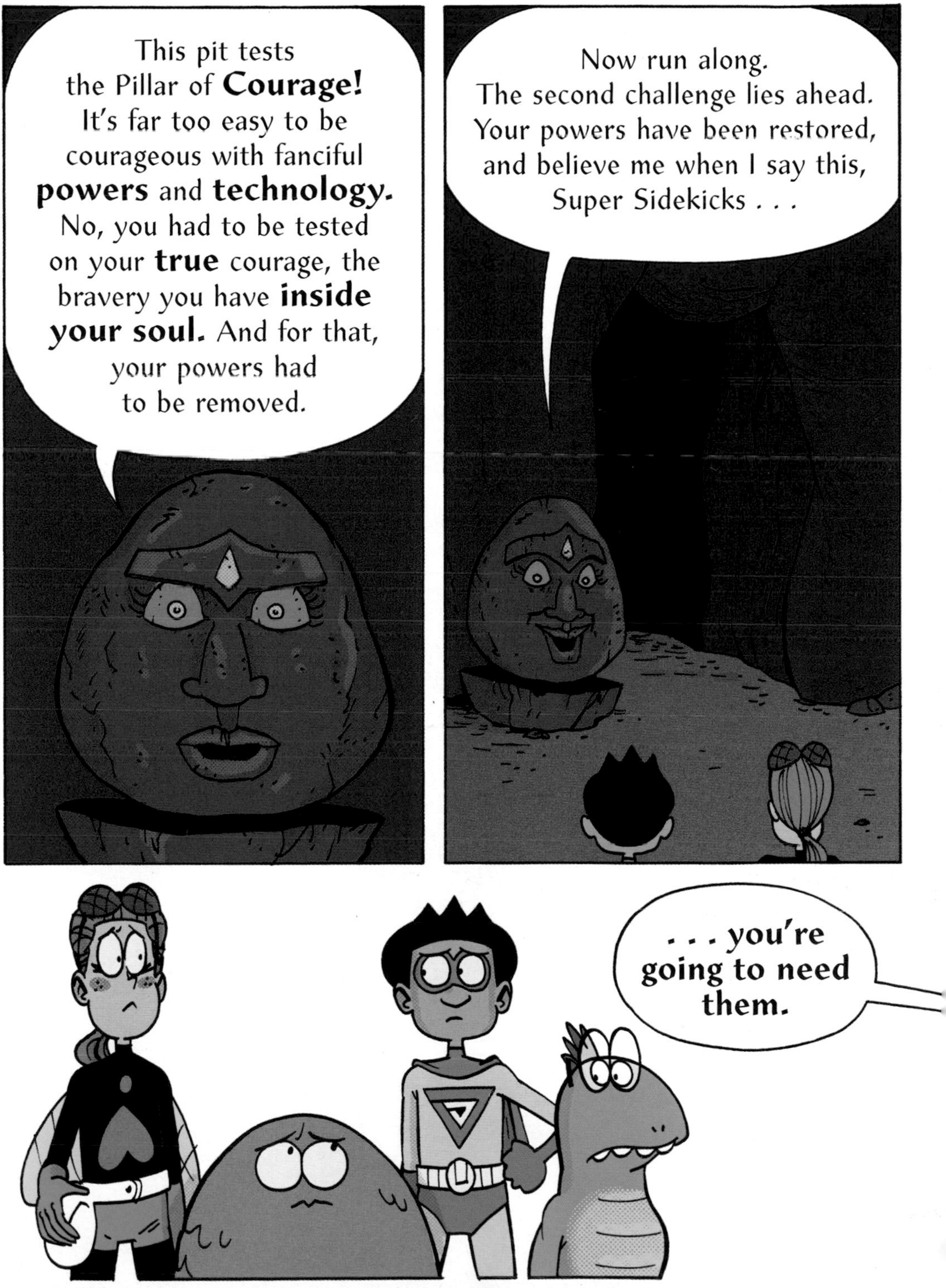
This pit tests the Pillar of Courage! It's far too easy to be courageous with fanciful powers and technology. No, you had to be tested on your true courage, the bravery you have inside your soul. And for that, your powers had to be removed.
Now run along. The second challenge lies ahead. Your powers have been restored, and believe me when I say this, Super Sidekicks . . .
. . . you're going to need them.

Chapter

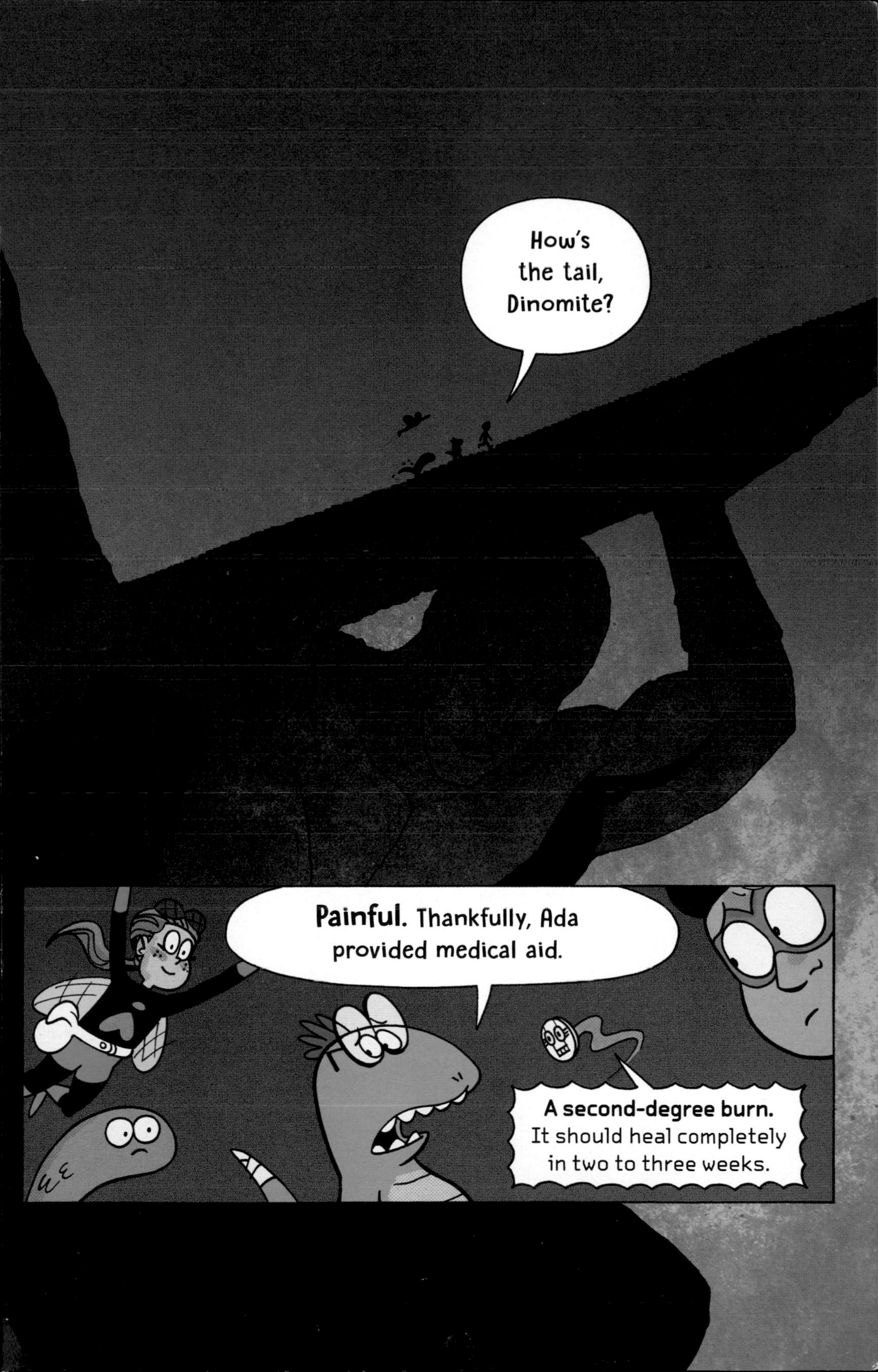
How's the tail, Dinomite?
Painful. Thankfully, Ada provided medical aid.
A second-degree burn. It should heal completely in two to three weeks.

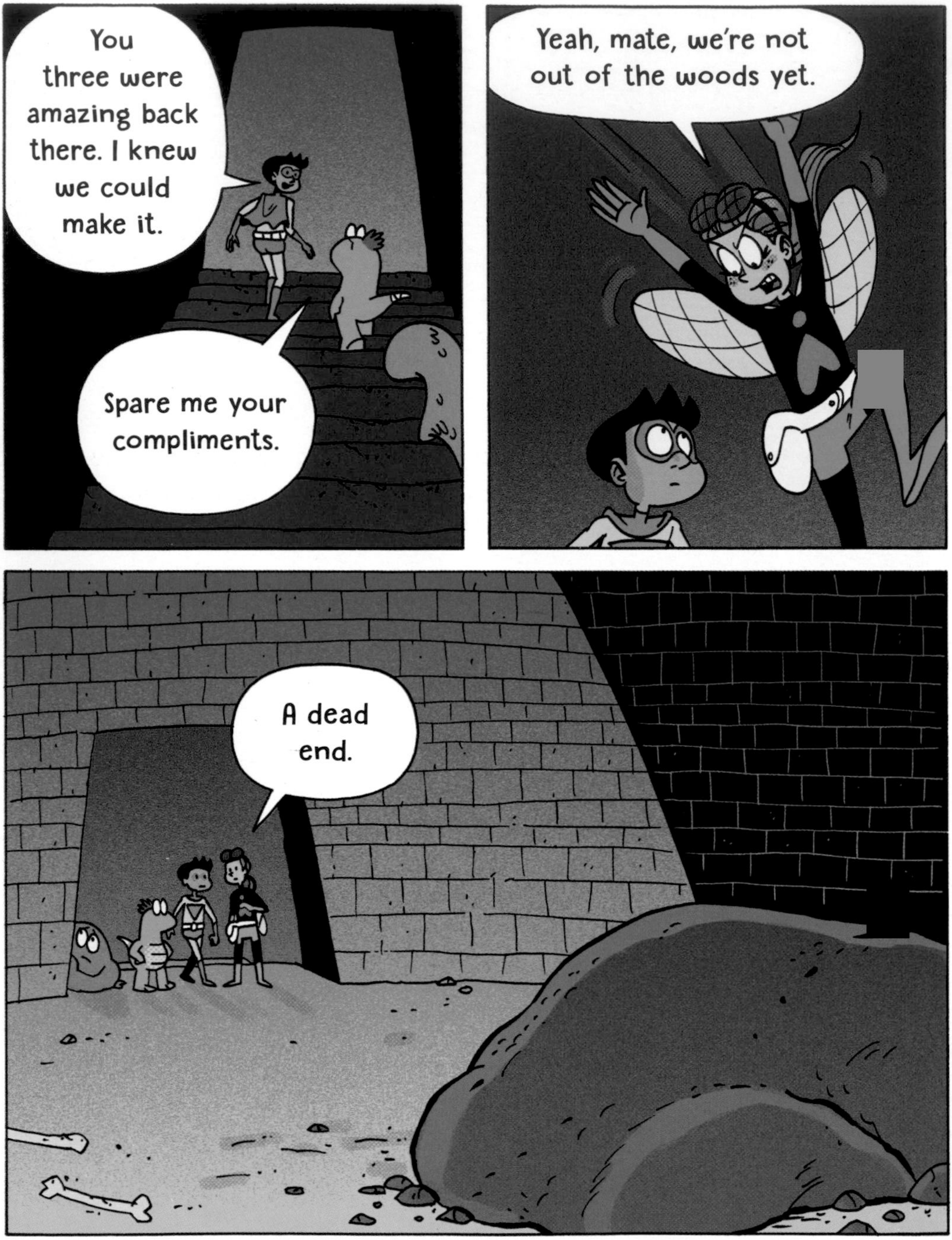
You three were amazing back there. I knew we could make it.
Spare me your compliments.
Yeah, mate, we're not out of the woods yet.
A dead end.

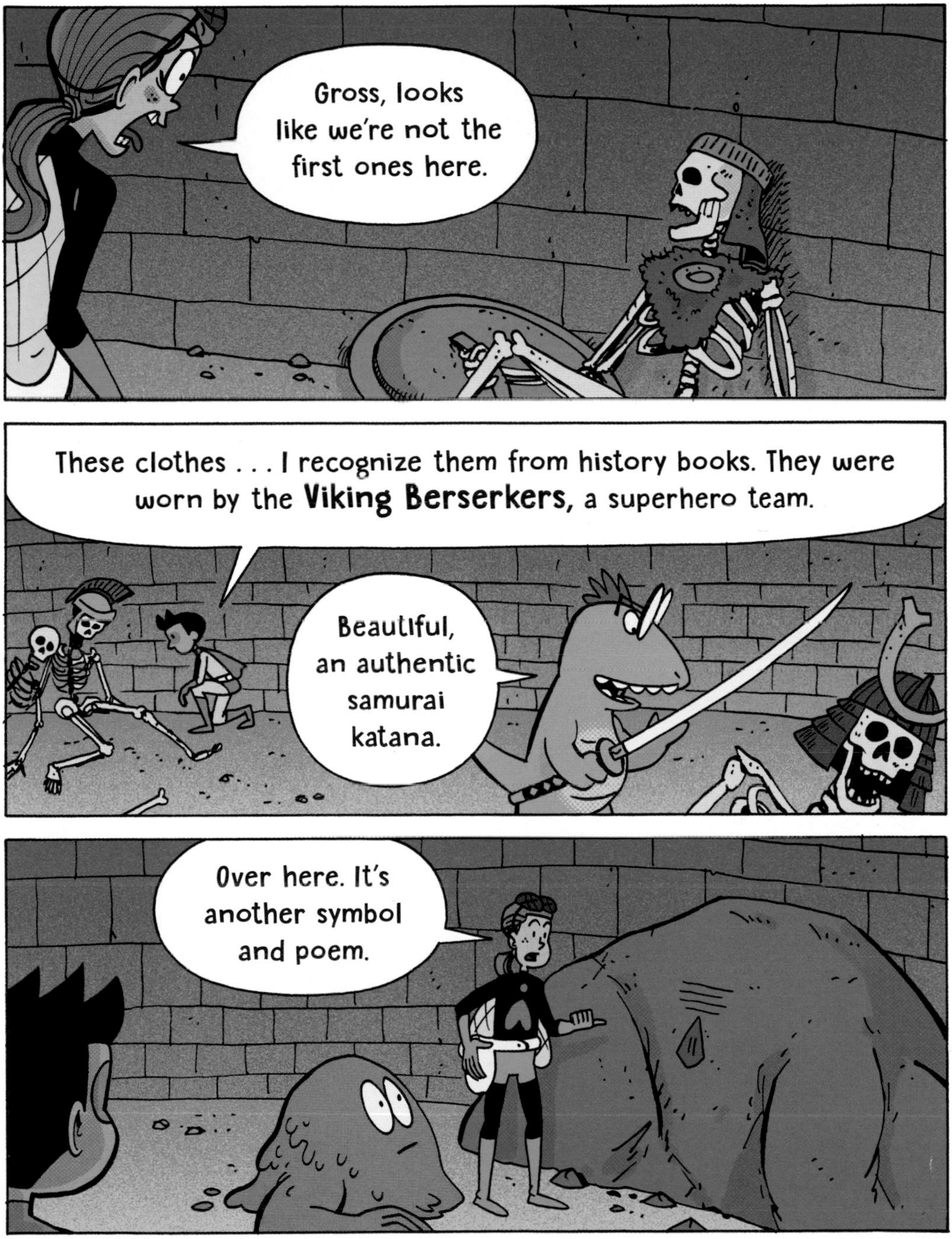
Gross, looks like we're not the first ones here.
These clothes . . . I recognize them from history books. They were worn by the **Viking Berserkers**, a superhero team.
Beautiful, an authentic samurai katana.
Over here. It's another symbol and poem.

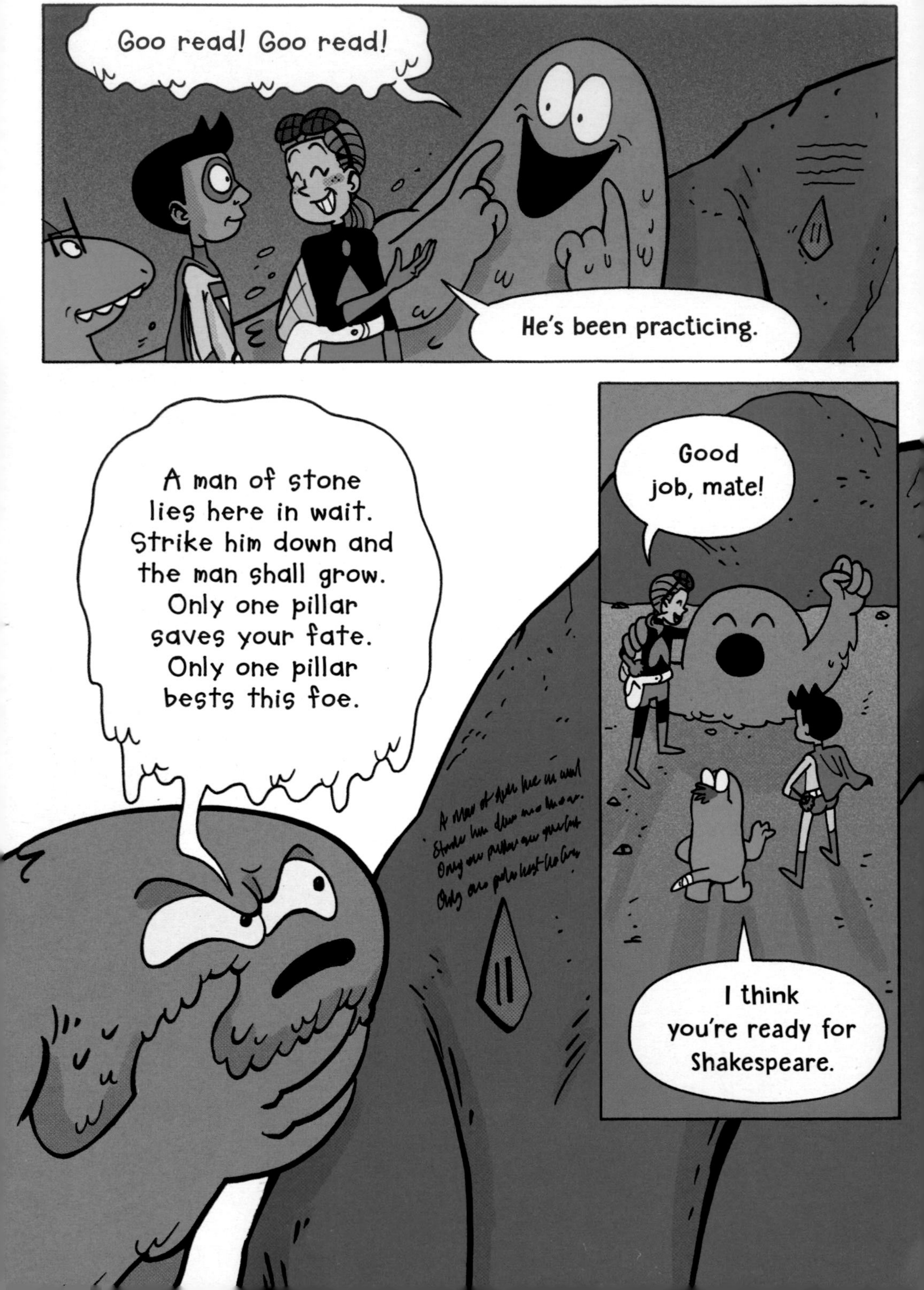
Goo read! Goo read!
He's been practicing.
A man of stone lies here in wait. Strike him down and the man shall grow. Only one pillar saves your fate. Only one pillar bests this foe.
Good job, mate!
I think you're ready for Shakespeare.

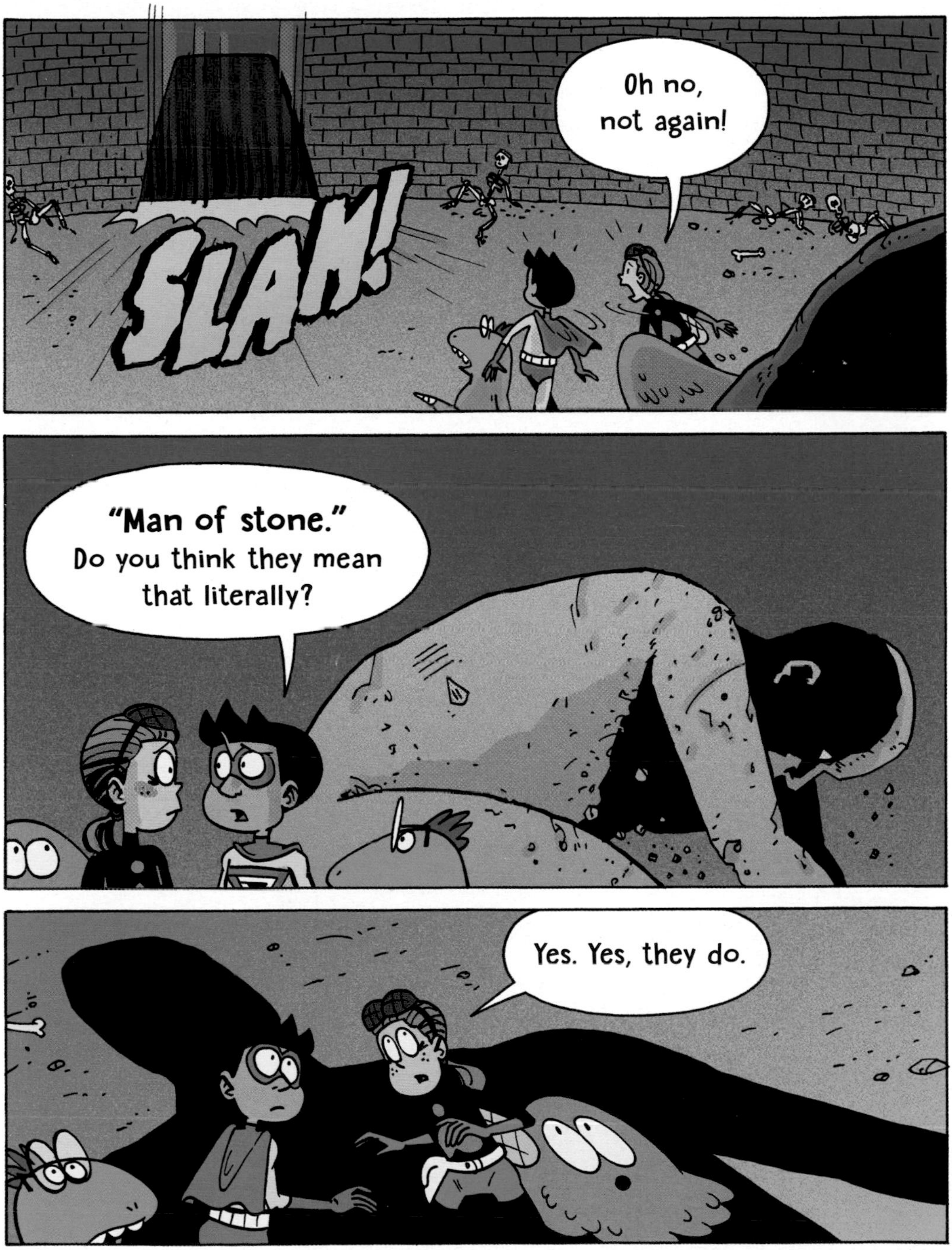
SLAM!
Oh no, not again!
"Man of stone." Do you think they mean that literally?
Yes. Yes, they do.

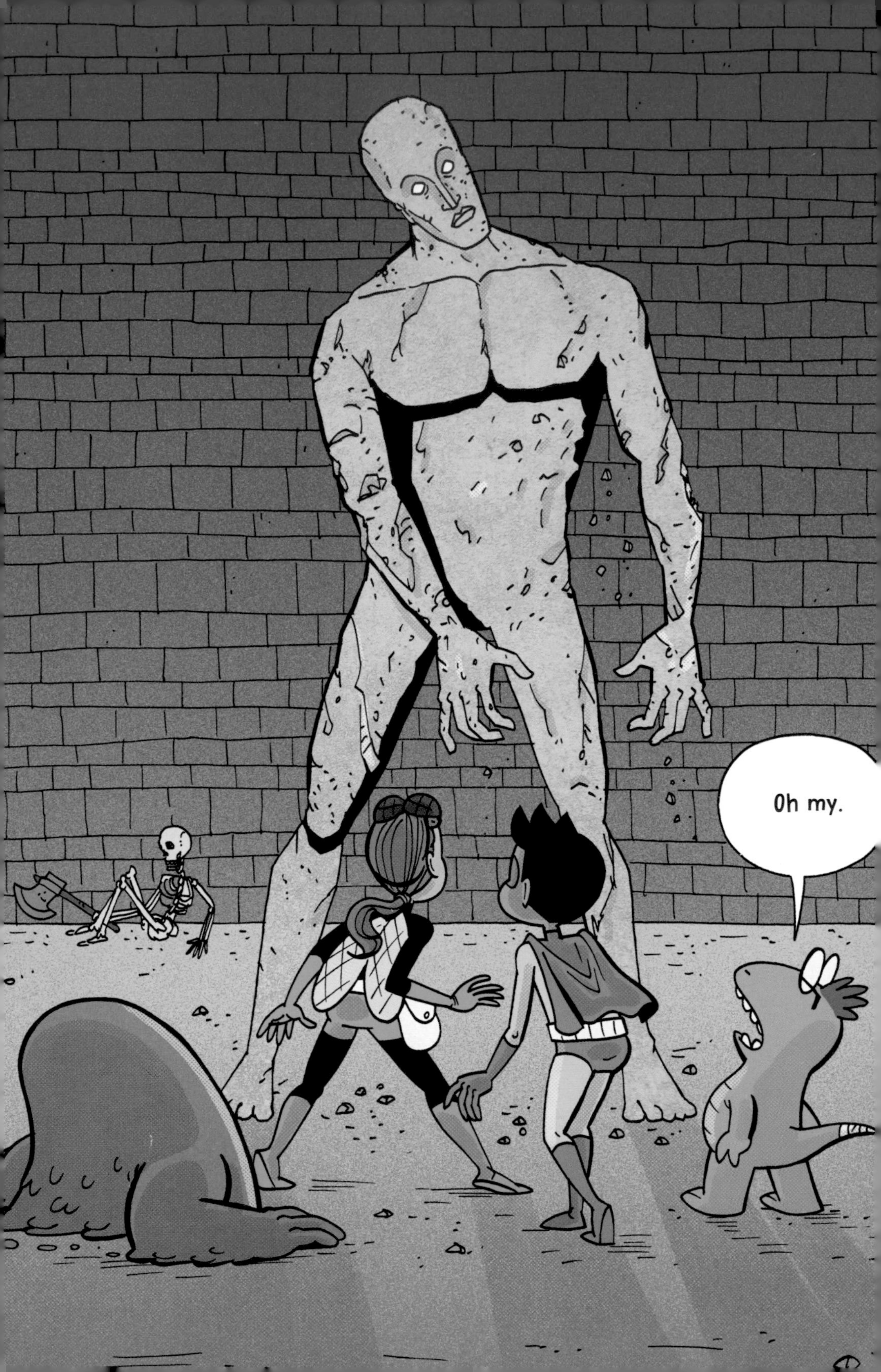
Oh my.

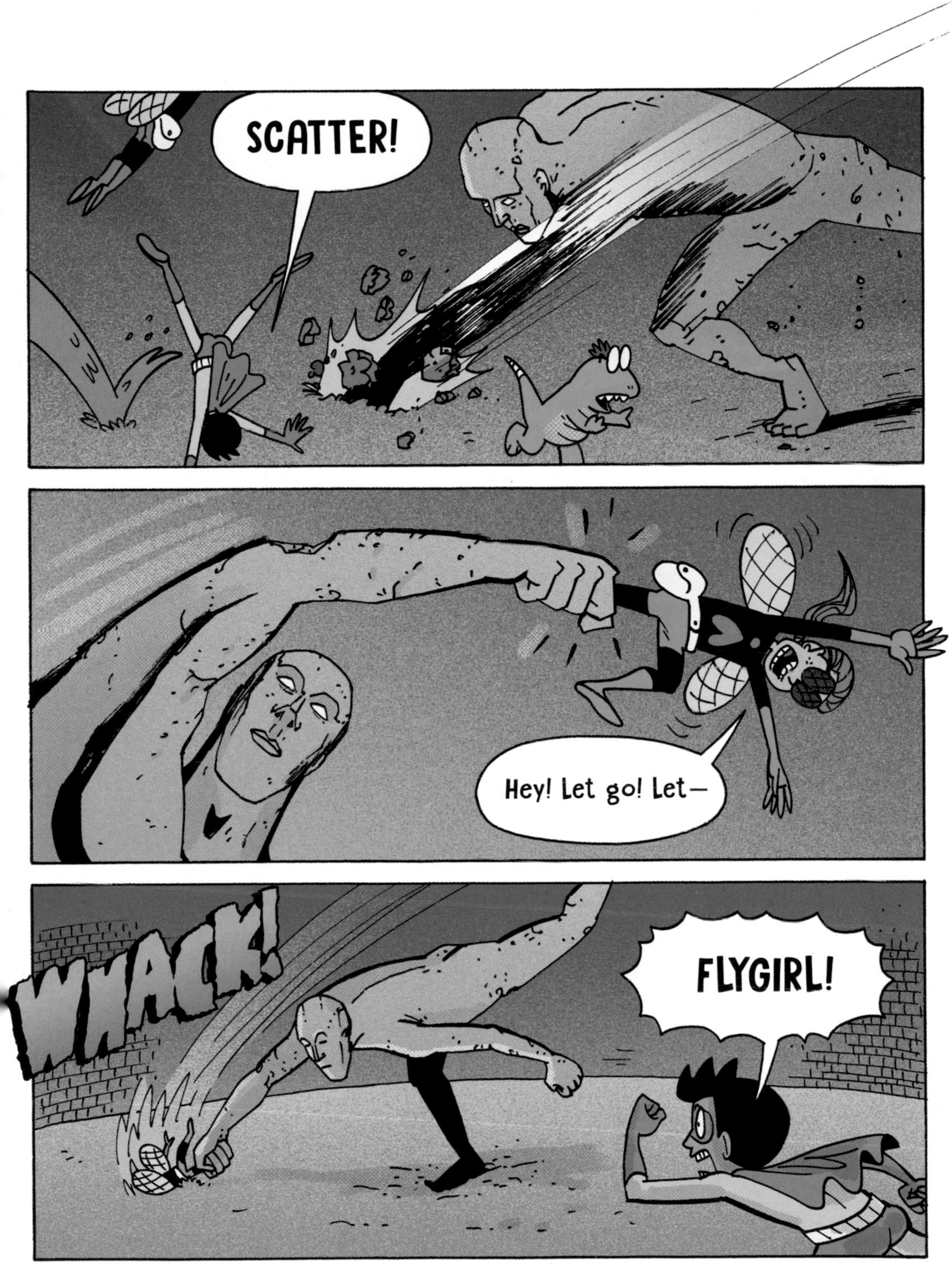
SCATTER!
Hey! Let go! Let—
WHACK!
FLYGIRL!

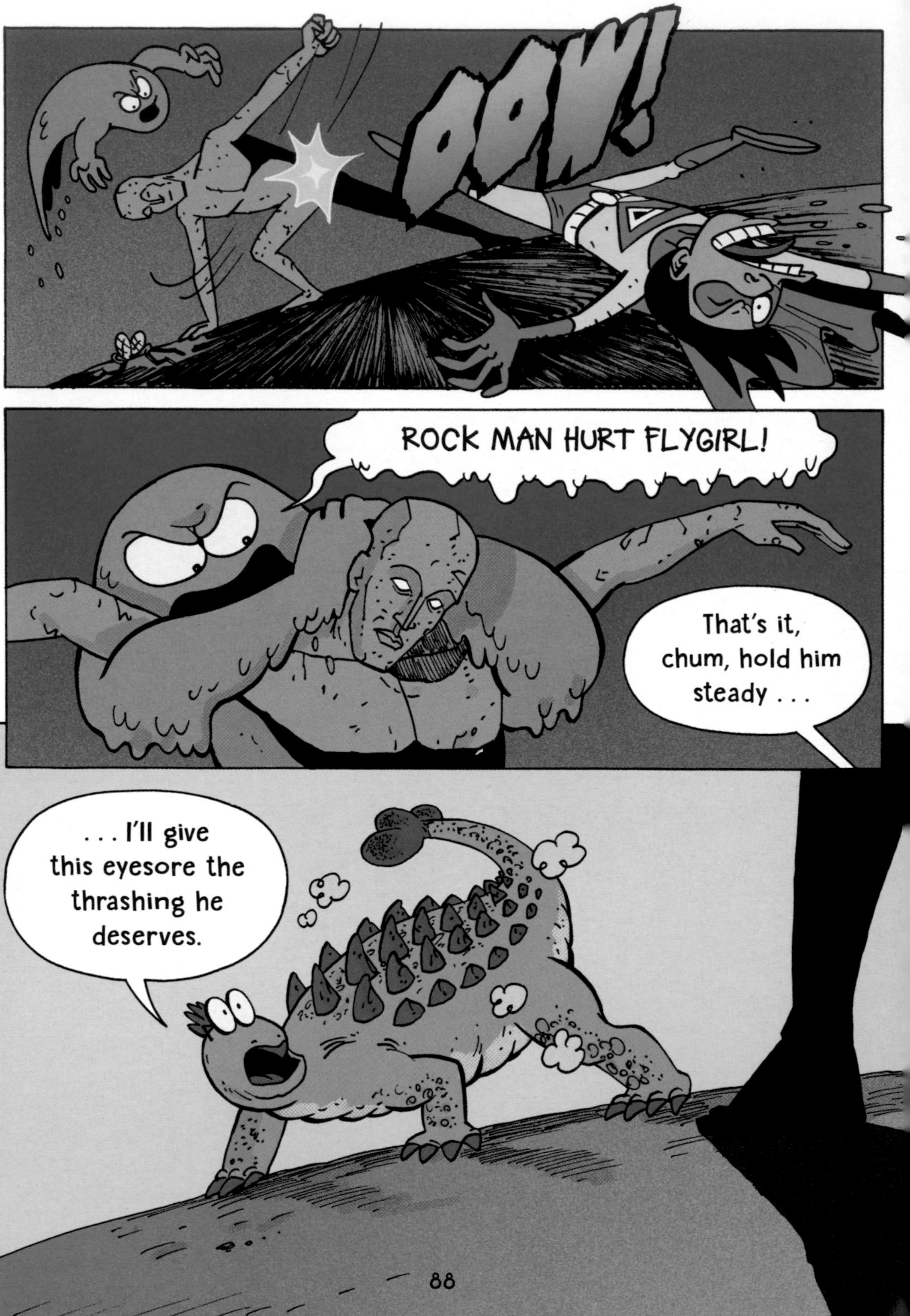
OOW!
ROCK MAN HURT FLYGIRL!
That's it, chum, hold him steady . . .
. . . I'll give this eyesore the thrashing he deserves.

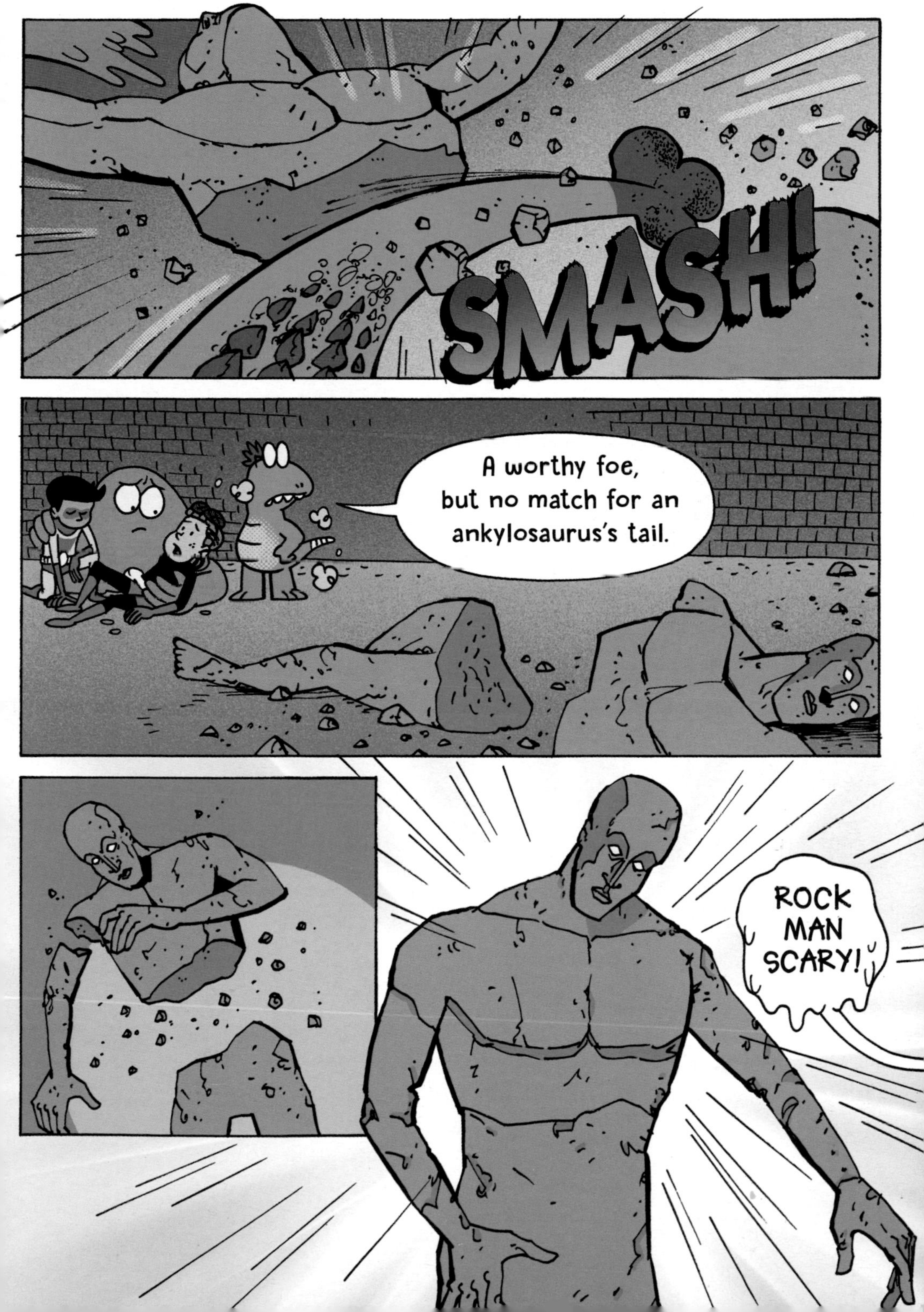
SMASH!
A worthy foe, but no match for an ankylosaurus's tail.
ROCK MAN SCARY!

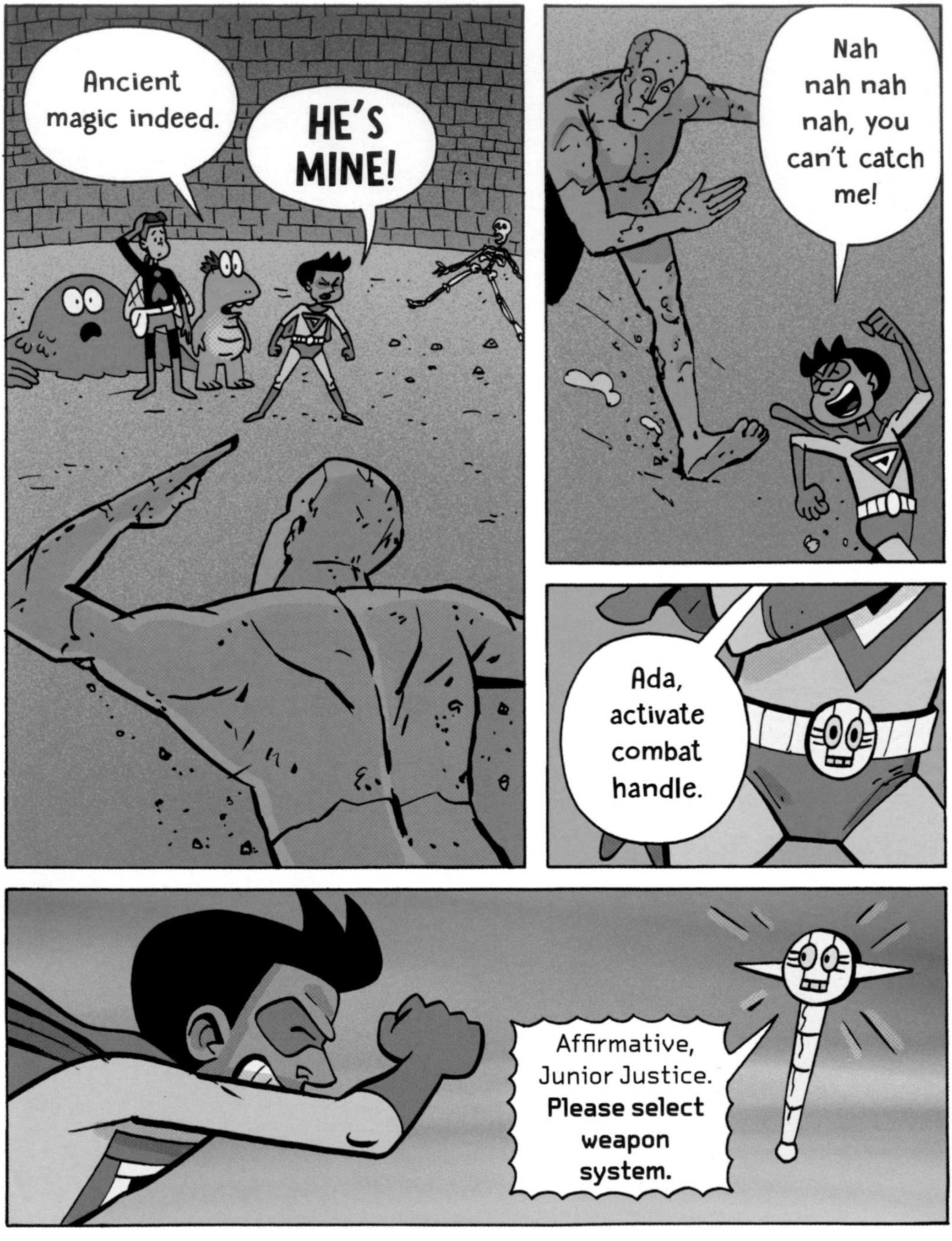
Ancient magic indeed.
HE'S MINE!
Nah nah nah nah, you can't catch me!
Ada, activate combat handle.
Affirmative, Junior Justice. **Please select weapon system.**

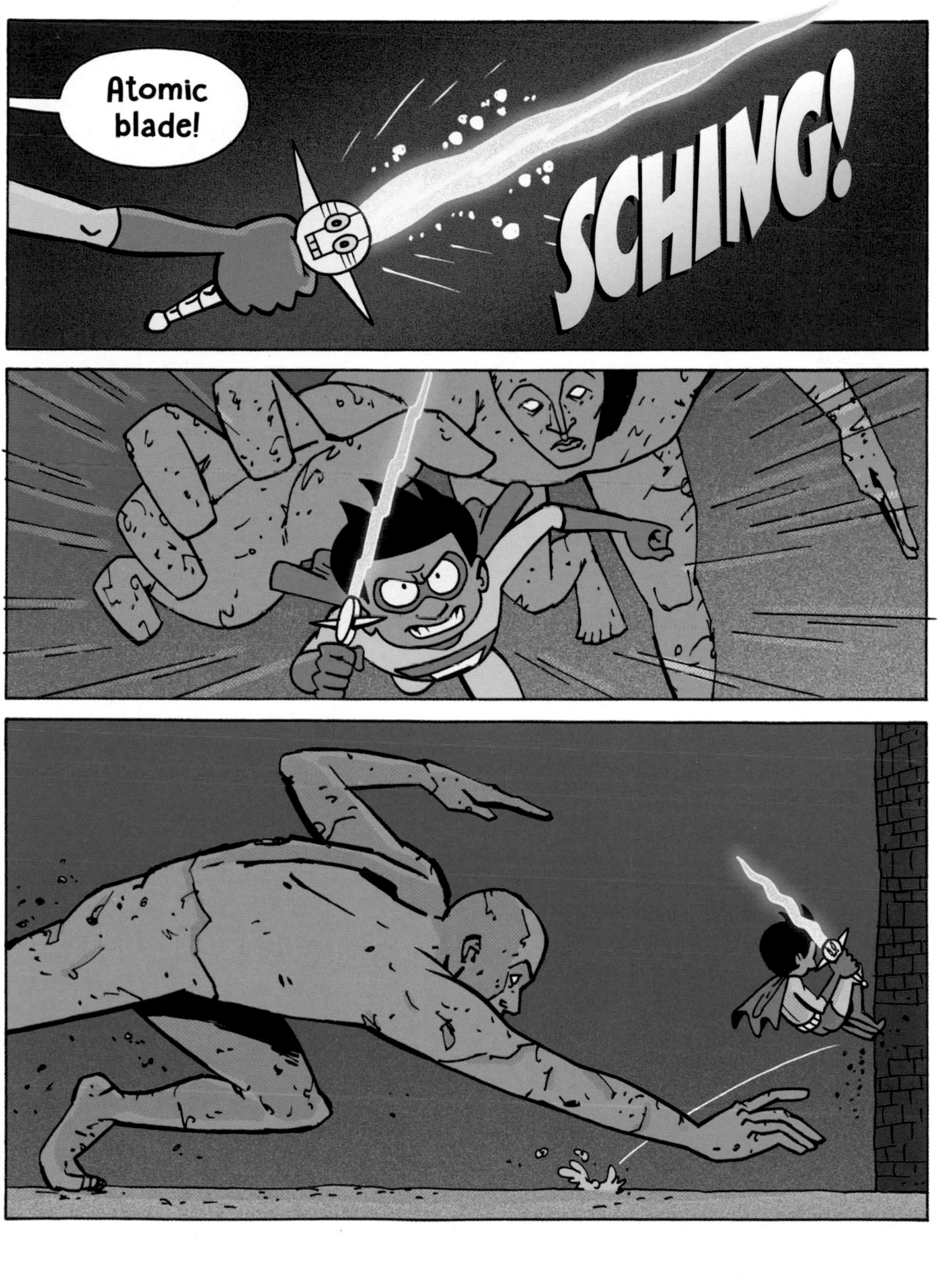
Atomic blade!
SCHING!

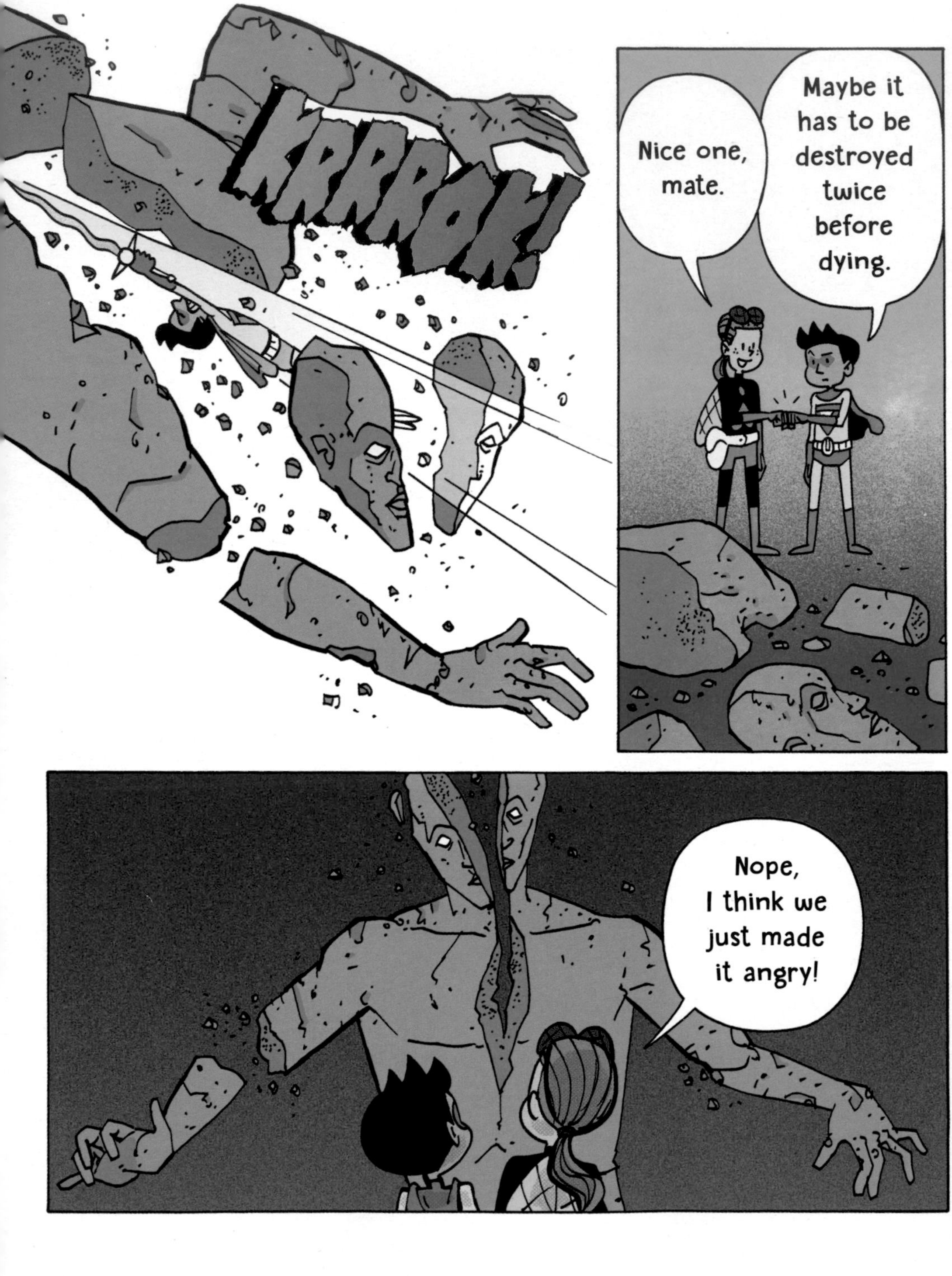
KRRRAK!
Nice one, mate.
Maybe it has to be destroyed twice before dying.
Nope, I think we just made it angry!

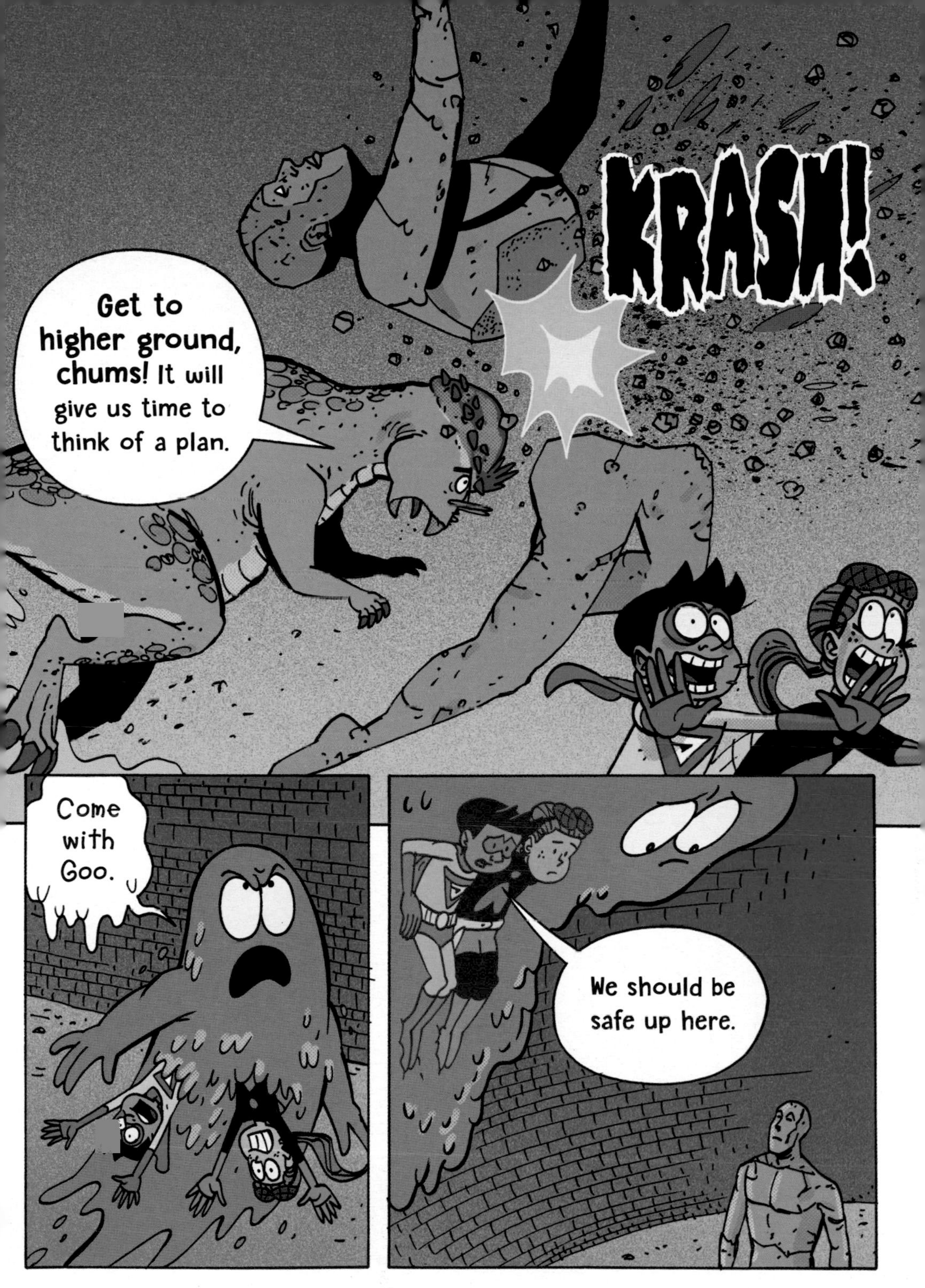
KRASH!
Get to higher ground, chums! It will give us time to think of a plan.
Come with Goo.
We should be safe up here.

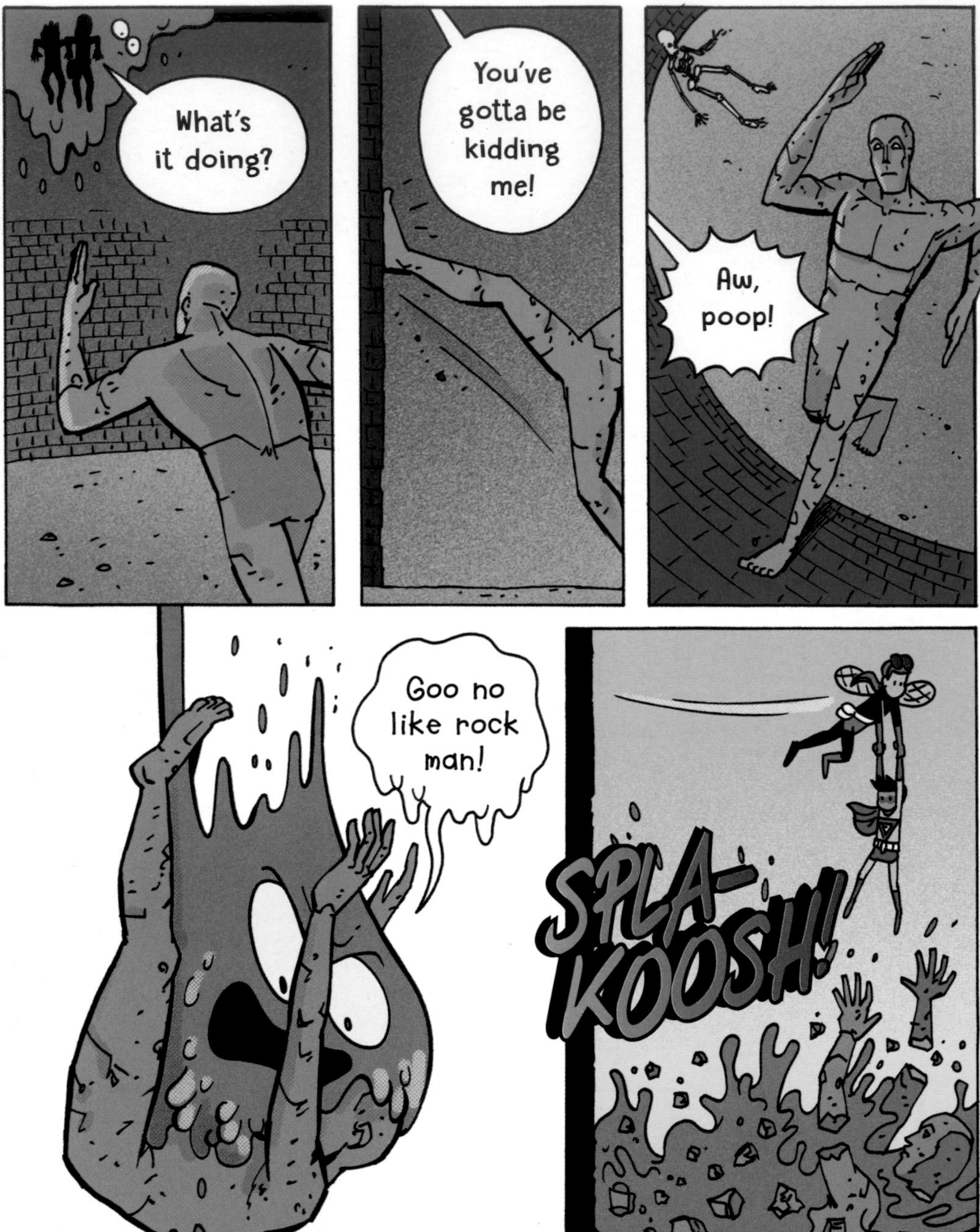
What's it doing?
You've gotta be kidding me!
Aw, poop!
Goo no like rock man!
SPLA-KOOSH!

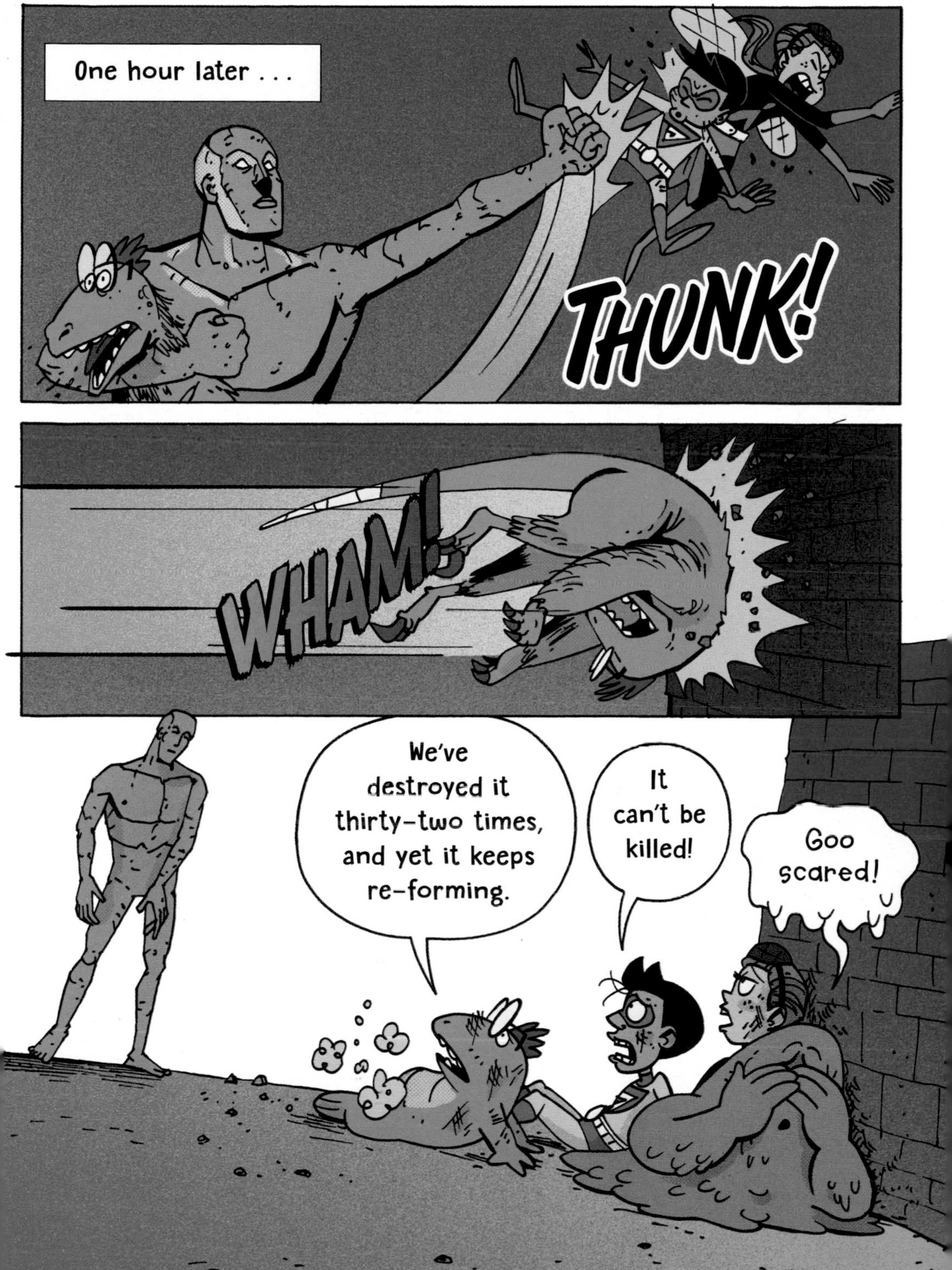
One hour later . . .
THUNK!
WHAM!
We've destroyed it thirty-two times, and yet it keeps re-forming.
It can't be killed!
Goo scared!

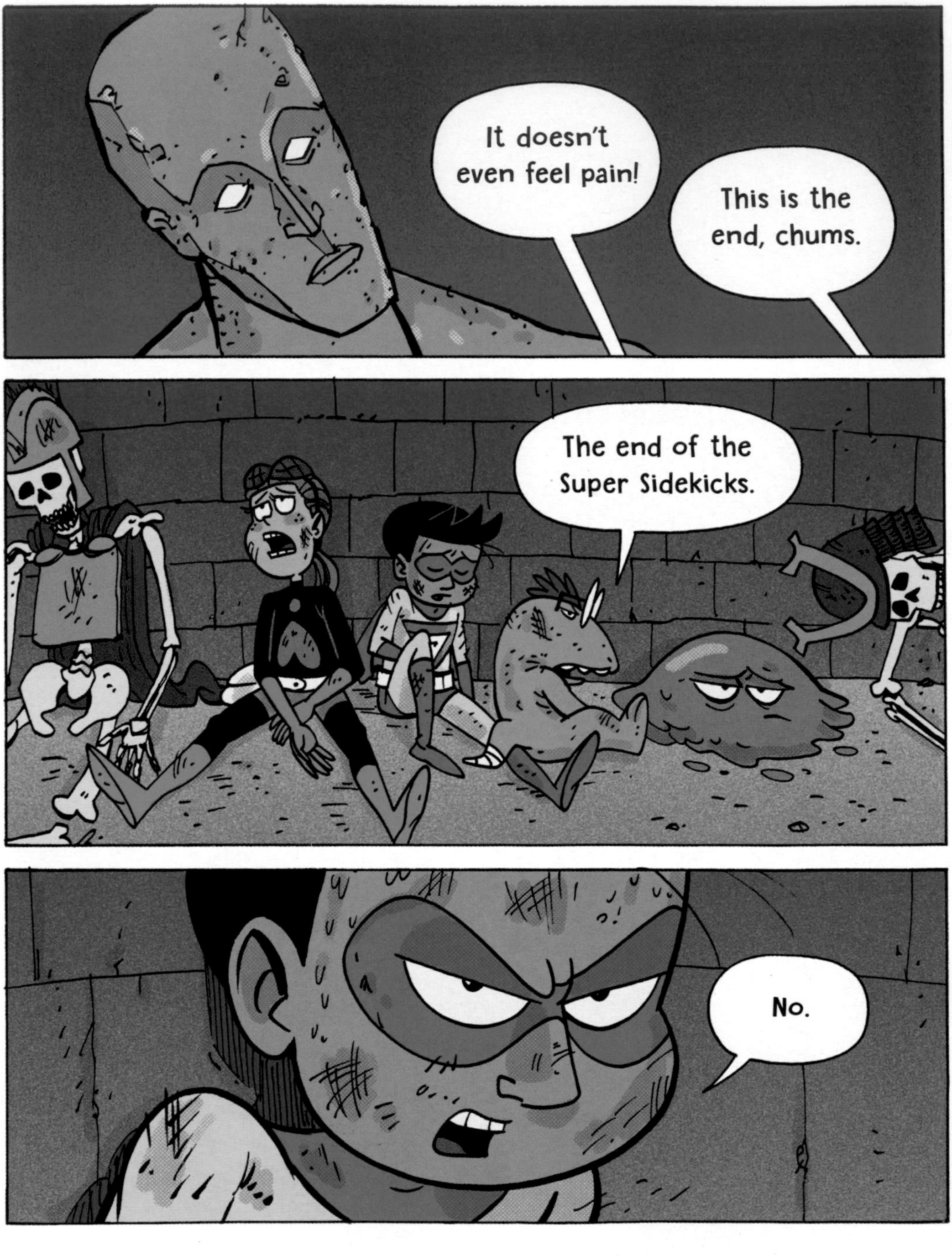
It doesn't even feel pain!
This is the end, chums.
The end of the Super Sidekicks.
No.

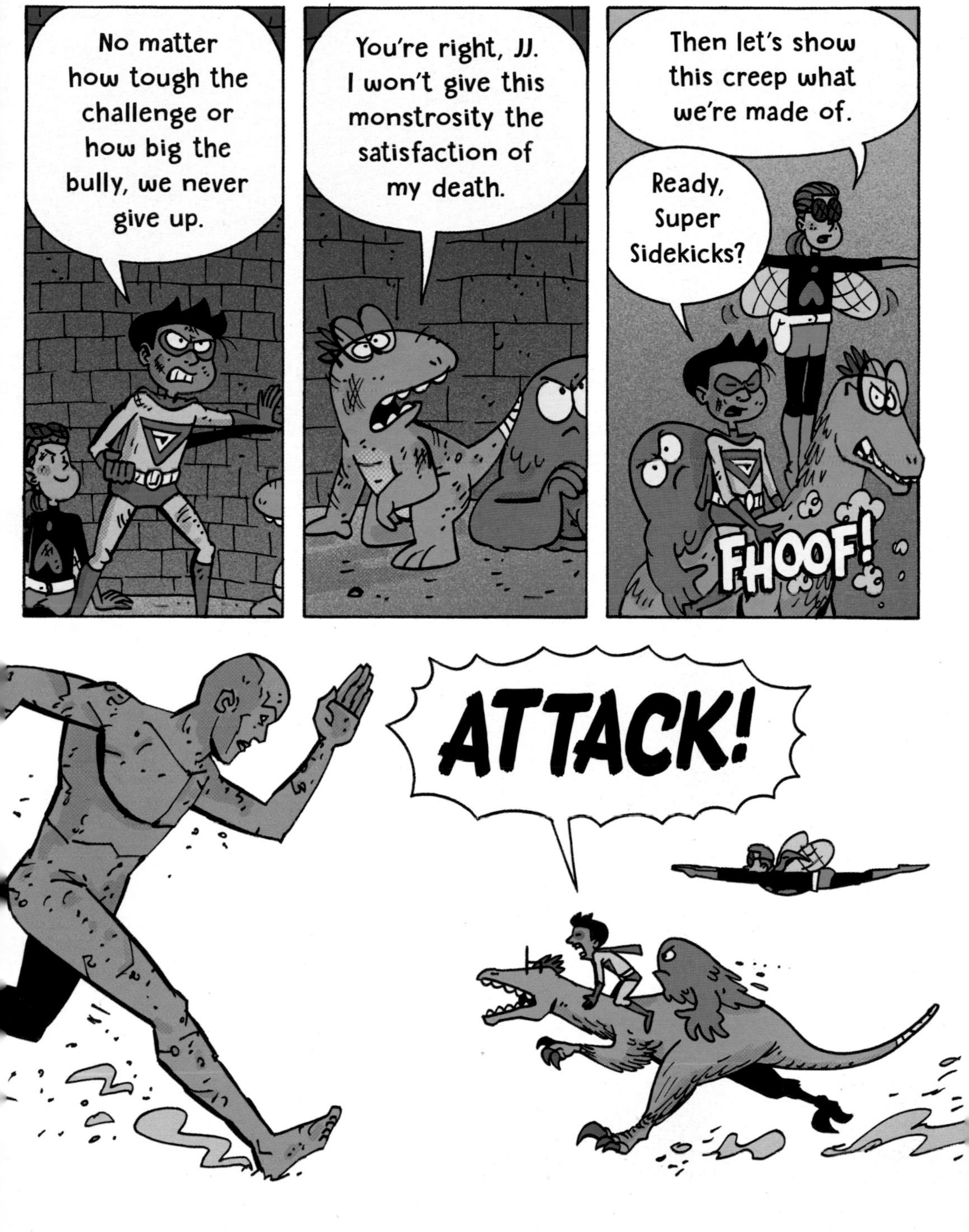
No matter how tough the challenge or how big the bully, we never give up.
You're right, JJ. I won't give this monstrosity the satisfaction of my death.
Then let's show this creep what we're made of.
Ready, Super Sidekicks?
FHOOF!
ATTACK!

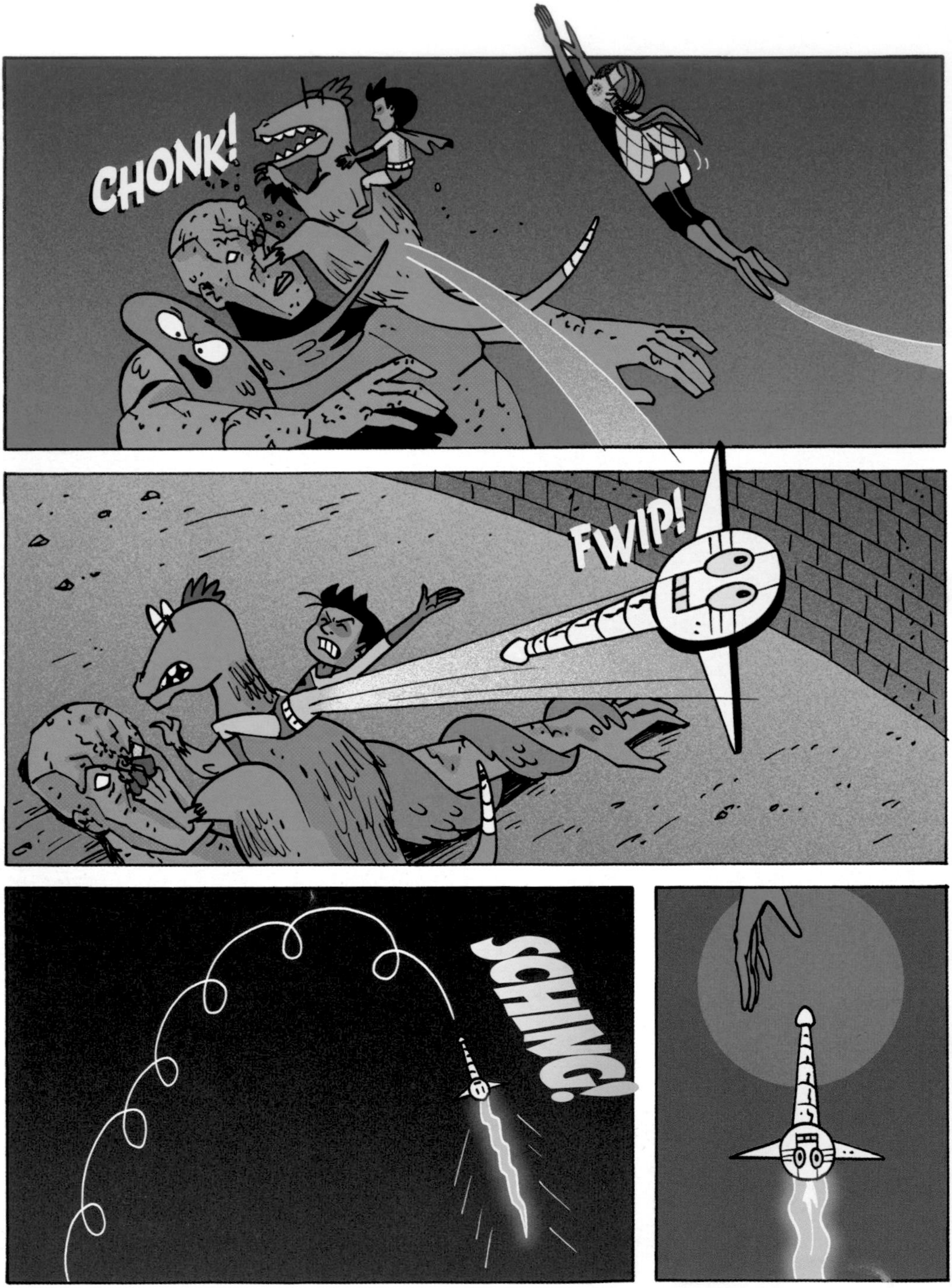
CHONK!
FWIP!
SCHING!

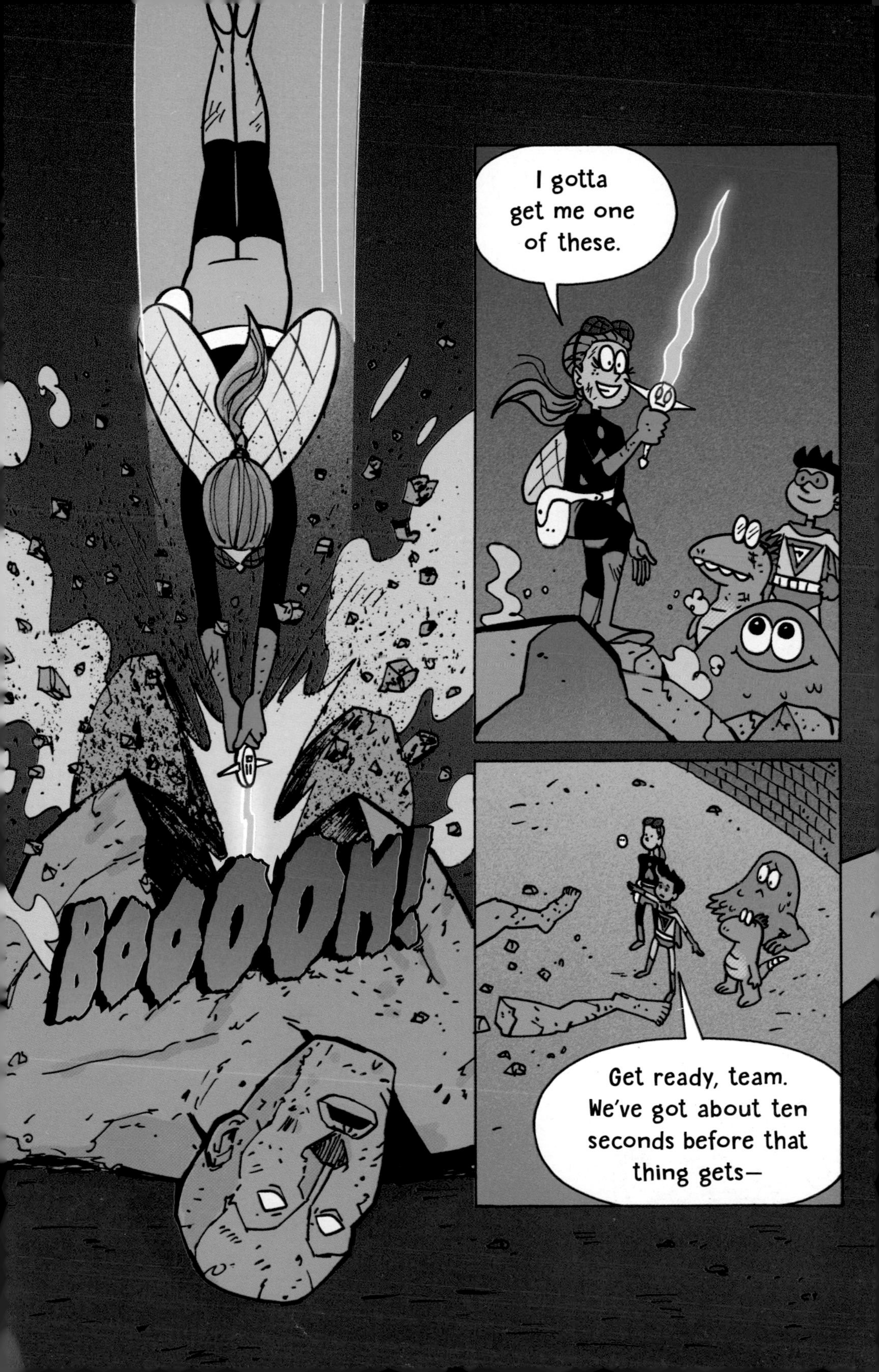
BOOOOM!
I gotta get me one of these.
Get ready, team. We've got about ten seconds before that thing gets—

BRAVO!

Stop doing that, Bakoo!

It . . . it's finally dead?

Yes! The man of stone takes thirty-three kills to be defeated.

Many more powerful and experienced heroes than you have faced him. But they gave up too easily. They lacked one thing which you four have just demonstrated: **PERSISTENCE!**

That is the second **Pillar of Heroism.** The will to not give up against overwhelming odds. The tenacity to get back up again and again, no matter the challenge. **That is what a true hero does.**

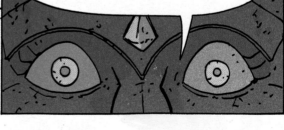

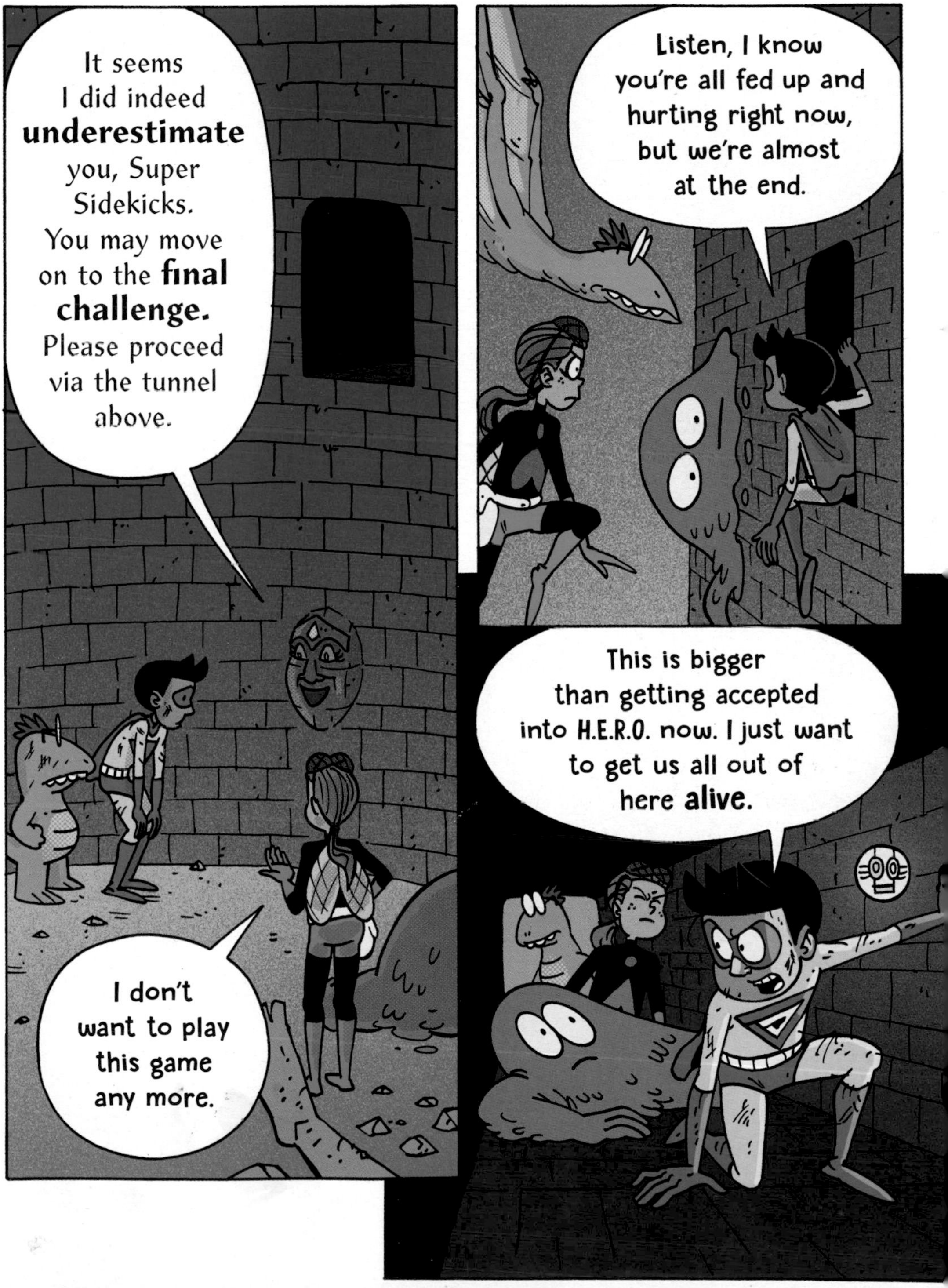
It seems I did indeed **underestimate** you, Super Sidekicks. You may move on to the **final challenge.** Please proceed via the tunnel above.
I don't want to play this game any more.
Listen, I know you're all fed up and hurting right now, but we're almost at the end.
This is bigger than getting accepted into H.E.R.O. now. I just want to get us all out of here **alive.**

Judging by the first two challenges, the last one is gonna be tough as heck.

Whatever it is, we'll face it together.

Up here . . . it's some kind of trapdoor. With another poem.

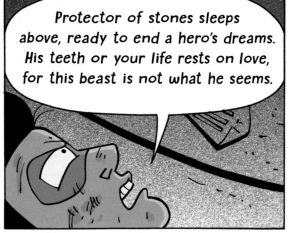

Protector of stones sleeps above, ready to end a hero's dreams. His teeth or your life rests on love, for this beast is not what he seems.

Love? That's one word I wasn't expecting.

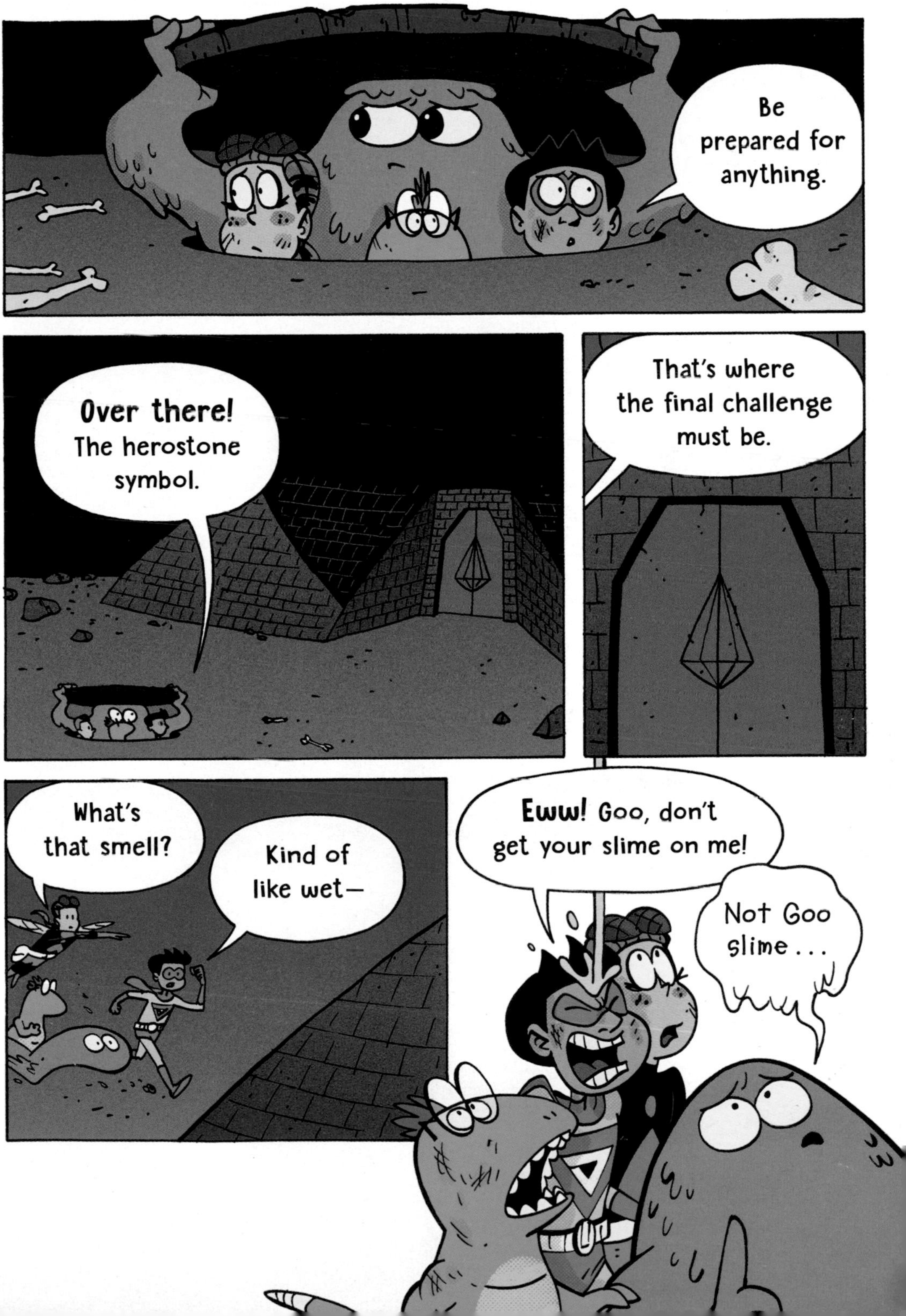
Be prepared for anything.
Over there! The herostone symbol.
That's where the final challenge must be.
What's that smell?
Kind of like wet—
Eww! Goo, don't get your slime on me!
Not Goo slime . . .

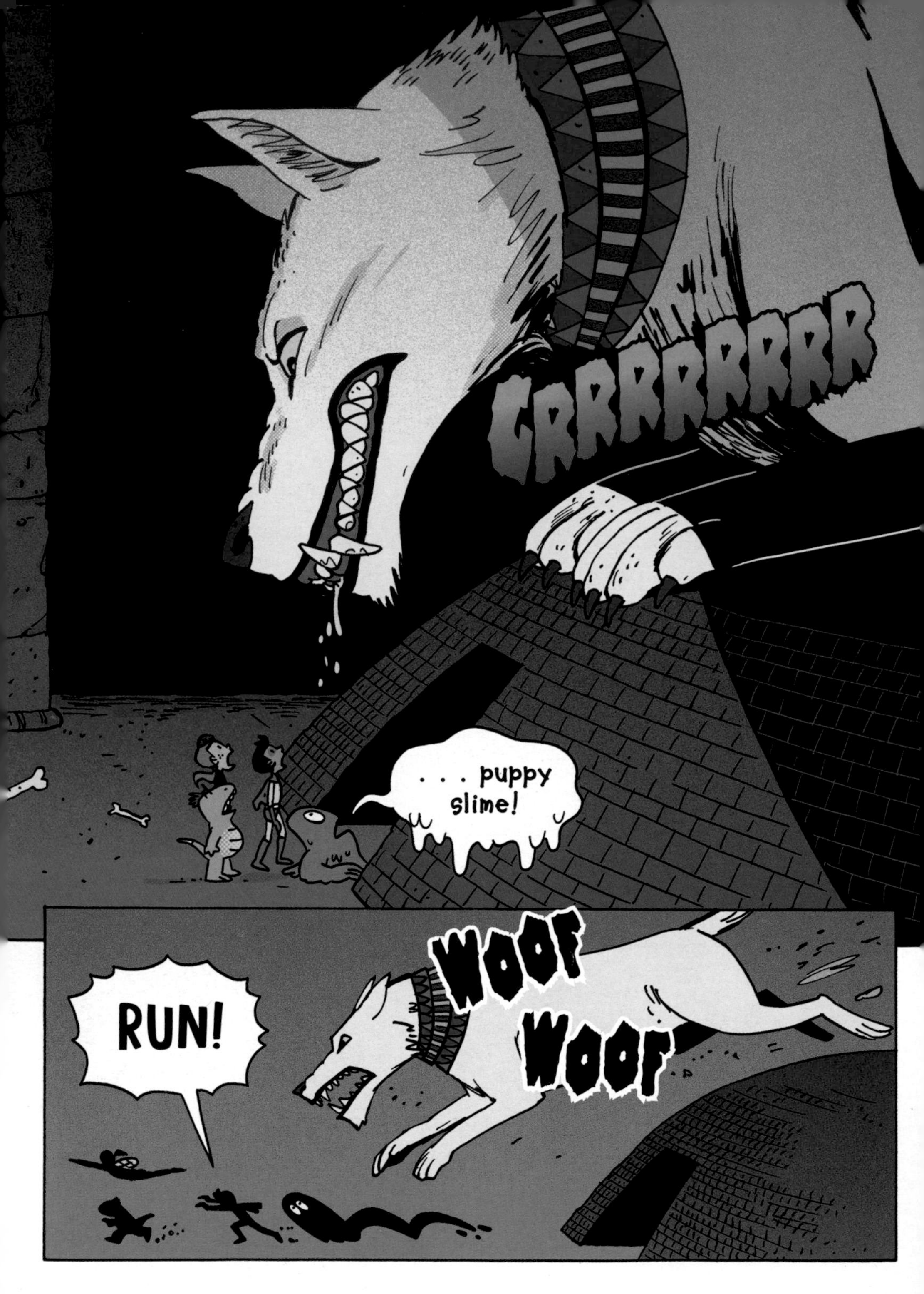
GRRRRRRRRR
. . . puppy slime!
RUN!
WOOF
WOOF

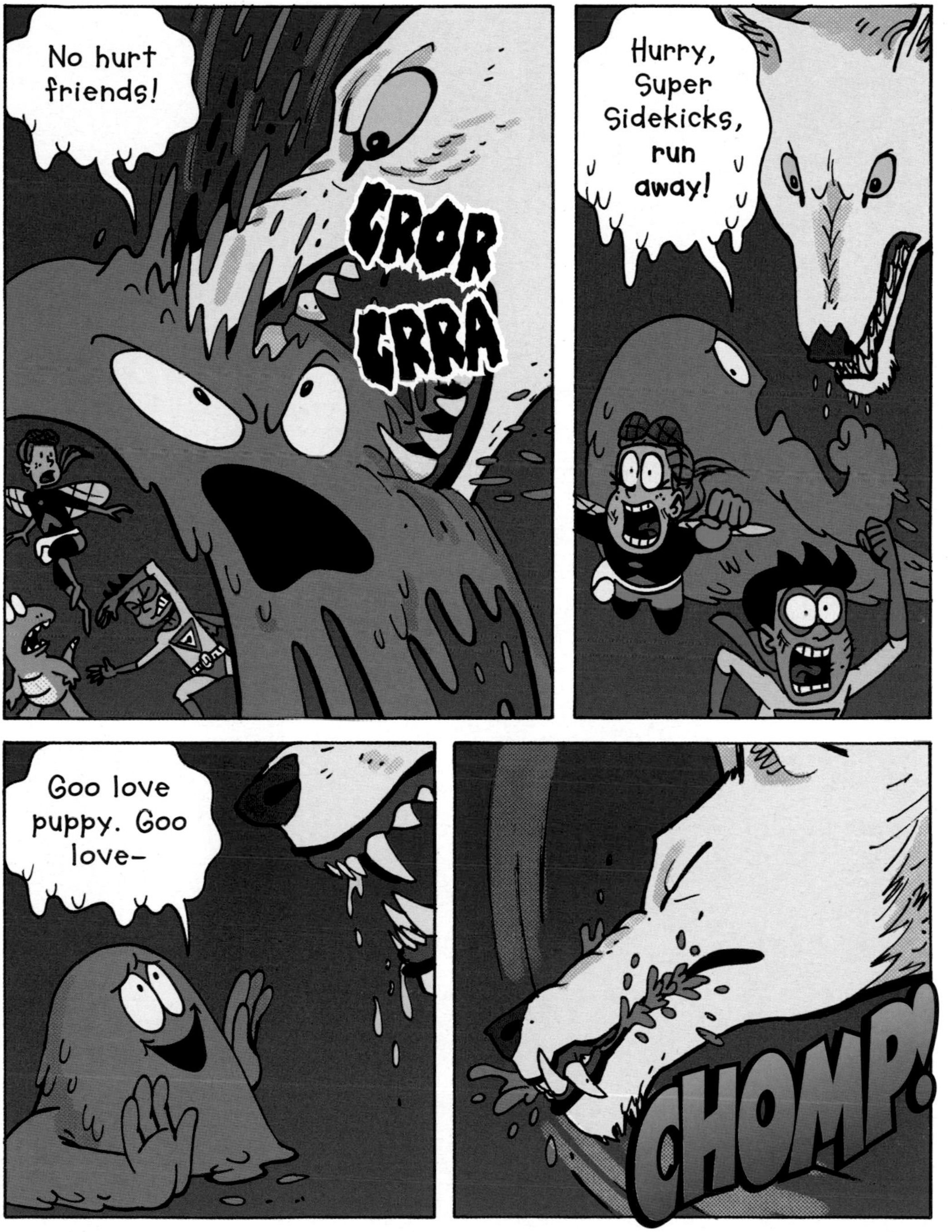
No hurt friends!
CROR CRRA
Hurry, Super Sidekicks, run away!
Goo love puppy. Goo love-
CHOMP!

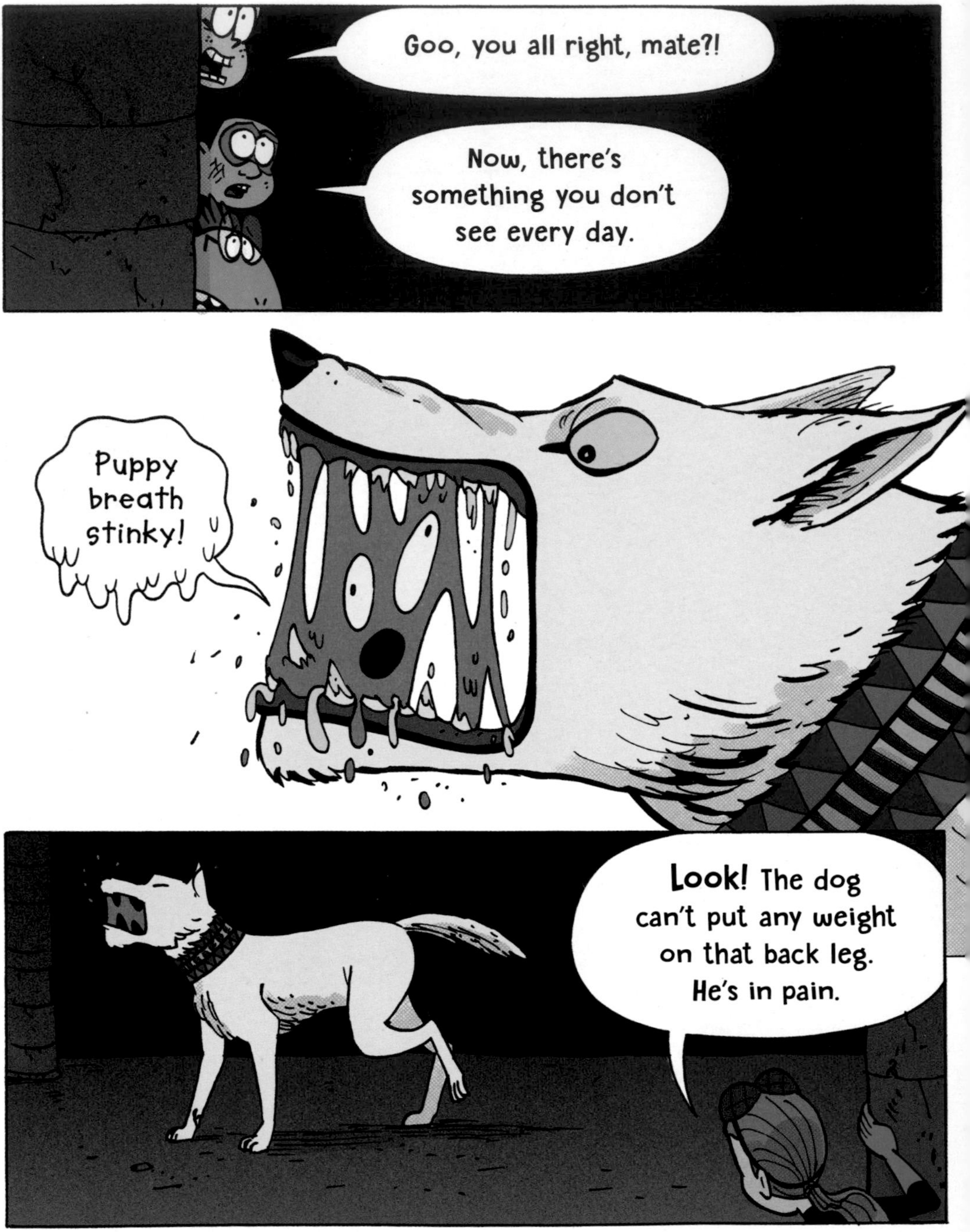
Goo, you all right, mate?!
Now, there's something you don't see every day.
Puppy breath stinky!
Look! The dog can't put any weight on that back leg. He's in pain.

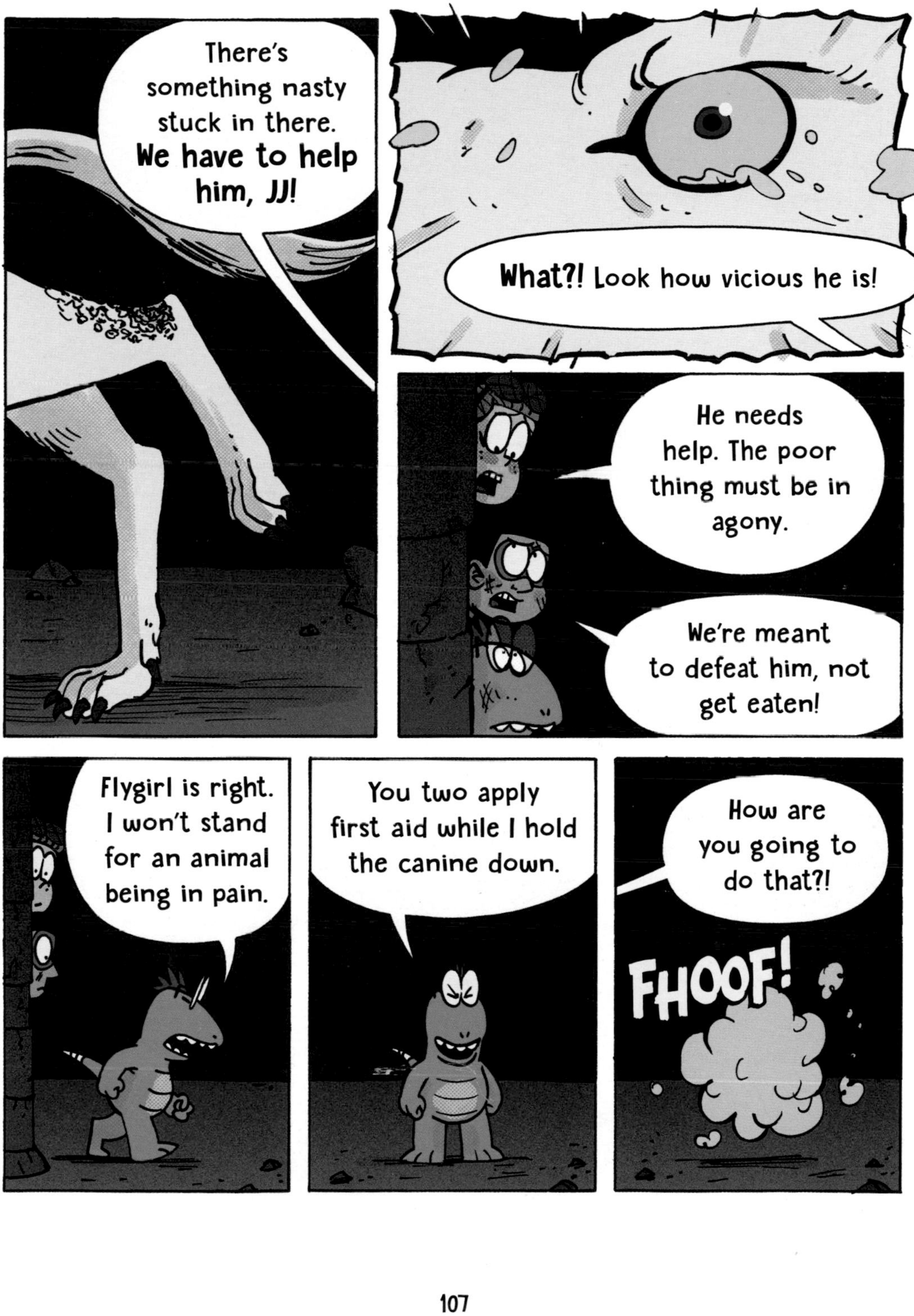
There's something nasty stuck in there. We have to help him, JJ!
What?! Look how vicious he is!
He needs help. The poor thing must be in agony.
We're meant to defeat him, not get eaten!
Flygirl is right. I won't stand for an animal being in pain.
You two apply first aid while I hold the canine down.
How are you going to do that?!
FHOOF!

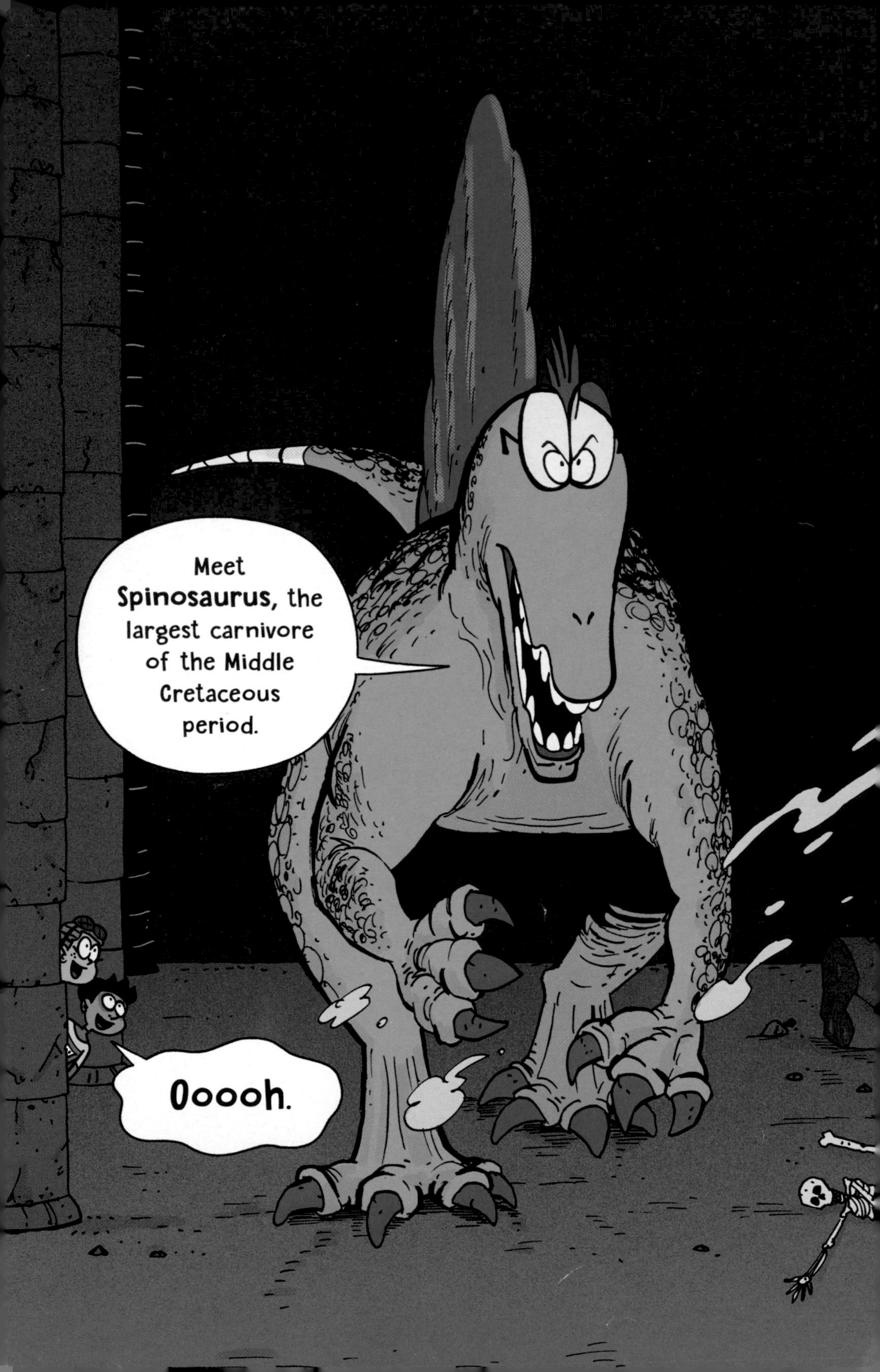
Meet Spinosaurus, the largest carnivore of the Middle Cretaceous period.
Ooooh.

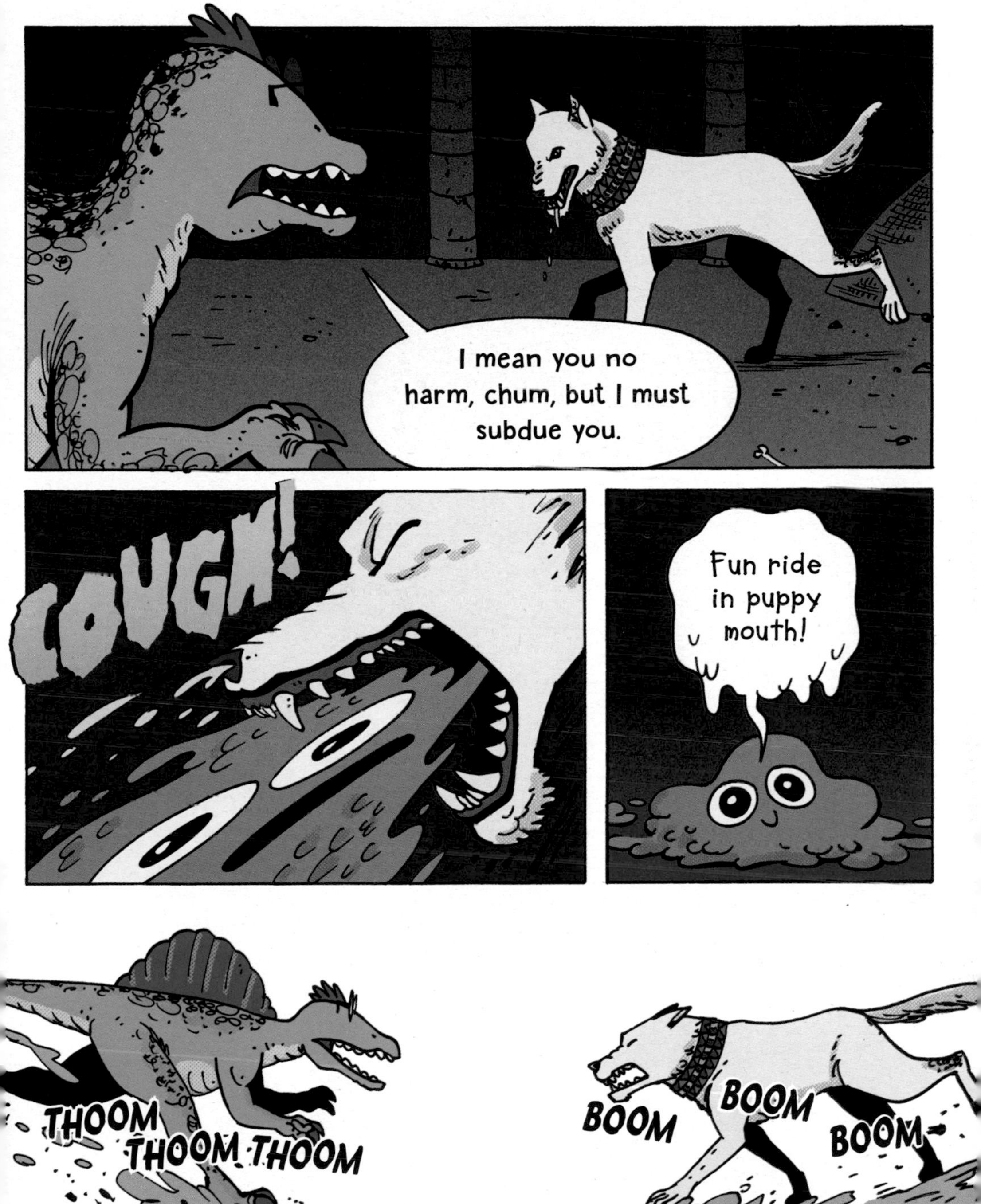
I mean you no harm, chum, but I must subdue you.
COUGH!
Fun ride in puppy mouth!
THOOM
THOOM THOOM
BOOM
BOOM
BOOM

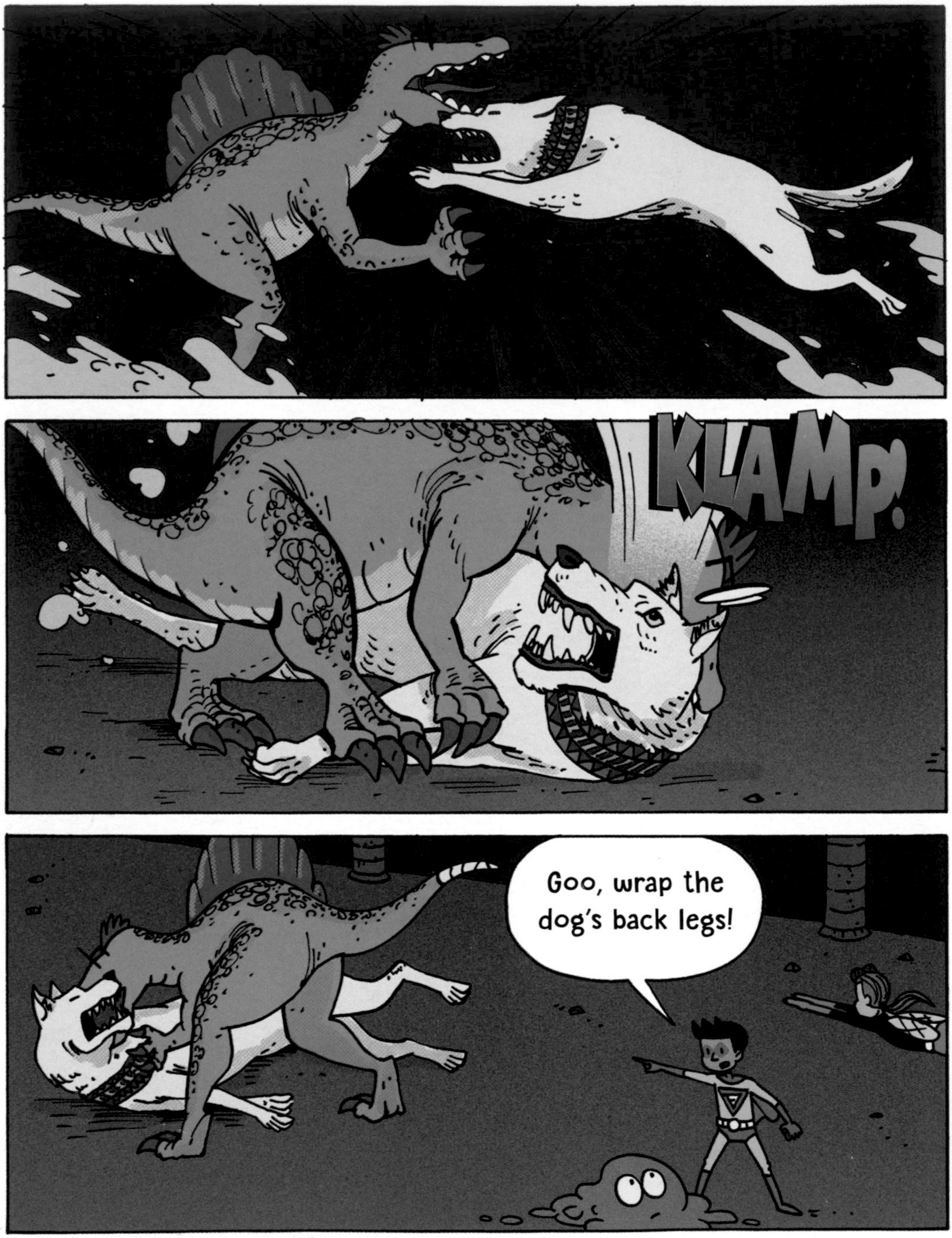
KLAMP!
Goo, wrap the dog's back legs!

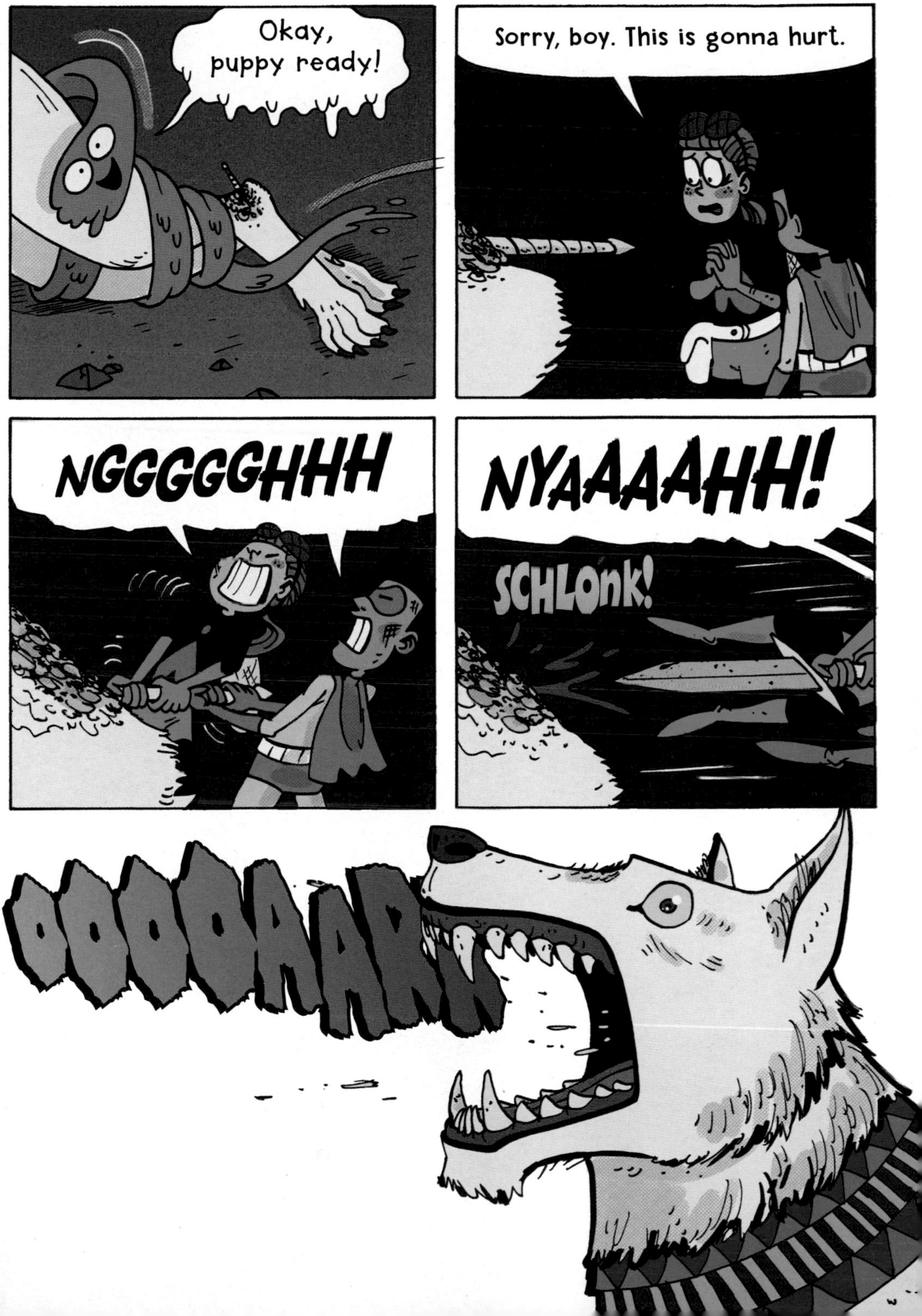
Okay, puppy ready!
Sorry, boy. This is gonna hurt.
NGGGGGHHH
NYAAAAHH!
SCHLONK!
OOOOAARR

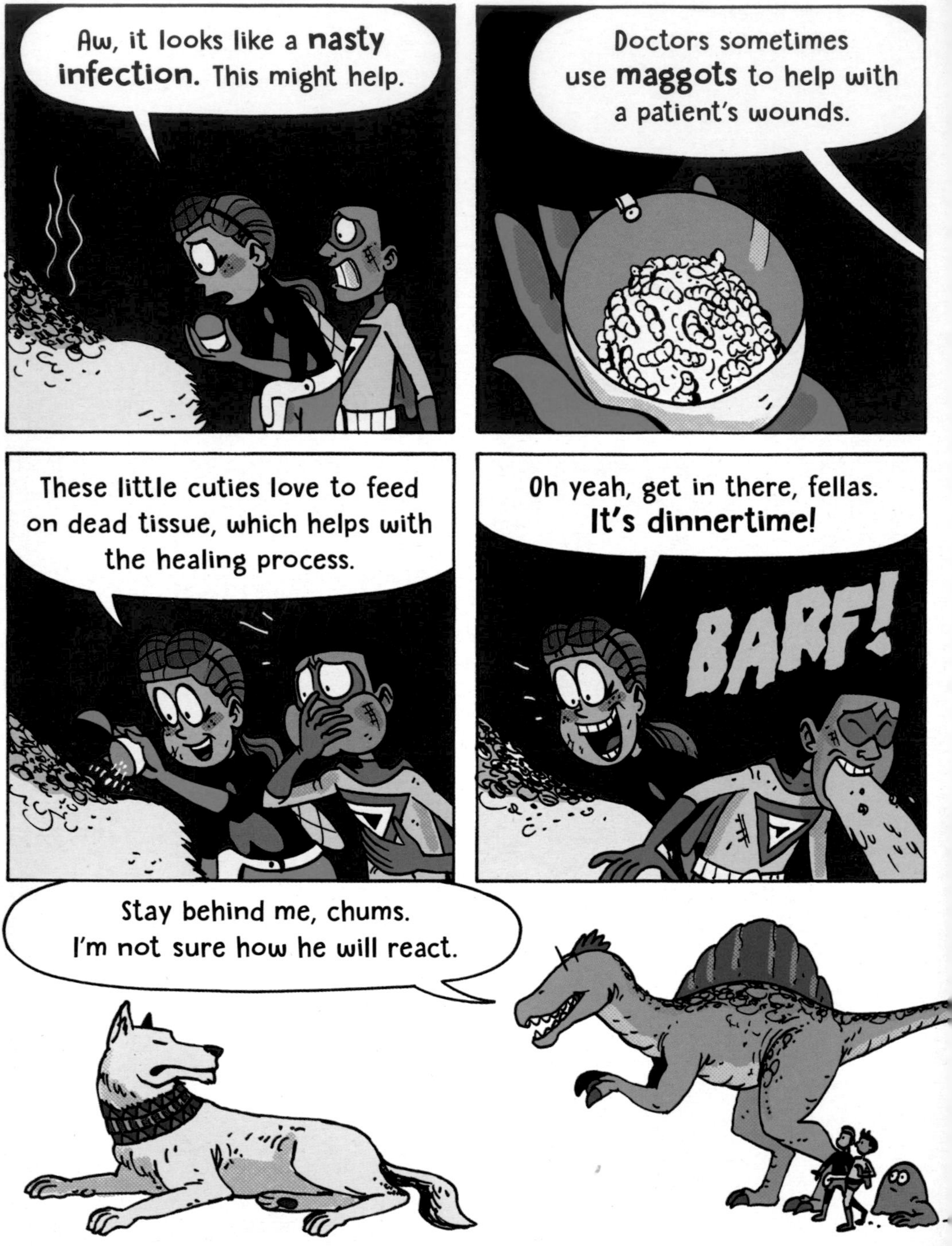

Aw, it looks like a **nasty infection.** This might help.
Doctors sometimes use **maggots** to help with a patient's wounds.
These little cuties love to feed on dead tissue, which helps with the healing process.
Oh yeah, get in there, fellas. **It's dinnertime!**
BARF!
Stay behind me, chums. I'm not sure how he will react.

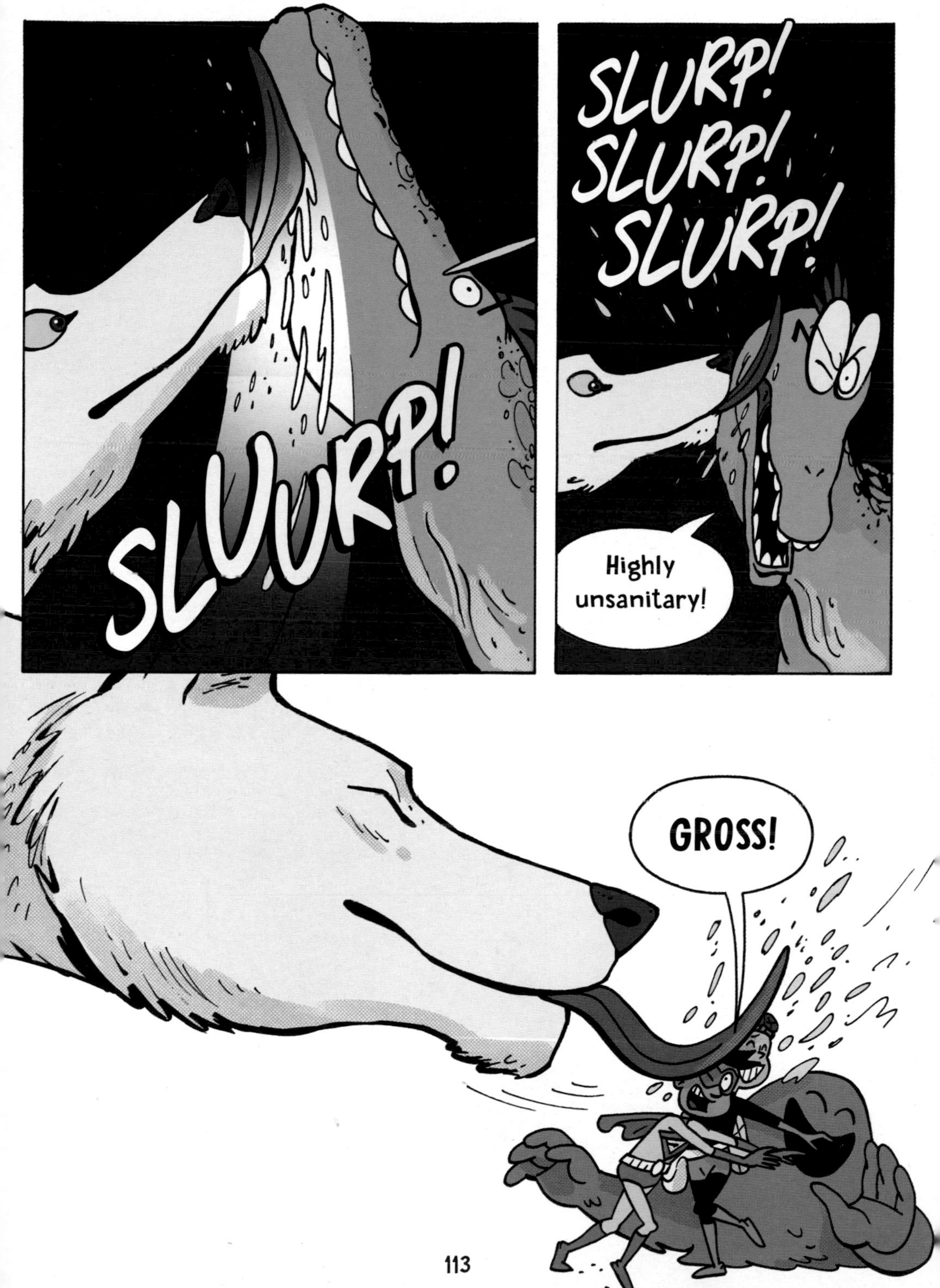
SLUURP!
SLURP! SLURP! SLURP!
Highly unsanitary!
GROSS!

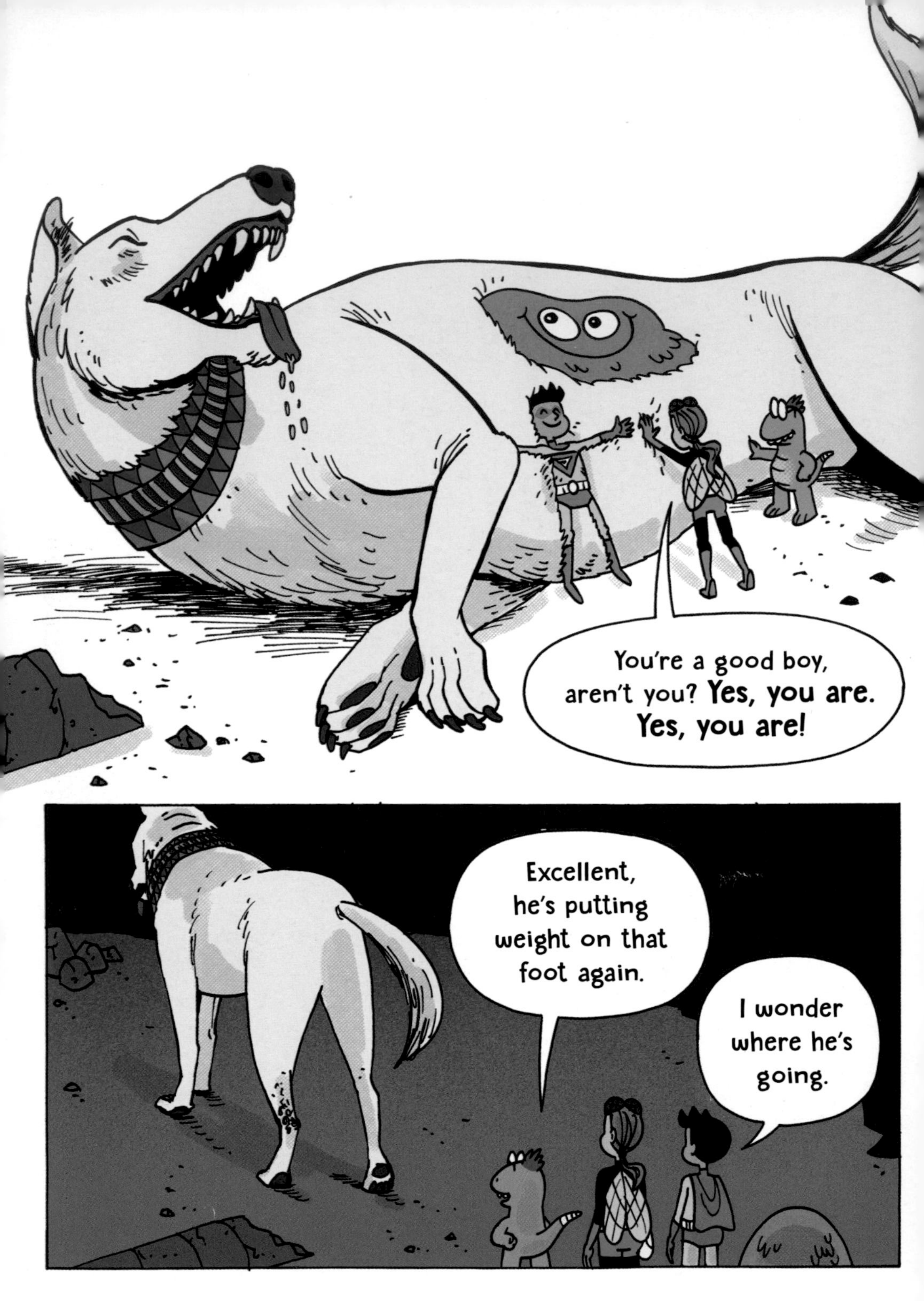
You're a good boy, aren't you? **Yes, you are. Yes, you are!**
Excellent, he's putting weight on that foot again.
I wonder where he's going.

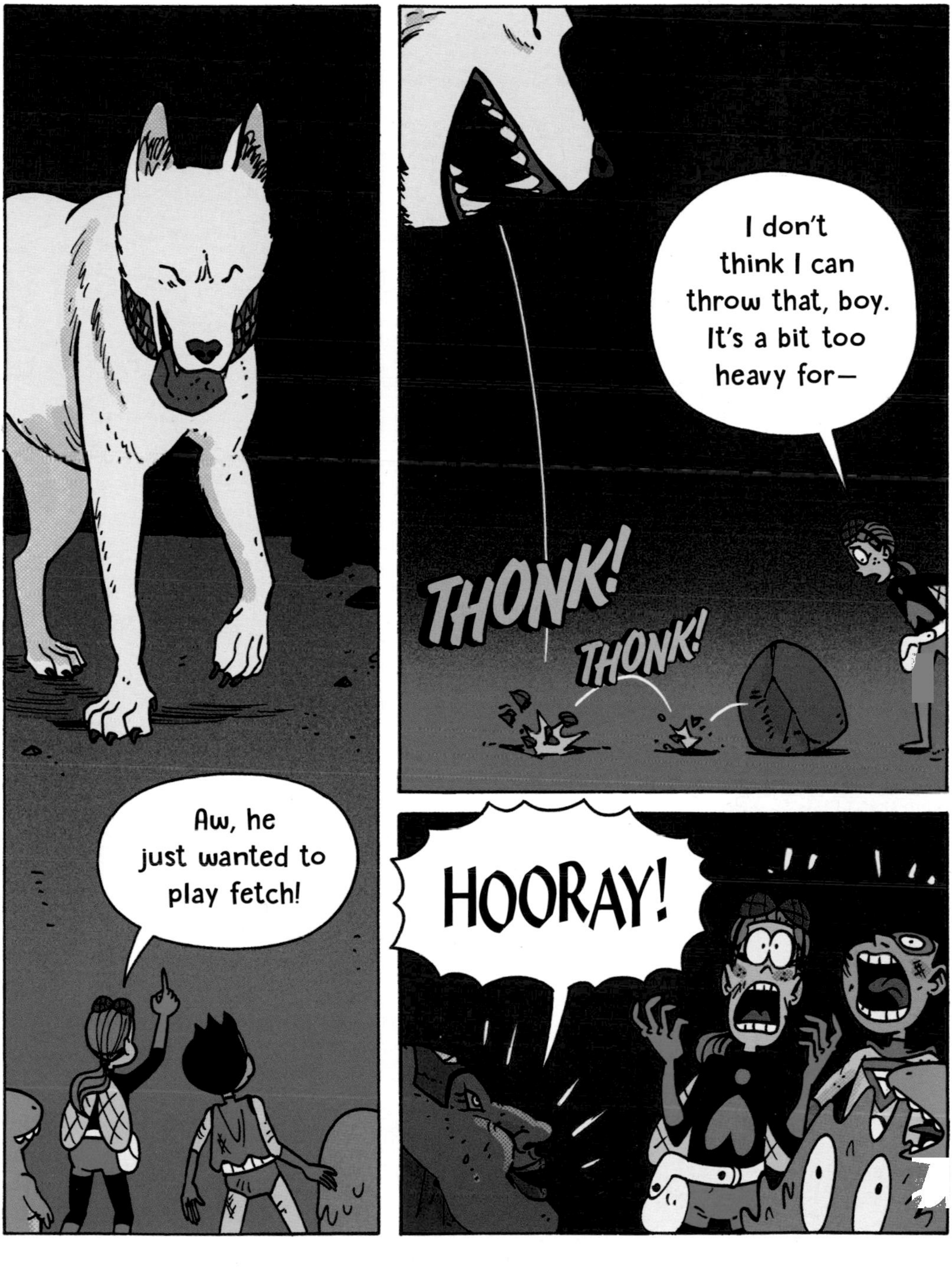
I don't think I can throw that, boy. It's a bit too heavy for—
THONK!
THONK!
Aw, he just wanted to play fetch!
HOORAY!

I can't thank you enough, Super Sidekicks. That silly sword has been stuck in Goliath's paw for more than **one hundred years!**

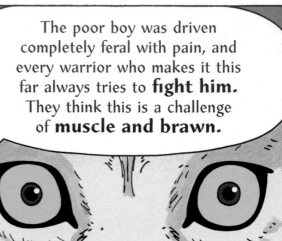

The poor boy was driven completely feral with pain, and every warrior who makes it this far always tries to **fight him.** They think this is a challenge of **muscle and brawn.**

No, this is a challenge of **compassion and empathy!** A true hero would have seen the pain he was in and helped. Just like you did.

Kindness in a hero is just as important as strength.

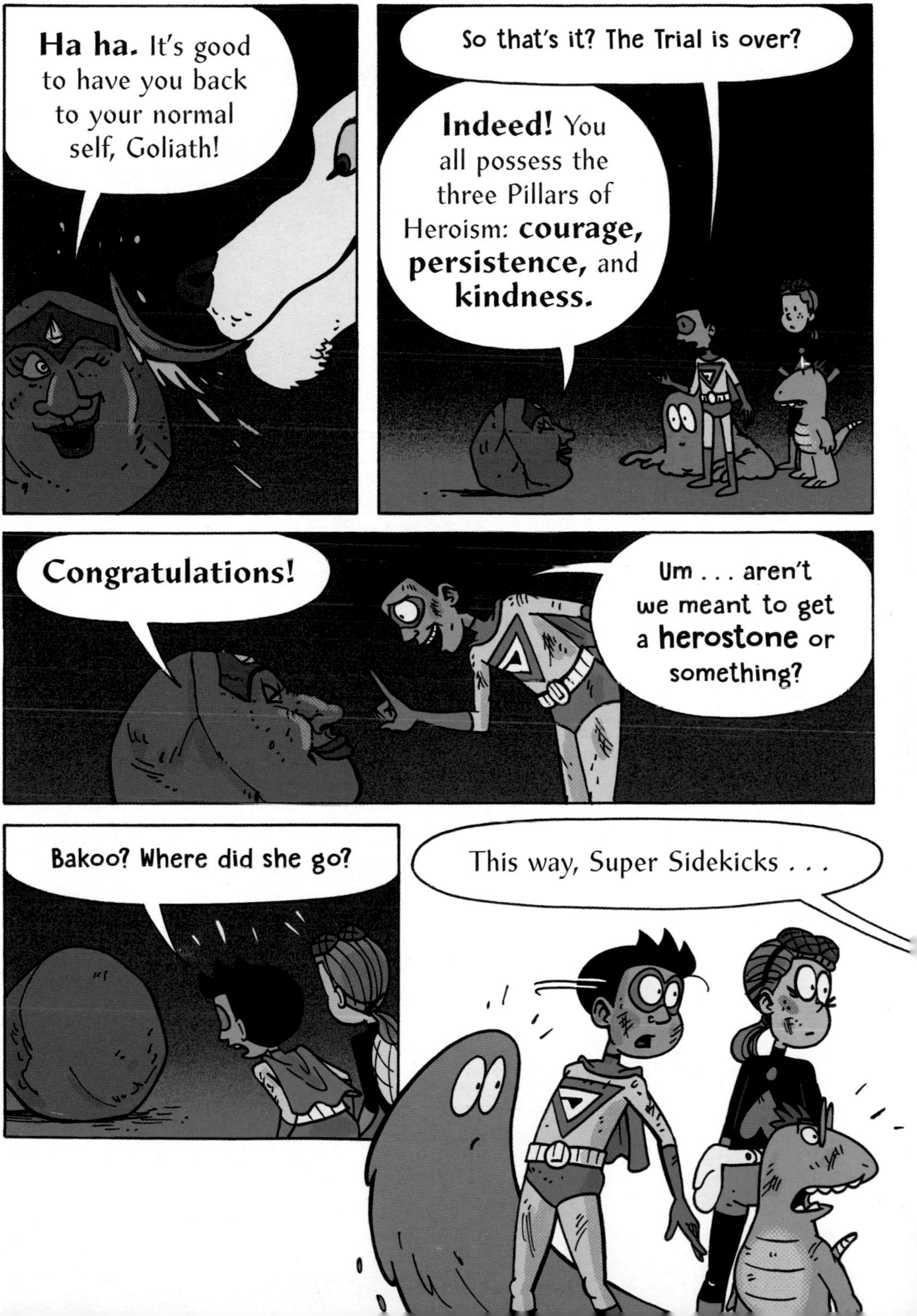
Ha ha. It's good to have you back to your normal self, Goliath!
So that's it? The Trial is over?
Indeed! You all possess the three Pillars of Heroism: courage, persistence, and kindness.
Congratulations!
Um . . . aren't we meant to get a herostone or something?
Bakoo? Where did she go?
This way, Super Sidekicks . . .

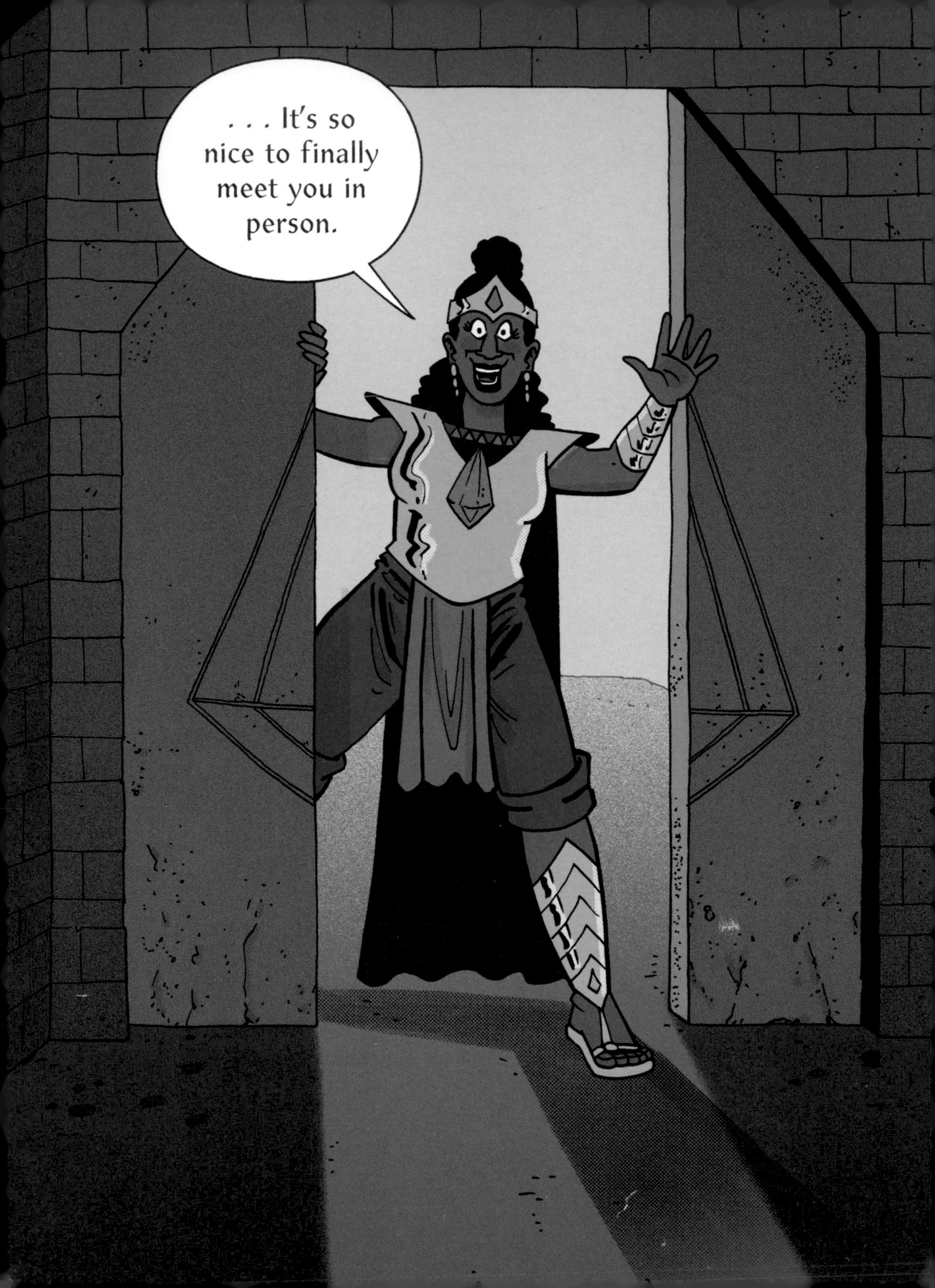
. . . It's so nice to finally meet you in person.

Chapter

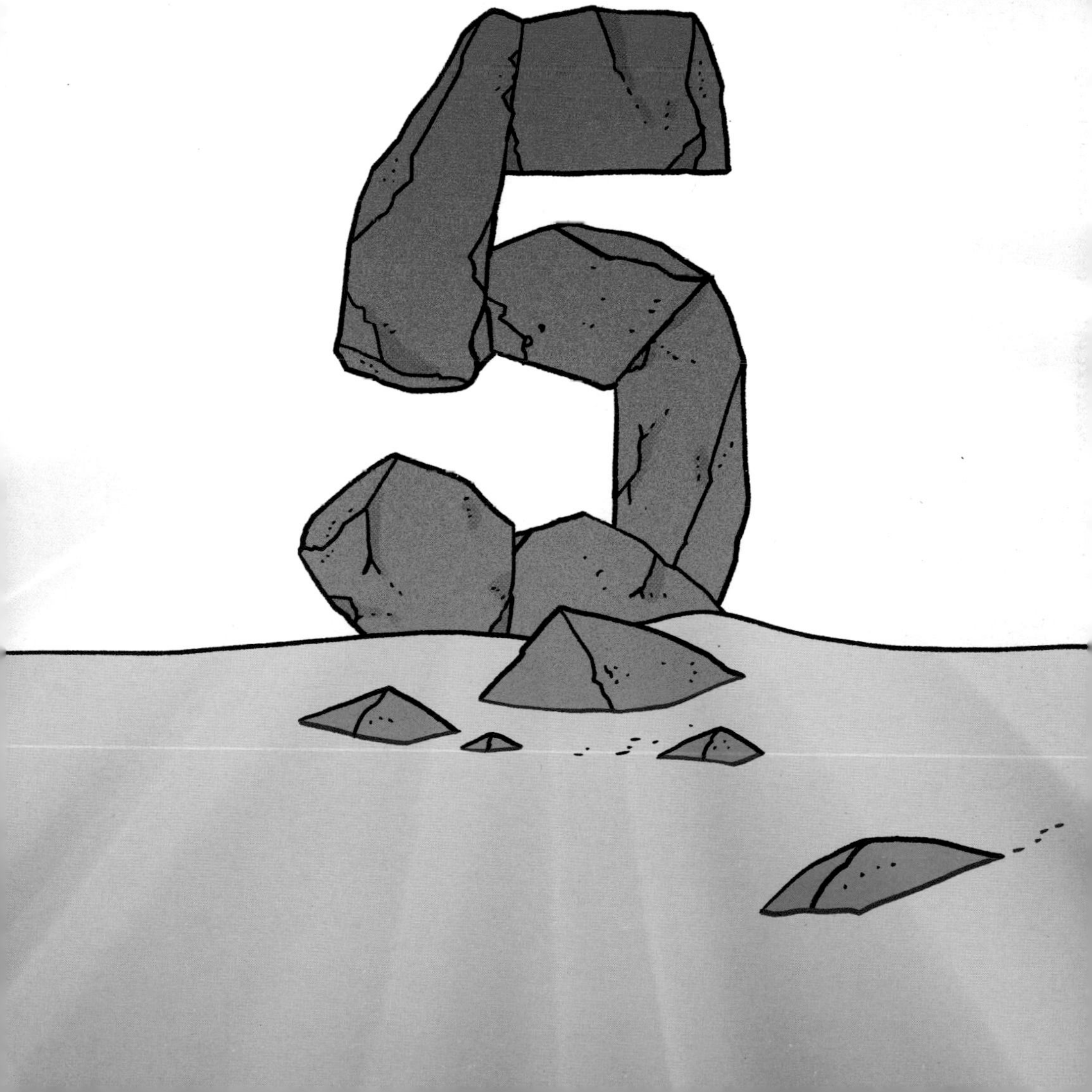
5

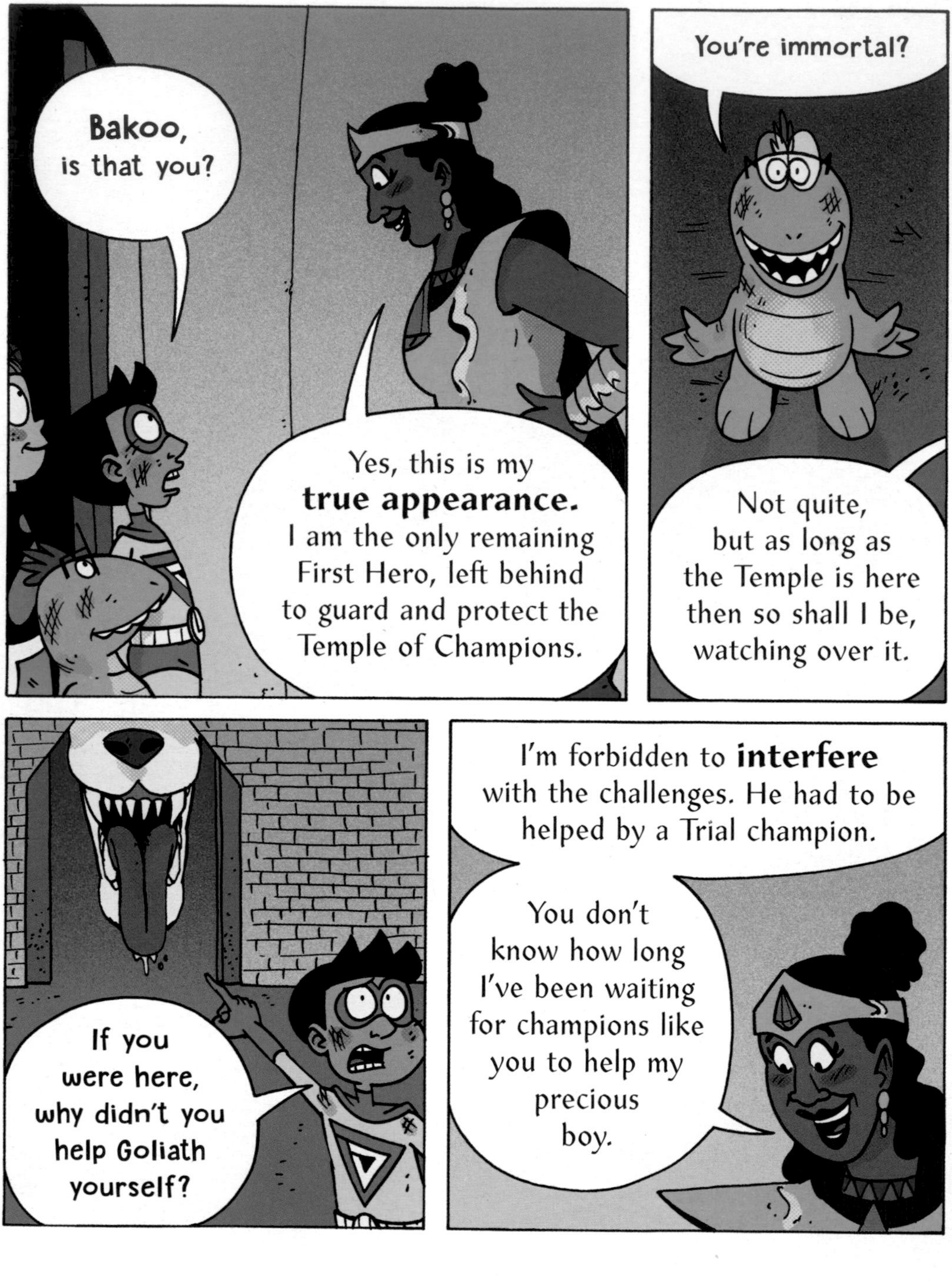
Bakoo, is that you?
Yes, this is my **true appearance.** I am the only remaining First Hero, left behind to guard and protect the Temple of Champions.
You're immortal?
Not quite, but as long as the Temple is here then so shall I be, watching over it.
If you were here, why didn't you help Goliath yourself?
I'm forbidden to **interfere** with the challenges. He had to be helped by a Trial champion.
You don't know how long I've been waiting for champions like you to help my precious boy.

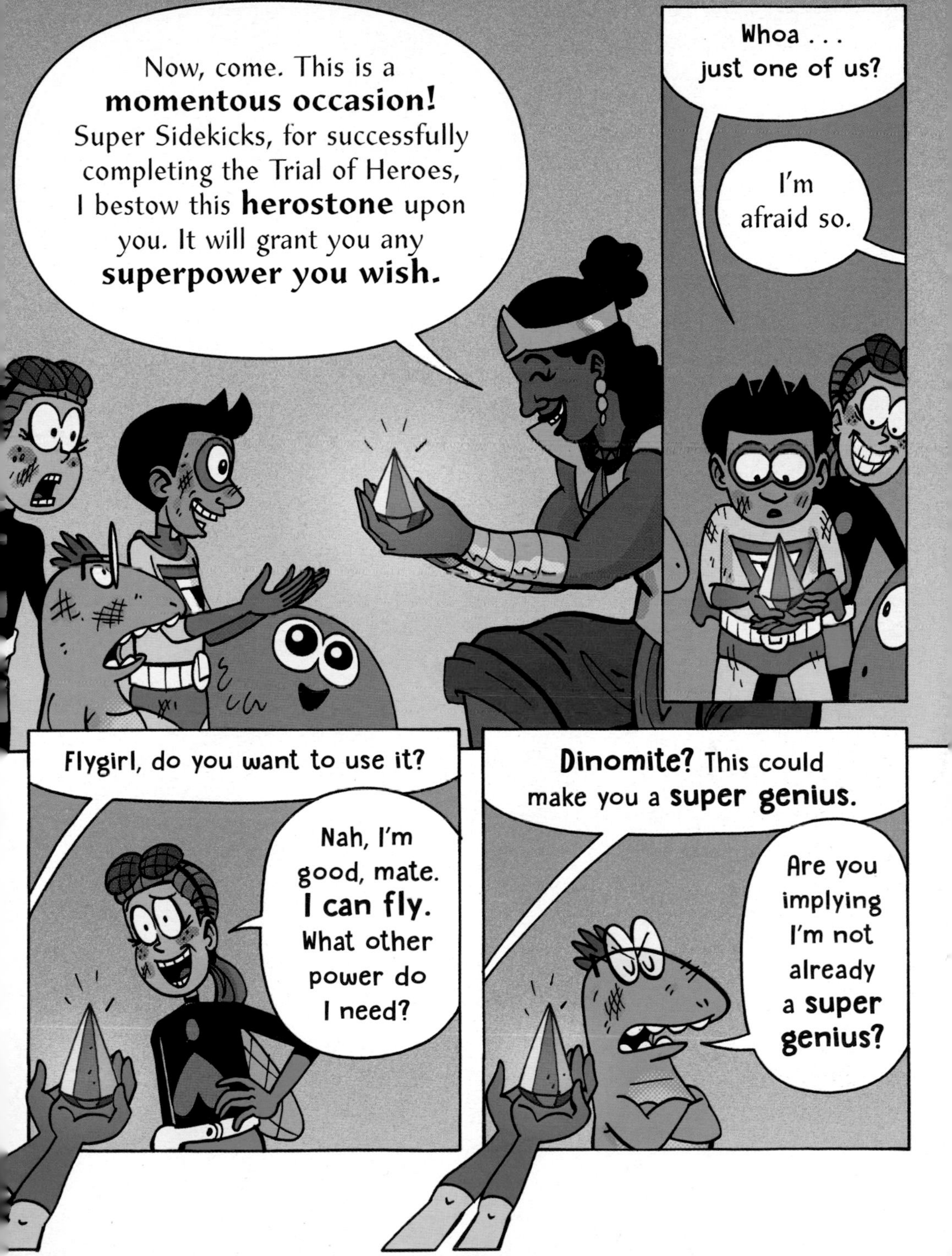
Now, come. This is a **momentous occasion!** Super Sidekicks, for successfully completing the Trial of Heroes, I bestow this **herostone** upon you. It will grant you any **superpower you wish.**
Whoa . . . just one of us?
I'm afraid so.
Flygirl, do you want to use it?
Nah, I'm good, mate. **I can fly.** What other power do I need?
Dinomite? This could make you a **super genius.**
Are you implying I'm not already a **super genius?**

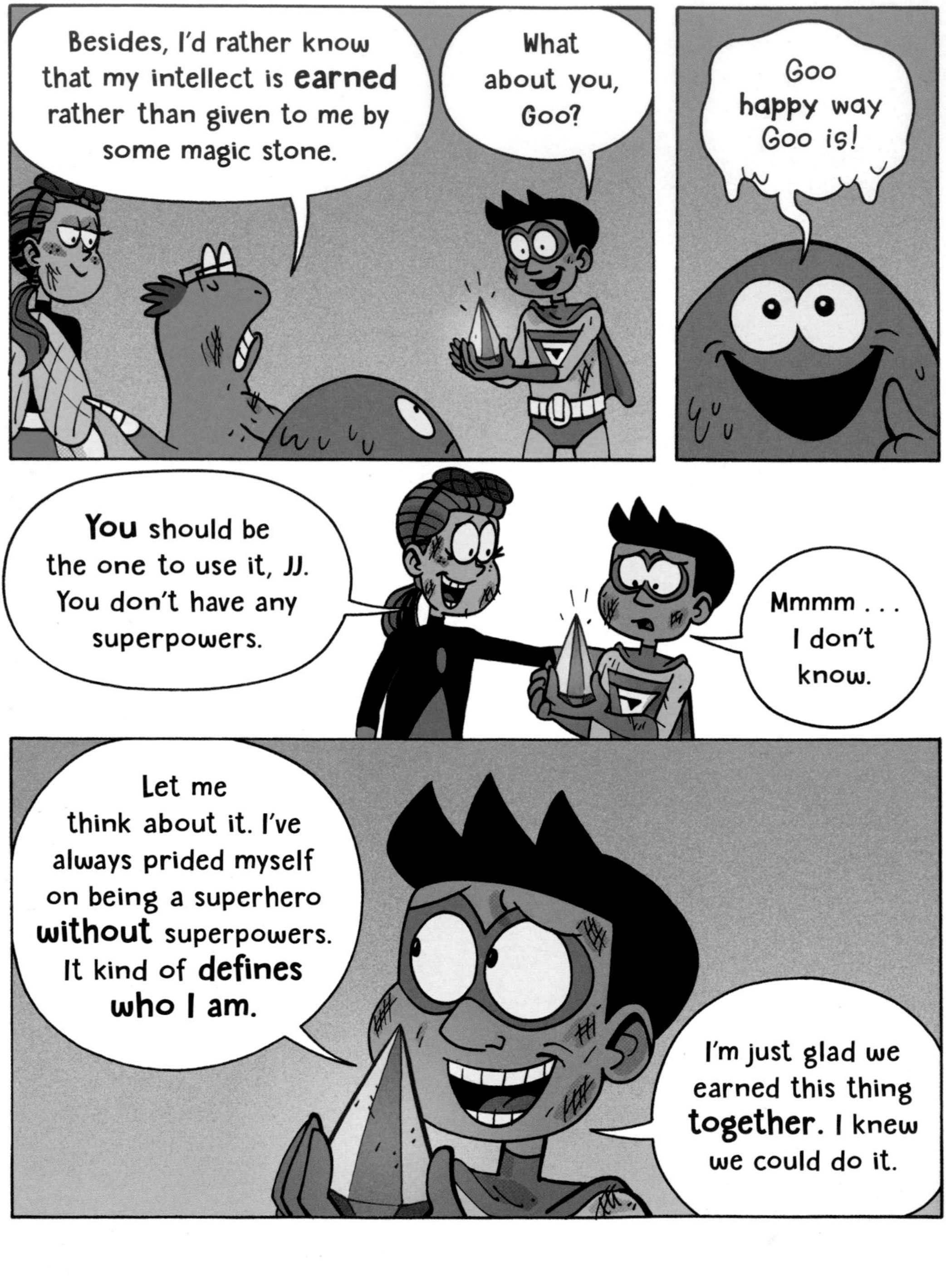
Besides, I'd rather know that my intellect is earned rather than given to me by some magic stone.
What about you, Goo?
Goo happy way Goo is!
You should be the one to use it, JJ. You don't have any superpowers.
Mmmm . . . I don't know.
Let me think about it. I've always prided myself on being a superhero without superpowers. It kind of defines who I am.
I'm just glad we earned this thing together. I knew we could do it.

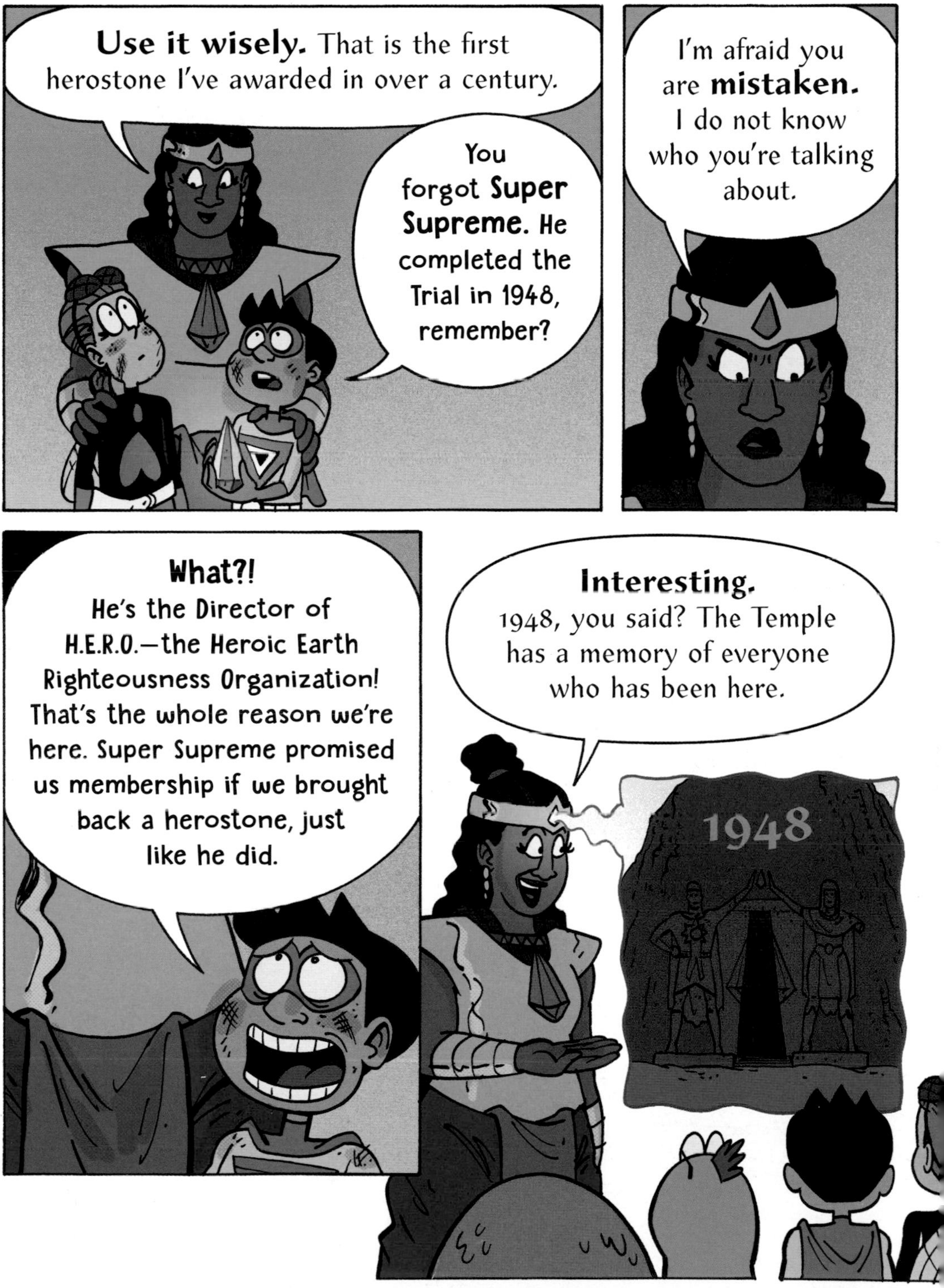
Use it wisely. That is the first herostone I've awarded in over a century.
You forgot Super Supreme. He completed the Trial in 1948, remember?
I'm afraid you are mistaken. I do not know who you're talking about.
What?! He's the Director of H.E.R.O.—the Heroic Earth Righteousness Organization! That's the whole reason we're here. Super Supreme promised us membership if we brought back a herostone, just like he did.
Interesting. 1948, you said? The Temple has a memory of everyone who has been here.
1948

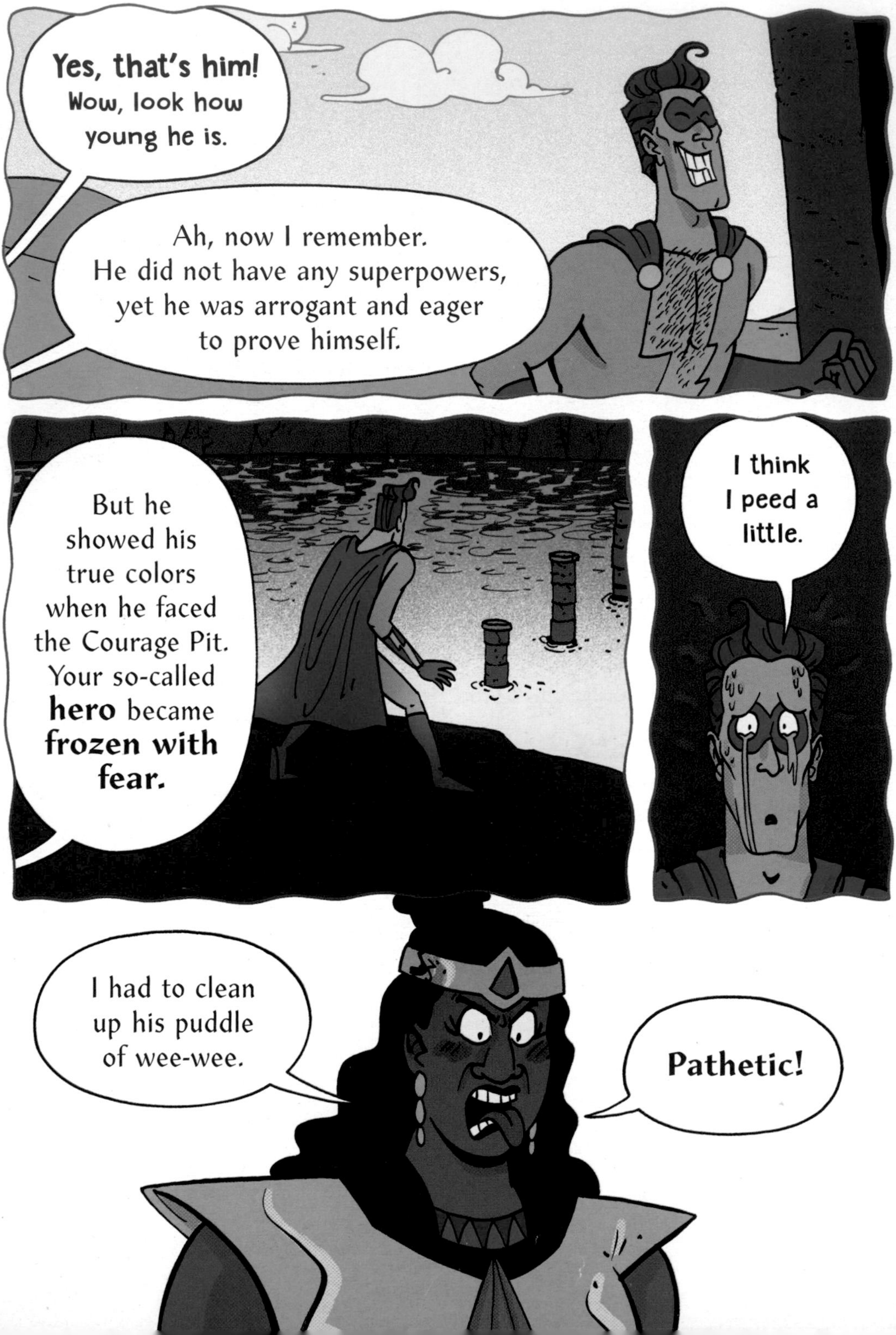
Yes, that's him! Wow, look how young he is.
Ah, now I remember. He did not have any superpowers, yet he was arrogant and eager to prove himself.
But he showed his true colors when he faced the Courage Pit. Your so-called **hero** became **frozen with fear.**
I think I peed a little.
I had to clean up his puddle of wee-wee.
Pathetic!

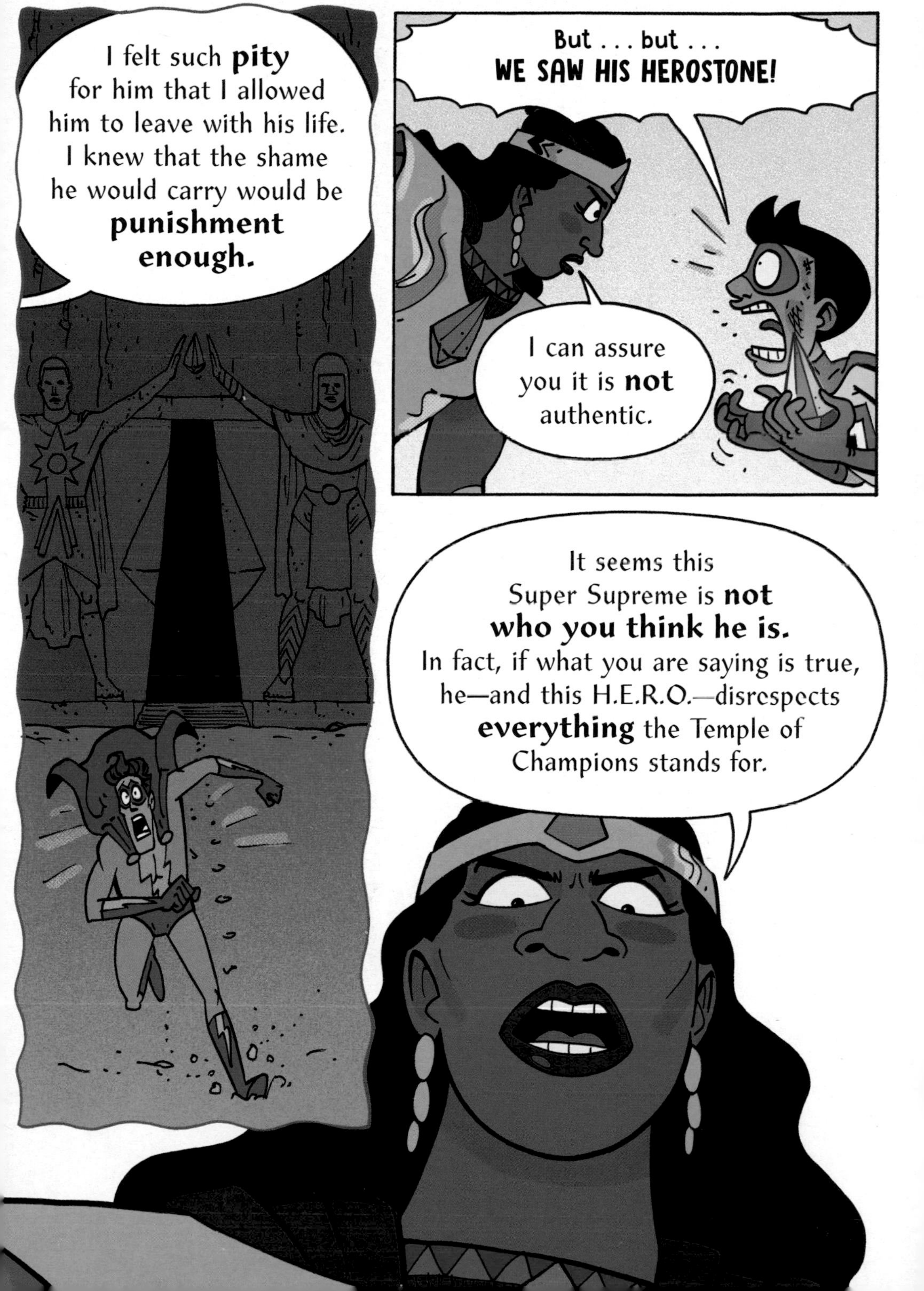
I felt such **pity** for him that I allowed him to leave with his life. I knew that the shame he would carry would be **punishment enough.**
But . . . but . . . **WE SAW HIS HEROSTONE!**
I can assure you it is **not** authentic.
It seems this Super Supreme is **not who you think he is.** In fact, if what you are saying is true, he—and this H.E.R.O.—disrespects **everything** the Temple of Champions stands for.

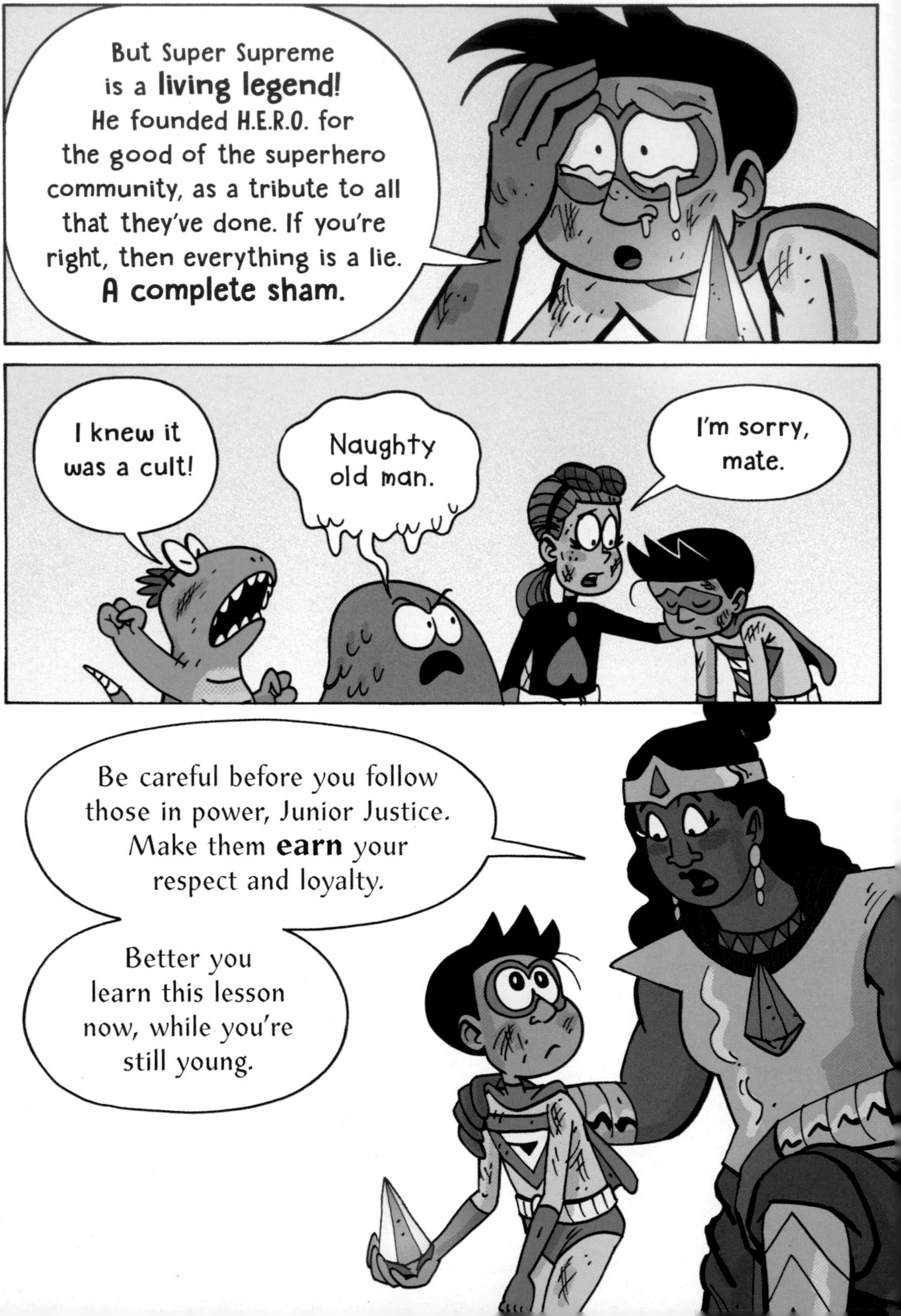
But Super Supreme is a **living legend!** He founded H.E.R.O. for the good of the superhero community, as a tribute to all that they've done. If you're right, then everything is a lie. **A complete sham.**
I knew it was a cult!
Naughty old man.
I'm sorry, mate.
Be careful before you follow those in power, Junior Justice. Make them **earn** your respect and loyalty.
Better you learn this lesson now, while you're still young.

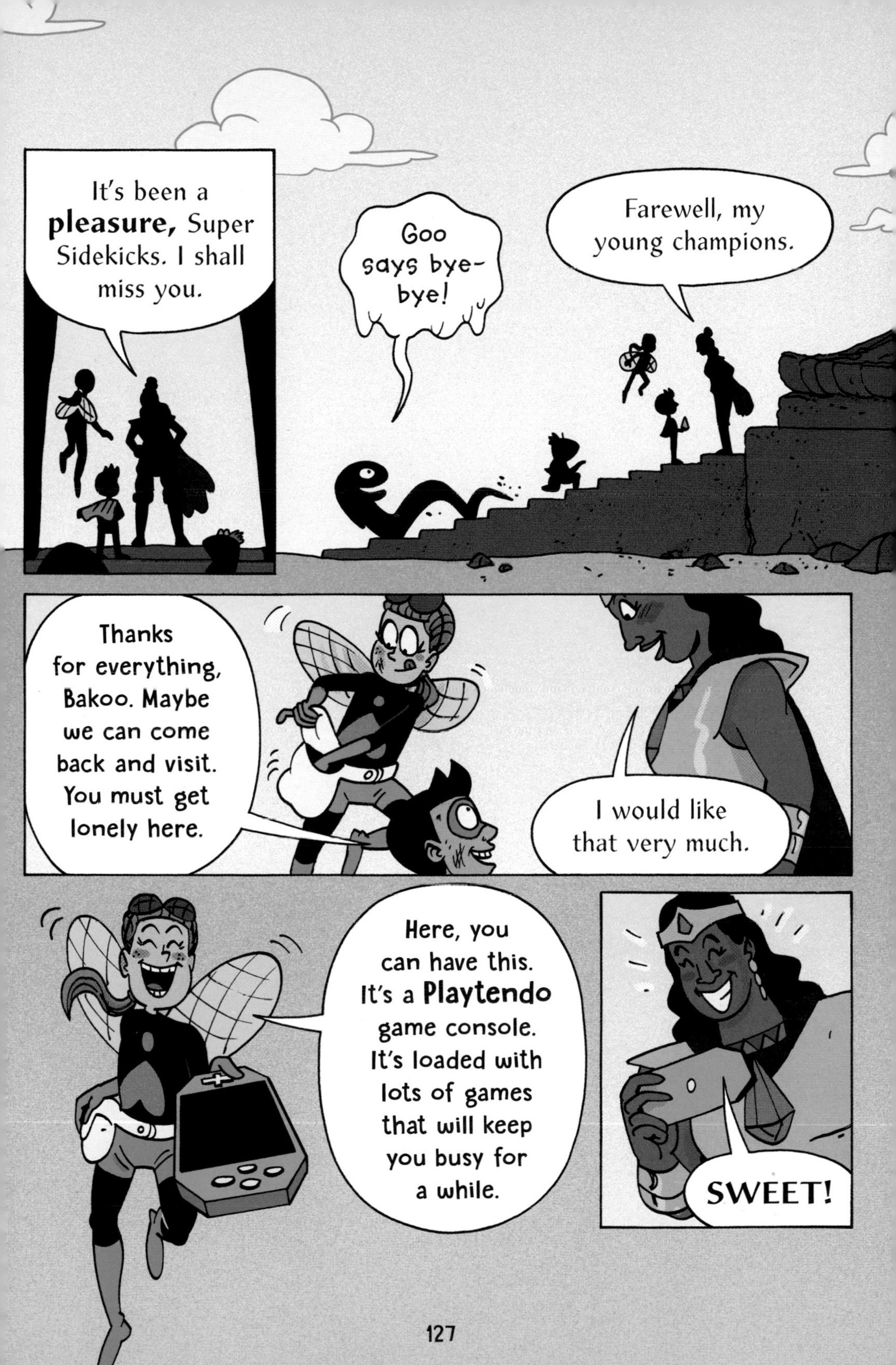

It's been a **pleasure,** Super Sidekicks. I shall miss you.
Goo says bye-bye!
Farewell, my young champions.
Thanks for everything, Bakoo. Maybe we can come back and visit. You must get lonely here.
I would like that very much.
Here, you can have this. It's a **Playtendo** game console. It's loaded with lots of games that will keep you busy for a while.
SWEET!

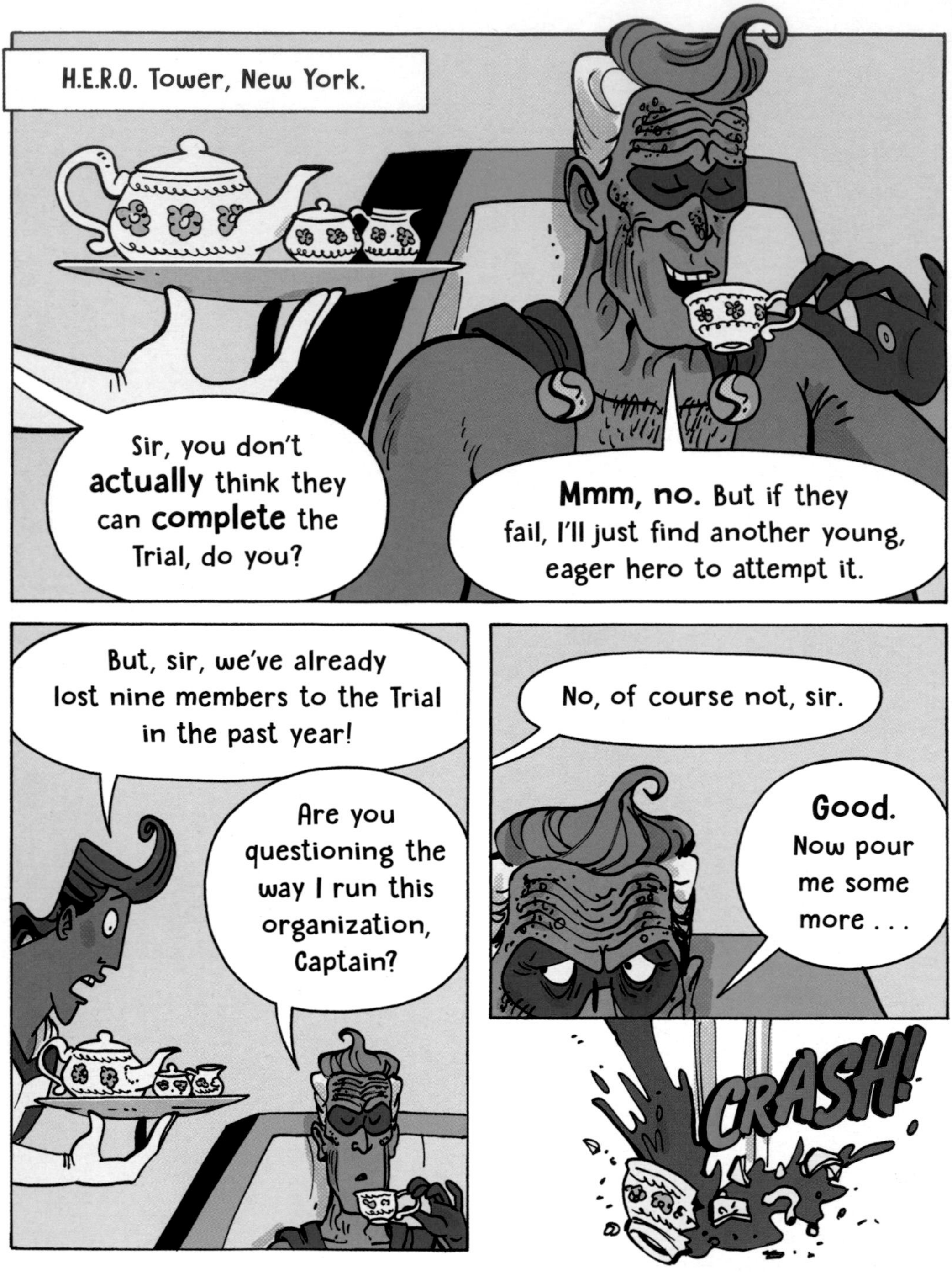
H.E.R.O. Tower, New York.
Sir, you don't **actually** think they can **complete** the Trial, do you?
Mmm, no. But if they fail, I'll just find another young, eager hero to attempt it.
But, sir, we've already lost nine members to the Trial in the past year!
Are you questioning the way I run this organization, Captain?
No, of course not, sir.
Good. Now pour me some more . . .
CRASH!

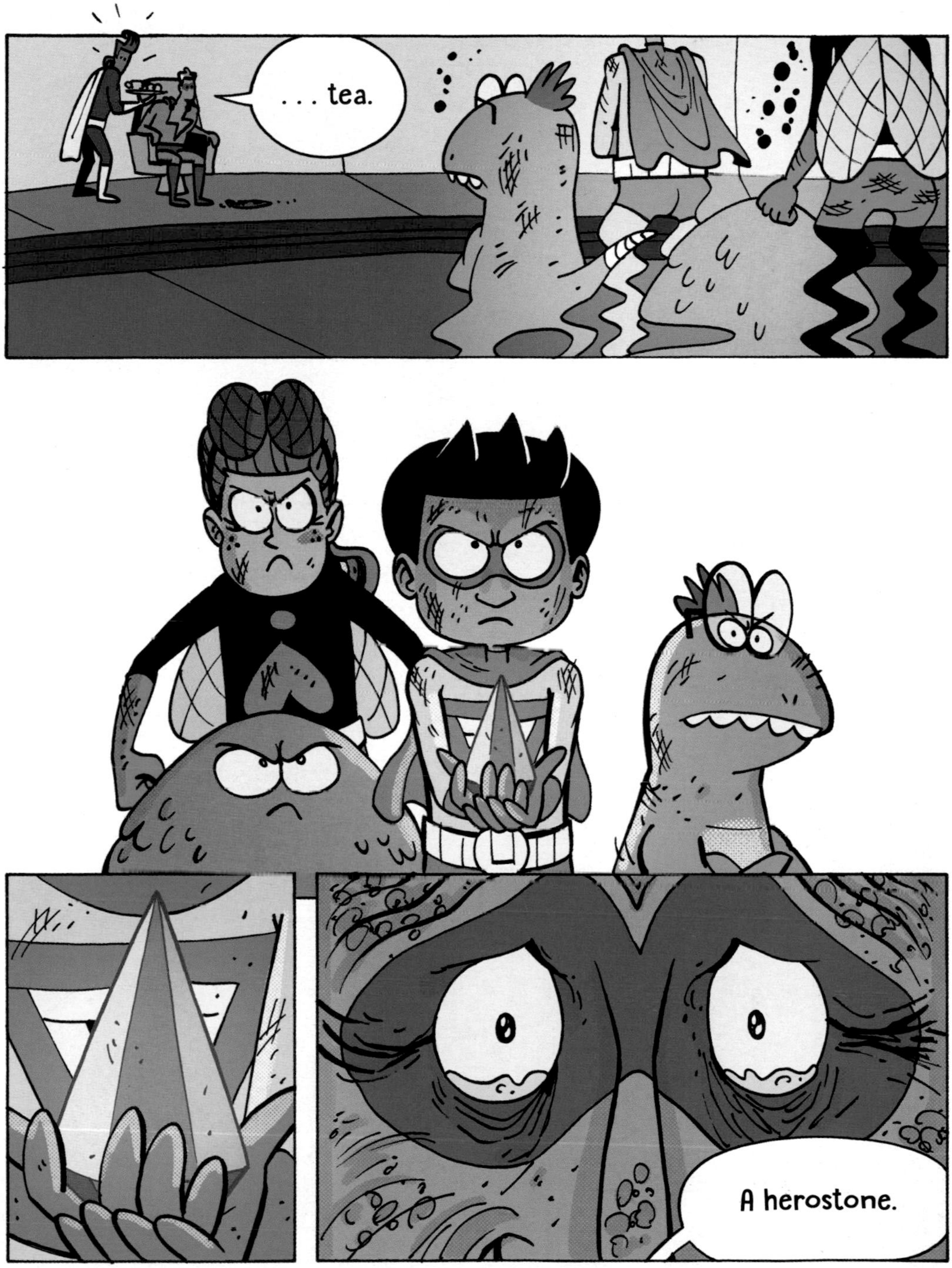
. . . tea.
A herostone.

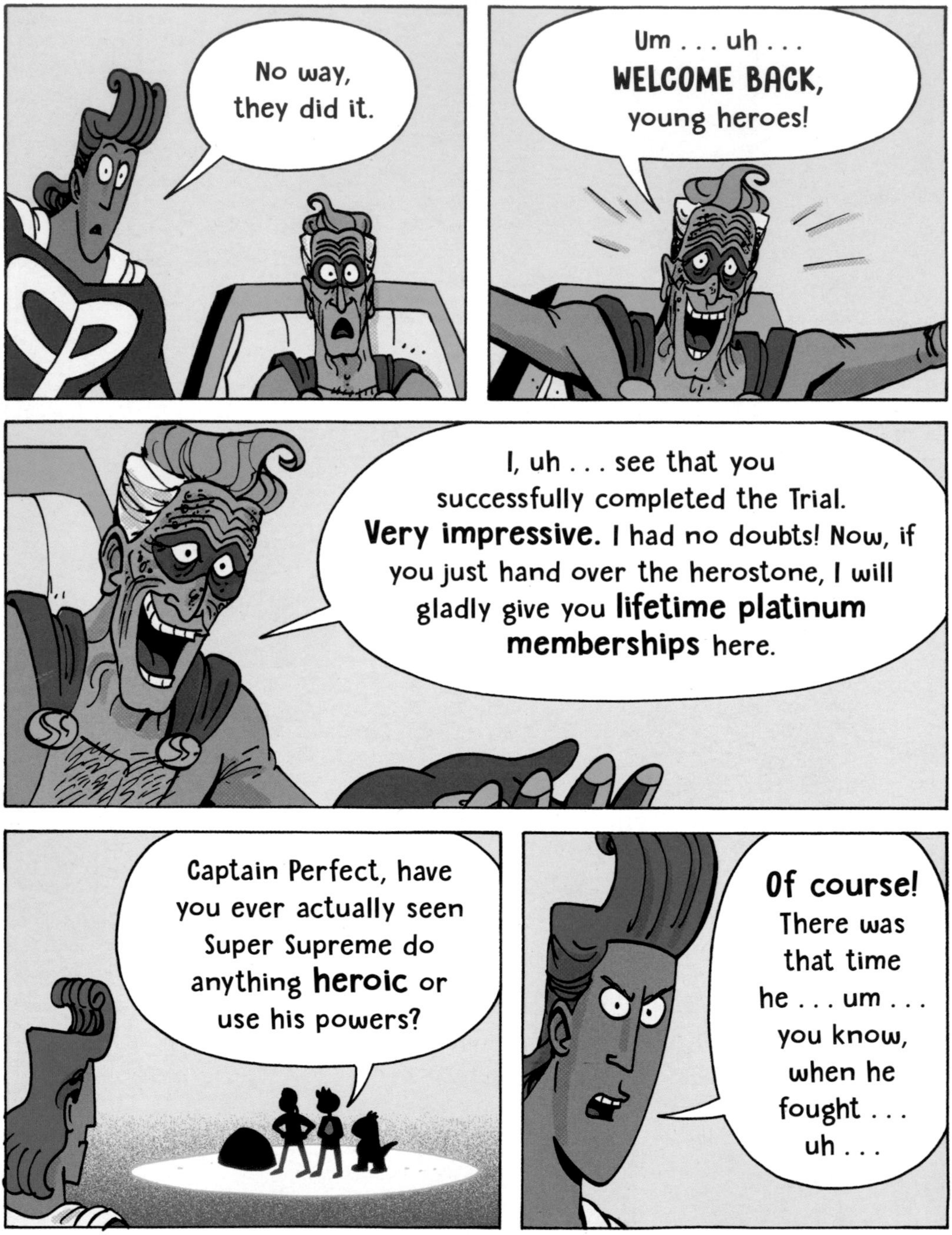
No way, they did it.
Um . . . uh . . . WELCOME BACK, young heroes!
I, uh . . . see that you successfully completed the Trial. Very impressive. I had no doubts! Now, if you just hand over the herostone, I will gladly give you lifetime platinum memberships here.
Captain Perfect, have you ever actually seen Super Supreme do anything heroic or use his powers?
Of course! There was that time he . . . um . . . you know, when he fought . . . uh . . .

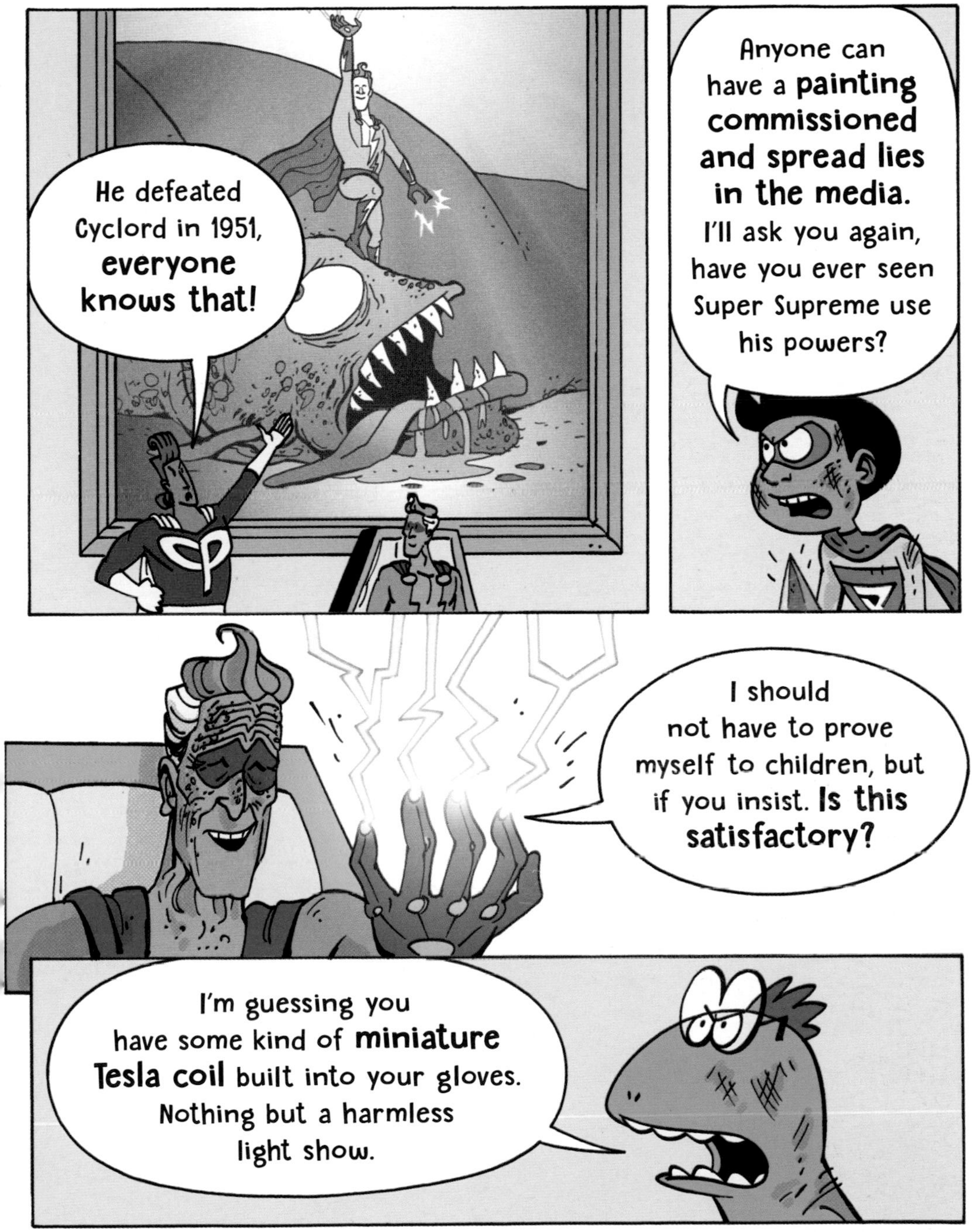
He defeated Cyclord in 1951, everyone knows that!
Anyone can have a painting commissioned and spread lies in the media. I'll ask you again, have you ever seen Super Supreme use his powers?
I should not have to prove myself to children, but if you insist. Is this satisfactory?
I'm guessing you have some kind of miniature Tesla coil built into your gloves. Nothing but a harmless light show.

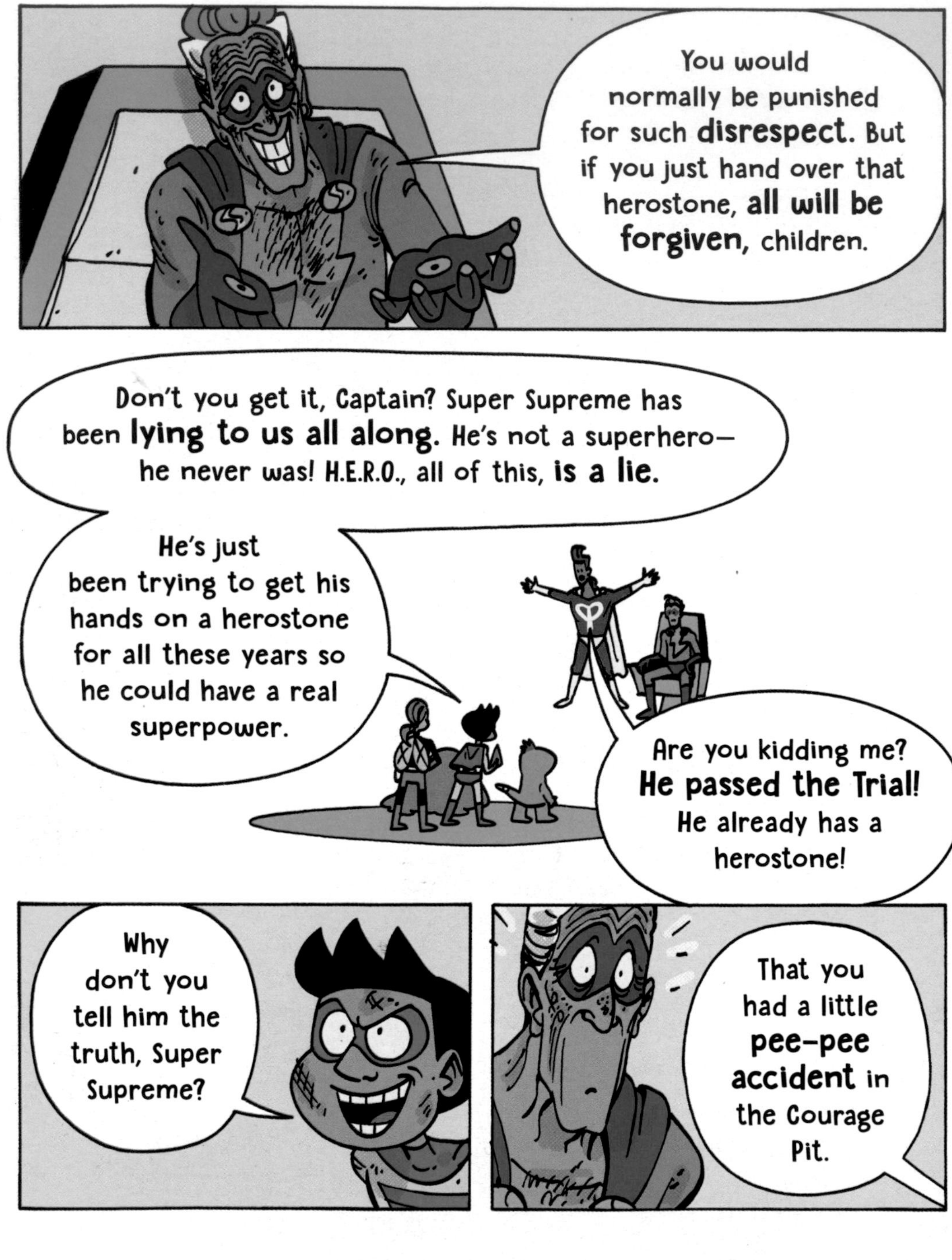
You would normally be punished for such disrespect. But if you just hand over that herostone, all will be forgiven, children.
Don't you get it, Captain? Super Supreme has been lying to us all along. He's not a superhero—he never was! H.E.R.O., all of this, is a lie.
He's just been trying to get his hands on a herostone for all these years so he could have a real superpower.
Are you kidding me? He passed the Trial! He already has a herostone!
Why don't you tell him the truth, Super Supreme?
That you had a little pee-pee accident in the Courage Pit.

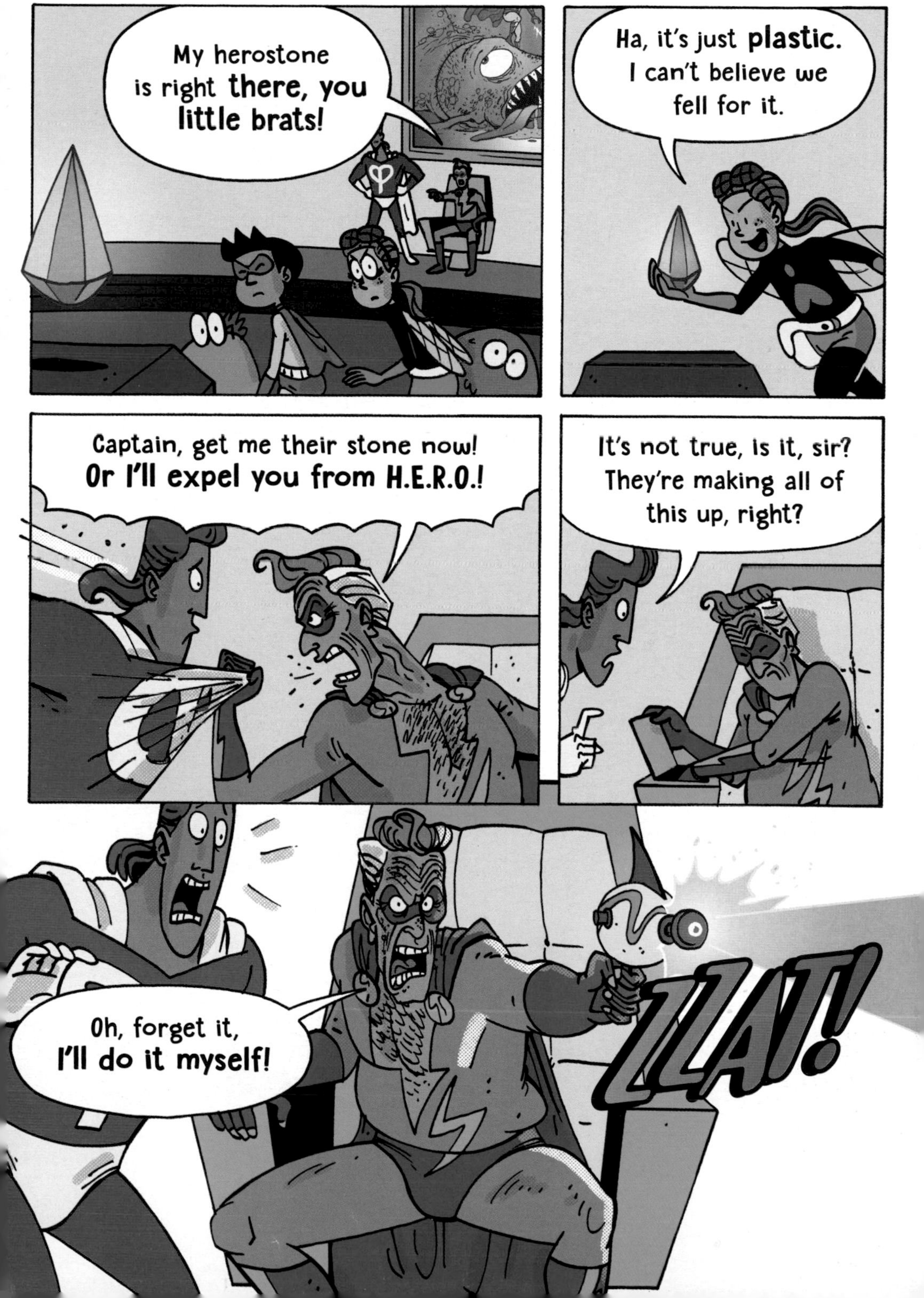
My herostone is right there, you little brats!
Ha, it's just plastic. I can't believe we fell for it.
Captain, get me their stone now! Or I'll expel you from H.E.R.O.!
It's not true, is it, sir? They're making all of this up, right?
Oh, forget it, I'll do it myself!
ZZAT!

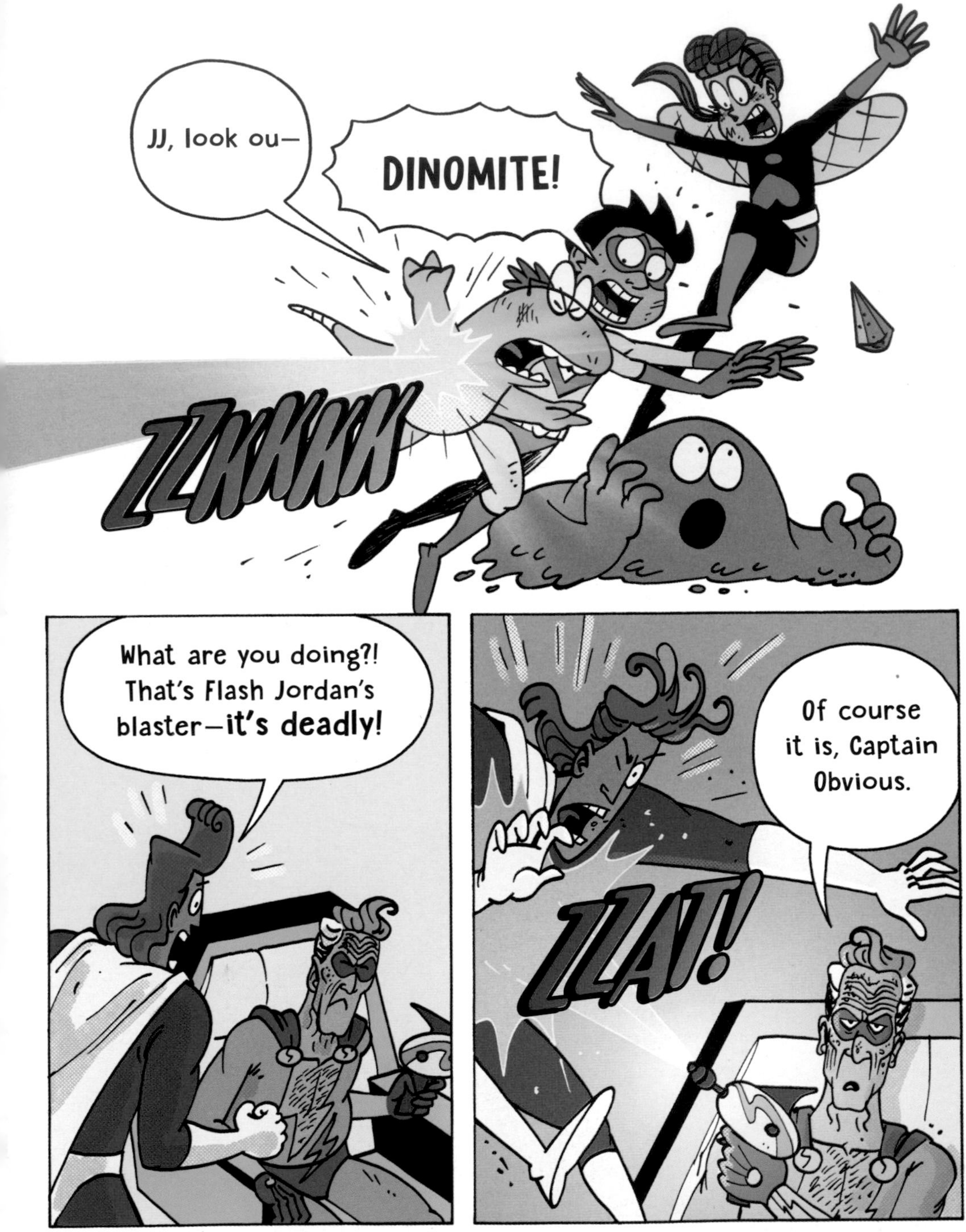
JJ, look ou—
DINOMITE!
ZZAKKKK
What are you doing?! That's Flash Jordan's blaster—it's deadly!
ZZAT!
Of course it is, Captain Obvious.

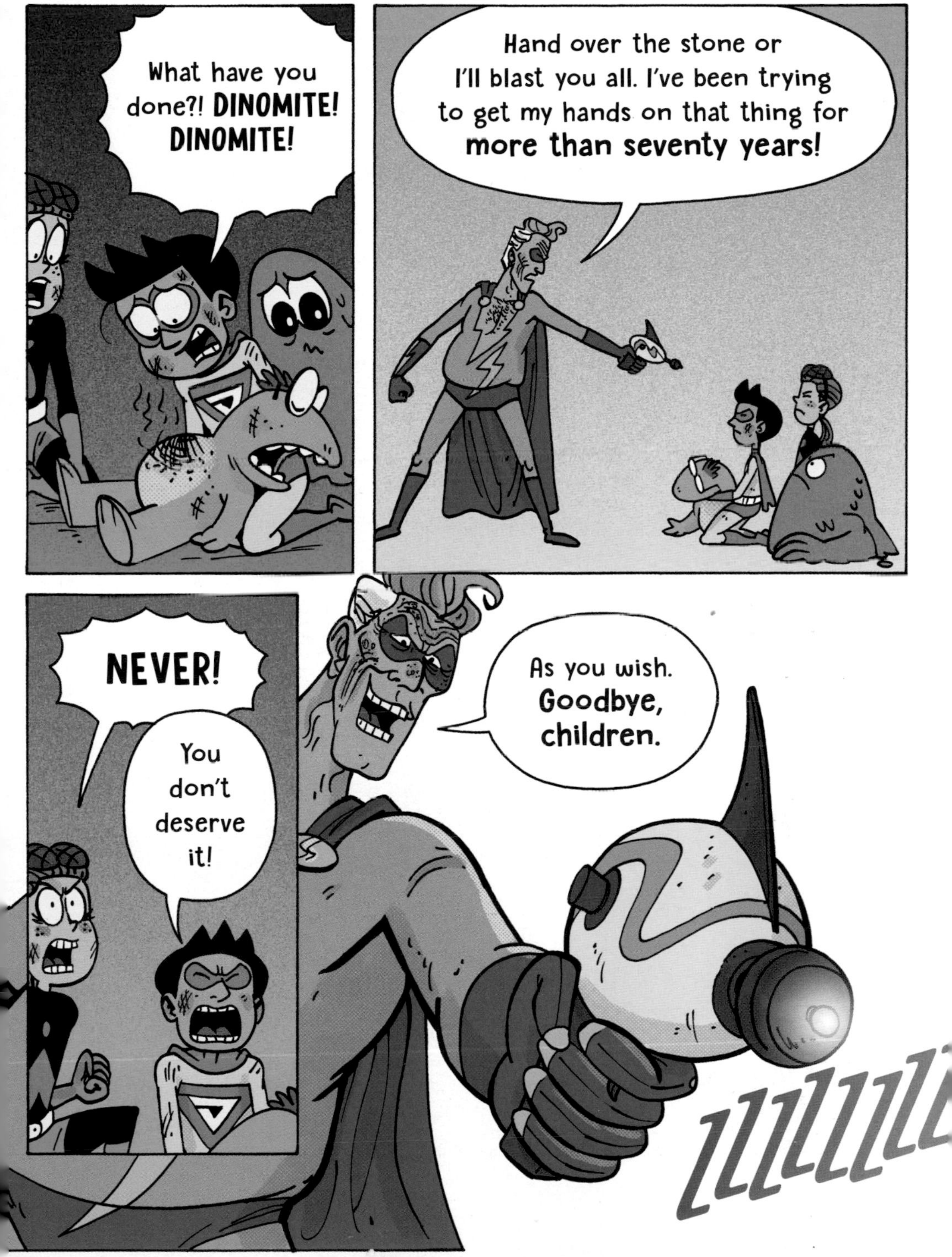
What have you done?! DINOMITE! DINOMITE!
Hand over the stone or I'll blast you all. I've been trying to get my hands on that thing for more than seventy years!
NEVER!
You don't deserve it!
As you wish. Goodbye, children.
ZZZZZZZ

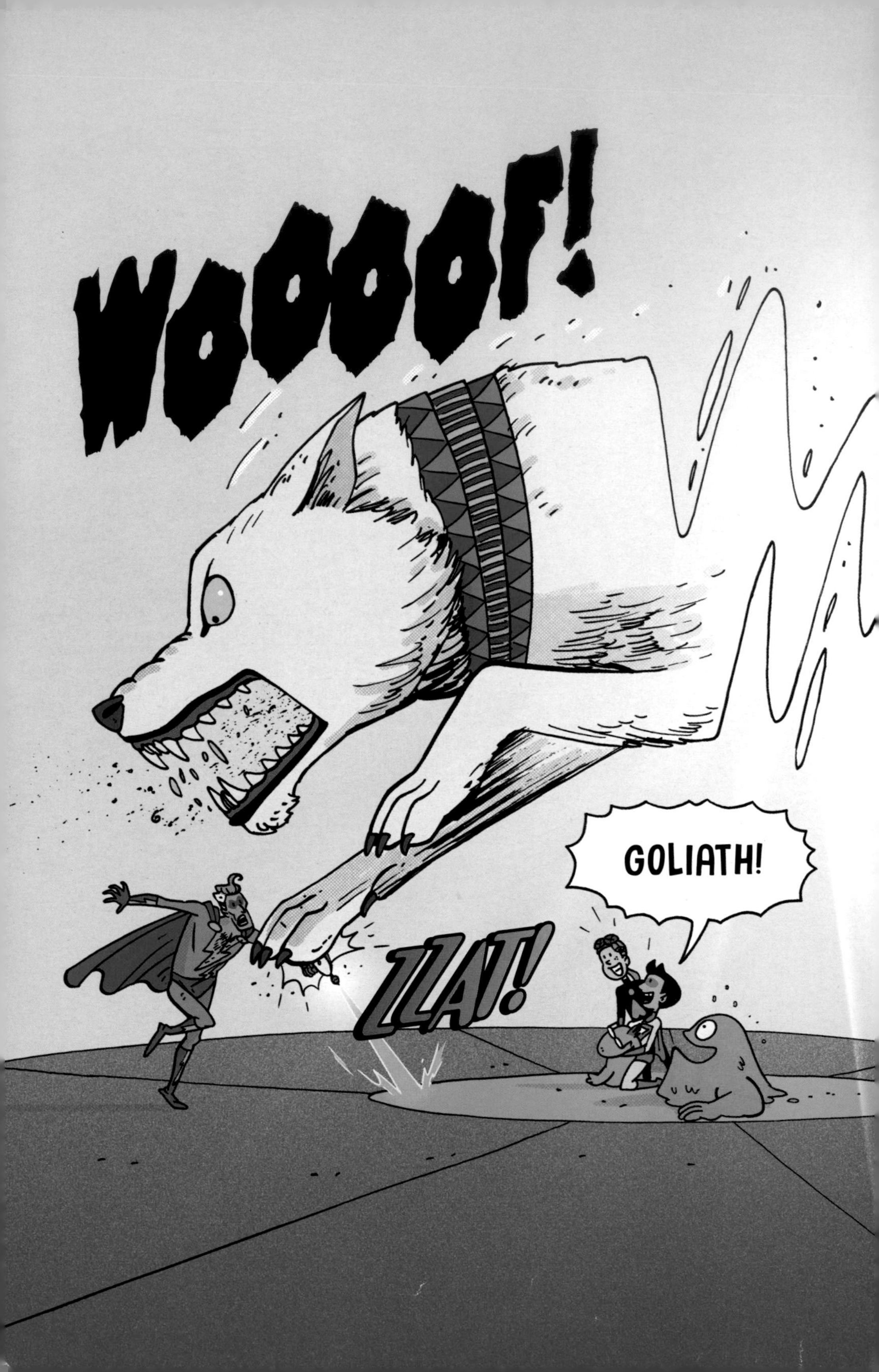
WOOOOF!
GOLIATH!
ZZAT!

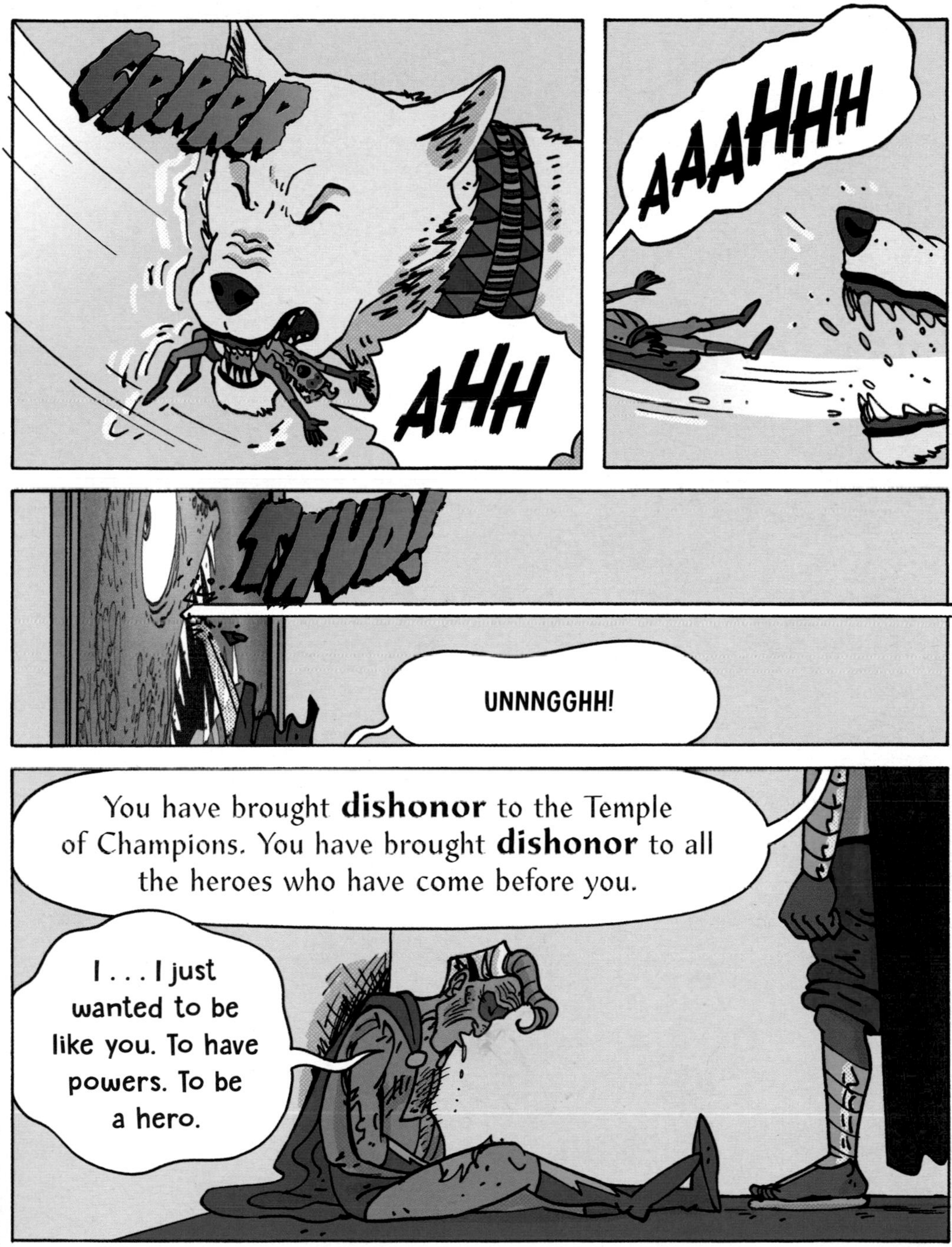
GRRRR
AHH
AAAHHH
THUD!
UNNNGGHH!
You have brought **dishonor** to the Temple of Champions. You have brought **dishonor** to all the heroes who have come before you.
I . . . I just wanted to be like you. To have powers. To be a hero.

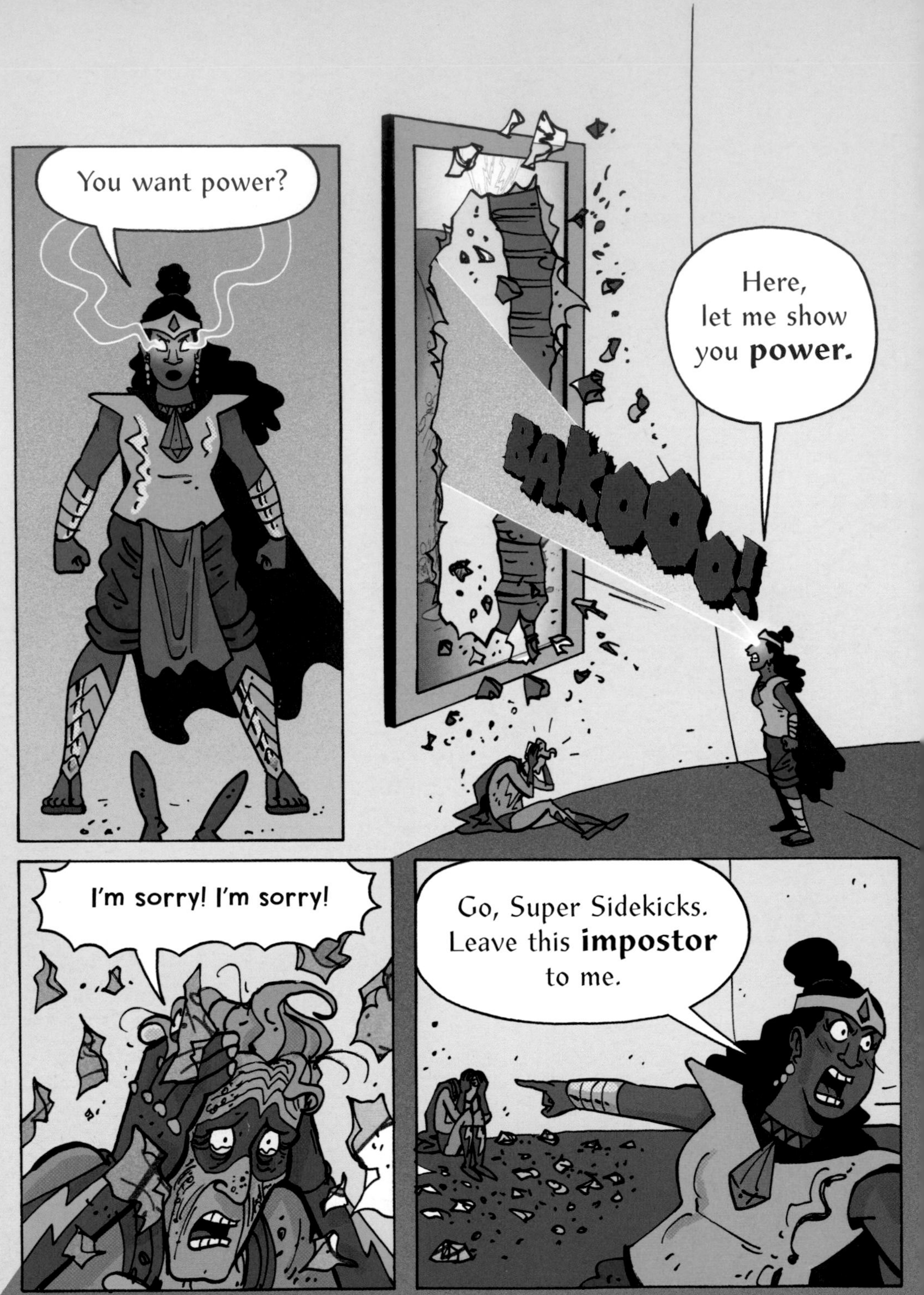
You want power?
Here, let me show you power.
BAKOOOO!!
I'm sorry! I'm sorry!
Go, Super Sidekicks. Leave this impostor to me.

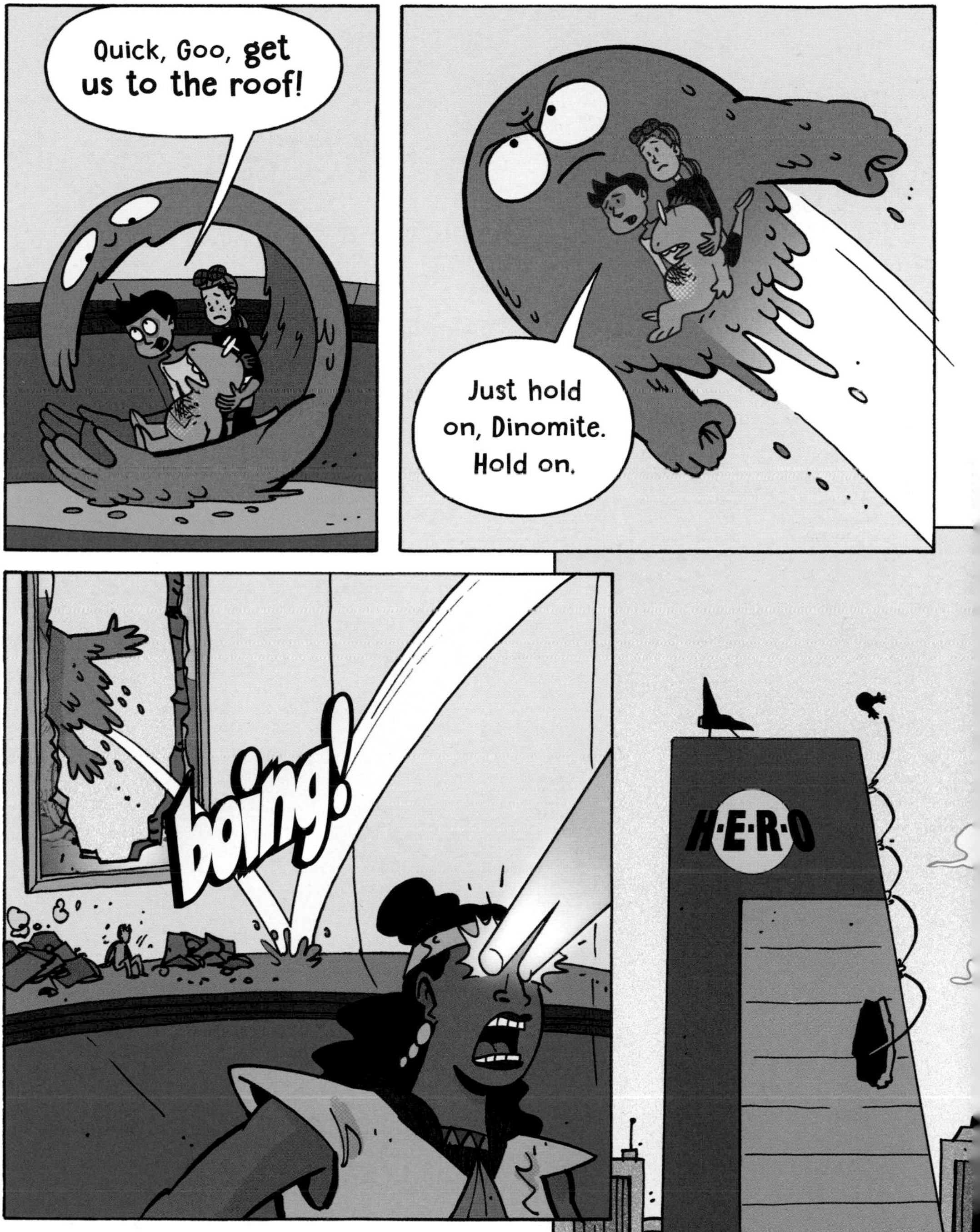
Quick, Goo, get us to the roof!
Just hold on, Dinomite. Hold on.
boing!
H·E·R·O

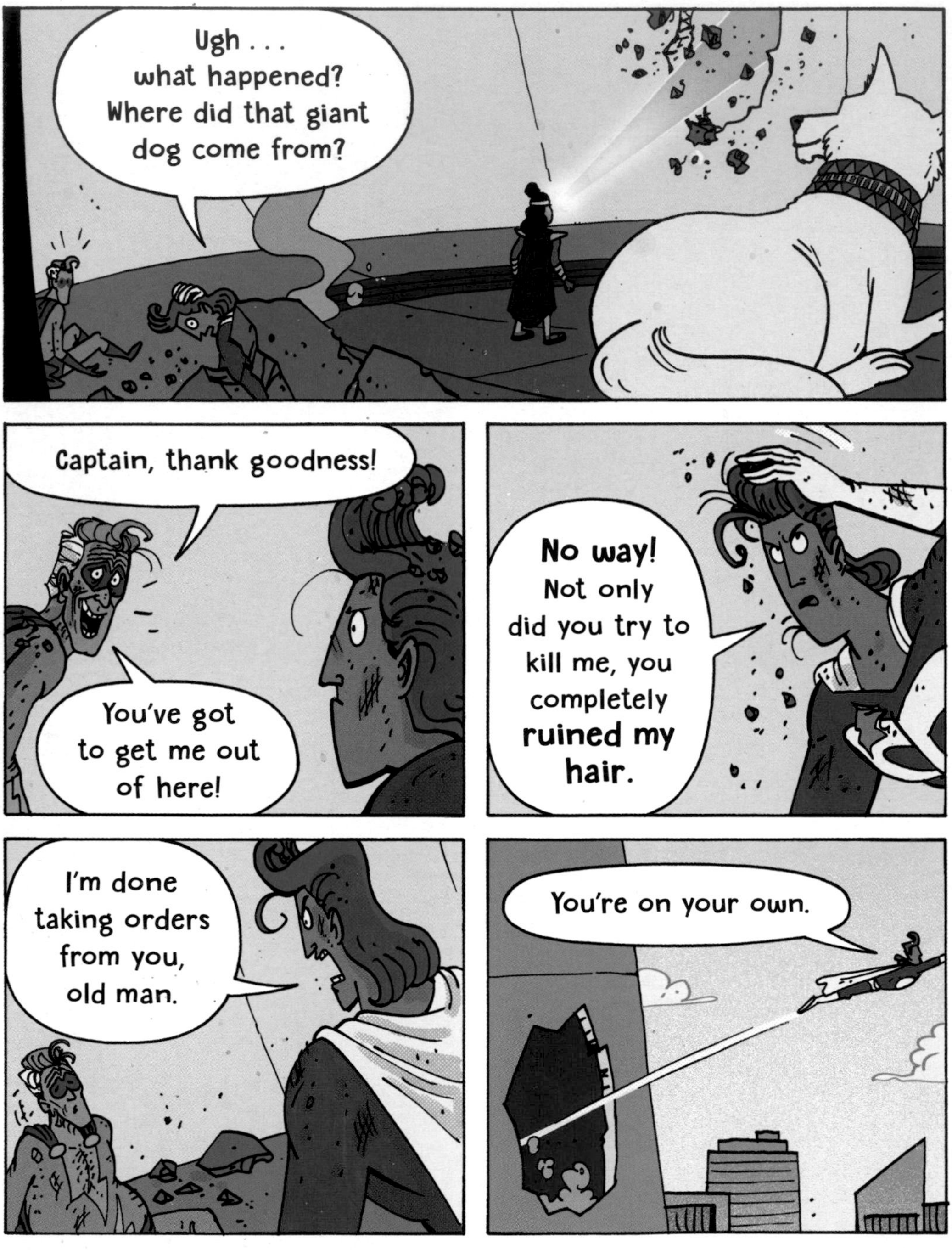
Ugh . . . what happened? Where did that giant dog come from?
Captain, thank goodness!
You've got to get me out of here!
No way! Not only did you try to kill me, you completely ruined my hair.
I'm done taking orders from you, old man.
You're on your own.

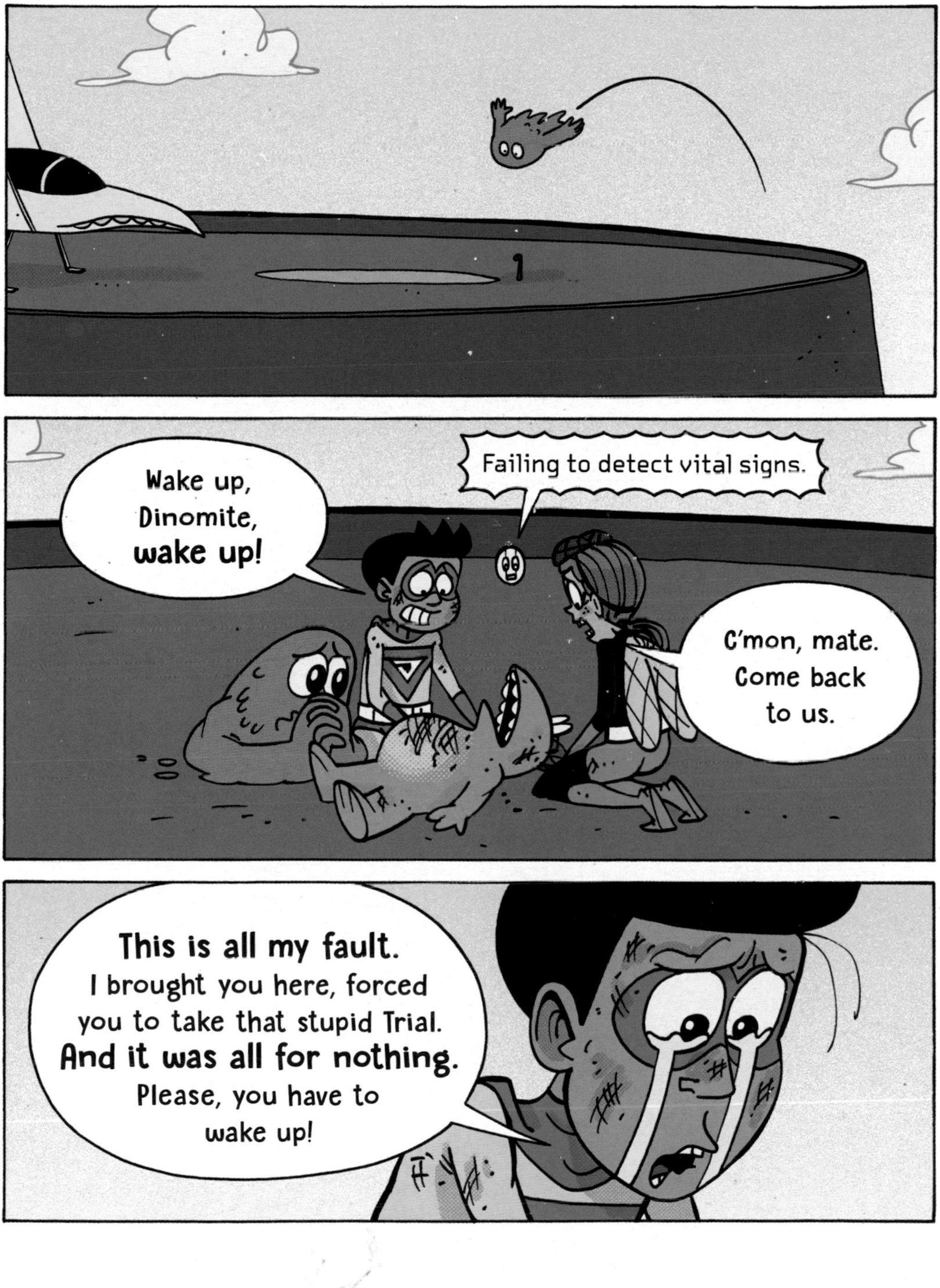
Wake up, Dinomite, wake up!
Failing to detect vital signs.
C'mon, mate. Come back to us.
This is all my fault. I brought you here, forced you to take that stupid Trial. And it was all for nothing. Please, you have to wake up!

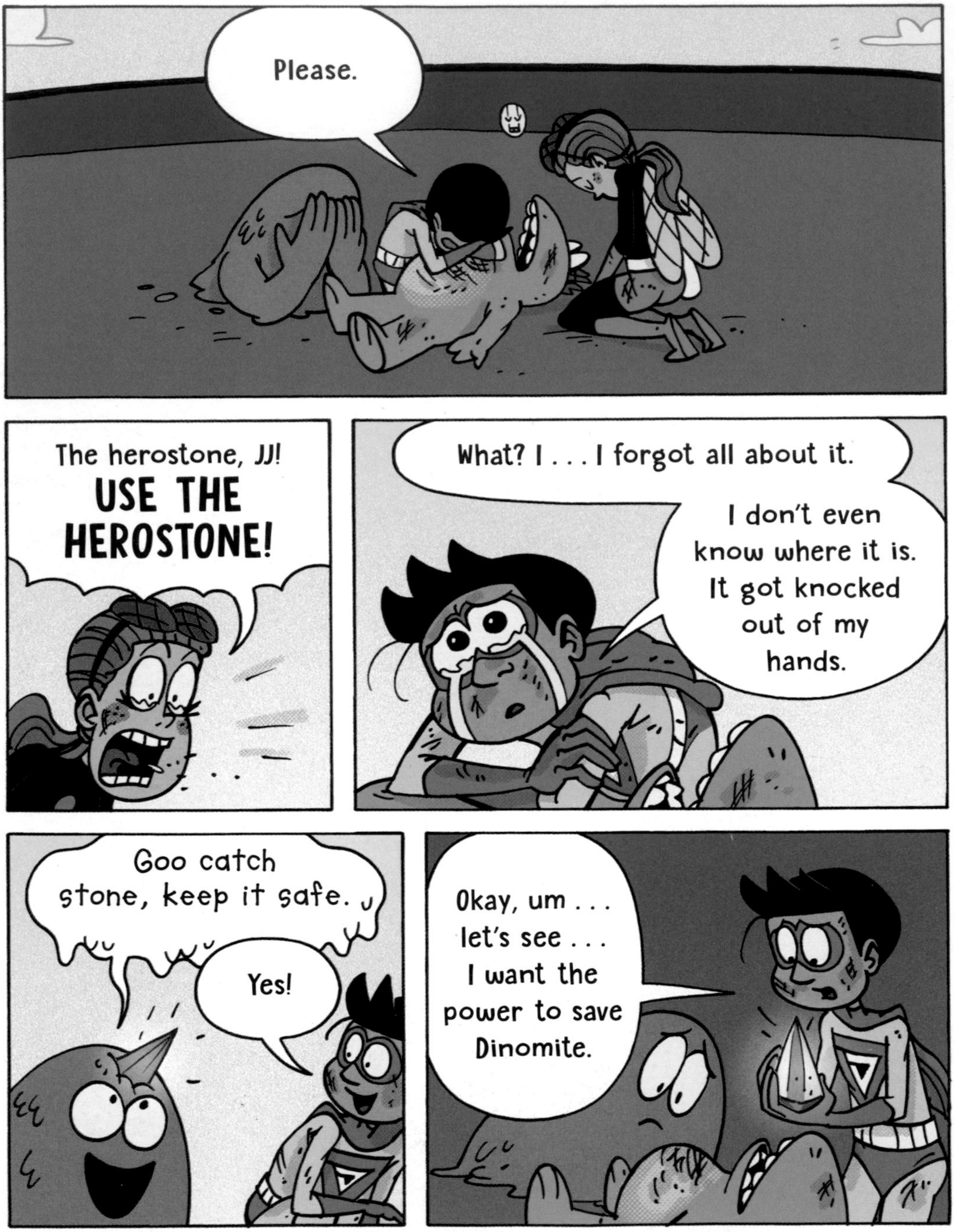
Please.
The herostone, JJ! USE THE HEROSTONE!
What? I . . . I forgot all about it.
I don't even know where it is. It got knocked out of my hands.
Goo catch stone, keep it safe.
Yes!
Okay, um . . . let's see . . . I want the power to save Dinomite.

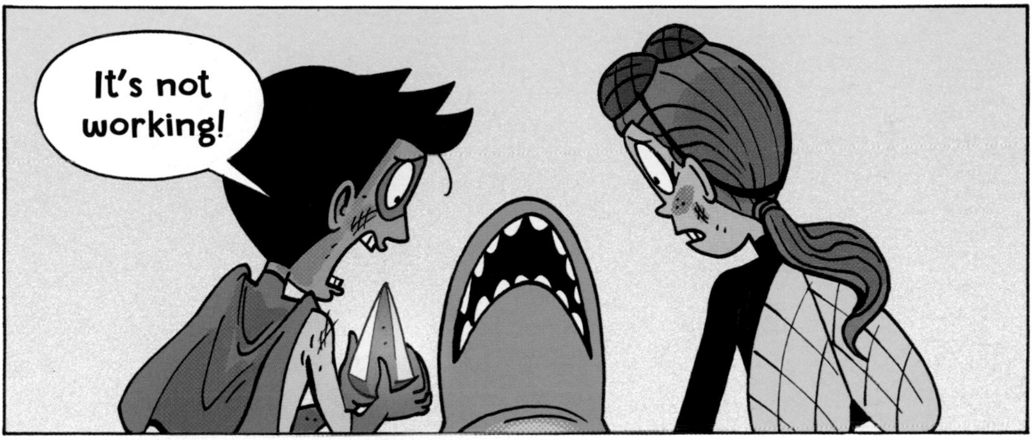
It's not working!

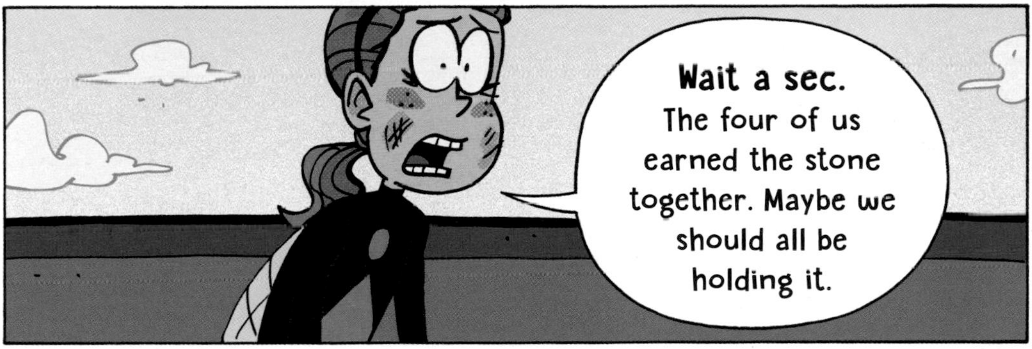
Wait a sec. The four of us earned the stone together. Maybe we should all be holding it.

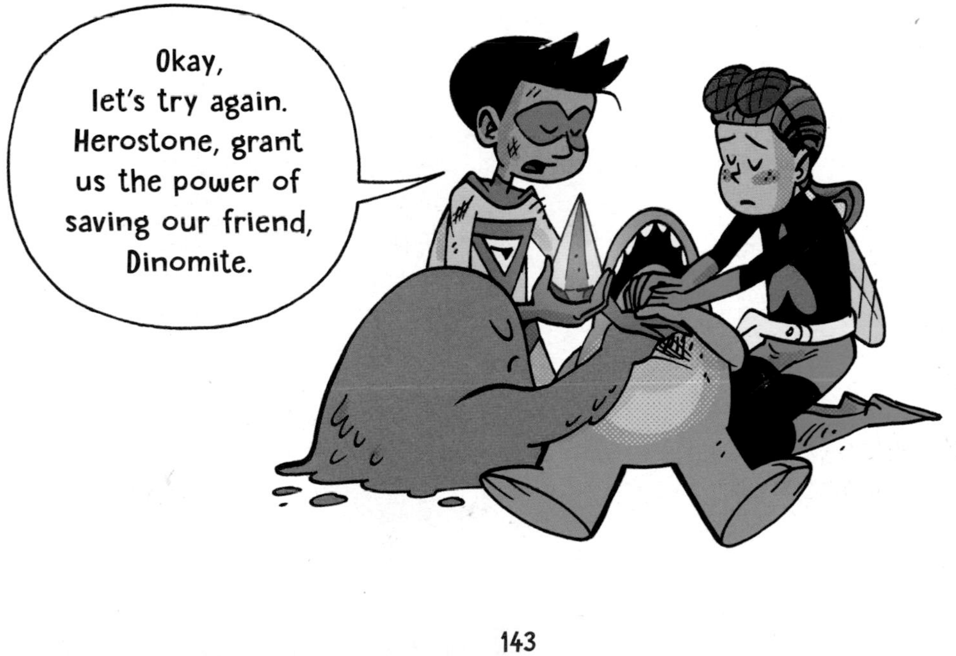
Okay, let's try again. Herostone, grant us the power of saving our friend, Dinomite.

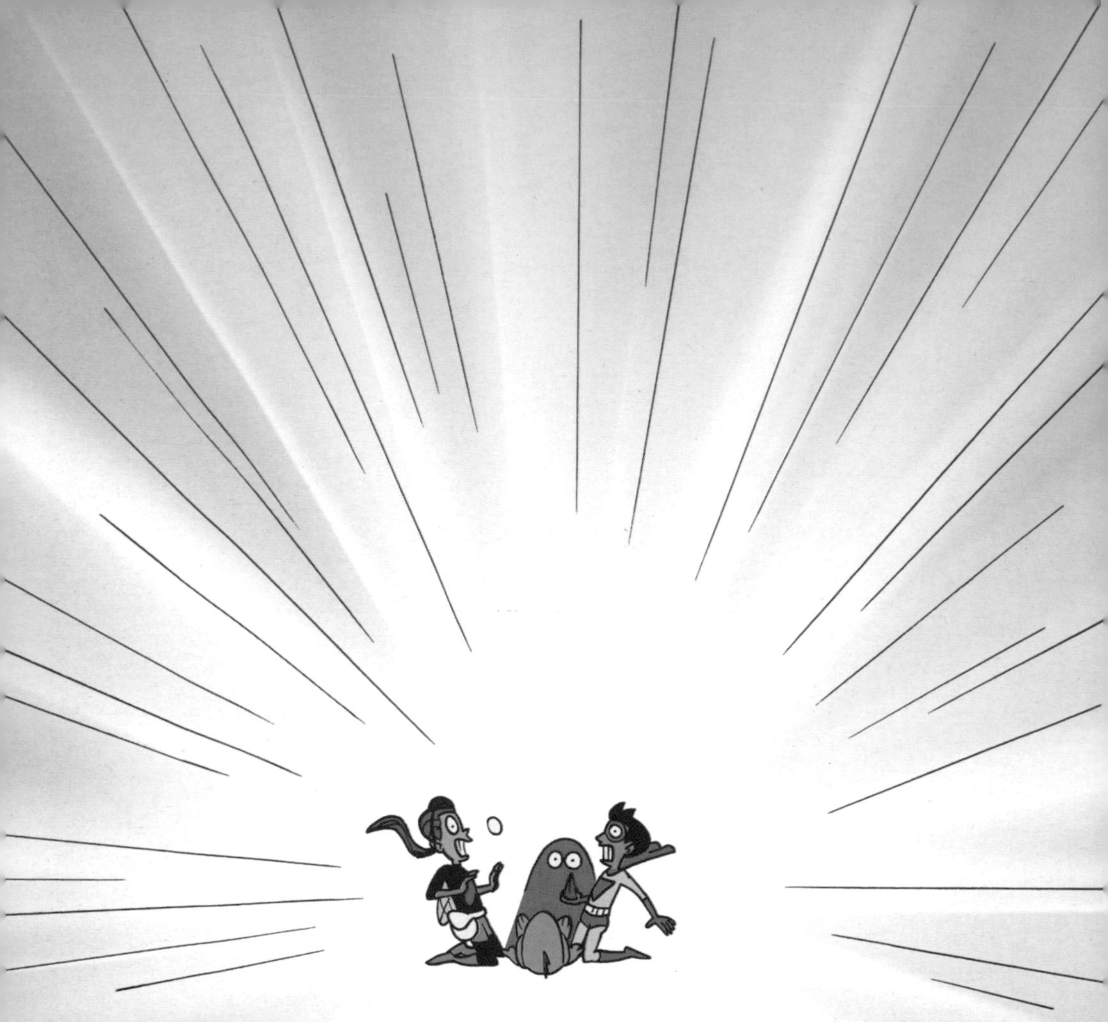

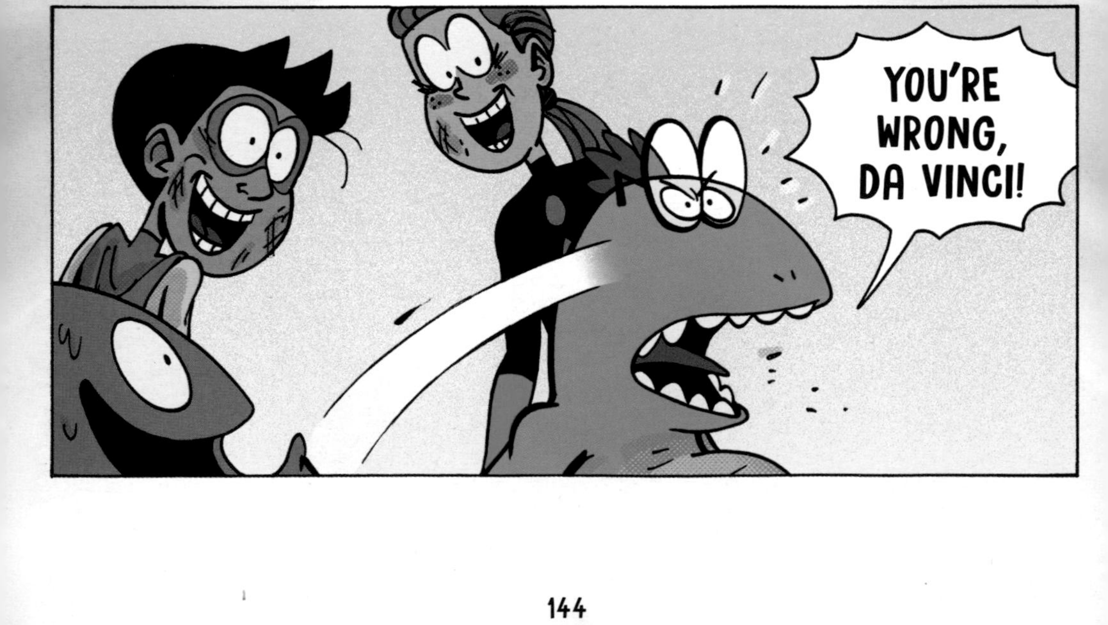
YOU'RE WRONG, DA VINCI!

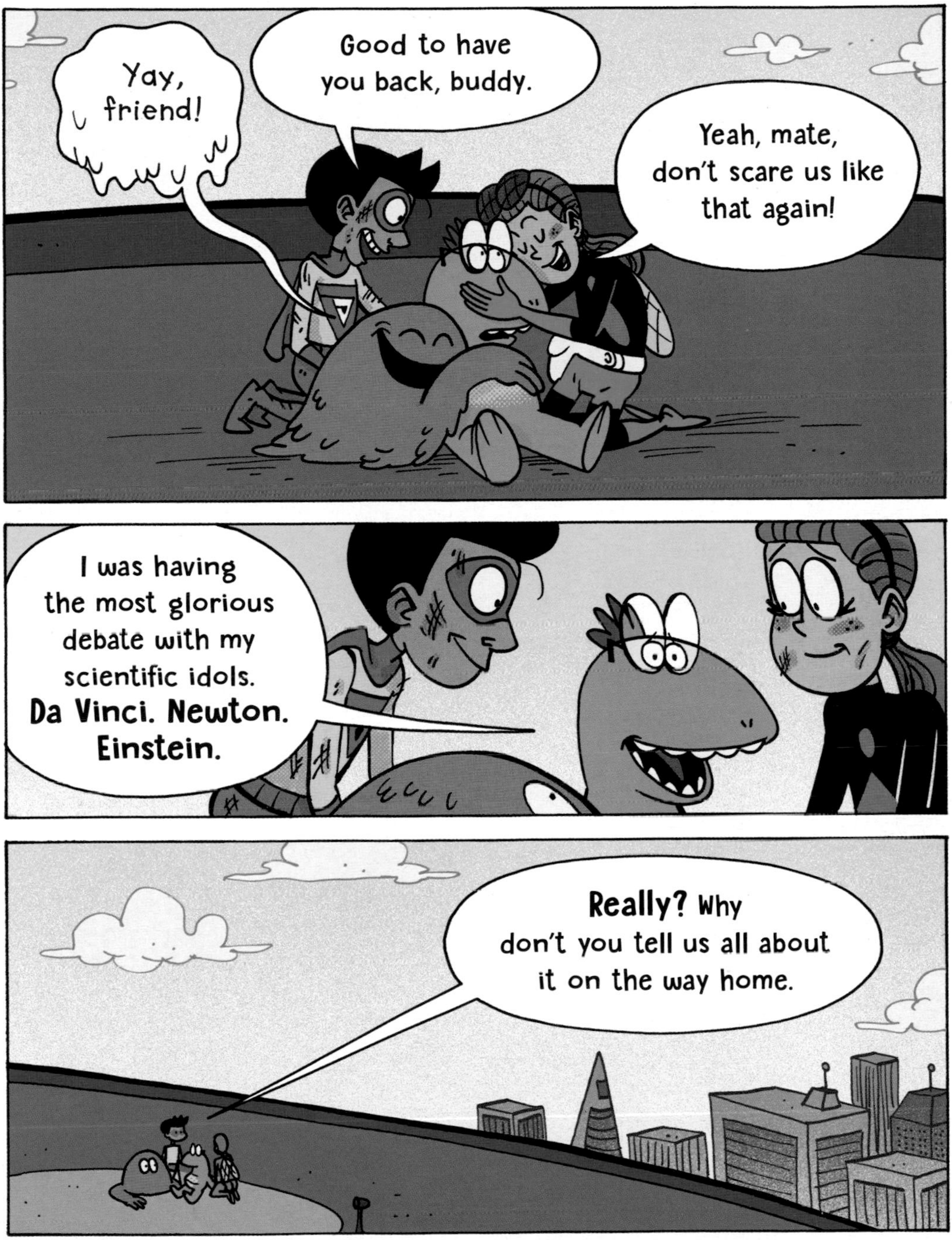
Yay, friend!
Good to have you back, buddy.
Yeah, mate, don't scare us like that again!
I was having the most glorious debate with my scientific idols. **Da Vinci. Newton. Einstein.**
Really? Why don't you tell us all about it on the way home.

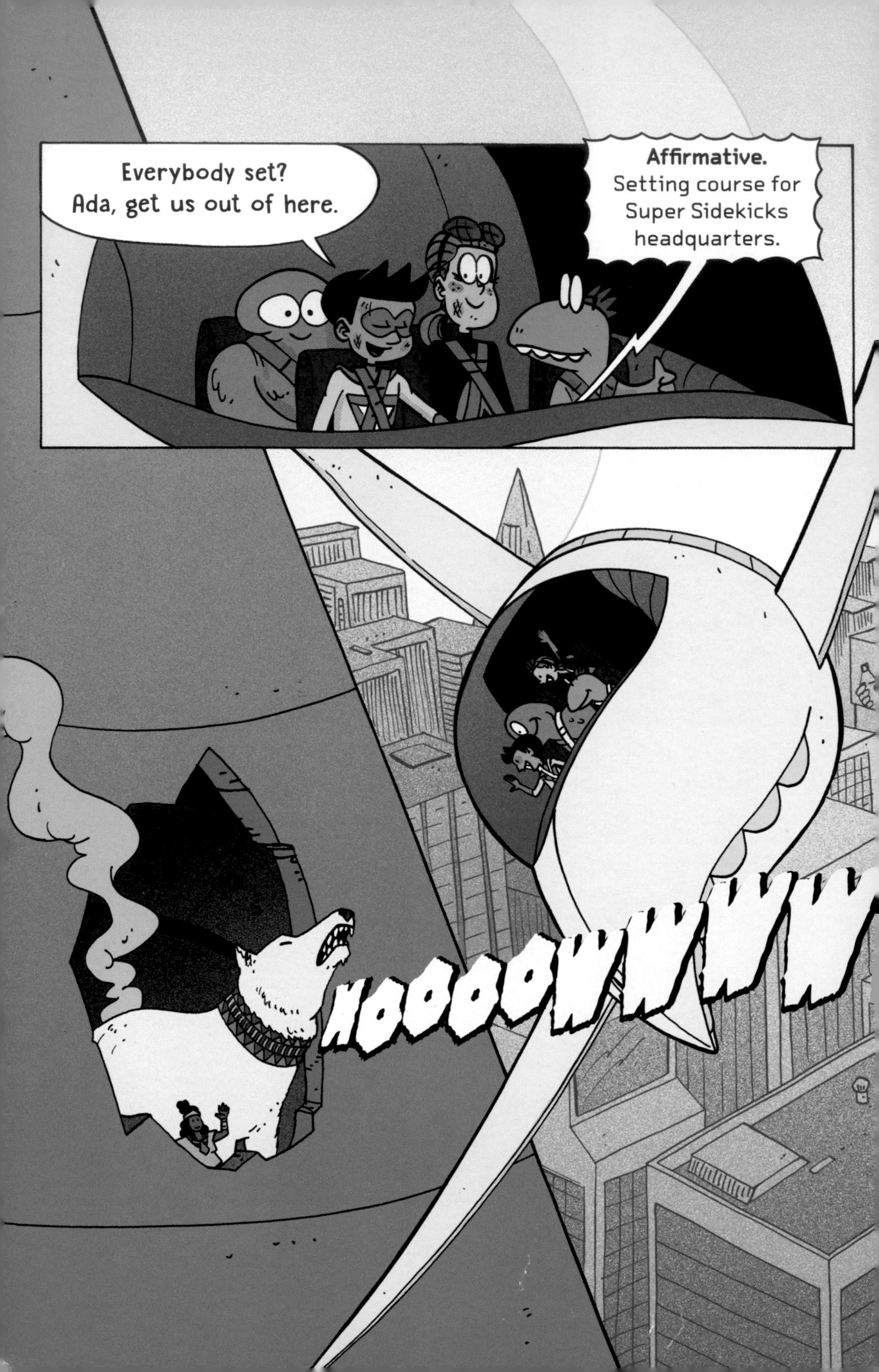
Everybody set? Ada, get us out of here.
Affirmative. Setting course for Super Sidekicks headquarters.
HOOOOOWWWWW

Chapter

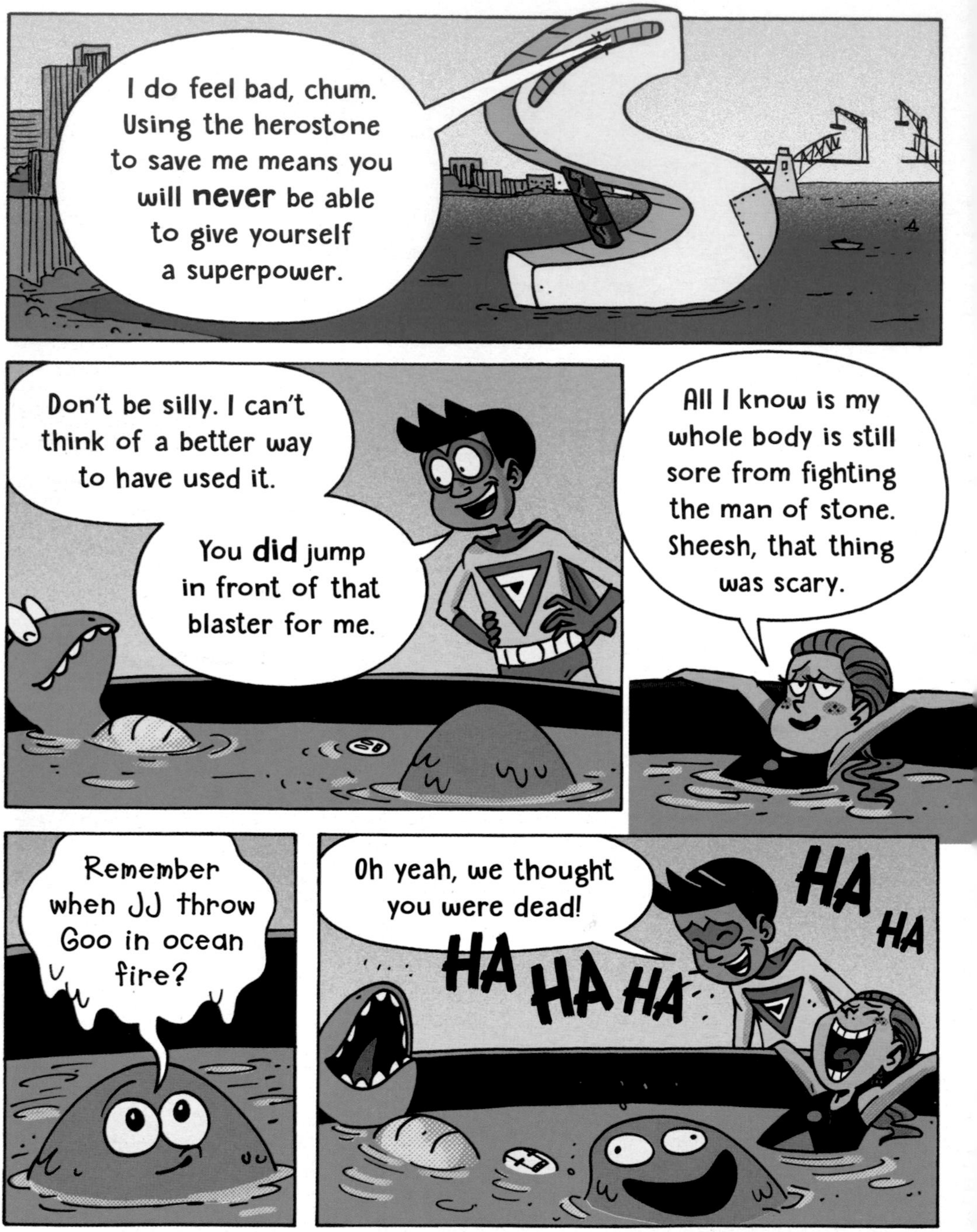
I do feel bad, chum. Using the herostone to save me means you will **never** be able to give yourself a superpower.
Don't be silly. I can't think of a better way to have used it.
You **did** jump in front of that blaster for me.
All I know is my whole body is still sore from fighting the man of stone. Sheesh, that thing was scary.
Remember when JJ throw Goo in ocean fire?
Oh yeah, we thought you were dead!
HA HA HA
HA HA

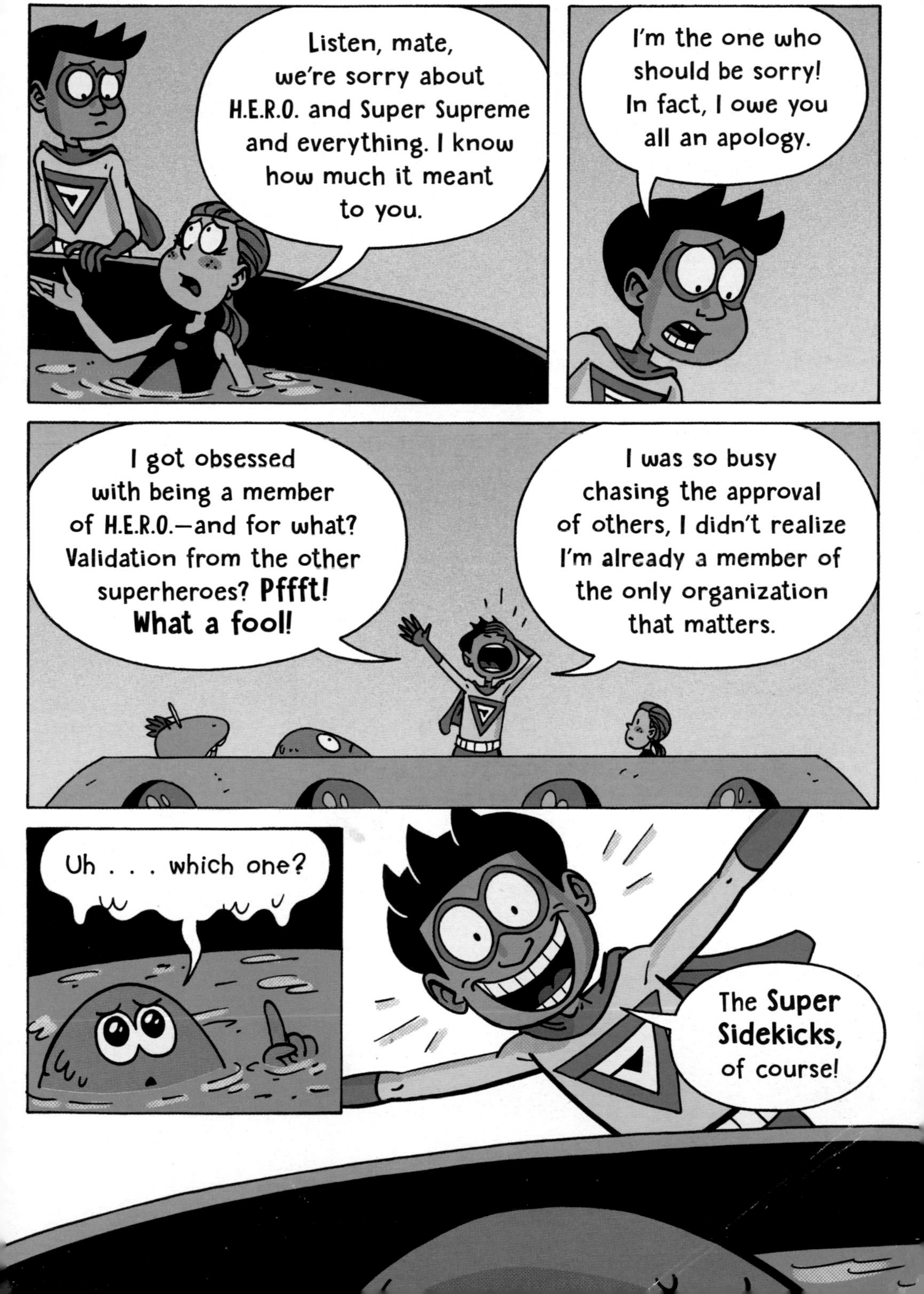
Listen, mate, we're sorry about H.E.R.O. and Super Supreme and everything. I know how much it meant to you.
I'm the one who should be sorry! In fact, I owe you all an apology.
I got obsessed with being a member of H.E.R.O.—and for what? Validation from the other superheroes? Pffft! What a fool!
I was so busy chasing the approval of others, I didn't realize I'm already a member of the only organization that matters.
Uh . . . which one?
The Super Sidekicks, of course!

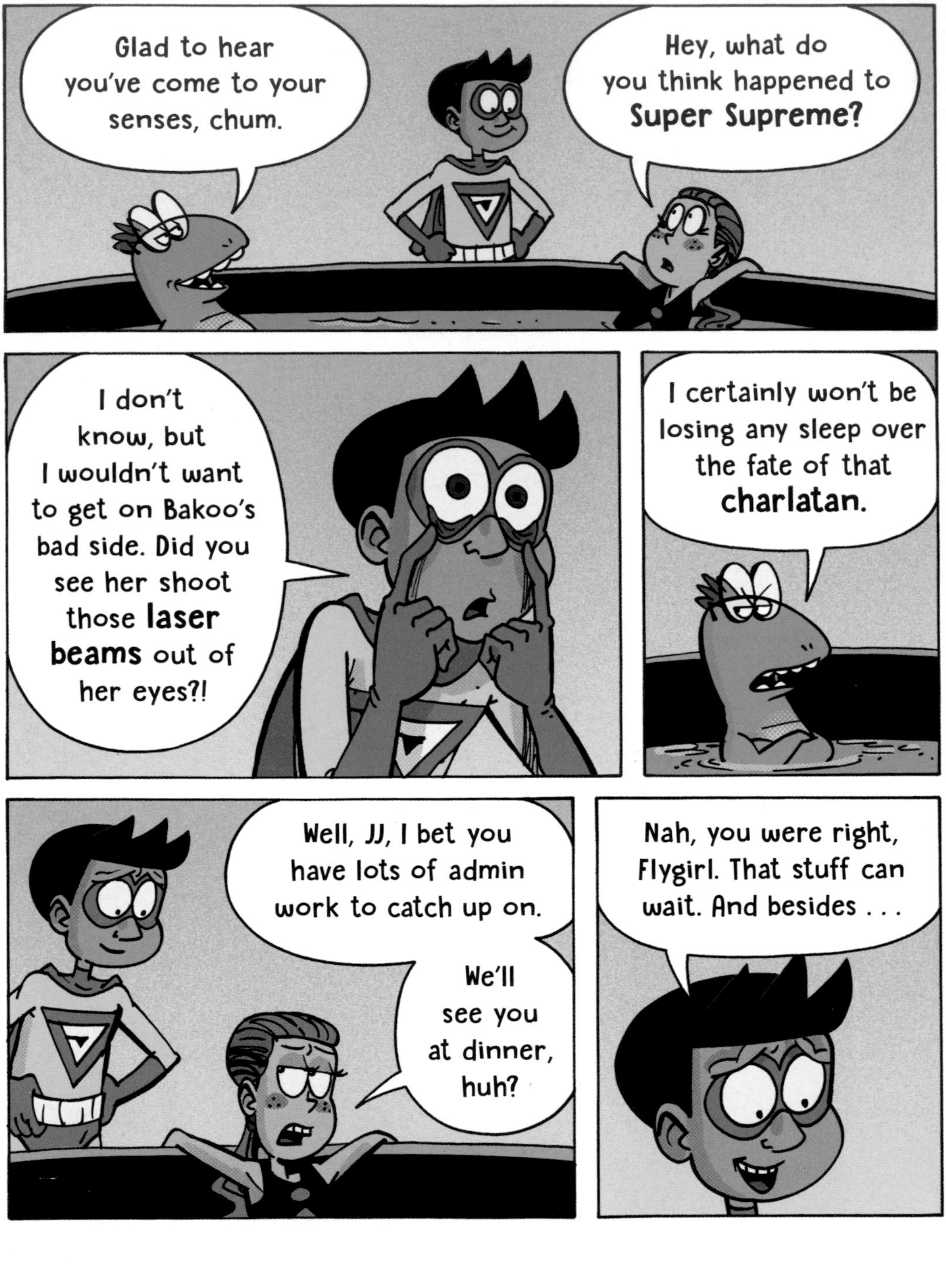
Glad to hear you've come to your senses, chum.
Hey, what do you think happened to **Super Supreme?**
I don't know, but I wouldn't want to get on Bakoo's bad side. Did you see her shoot those **laser beams** out of her eyes?!
I certainly won't be losing any sleep over the fate of that **charlatan.**
Well, JJ, I bet you have lots of admin work to catch up on.
We'll see you at dinner, huh?
Nah, you were right, Flygirl. That stuff can wait. And besides . . .

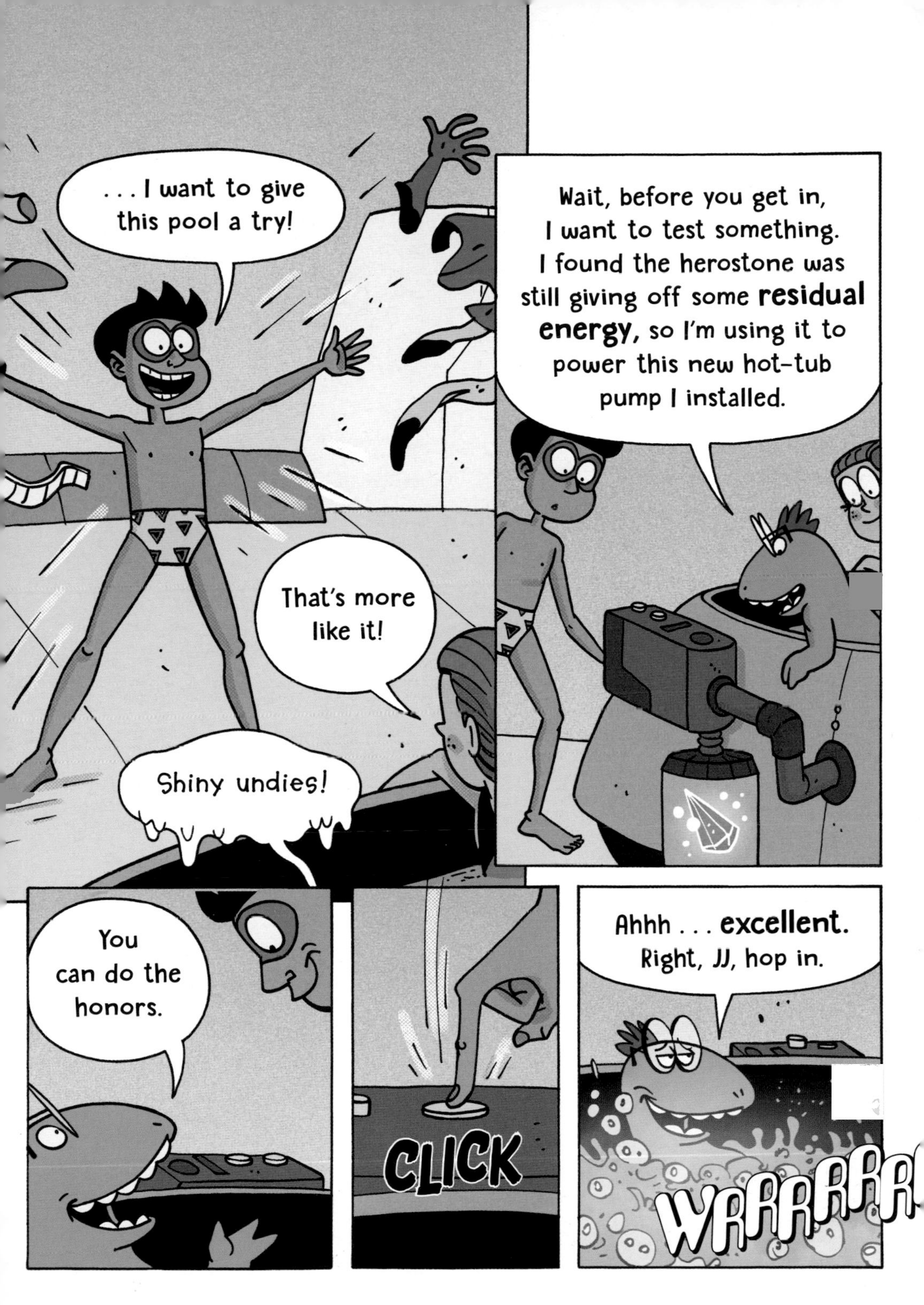
. . . I want to give this pool a try!
That's more like it!
Shiny undies!
Wait, before you get in, I want to test something. I found the herostone was still giving off some **residual energy,** so I'm using it to power this new hot-tub pump I installed.
You can do the honors.
CLICK
Ahhh . . . **excellent.** Right, JJ, hop in.
WRRRRRR

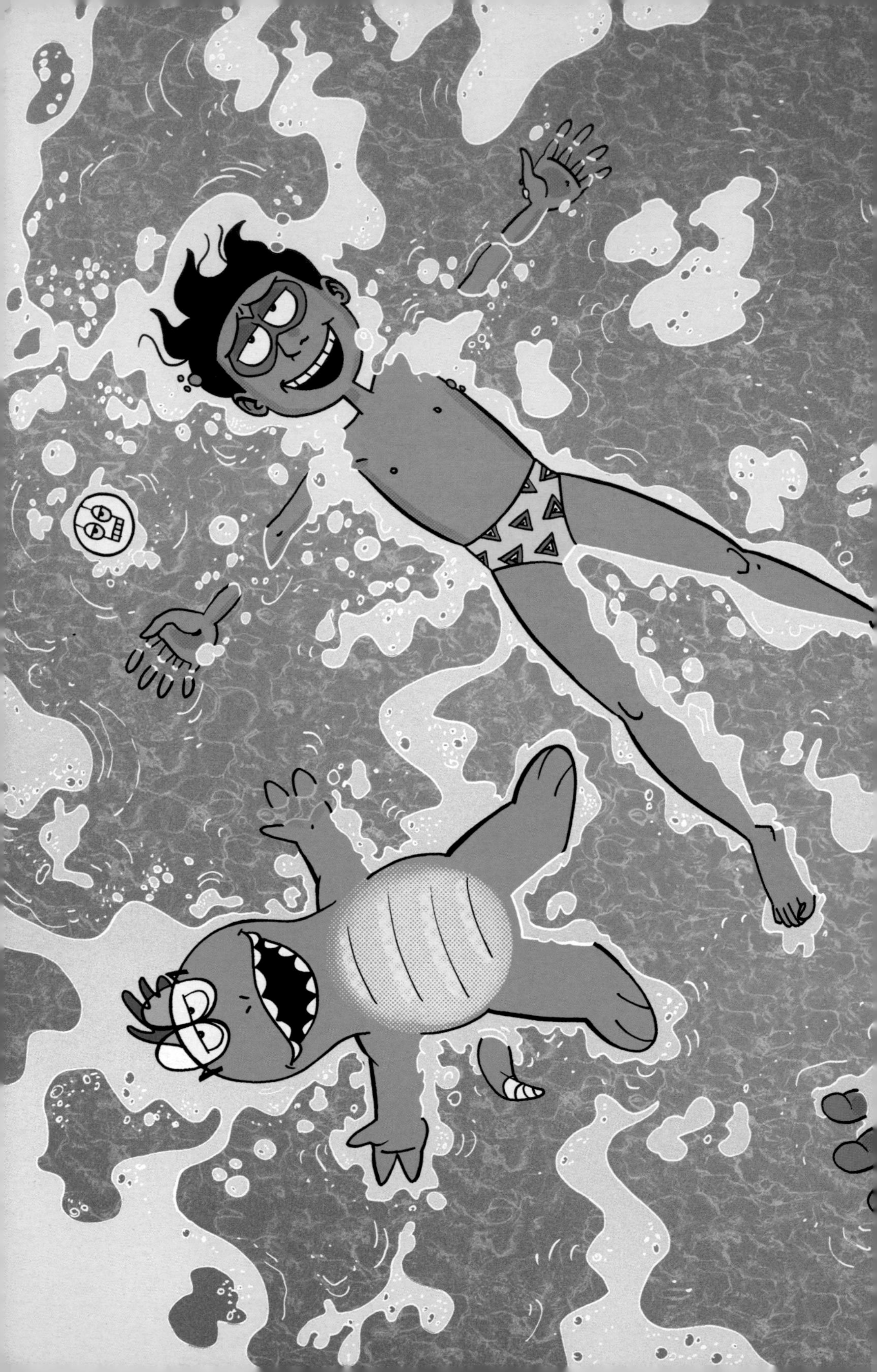

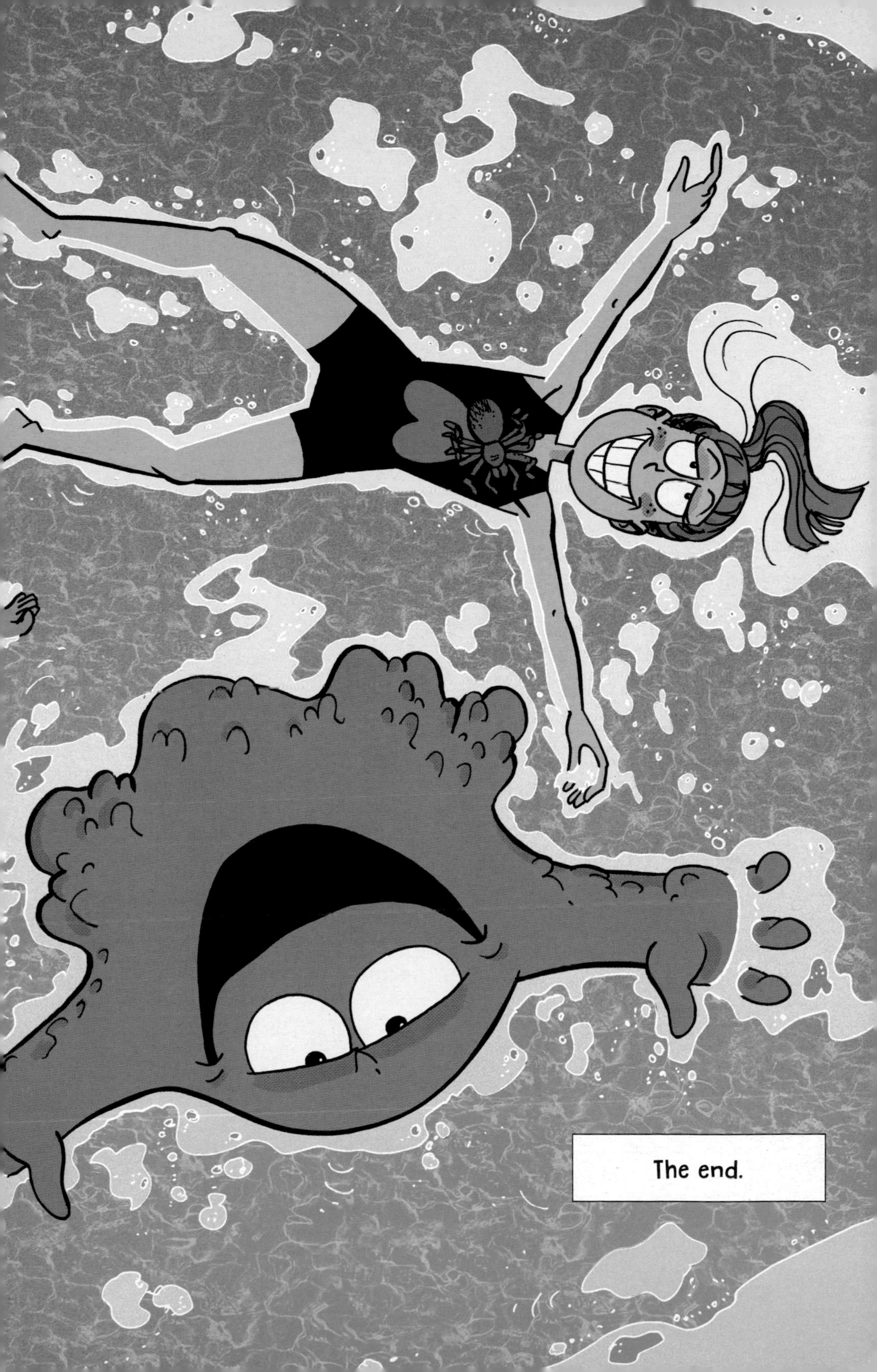
The end.

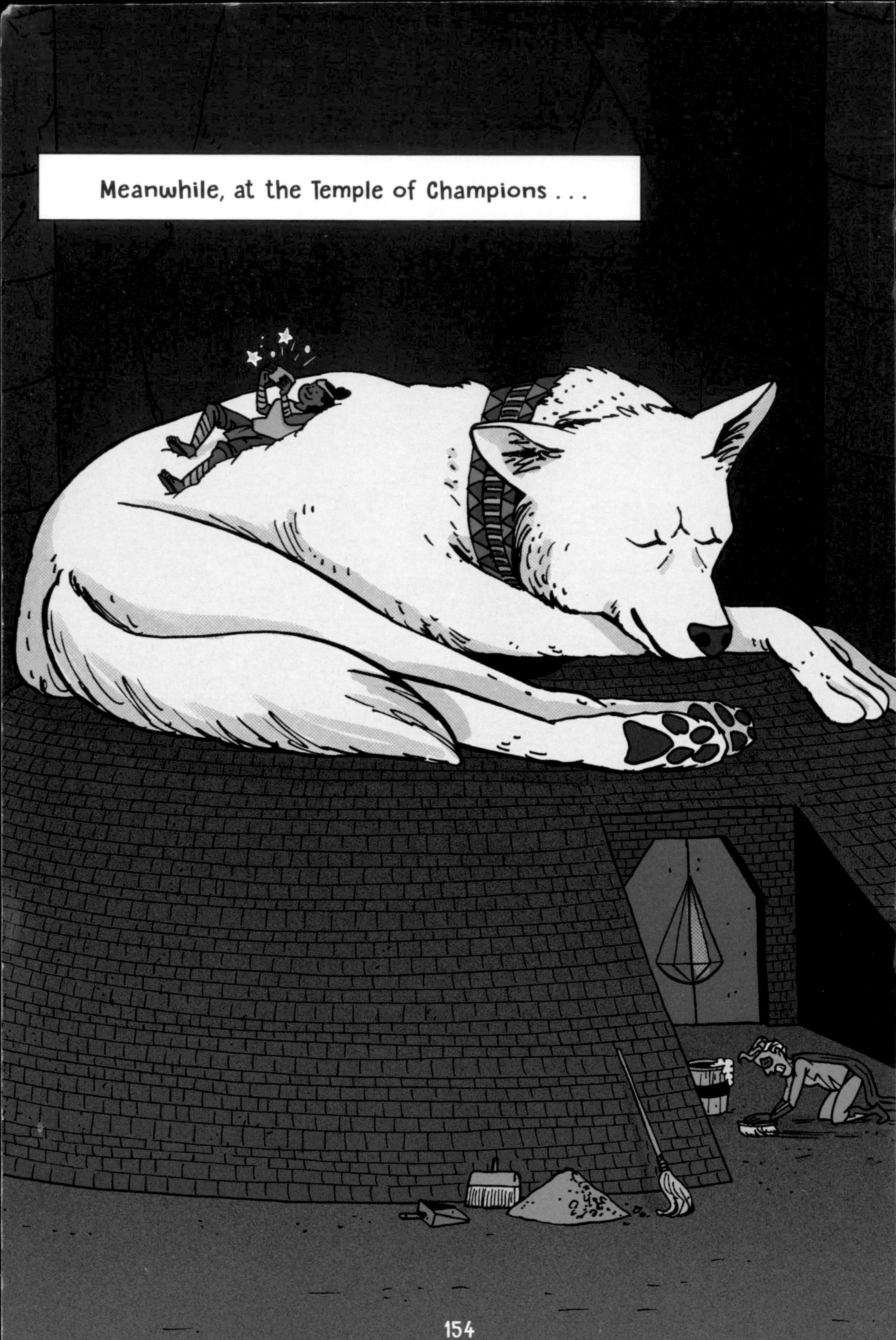
Meanwhile, at the Temple of Champions . . .

HOW HEROES ARE MADE

All heroes have origin stories. Check out how Gavin Aung Than takes the Super Sidekicks from early sketches to final art. It's super!

THUMBNAILS → PENCILS → INKS

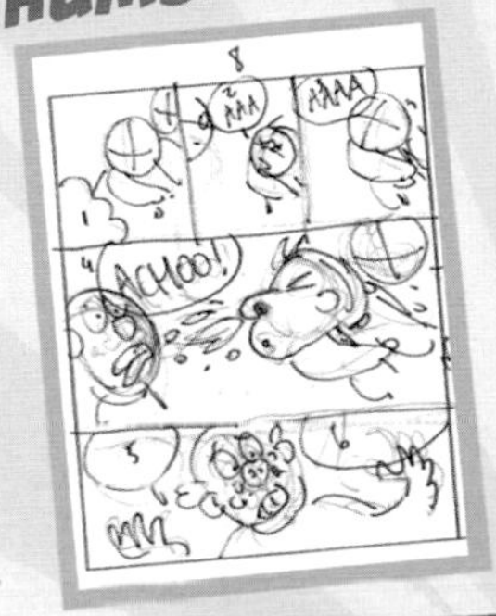
ACHOO!

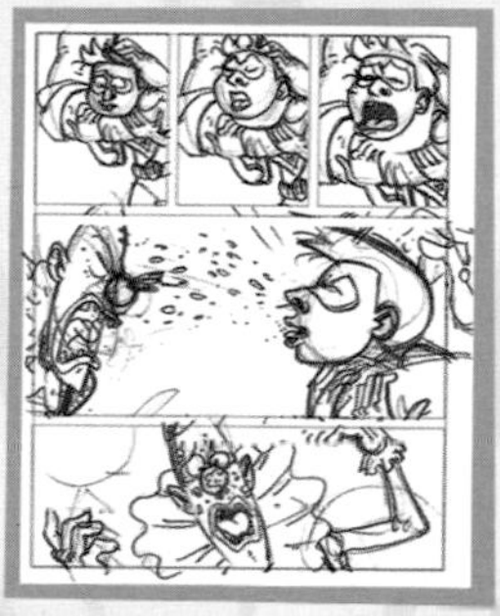

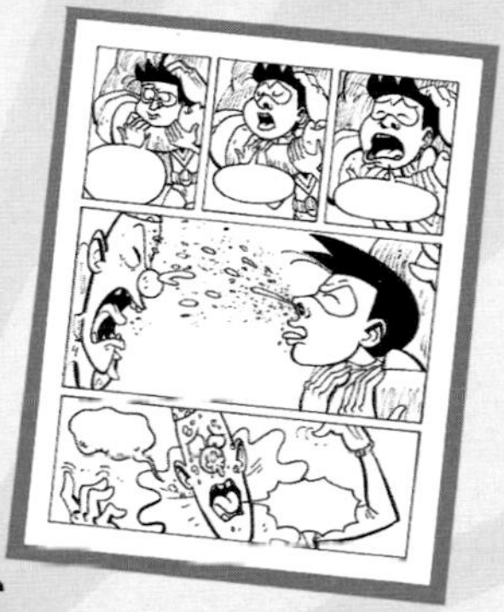

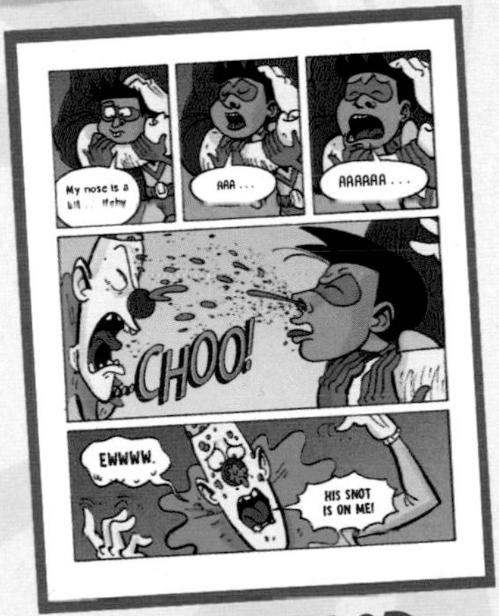
My nose is a bit . . . itchy
AAA . . .
AAAAAA . . .
...CHOO!
EWWWW.
HIS SNOT IS ON ME!

FULL COLOR
(BY SARAH STERN)

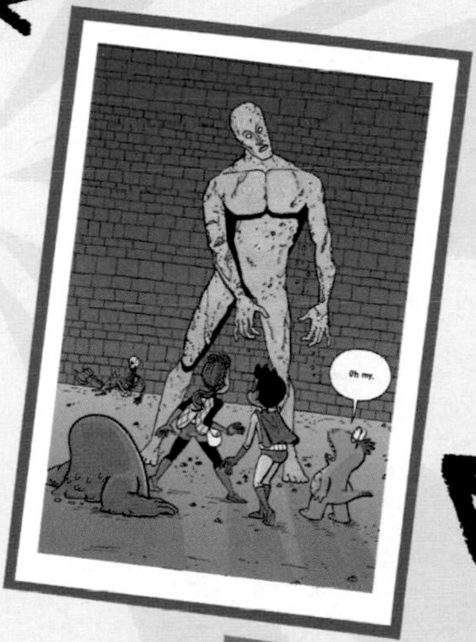
Oh my.

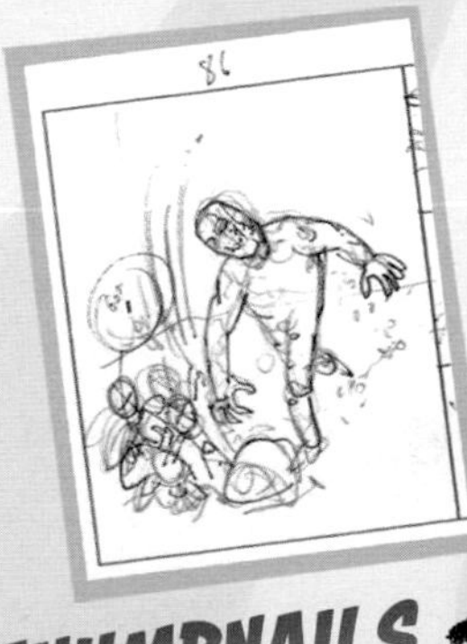

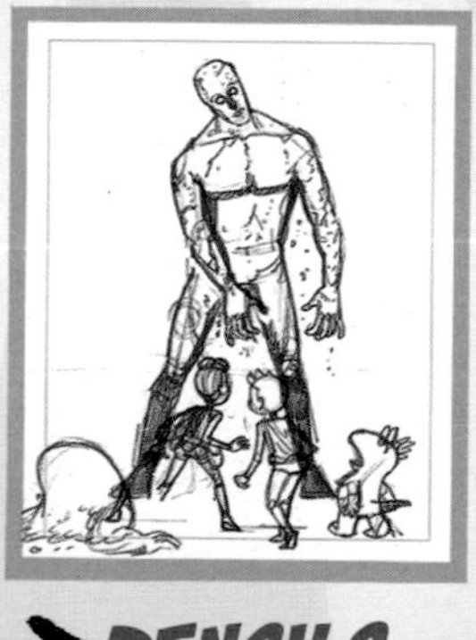

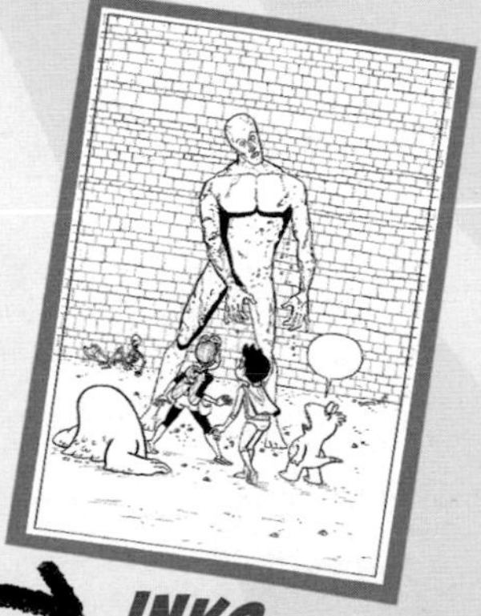

THUMBNAILS → PENCILS → INKS

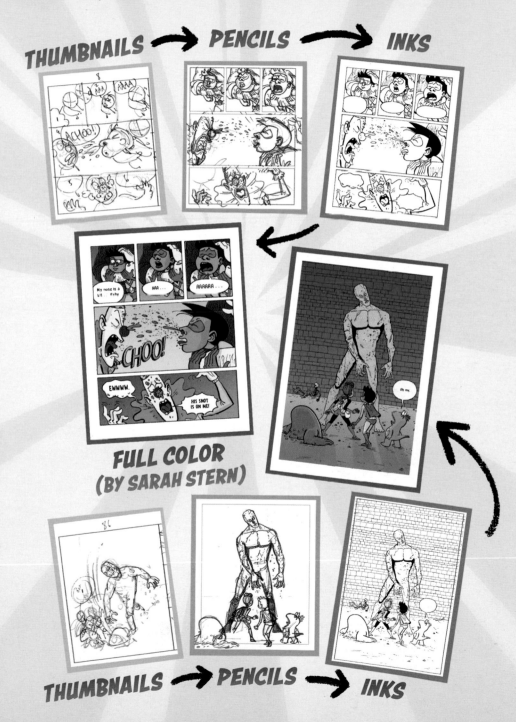

Gavin Aung Than is a *New York Times* bestselling cartoonist and the creator of the Super Sidekicks series. He once attempted the Trial of Heroes but got a heat rash in the desert and had to turn back before making it to the Temple of Champions.

Visit Gav's website at aungthan.com and follow him on social media!

@ZenPencils

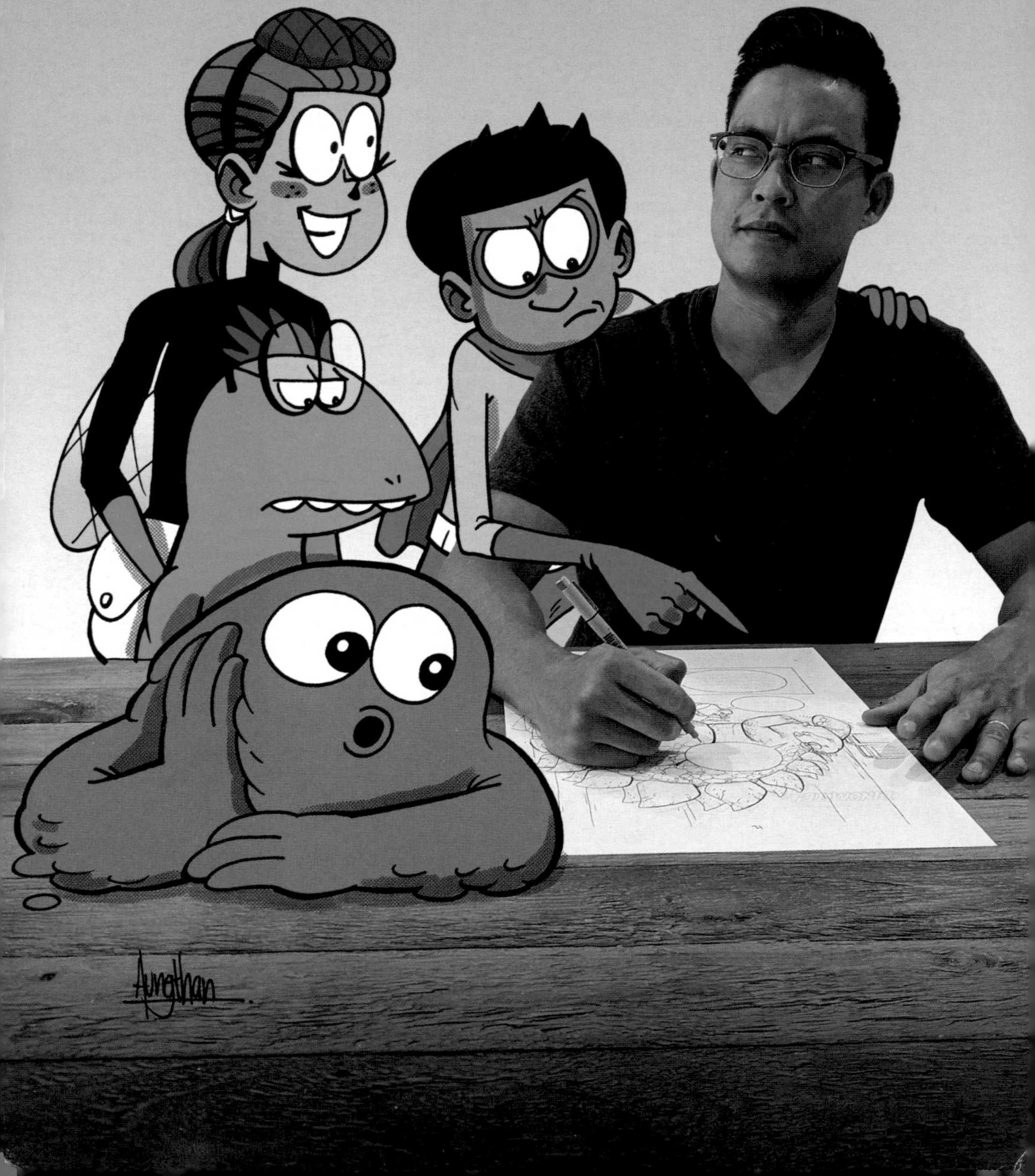
Aungthan